Peregrine's Progress

by Jeffery Farnol

Copyright © 3/17/2016
Jefferson Publication

ISBN-13: 978-1530609352

Table of Contents

CHAPTER I

INTRODUCING MYSELF

"Nineteen to-day, is he!" said my uncle Jervas, viewing me languidly through his quizzing-glass. "How confoundedly the years flit! Nineteen—and on me soul, our poor youth looks as if he hadn't a single gentlemanly vice to bless himself with!"

"Not one, Jervas, my boy," quoth my uncle George, shaking his comely head at me. "Not one, begad, and that's the dooce of it! It seems he don't swear, he don't drink, he don't gamble, he don't make love, he don't even—"

"Don't, George," exclaimed my aunt Julia in her sternest tone, her handsome face flushed, her stately back very rigid.

"Don't what, Julia?"

"Fill our nephew's mind with your own base masculine ideas—I forbid."

"But damme—no, Julia, no—I mean, bless us! What's to become of a man—what's a man to do who don't—"

"Cease, George!"

"But he's almost a man, ain't he?"

"Certainly not; Peregrine is—my nephew—"

"And ours, Julia. We are his legal guardians besides—"

"And set him in my care until he comes of age!" retorted my aunt defiantly.

"And there, happy youth, is his misfortune!" sighed my uncle Jervas.

"Misfortune?" echoed my aunt in whisper so awful that I, for one, nearly trembled. "Misfortune!" she repeated. "Hush! Silence! Not a word! I must think this over! Misfortune!"

In the dreadful pause ensuing, I glanced half-furtively from one to other of my three guardians; at my uncle Jervas, lounging gracefully in his chair, an exquisite work of art from glossy curls to polished Hessians; at my uncle George, standing broad back to the mantel, a graceful, stalwart figure in tight-fitting riding-coat, buckskins and spurred boots; at my wonderful aunt, her dark and statuesque beauty as she sat, her noble form posed like an offended Juno, dimpled chin on dimpled fist, dark brows bent above long-lashed eyes, ruddy lips close-set and arched foot tapping softly beneath the folds of her ample robe.

"His misfortune!" she repeated for the fourth time, softly and as to herself. "And ever have I striven to be to him the tender mother he never knew, to stand in place of the father he never saw!"

"I'm sure of it, Julia!" said my uncle George, fidgeting with his stock.

"His misfortune! And I have watched over him with care unfailing—"

"Er—of course, yes—not a doubt of it, Julia," said uncle George, fiddling with a coat button.

"His upbringing has been the passion of my life—"

"I'm sure of it, Julia, your sweet and—er—womanly nature—"

"George, have the goodness not to interrupt!" sighed my aunt, with a little gesture of her hand. "I have furthermore kept him segregated from all that could in any way vitiate or vulgarise; he has had the ablest tutors and been my constant companion, and to-day—I am told—all this is but his misfortune. Now and therefore. Sir Jervas Vereker, pray explain yourself."

"Briefly and with joy, m'dear Julia," answered my uncle Jervas, smiling sleepily into my aunt's fierce black eyes. "I simply mean that your meticulous care of our nephew has turned what should have been an ordinary and humanly promising, raucous and impish hobbledehoy into a very precise, something superior, charmingly prim and modest, ladylike young fellow—"

"Ladyli—!" My stately aunt came as near gasping as was possible in such a woman, then her stately form grew more rigidly statuesque, her mouth and chin took on that indomitable look I knew so well, and she swept the speaker with the blasting fire of her fine black eyes. "Sir Jervas Vereker!" she exclaimed at last, and in tones of such chilling haughtiness that I, for one, felt very like shivering. There fell another awful silence, aunt Julia sitting very upright, hands clenched on the arms of her chair, dark brows bent against my uncle Jervas, who met her withering glance with all his wonted impassivity, while my uncle George, square face slightly flushed, glanced half-furtively from one to the other and clicked nervous heels together so that his spurs jingled.

"George!" exclaimed my aunt suddenly. "In heaven's name, cease rattling your spurs as if you were in your native stables."

"Certainly, m'dear Julia!" he mumbled, and stood motionless and abashed.

"'Pon me life, Julia," sighed my uncle Jervas, "I swear the years but lend you new graces; time makes you but the handsomer—"

"Begad, but that's the very naked truth, Julia!" cried uncle George. "You grow handsomer than ever."

"Tush!" exclaimed my aunt, yet her long lashes drooped suddenly.

"Your hair is—" said uncle Jervas.

5

"Wonderful!" quoth uncle George. "Always was, begad!"

"Tchah!" exclaimed my aunt.

"Your hair is as silky," pursued my uncle Jervas, "as abundant and as black as—"

"As night!" added uncle George.

"A fiddlestick!" exclaimed my aunt.

"A raven's wing!" pursued my uncle Jervas. "Time hath not changed the wonder of it—"

"Phoh!" exclaimed my aunt.

"Devil a white hair to be seen, Julia!" added uncle George.

"While as for myself, Julia," sighed my uncle Jervas, "my fellow discovered no fewer than four white hairs above my right ear this morning, alas! And look at poor George—as infernally grey as a badger."

"I think," said my aunt, leaning back in her chair, "I think we were discussing my nephew Peregrine—"

"Our mutual ward—precisely, Julia."

"Aye," quoth uncle George, "we are legal guardians of the lad and—"

"Fie, George!" cried aunt Julia. "A vulgar word, an unseemly word!"

"Eh? Word, Julia? What word?"

"'Lad'!" exclaimed my aunt, frowning. "A most obnoxious word, applicable only to beings with pitchforks and persons in sleeved waistcoats who chew straws and attend to horses. Lads pertain only to your world! Peregrine never was, will, or could be such a thing!"

"Good God!" exclaimed my uncle George feebly, and groped for his short, crisp-curling whisker with fumbling fingers.

"Peregrine never was, will, or could be such a thing!" repeated my aunt in a tone of finality.

"Then what the dev—"

"George!"

"I should say then—pray, Julia, what the—hum—ha—is he?"

"Being my nephew, he is a young gentleman, of course!"

"Ha!" quoth my uncle George.

"Hum!" sighed my uncle Jervas. "A gentleman is usually a better man for having been a lad! As to our nephew—"

"Pray, Jervas," said aunt Julia, lifting white imperious hand, "suffer me one word, at least; in justice to myself I can sit mute no longer—"

"Mute?" exclaimed uncle George, grasping whisker again. "Mute, were you, Julia; oh, begad, why then—"

"George—silence—I plead!" said my aunt, and folding her white hands demurely on her knee gazed down at them wistfully beneath drooping lashes.

"Proceed, Julia," quoth my uncle Jervas, "your voice is music to my soul—"

"Mine too!" added uncle George, "mine too, dooce take me if 't isn't!"

MY AUNT (her voice soft and plaintively sad). For nineteen happy years I have devoted myself to caring for my nephew Peregrine, body and mind. My every thought has been of him or for him, my love has been his shield against discomforts, bodily ailments and ills of the mind—

MY UNCLE JERVAS. And precisely there, Julia, lies his happy misfortune. You have thought for him so effectively he has had small scope to think for himself; cared for him so sedulously that he shall hardly know how to take care of himself; sheltered him so rigorously that, once removed from the sphere of your strong personality, he would be pitifully lost and helpless. In short, he is suffering of a surfeit of love, determined tenderness and pertinacious care—in a word, Julia, he is over-Juliaized!

MY UNCLE GEORGE (a little diffidently, and jingling his spurs). B'gad, and there ye have it, sweet soul—d'ye see—

MY AUNT (smiting him speechless with flashing eye). I—am—not your sweet soul. And as for poor dear Peregrine—

MY UNCLE JERVAS. The poor youth is become altogether too preternaturally dignified, too confounded sober, solemn and sedate for this mundane sphere; he needs more—

UNCLE GEORGE. Brimstone and the devil!

MY AUNT (freezingly). George Vereker!

UNCLE JERVAS. Wholesome ungentleness.

UNCLE GEORGE (hazarding the suggestion). An occasional black eye—bloody nose, d'ye see, Julia, healthy bruise or so—

MY AUNT. Mr. Vereker!

UNCLE GEORGE (groping for whisker). What I mean to say is, Julia, a—ha—hum! (Subsides.)

UNCLE JERVAS. George is exactly right, Julia. Our nephew is well enough in many ways, I'll admit, but corporeally he is no Vereker; he fills the eye but meanly—

MY AUNT (in tones of icy gloom). Sir Jervas—explain!

UNCLE JERVAS. Well, my dear Julia, scan him, I beg; regard him with an observant eye, the eye not of a doting woman but a dispassionate critic—examine him!

(Here I sank lower in my great chair.)

MY AUNT. If Peregrine is not so—large as your robust self or so burly as—monstrous George, am I to blame?

MY UNCLE JERVAS. The adjective robust as applied to myself is, I think, a trifle misplaced. I suggest the word "elegant" instead.

MY AUNT (patient and sighful). What have you to remark, George Vereker?

UNCLE GEORGE (measuring me with knowing eye). I should say he would strip devilish—I mean—uncommonly light—

MY AUNT (in murmurous horror). Strip? An odious suggestion! Only ostlers, pugilists, and such as yourself, George, would stoop to do such a thing! Oh, monstrous!

UNCLE GEORGE (pathetically). No, no, Julia m'dear, you mistake; to "strip" is a term o' the "fancy"—milling, d'ye see—fibbing is a very gentlemanly art, assure you; I went three rounds with the "Camberwell Chicken" before I—

My AUNT (scornfully). Have done with your chickens, sir—

UNCLE GEORGE (ruefully). B'gad, he nearly did for me—naked mauleys, you'll understand. In—

MY AUNT (covers ears). Horrors! this ribaldry, George Vereker!

UNCLE GEORGE. O Lord! (Sinks into chair and gloomy silence.)

MY UNCLE JERVAS (rising gracefully, taking aunt Julia's indignant hands and kissing them gallantly). George is perfectly right, dear soul. Our Peregrine requires a naked mauley (clenches Aunt Julia's white hand into a fist)—something like this, only bigger and harder—applied to his torso—

UNCLE GEORGE. Of course, above the belt, you'll understand, Julia! Now the Camberwell Chicken—

MY UNCLE JERVAS. Applied, I say, with sufficient force to awake him to the stern—shall we say the harsh realities of life.

AUNT JULIA. Life can be real without sordid brutality.

UNCLE JERVAS. Not unless one is blind and deaf, or runs away and hides from his fellows like a coward; for brutality, alas, is a very human attribute and slumbers more or less in each one of us, let us deny it how we will.

UNCLE GEORGE. True enough, Jervas, and as you'll remember when I fought the "Camberwell Chicken," my right ogle being closed and claret flowing pretty freely, the crowd afraid of their money—

MY AUNT (coldly determined). Enough! My nephew shall never experience such horrors or consort with such brutish ruffians.

UNCLE GEORGE. Then he'll never be a man, Julia.

MY AUNT. Nature made him that. I intend him for a poet.

Here my uncle George rose up, sat down and rose again, striving for speech, while uncle Jervas smiled and dangled his eyeglass.

MY UNCLE GEORGE (breathing heavily). That's done it, Jervas, that's one in the wind. A poet! Poor, poor lad.

MY AUNT (triumphantly). He has written some charming sonnets, and an ode to a throstle that has been much admired.

UNCLE GEORGE (faintly). Ode! B'gad! Throstle!

MY UNCLE JERVAS. He trifles with paints and brushes, too, I believe?

MY AUNT. Charmingly! He may dazzle the world with a noble picture yet; who knows?

MY UNCLE JERVAS. Oh, my dear Julia, who indeed! He has a pronounced aversion for most manly sports, I believe: horses, for instance—

MY AUNT. He rides with me occasionally, but as for your inhuman hunting and racing—certainly not!

UNCLE GEORGE. And before we were his age, I had broken my collarbone and you had won the county steeplechase from me by a head, Jervas. Ha, that was a race, lad, never enjoyed anything more unless it was when the "Camberwell Chicken" went down and couldn't come up to time and the crowd—

AUNT JULIA. You were both so terribly wild and reckless!

UNCLE JERVAS. No, my sweet woman, just ordinary healthy young animals.

AUNT JULIA. My nephew is a young gentleman.

UNCLE GEORGE. Ha!

UNCLE JERVAS. H'm! A gentleman should know how to use his fists—there is Sir Peter Vibart, for instance.

UNCLE GEORGE. And to shoot straight, Julia.

UNCLE JERVAS. And comport himself in the society of the Sex. Yet you keep Peregrine as secluded as a young nun.

MY AUNT. He prefers solitude. Love will come later.

UNCLE JERVAS. Most unnatural! Before I was Peregrine's age I had been head over ears in and out of love with at least—

MY AUNT. Reprobate!

UNCLE GEORGE. So had I, Julia. There was Mary—or was it Ann—at least if it wasn't Ann it was Betty or Bessie; anyhow, I know she was—

AUNT JULIA. Rake!

UNCLE JERVAS. Remember, we were very young and had never been privileged to behold the Lady Julia Conroy—

UNCLE GEORGE. Begad, Julia—and there y'have it!

MY AUNT. We were discussing my nephew, I think!

MY UNCLE JERVAS. True, Julia, and I was about to remark that since you refuse to send him up to Oxford or Cambridge, the only chance I see for him is to quit your apron strings and go out into the world to find his manhood if he can.

My aunt turned upon the speaker, handsome head upflung, but, ere she could speak, the grandfather clock in the corner rang the hour in its mellow chime. Thereupon my aunt rose to her stately height and reached out to me her slender, imperious hand.

"Peregrine, it is ten o'clock. Good night, dear boy!" said she and kissed me. Thereafter, having kissed the hand that clasped mine, I bowed to my two uncles and went dutifully to bed.

CHAPTER II

TELLS HOW AND WHY I SET FORTH UPON THE QUEST IN QUESTION

"Ladylike!" said I to myself, leaning forth from my chamber window into a fragrant summer night radiant with an orbed moon. But for once I was heedless of the ethereal beauty of the scene before me and felt none of that poetic rapture that would otherwise undoubtedly have inspired me, since my vision was turned inwards rather than out and my customary serenity hatefully disturbed.

"Ladylike!"

Thus, all unregarding, I breathed the incense of flowery perfumes and stared blindly upon the moon's splendour, pondering this hateful word in its application to myself. And gradually, having regard to the manifest injustice and bad taste of the term, conscious of the affront it implied, I grew warm with a righteous indignation that magnified itself into a furious anger against my two uncles.

"Damn them! Damn them both!" exclaimed I and, in that moment, caught my breath, shocked, amazed, and not a little ashamed at this outburst, an exhibition so extremely foreign to my usually placid nature.

'To swear is a painful exhibition of vulgarity, and passion uncontrolled lessens one's dignity and is a sign of weakness.'

Remembering this, one of my wonderful aunt's incontrovertible maxims, I grew abashed (as I say) by reason of this my deplorable lapse. And yet:

"'Ladylike!'"

I repeated the opprobrious epithet for the third time and scowled up at the placid moon.

And this, merely because I had a shrinking horror of all brutal and sordid things, a detestation for anything smacking of vulgarity or bad taste. To me, the subtle beauty of line or colour, the singing music of a phrase, were of more account than the reek of stables or the whooping clamour and excitement of the hunting-field, my joys being rather raptures of the soul than the more material pleasures of the flesh.

"And was it," I asked myself, "was it essential to exchange buffets with a 'Camberwell Chicken,' to shoot and be shot at, to spur sweating and unwilling horses over dangerous fences—were such things truly necessary to prove one's manhood? Assuredly not! And yet—'Ladylike!'"

Moved by a sudden impulse I turned from the lattice to the elegant luxuriousness of my bedchamber, its soft carpets, rich hangings and exquisite harmonies of colour; and coming before the cheval mirror I stood to view and examine myself as I had never done hitherto, surveying my reflection not with the accustomed eyes of Peregrine Vereker, but rather with the coldly appraising eyes of a stranger, and beheld this:

A youthful, slender person of no great stature, clothed in garments elegantly unostentatious.

His face grave and of a saturnine cast—but the features fairly regular.

His complexion sallow—but clear and without blemish.

His hair rather too long—but dark and crisp-curled.

His brow a little too prominent—but high and broad.

His eyes dark and soft—but well-opened and direct.

His nose a little too short to please me—but otherwise well-shaped.

His mouth too tender in its curves—but the lips close and firm.

His chin too smoothly rounded, at a glance—but when set, looks determined enough.

His whole aspect not altogether unpleasing, though I yearned mightily to see him a few inches taller.

Thus then I took dispassionate regard to, and here as dispassionately set down, my outer being; as to my inner, that shall appear, I hope, as this history progresses.

I was yet engaged on this most critical examination of my person when I was interrupted by the sound of footsteps on the flagged terrace beneath my open window and the voices of my two uncles as they passed slowly to and fro, each word of their conversation very plain to hear upon the warm, still air. Honour should have compelled me to close my ears or the lattice; had I done so, how different might this history have been, how utterly different my career. As it was, attracted by the sound of my own name, I turned from contemplation of my person and, coming to the window, leaned out again.

"Poor Peregrine," said my uncle George for the second time.

"Why the pity, George? Curse and confound it, wherefore the pity? Our youth is a perfect ass, an infernal young fish, a puppy-dog—pah!"

"Aye, but," quoth my uncle George (and I could distinguish the faint jingle of his spurs), "we roasted him devilishly to-night between us, Jervas, and never a word out o' the lad—"

"Egad, Julia did the talking for him—"

"Ha, yes—dooce take me, she did so!" exclaimed uncle George. "What an amazingly magnificent creature she is—"

"And did ye mark our youth's cool insolence, his disdainful airs—the cock of his supercilious nose—curst young puppy!"

"Most glorious eyes in Christendom," continued my uncle George, "always make me feel so dooced—er—so curst humble—no, humble's not quite the word; what I do mean is—"

"Fatuous, George?" suggested Uncle Jervas a trifle impatiently.

"Unworthy—yes, unworthy and er—altogether dooced, d'ye see—her whole life one of exemplary self-sacrifice and so forth, d'ye see, Jervas—"

"Exactly, George! Julia will never marry, we know, while she has this precious youth to pet and pamper and cherish—"

"Instead of us, Jervas!"

"Us? George, don't be a fool! She couldn't wed us both, man!"

"Why, no!" sighed uncle George. "She'd ha' to be content wi' one of us, to be sure, and that one would be—"

"Myself, George!"

"Aye!" quoth uncle George, sighing more gustily than ever. "Begad, I think it would, Jervas."

"Though, mark me, George, I have sometimes thought she has the preposterous lack of judgment to prefer you."

"No—did you though!" exclaimed my uncle George, spurs jingling again. "B'gad, and did you though—dooce take me!"

"Aye, George, I did, but only very occasionally. Of course, were she free of this incubus Peregrine, free to live for her own happiness instead of his, I should have her wedded and wifed while you were thinking about it."

"Aye," sighed my uncle George, "you were always such an infernal dasher—"

"As it is, the boy will grow into a priggish, self-satisfied do-nothing, and she into an adoring, solitary old woman—"

"Julia! An old woman! Good God! Hush, Jervas—it sounds dooced indecent!"

"But true, George, devilish true! Here's Julia must grow into a crotchety old female, myself into a solitary, embittered recluse, and you into a lonely, doddering old curmudgeon—and all for sake of this damned lad—"

At this, stirred by sudden impulse, I thrust my head out of the window and hemmed loudly, whereupon they halted very suddenly and stood staring up at me, their surprised looks plain to see by reason of the brilliant moon.

"Pardon me, my dear uncles," said I, bowing to them as well as I might, "pardon me, but I venture to think not—"

"Now 'pon me everlasting soul!" exclaimed my uncle Jervas, fumbling for his eyeglass. "What does the lad mean?"

"With your kind attention, he will come down and explain," said I, and clambering through the casement, I descended forthwith, hand over hand, by means of the ivy stems that grew very thick and strong hereabouts.

Reaching the terrace, I paused to brush the dust from knee and elbow while my uncle Jervas, lounging against the balustrade, viewed me languidly through his glass, and uncle George stared at me very round of eye and groped at his close-trimmed whisker.

"Sirs," said I, glancing from one to other, "I regret that I should appear to you as a 'fish,' a 'puppy' and a 'self-satisfied do-nothing,' but I utterly refuse to be considered either an 'incubus' or a 'damned lad'!"

"Oh, the dooce!" ejaculated uncle George.

"To the which end," I proceeded, "I propose to remove myself for a while—let us say for six months or thereabouts—on a condition."

"Remove yourself, nephew?" repeated uncle Jervas, peering at me a little more narrowly. "Pray where?"

"Anywhere, sir. I shall follow the wind, tramp the roads, consort with all and sundry, open the book of Life and endeavour to learn of man by man himself."

"Very fine!" said my uncle Jervas,—"and damned foolish!"

"In a word," I continued, "I propose to follow your very excellent advice, Uncle Jervas, and go out into the world to find my manhood if I can! That was your phrase, I think?"

"Ah, and when, may I ask?"

"At once, sir. But, as I said before—on a condition."

"Hum!" quoth my uncle Jervas, dropping his glass to tenderly stroke his somewhat too prominent chin.

"And might we humbly venture to enquire as to the condition?"

"Merely this, sir; so soon as Aunt Julia is freed of her incubus—so soon as I am gone—you will see to it she is not lonely. You will woo her, beginning at once, both together or turn about, because I would not have her—this best, this noblest and most generous of women—forfeit anything of happiness on my account; because, having neither father nor mother that I ever remember, the love and reverence that should have been theirs I have given to her."

"Lord!" exclaimed my uncle George, clashing his spurs suddenly. "Lord love the lad—begad—oh, the dooce!"

As for uncle Jervas, forgetting his languor, he stood suddenly erect, frowning, his chin more aggressive than ever.

"You haven't been drinking, have you, Peregrine?" he demanded.

"No, sir!"

"Then you must be mad!"

"I think not, sir. Howbeit, I shall go!"

"Preposterousandamridiculous!" he exclaimed in a breath.

"Possibly, sir!" quoth I, squaring my shoulders resolutely. "But my mind is resolved—"

"Julia—your aunt, will never permit such tom-fool nonsense, boy!"

"I am determined, sir!" said I, folding my arms. "I go for her sake—her future happiness—"

"Happiness?" cried my uncle George, pulling at his whisker, "'t would break her heart, Perry; she'd grieve, boy, aye, begad she would—she'd grieve, as I say, and—grieve, d'ye see—"

"Then you must comfort her—you or Uncle Jervas, or both! Woo her, win her whoever can, only make her happy—that happiness she has denied herself for my sake, all these years. This you must do—it is for this I am about to sacrifice the joy of her companionship, the gentle quiet and luxury of home to pit myself, alone and friendless, against an alien world. This, my dear uncles," said I, finding myself not a little moved as I concluded, "this is my prayer, that, through one of you she may find a greater happiness than has ever been hers hitherto."

"Tush, boy!" murmured my uncle Jervas, lounging gracefully against the balustrade of the terrace again, "Tush and fiddle-de-dee! If you have done with these heroics, let us get to our several beds like common-sense beings," and he yawned behind a white and languid hand.

His words stung me, I will own; but it was not so much these that wrought me to sudden, cold fury, as that contemptuous yawn. Even as I stood mute with righteous indignation, all my finer feelings thus wantonly outraged, he yawned again.

"Come, Peregrine," he mumbled sleepily, "come you in to bed, like a sensible lad."

"Uncle Jervas," said I, smiling up at him as contemptuously as possible, "I will see you damned first!"

"Good God!" exclaimed my uncle George, and letting go his whisker he fell back a step, staring down at me as if he had never seen me before in all his life. Uncle Jervas, on the contrary, regarded me silently awhile, then I saw his grim lips twitch suddenly and he broke into a peal of softly modulated laughter.

"Our sucking dove can roar, it seems, George—our lamb can bellow on occasion. On me soul, I begin to hope we were perhaps a trifle out in our estimation of him. There was an evil word very well meant and heartily expressed!" And he laughed again; then his long arm shot out, though whether to cuff or pat my head I do not know nor stayed to enquire, for, eluding that white hand, I vaulted nimbly over the balustrade and, from the flower bed below, bowed to him with a flourish.

"Uncle Jervas," said I, "pray observe that I bow to your impertinence, by reason of your age; may God mend your manners, sir! Uncle George, farewell. Uncles both, heaven teach you to be some day more worthy my loved aunt Julia!" Saying which, I turned and strode resolutely away across the shadowy park, not a little pleased with myself.

I was close upon the gates that opened upon the high road when, turning for one last look at the great house that had been my home, I was amazed and somewhat disconcerted to find my two uncles hastening after me; hotfoot they came, at something betwixt walk and run, their long legs covering the ground with remarkable speed. Instinctively I began to back away and was deliberating whether or not to cast dignity to the winds and take to my heels outright, when my uncle George hailed me, and I saw he flourished a hat the which I recognised as my own.

"Hold hard a minute, Perry!" he called, spurs jingling with his haste.

"My good uncles," I called, "you are two to one—two very large, ponderous men; pray excuse me therefore if I keep my distance."

"My poor young dolt," quoth uncle Jervas a trifle breathlessly, "we merely desire a word with you—"

"Aye, just a word, Perry!" cried uncle George. "Besides, we've brought your hat and coat, d'ye see."

"You have no other purpose?" I enquired, maintaining my rearward movement.

"Dammit—no!" answered uncle Jervas.

"Word of honour!" cried uncle George.

At this I halted and suffered them to approach nearer.

"You do not meditate attempting the futility of force?" I demanded.

"We do not!" said uncle Jervas.

"Word of honour!" cried uncle George.

"On the contrary," continued uncle Jervas, handing me my silver-buttoned, frogged surtout, "I for one heartily concur and commend your decision in so far as concerns yourself—a trifle of hardship is good for youth and should benefit you amazingly, nephew—"

"B'gad, yes!" nodded uncle George. "Fine thing, hardship—if not too hard. So we thought it well to see that you did not go short of the—ah—needful, d'ye see."

"Needful, sir?" I enquired.

"Rhino, lad—chink, my boy!"

"Ha, to be sure," sighed uncle Jervas, noting my bewilderment. "These coarse metaphors are but empty sounds in your chaste ears, nephew—brother George is trying to say money. Do you happen to have a sufficiency of such dross about you, pray?" A search of my various pockets resulted in the discovery of one shilling and a groat. "Precisely as I surmised," nodded my uncle Jervas, "having had your every possible want supplied hitherto, money is a sordid vulgarity you know little about, yet, if you persist in adventuring your precious person into the world of men and action, you will find money a somewhat useful adjunct. In this purse are some twelve guineas or so—" here he thrust the purse into the right-hand pocket of my coat.

"And six in this, Perry!" said uncle George, thrusting his purse into my left pocket.

"So here are eighteen-odd guineas," quoth uncle Jervas, "a paltry and most inadequate sum, perhaps, but these should last you a few days—with care, or at least until, wearying of hardship, you steal back into the silken lap of luxury."

"And look 'ee, Perry lad," added uncle George, clapping me on the shoulder and eyeing me a little anxiously, "come back soon, boy—soon, d'ye see—"

"He will, George, he will!" nodded uncle Jervas.

"He looks damnably solitary, somehow, Jervas."

"And small, George."

"Sirs," said I, "for my lack of size, blame nature. As to loneliness—'my mind to me my kingdom is,' and one peopled by a thousand loved friends, or of what avail the reading of books?"

"Books? M—yes, precisely!" quoth my uncle George, ruffling up his thick curls and eyeing me askance. "But what are we to tell your aunt Julia?"

"Nothing, sir. At the first inn I stop at I will write her fully regarding my departure and future plans—"

"But—oh, curse it. Perry," exclaimed uncle George, fumbling for his whisker, "she'll be sure to blame us, aye, she will so, b'gad d'ye see—"

"Not when she reads my letter, sir. Indeed I feel—nay, I know that my absence will but serve to draw you nearer together, all three, and I look forward with assured hope to seeing her happily wedded to—to one or other of you when—when I return—"

"Lord love me!"

"Now on me immortal soul!" exclaimed my two uncles in one breath.

"My dear sirs," I continued, "I have long suspected your passion for my peerless aunt, nor do I venture to blame you—"

"Blame, b'gad!" exclaimed my uncle George faintly.

"To-night I chanced to overhear words pass between you that put the matter beyond doubt—"

"Impertinent young eavesdropper!" exclaimed my uncle Jervas, very red in the face.

"Thus, in taking my departure, I can but wish you every happiness. But before I go, I would beg of you to satisfy me on a point of family history—if you will. My parents died young, I believe?"

"They did!" answered my uncle Jervas in strangely repressed voice.

"Very young!" sighed my uncle George.

"And what—how came they to die?" I questioned.

"Your mother died of—a broken heart, Peregrine," said uncle Jervas.

"Sweet child!" added uncle George.

"Then I pray that God in His mercy has mended it long ere this," said I. "And my father, sirs,—how came he by death so early?"

Here my two uncles exchanged looks as though a little at a loss.

"Has your aunt never told you?" enquired my uncle Jervas.

"Never, sir! And her distress forbade my questioning more than the once. But you are men and so I ask you how did your brother and my father die?"

"Shot in a duel, lad, killed on the spot!" said my uncle George, and I saw his big hand clench itself into a quivering fist. "They fought in a little wood not so far from here—such a lad he was—our fag at school, d'ye see. I remember they carried him up these very steps—and the sun so bright—and he had scarcely begun to live—"

"And the bullet that slew him," added my uncle Jervas, "just as surely killed your mother also."

"Yes!" said I. "And whose hand sped that bullet?"

"He is dead!" murmured my uncle Jervas, gazing up at the placid moon. "Dead and out of reach—years ago."

"Aye—he died abroad," added uncle George, "Brussels, I think, or Paris—or was it Vienna—anyhow he—is dead!"

"And—out of reach!" murmured uncle Jervas, still apparently lost in contemplation of the moon.

"As to yourself, dear, foolish lad," said uncle George, laying his hand upon my shoulder, "if go you will, come back soon! And should you meet trouble—need a friend—any assistance, d'ye see, you can always find me at the Grange."

"Or a letter to me, Peregrine, directed to my chambers in St. James's Street, will always bring you prompt advice in any difficulty and, what is better, perhaps—money. Moreover, should you wish to see the town or aspire socially, you will find I can be of some small service—"

"My dear uncles," I exclaimed, grasping their hands in turn, "for this kind solicitude God bless you both again and—good-bye!"

So saying, I turned (somewhat hastily) and went my way; but after I had gone some distance I glanced back to behold them watching me, motionless and side by side; hereupon, moved by their wistful attitude, I forgot my dignity and, whipping off my hat, I flourished it to them above my head ere a bend in the drive hid them from my view.

CHAPTER III

WHEREIN THE READER SHALL FIND SOME DESCRIPTION OF AN EXTRAORDINARY TINKER

I went at a good, round pace, being determined to cover as much distance as possible ere dawn, since I felt assured that so soon as my indomitable aunt Julia discovered my departure she would immediately head a search party in quest of me; for which cogent reason I determined to abandon the high road as soon as possible and go by less frequented byways.

A distant church clock chimed the hour and, pausing to hearken, I thrilled as I counted eleven, for, according to the laws which had ordered my life hitherto, at this so late hour I should have been blissfully asleep between lavender-scented sheets. Indeed my loved aunt abhorred the night air for me, under the delusion that I suffered from a delicate chest; yet here was I out upon the open road and eleven o'clock chiming in my ears. Thus as I strode on into the unknown I experienced an exhilarating sense of high adventure unknown till now.

It was a night of brooding stillness and the moon, high-risen, touched the world about me with her magic, whereby things familiar became transformed into objects of wonder; tree and hedgerow took on shapes strange and fantastic; the road became a gleaming causeway whereon I walked, godlike, master of my destiny. Beyond meadow and cornfield to right and left gloomed woods, remote and full of mystery, in whose enchanted twilight elves and fairies might have danced or slender dryads peeped and sported. Thus walked I in an ecstasy, scanning with eager eyes the novel beauties around me, my mind full of the poetic imaginations conjured up by the magic of this midsummer night, so that I yearned to paint it, or set it to music, or write it into adequate words; and knowing this beyond me, I fell to repeating Milton's noble verses the while:

"I walk unseen
On the dry smooth-shaven green,
To behold the wand'ring moon
Riding near her highest noon,
Like one that had been led astray
Through the heaven's wide pathless way."

After some while I espied a stile upon my right and climbing this, I crossed a broad meadow to a small, rustic bridge spanning a stream that flowed murmurous in the shade of alder and willow. Being upon this bridge, I paused to look down upon these rippling waters and to watch their flash and sparkle where the moon caught them.

And hearkening to the melodious voice of this streamlet, I began to understand how great poems were written and books happened. At last I turned and, crossing the bridge, went my way, pondering on Death, of which I knew nothing, and on Life, of which I knew little more, and so at last came to the woods.

On I went amid the trees, following a grassy ride; but as I advanced, this grew ever narrower and I walked in an ever-deepening gloom, wherefore I turned about, minded to go back, but found myself quite lost and shut in, what with the dense underbrush around me and the twisted, writhen branches above, whose myriad leaves obscured the moon's kindly beam. In this dim twilight I pushed on then, as well as I might, often running foul of unseen obstacles or pausing to loose my garments from clutching thorns. Sudden there met me a wind, dank and chill, that sighed fitfully near and far, very dismal to hear.

And now, as I traversed the gloom of these leafy solitudes, what must come into my head but murders, suicides and death in lonely places. I remembered that not so long ago the famous Buck and Corinthian Sir Maurice Vibart had been found shot to death in just such another desolate place as this. And there was my own long-dead father!

"They fought in a little wood not so far from here!"

These, my uncle George's words, seemed to ring in my ears and, shivering, I stopped to glance about me full of sick apprehension. For all I knew, this might be the very wood where my youthful father had staggered and fallen, to tear at the tender grass with dying fingers; these sombre, leafy aisles perhaps had echoed to the shot—his gasping moan that had borne his young spirit up to the Infinite! At this thought, Horror leapt upon me, wherefore I sought to flee these gloomy shades, only to trip and fall heavily, so that I lay breathless and half-stunned, and no will to rise.

It was at this moment, lying with my cheek against Mother Earth, that I heard it,—a strange, uncanny sound that brought me to my hands and knees, peering fearfully into the shadows that seemed to be deepening about me moment by moment.

With breath held in check I crouched there, straining my ears for a repetition of this unearthly sound that was like nothing I had ever heard before,—a quick, light, tapping chink, now in rhythm, now out, now ceasing, now recommencing, so that I almost doubted but that this wood must be haunted indeed.

Suddenly these foolish apprehensions were quelled somewhat by the sound of a human voice, a full, rich voice, very deep and sonorous, upraised in song; and this voice being so powerful and the night so still, I could hear every word.

"A tinker I am, O a tinker am I,
A tinker I'll live, and a tinker I'll die;
If the King in his crown would change places wi' me
I'd laugh so I would, and I'd say unto he:
'A tinker I am, O a tinker am I,
A tinker I'll live, and a tinker I'll'—"

The voice checked suddenly and I cowered down again as in upon me rushed the shadows, burying me in a pitchy gloom so that my fears racked me anew, until I bethought me this sudden darkness could be no more than a cloud veiling the moon, and I waited, though very impatiently, for her to light me again.

Now as I crouched there, I beheld a light that was not of the moon, but a red and palpitant glow that I judged must be caused by a fire at no great distance; therefore I arose and made my way towards it as well as I could for the many leafy obstacles that beset my way. And thus at last I came upon a glade where burned a fire and beyond this, flourishing a tin kettle in highly threatening fashion, stood a small, fierce-eyed man.

"Hold hard!" quoth he in mighty voice, peering at me over the fire. "I've a blunderbuss here and two popps, so hold hard or I'll be forced to brain ye wi' this here kettle. Now then—come forward slow, my covey, slow, and gi'e us a peep o' you *churi*—step cautious now or I'll be the gory death o' you!"

12

Not a little perturbed by these ferocious expressions, I advanced slowly and very unwillingly into the firelight and, halting well out of his reach, spoke in tone as conciliatory as possible.

"Pray pardon my intrusion, but—"

"Your what?" he demanded, while his quick, bright eyes roved over my shrinking person.

"Intrusion," I repeated, "and now, if you will kindly allow—"

"Intrusion," quoth he, mouthing the word, "intrusion! Why, here's one as don't come my way often! Intrusion! 'T is a good word and rhymes wi' confusion, don't it?"

"It does!" said I, wondering at his manner.

"And 'oo might you be—and what?" he questioned, beckoning me nearer with a motion of the kettle.

"One who has lost his way—"

"In silver buttons an' a jerry 'at—hum! You're a young nob, you are, a swell, a tippy, a go—that's what you are! Wherefore and therefore I ask what you might be a-doing in this here wood at midnight's lone hour?"

"I am lost—"

"Aha!" said he, eyeing me dubiously and scratching his long, blue chin with the spout of his kettle. "A young gent in a jerry 'at—lost an' wandering far from a luxurious 'ome in a wood at midnight! And wherefore? It ain't murder, is it? You aren't been doing to death any pore, con-fiding young fe-male, have ye?"

"Good God—no!" I answered in indignant horror.

"Why then, you don't 'appen to ha' been robbing your rich uncle and now on your way to London wi' the family jew-ells to make your fortun', having set fire to the fam-ly mansion to cover the traces o' your dark an' desp'ret doin's?"

"Certainly not!"

"Ha!" said he, with rueful shake of his head, "I knew it—from the first. I suppose you'll tell me you ain't even forged your 'oary-'eaded grandfather's name for to pay off your gambling debts and other gentlemanly dissipations—come now?"

"No," said I, a little haughtily, "I am not the rogue and scoundrel you seem determined to take me for."

"True!" he sighed. "And what's more, you ain't even got the look of it. Life's full o' disapp'intments to a romantic soul like me and not half so inter-esting as a good nov-el. Now if you'd only 'appened to be a murderer reeking wi' crime an' blood—but you ain't, you tell me?" he questioned, his keen eyes twinkling more brightly than ever.

"I am not!"

"Why, very well then!" said he, nodding and seating himself upon a small stool. "So be it, young master, and if you'm minded to talk wi' a lonely man an' share his fire, sit ye down an' welcome. Though being of a nat'rally enquiring turn o' mind, I'd like to know what you've been a-doing or who, to be hiding in this wood at this witching hour when graves do yawn?"

"I might as well ask you why you sit mending a kettle and singing?"

"Because I'm a tinker an' foller my trade, an' trade's uncommon brisk hereabouts. But as to yourself—"

"You are a strange tinker, I think!" said I, to stay his questioning.

"And why strange?"

"You quote Shakespeare, for one thing—"

"Aha! That's because, although I'm a tinker, I'm a literary cove besides. I mend kettles and such for a living and make verses for a pleasure!"

"What, are you a poet?"

"'Ardly that, young sir, 'ardly that!" said he, rubbing his chin with the shaft of his hammer. "No, 'ardly a poet, p'raps,—but thereabouts. My verses rhyme an' go wi' a swing, which is summat, arter all, ain't it? I made the song I was a-singing so blithe an' 'earty—did ye like it?"

"Indeed, yes."

"No, but did ye though?" he questioned wistfully, slanting his head at me. "Honest an' true?"

"Honest and true!"

At this, his bright eyes danced and a smile curved his grim lips; setting by hammer and kettle, he rose and disappeared into the small dingy tent behind him, whence he presently emerged bearing a large case-bottle, which he uncorked and proffered to me.

"Rum!" said he, nodding. "Any cove as likes verses, 'specially my verses, is a friend—so drink hearty, friend, to our better acquaintance."

"Thank you, but I never drink!"

"Lord!" he exclaimed, and stood bottle in hand, like one quite at a loss; whereupon, perceiving his embarrassment, I took the bottle and swallowed a gulp for good-fellowship's sake and straightway gasped.

"Why, 'tis a bit strong," quoth he, "but for the concocting, or, as you might say, com-posing o' verses there's nothing like a drop o' rum, absorbed moderate, to hearten the muse now and then—here's health an' long life!"

Having said which, he swallowed some of the liquor in turn, sighed, corked the bottle and, having deposited it in the little tent, sat down to his work again with a friendly nod to me.

"Young sir," quoth he, "'tis very plain you are one o' the real sort wi' nothing flash about you, therefore I am the more con-sarned on your account, and wonder to see the likes o' you sitting alongside the likes o' me at midnight in Dead Man's Copse—"

"Dead Man's Copse!" I repeated, glancing into the shadows and drawing nearer the fire. "It is a very dreadful name—"

13

"But very suitable, young sir. There's many a dead 'un been found hereabouts, laying so quiet an' peaceful at last—pore souls as ha' found this big world and life too much for 'em an' have crept here to end their misery—and why not? There's the poor woman that's lost, say, and wandering in the dark, but with her tired eyes lifted up to the kindly stars; so she struggles on awhile, but by an' by come storm clouds an' one by one the stars go out till only one remains, a little twinkling light that is for her the very light of Hope itself—an' presently that winks an' goes, an' with it goes Hope as well, an' she—poor helpless, weary soul—comes a-creeping into some quiet place like this, an' presently only her poor, bruised body lies here, for the soul of her flies away—up an' up a-singing an' a-carolling—back to the stars!"

"This is a great thought—that the soul may not perish!" said I, staring into the Tinker's earnest face.

"Ah, young sir, where does the soul come from—where does it go to? Look yonder!" said he, pointing upwards with his hammer where stars twinkled down upon us through the leaves. "So they've been for ages, and so they will be, winking down through the dark upon you an' me an' others like us, to teach us by their wisdom. An' as to our souls—Lord, I've seen so many corpses in my time I know the soul can't die. Corpses? Aye, by goles, I'm always a-finding of 'em. Found one in this very copse none so long ago—very young she was—poor, lonely lass! Ah, well! Her troubles be all forgot, long ago. An' here's the likes o' you sitting along o' the likes o' me in a wood at midnight—you as should be snug in sheets luxoorious, judging by your looks—an' wherefore not, young friend?"

Now there was about this small, quick, keen-eyed tinker a latent kindliness, a sympathy that attracted me involuntarily, so that, after some demur, I told him my story in few words as possible and careful to suppress all names. Long before I had ended he had laid by hammer and kettle and turned, elbows on knees and chin on sinewy fists, viewing me steadfastly where I sat in the fireglow.

"So you make verses likewise, do you?" he questioned, when I had done.

"Yes."

"And can paint pic-toors, beside?"

"Yes—of a sort!" I answered, finding myself suddenly and strangely diffident.

"An' you so young!" said he in hushed and awestruck tones. "Have you writ many poems, sir?"

"I have published only one volume so far."

"Lord!" he whispered. "Published a vollum—in print—a book! Ah—what wouldn't I give t' see my verses in print—in a book—to know they were good enough—"

"Ah, pray don't mistake!" said I hastily, my new diffidence growing by reason of his unfeigned and awestruck wonder. "I published them myself—no bookseller would take them, so I—I paid to have them printed."

"And did it cost much—very much?" he enquired eagerly. "Anywhere near, well, say—five pound?"

"A great deal nearer a hundred!"

"A hun—" he gasped. "By goles!" he ejaculated after a moment, "poetry comes expensive, don't it? A hundred pound! Lord love me, I don't make so much in a year! So I'll never see any o' my verses in a book, 'tis very sure. Ah, well," said he with a profound sigh, "that won't stop me a-thinking or a-making of 'em, will it?"

"And what do you write about?" I enquired, vastly interested.

"All sorts o' things—common things, trees an' brooks, fields an' winding roads, and then—there's always the stars. Wrote one about 'em this very week, if you'd care to—"

"I should," cried I eagerly. "Indeed I should!"

"Should you, friend?" said he, fumbling in a pocket of his sleeved waistcoat. "Why, then, so you shall, though there ain't much of it, which is p'raps just as well!"

From his pocket he brought forth a strange collection of oddments whence he selected a crumpled wisp of paper; this he smoothed out and bending low to the fire, read aloud as follows:

"When night comes down, where'er I be
I want no roof to shelter me;
I love to lie where I may see
The blessed stars.

"Though I am one not over-wise
They seem to me like friendly eyes That watch us kindly from the skies,
These winking stars.

"Though I've no friend to share my woe
And bitter tears unseen may flow,
To soothe my grief I silent go
To tell the stars.

"And when my time shall come to die
I care not where my flesh shall lie
Because I know my soul shall fly
Back to the stars!"

"Did you write that?" I exclaimed.

"Aye, I did!" he answered, a little anxiously. "Rhymes true, don't it?"

"Yes."

"Goes wi' a swing, don't it?"

"Yes."

"Very well then; what more can you want in a verse?"

"But you've got more—much more!"

"What more?"

"A great deal! Atmosphere, for one thing—"

"Why, 't was writ under a hedge," he explained. "And now, friend, p'raps you'll oblige me wi' one o' yourn?"

"Indeed I would rather not," said I, finding myself oddly ill at ease for once.

"Come, fair is fair!" he urged. Hereupon, after some little reflection, I began reciting this, one of my latest efforts:

"Hail, gentle Dian, goddess-queen
Throned 'mid th' Olympian vasts
Majestic, splendidly serene
'Spite Boreas' rageful blasts.
Immaculate, 'midst starry fires
Incalculable thou—"

here I stopped suddenly and bowed my head.

"Why, what now, young sir; what's wrong?" questioned the Tinker.

"Everything!" said I miserably. "This is not poetry!"

"It—sounds very fine!" said the Tinker kindly.

"But it is just sound and nothing more—it is fatuous—trivial—it has no soul, no meaning, nothing of value—I shall never be a poet!" And knowing this for very truth, there was born in me a humility wholly unknown until this moment.

"Nay—never despond, friend!" quoth the Tinker, laying his hand on my bowed shoulder. "For arter all you've got what I ain't got—words! All you need is to suffer a bit, mind an' body, an' not so much for yourself as for some one or something else. Nobody can expect to be a real poet, I think, as hasn't suffered or grieved over summat or some one! So cheer up; suffering's bound to come t' ye soon or late; 'tis only to be expected in this world. Meanwhile how are ye going to live?"

"I haven't thought of it yet."

"Hum! Any money?"

"Only eighteen guineas."

"Why, 'tis a tidy sum! But even eighteen pound can't last for ever, an' when 'tis all gone—how then?"

"I don't know."

"Hum!" quoth the Tinker again and sat rubbing his chin and staring into the fire, while I, lost in my new humility, wondered if my painting was not as futile as my poetry.

"Can ye work?" enquired my companion suddenly.

"I think so!"

"What at?"

"I don't know!"

"Hum! Any trade or profession?"

"None!"

"Ha! too well eddicated, I suppose. Well, 'tis a queer kettle o' fish, but so's life, yet, though heaviness endure for a night, j'y cometh in the morning, and mind, I'm your friend if you're so minded. And now, what I says is—let's to sleep, for I must be early abroad." Here he reached into the little tent and presently brought thence two blankets, one of which he proffered me, but the night being very hot and oppressive, I declined it and presently we were lying side by side, staring up at the stars. But suddenly upon the stillness, from somewhere amid the surrounding boskages that shut us in, came the sound of one sighing gustily, and I sat up, peering.

"All right, friend," murmured the Tinker drowsily; "'tis only my Diogenes!"

"And who is Diogenes?"

"My pony, for sure!"

"But why do you call him Diogenes?"

"Because Diogenes lived in a tub an'—he don't! Good night, young friend! Never thought o' writing a nov-el, I s'pose?" he enquired suddenly.

"Never! Why do you ask?"

"I met a young cove once, much like you only bigger, and this young cove threatened to write a nov-el an' put me into it. That was years ago, an' I've sold and read a good many nov-els since then, but never came across myself in ever a one on 'em."

"Good night!" said I and very presently heard him snore. But as for me I lay wakeful, busied with my thoughts and staring up at the radiant heaven. "No!" said I to myself at last, speaking my thought aloud, "No, I shall never be a poet!"

15

CHAPTER IV

IN WHICH I MEET A DOWN-AT-HEELS GENTLEMAN

I awoke uncomfortably warm, to find the high-risen sun pouring his dazzling beams full upon me while, hard by, the Tinker's fire yet smouldered; up I started to rub my eyes and stare about me upon the unfamiliar scene. Birds piped and chirped merrily amid the leaves above and around, a rabbit sat to watch me inquisitively, but otherwise I was alone, for the Tinker had vanished and his tent with him.

Now as I sat, feeling strangely lonely and disconsolate, I espied a bulbous parcel lying in reach and, opening this, found it to contain a small loaf, three slices of bacon and a piece of cheese, together with a folded paper whereon I deciphered these words inscribed in painfully neat characters.

YOUNG SIR:

What is one thing at night is another in the morning, so I have gone my way and taken my course appointed. If you should wish to meet me again, which would be strange, I think, you shall hear of me at the White Hart nigh to Sevenoaks, or the Chequers at Tonbridge or from mostly any of the padding kind, since the high road is my home and has been long. I am glad you liked my verses, I have more I could have read you and I think better of yours than you think I thought, though you have taken Lord Byron for your model I think and he is only a poet when he forgets to be a fine gentleman. May you prosper, young sir, and find your manhood which I reckon is none so far to seek. And this is the true desire of me.

Jeremiah Jarvis.

Tinker and occasionally literary cove.

I have left you some breakfast also fire to cook same, eat hearty. You will find a frying-pan in a cleft of the tree we slept under.

Thereupon, being much more hungry than was my wont, I came to the tree in question and presently found a roomy cleft where was the frying-pan, sure enough. And now, having made up the fire, I set about cooking my breakfast for the first time in my life and found it no great business, turning the rashers this way and that in the pan until what with their delectable sight and smell, my hunger grew to a voracious desire that amazed me by its intensity. So, placing the frying-pan on the grass between my knees, I began to eat with the aid of my penknife and a hunch of crusty bread, and never in all my days enjoyed anything more.

In due time, the bacon being despatched together with the greater part of the loaf and cheese, I lay propped against the tree, blinking in the sun and drowsily content. But this blissful aftermath was presently marred by haunting memories of tea, coffee and creamy chocolate until at last, roused by an insistent and ever-growing thirst, I arose, minded to seek some means of assuaging this appetite. Thus, having scrubbed out the frying-pan with a handful of bracken, I restored it to the tree and set out. After some little while I came on a brook bubbling pleasantly amid mossy stones and yet, though it looked sweet and clean enough, I could not bring myself to drink of it, being too proud-stomached, and must go wandering on, plagued by my thirst, until, chancing on the same brook or another, I could resist no longer, and stretching myself full-length upon the bank I stooped to the murmurous water and drank my fill and found it none so ill, although a little brackish.

As the day advanced, the cool wind died away so that what with the heat and this unwonted exercise I grew distressed and was about to cast myself down in the shade of a hedge, when I espied a small tavern bowered in trees some little distance along the road, very pleasant to see, and hasted thitherward accordingly. I was yet some distance away when I became aware that something untoward was afoot, for, borne to my ears, came a sound of excited voices, dominated all at once by one deep and hoarse and loud in virtuous indignation.

"Drunk me beer, I tell 'ee—every drop! Drunk me beer at one gullup so quick's a flash—the 'eartless ruffin!"

Hereupon rose an answering chorus.

"Throw 'im out! Duck 'im! Gi'e 'un one for 'isself!"

Reaching the tavern, I halted on the threshold of a low, wide chamber, floored with red tiles and furnished with oaken tables and benches, where I beheld some half-dozen angry country-fellows grouped about a solitary individual who fronted them in very desperate and determined manner, his back to the wall; an extremely down-at-heels gentleman this, who yet cocked his hat and glared about him with an air of polite ferocity.

"In half a pig's whisper," said he, squaring his arms belligerently, "in half a pig's whisper or less, blood will flow, gore will gush and spatter—" Here, chancing to catch sight of me in the doorway, he flourished off his hat, a miserably sorry-looking object, and bowed profoundly. "Aha, Sir Oswald," quoth he, "you arrive most aptly—in the very nick, the moment, the absolute tick! If you have a mind to see a little delicate fibbing, some scientific bruising as taught by the famous Natty Bell, foot and fist-work as exhibited by Glorious John, Jem Belcher and—"

"'E swallowed all my beer, 'e did, sir!" exclaimed a red-faced man in gaiters and smock-frock, "in one gullup—so quick no 'and could stay the deed! Stole me beer an' can't deny it—"

"No, by heaven!" exclaimed the down-at-heels gentleman. "I drank the fellow's beer, every drop—could have drunk more. Our fat and furious friend labours under a delusion, for to drink good beer with a man out of that man's own pot is surely a mark of high esteem—"

"Dang your 'steem!" cried the stout fellow, flourishing his empty tankard threateningly. "A chap as thieves a chap's beer is a chap as can't be no chap's friend! 'Ow about it, you chaps?" quoth he, appealing to his fellows. "Shall us let a chap thieve a chap's beer an' not kick that chap out where that chap belongs—'ow about it?" Whereupon came the answering chorus:

"Aye, Sim, go for 'im, lad—we'm wi' 'ee! Pitch 'im out! Duck 'im in th' 'orsepond!"

At this juncture spake one I deemed to be the landlord, a gloomy being who drooped above a small bar in one corner.

"Do as ye will, neighbours all, do as ye will—only don't break nothink—them as breaks, pays!"

"One moment, please!" said I, stepping forward. "If the gentleman committed the solecism complained of, it was, I am sure, not so much a wish to offend as an error of judgment—"

"Admirably expressed, sir!" exclaimed the gentleman in question. "And suffer me to add—the exigencies of fortune and circumstance!"

"Therefore," I continued, returning the gentleman's polite bow, "I shall be happy to make such restitution on his behalf as I may."

At this there fell a strange silence during which every eye was fixed on me in somewhat disconcerting fashion, feet shuffled, heads were scratched.

"Ax your pardon, sir—" said the red-faced man at last, rasping shaven chin with tankard rim, "but if you could manage to talk a little less furrin'—more plain English-like?"

"I mean I will buy more beer for you—and any one else who—"

"D'ye hear that, landlord?" cried a voice. "The genelman do mean pots all round!"

"Do ye mean that same, sir?" enquired the landlord, glooming and doubtful.

"I will pay for as many pots as they can drink, for good-fellowship's sake," said I, and laid down a coin.

"Spoken like a true sportsman, sir!" exclaimed the down-at-heels gentleman. "Sir Oswald, permit me to bring to your notice one Anthony—myself, once blooming gayest of the gay, now, alas! a faded blossom, cankered, sir, blighted, yet not to be trodden upon with impunity and always your most obliged, humble servant!" Here he paused to lift the brimming tankard the gloomy landlord had just set before him and bow to me across the creamy foam. "Sir Oswald, your health!" said he. "And may heaven preserve you from these three fatal F's—fathers, friends and females!" Having said which, he drank thirstily and thereafter sat frowning down at his broken boots beneath the brim of his woebegone hat, apparently lost in bitter thought. And beholding him thus, his flippancy forgotten, his air of dashing ferocity laid aside, I saw he was pale and thin and haggard and much younger than I had thought. Suddenly, chancing to meet my eye, his pale cheeks flushed painfully, then, squaring his drooping shoulders, he smote his hat more over one eye than ever, nodded gaily, sprang lightly to his feet and gripped at the table to steady himself.

"E'gad, sir," said he, laughing, "they brew uncommonly strong ale in these parts, it seems!"

"Yes!" said I, well knowing it was not this had so shaken him or caused his hands to quiver as he leaned. "I was thinking," I continued, "that with such ale a crust of bread and cheese might not be amiss?"

"Cheese!" he exclaimed fiercely. "Sir—I—I detest cheese!" But as he spoke I noticed his nearest hand had clenched itself into a quivering fist.

"Why, indeed," said I, furtively watching that telltale hand, "I myself should prefer a slice of roast beef—or a rasher of ham—"

"Ham!" he murmured softly as if to himself—and then in the same tone,
"Sir, I never eat ham, it is an abom—"

"'Am, sir?" sighed the gloomy landlord at this juncture, "if you gentleman was a-thinking of 'am, I've as fine a gammon as was ever smoked, leastways so my missus do say, so if you'm minded for a rasher or so—cut thick—an' say 'arf a dozen eggs—why, say the word, sir."

"The word is 'yes'—if this gentleman will honour me with his company," said I. Hereupon the down-at-heels gentleman shook his head, scowled into his tankard, sighed, and, meeting my eye, broke into a wry smile.

"With all the pleasure in life, sir!" said he.

Thus in a little while we were seated in a small, clean room with the ham and eggs smoking on a dish between us, whence emanated a savour most delectable.

"It smells very appetising!" said I, taking up knife and fork.

"So much so," said he, "so very much so, that before I accept more of your hospitality, it is as well you should know whom you would honour—" here I paused and stared down at the ham and eggs. "Sir, I am a thief!" Here I let fall the knife. "Three nights since, sir," he continued in the same passionless voice, "I broke into a farmhouse and stole a loaf and a piece of cheese. I should have stolen more but that I was interrupted and pursued. I lost the cheese clambering over a wall, the last of the loaf I finished yesterday morning, since when I have subsisted on air and an occasional mangel-wurzel—"

"Then surely it is time you ate something more substantial—this ham seems excellent and—"

"God love you, Sir Oswald—you're a trump!" he exclaimed and sitting down, fell to upon the food I had set before him.

"It is good ham!" said I.

"Sublime!" he answered, and seeing with what fervour he addressed himself to the viands, I troubled him with no further speech until, his plate empty, he leaned back in his chair and vented a sigh of blissful and utter content.

"For that—" he began haltingly, his voice a little hoarse, "for—your hospitality—accept the thanks of a starving wretch!"

"And my name is not Oswald!" said I.

"Of course not, but it answered very well with the fellows outside—nothing like a high-sounding name or title to awe your British rustic. And now," said he, with an expression half-whimsical, half-rueful, as he picked up his woebegone hat, "having by your courtesy eaten and drunk my fill, I will do my best to repay you by ridding you of my company."

"I was christened Peregrine," said I, reaching over to refill his tankard. Now at this he stood mute a space, and very still, only he fumbled nervously with his hat and I heard his breath catch oddly, wherefore I kept my gaze bent upon the jug in my hand.

"Sir," said he at last, speaking as with an effort, "when I stole the bread and cheese, I would have stolen—anything that had chanced in my reach—money—jewels—anything. I was mad and desperate with hunger. And yet many a poor rogue in the same circumstances did no more and their bodies dangle in chains on the highway. I have even contemplated turning footpad—"

17

"I think," said I, "you told me your name was Anthony—well, if you are going on, I will come with you, if I may."

"You will trust yourself—with me—in these solitary byways!"

"Of course," said I, rising, "because, in spite of everything, you are a gentleman!"

At this he turned very abruptly and strode to the latticed casement, while I, having summoned the landlord, paid the reckoning. Then, bidding the company good-day, we set forth together.

CHAPTER V

FURTHER CONCERNING THE AFORESAID GENTLEMAN, ONE ANTHONY

So we walked on together, side by side, through leafy byways and winding paths, past smiling cornfield and darkling wood; we talked of the Government, of country and town, of the Fashionable World and its most famous denizens, concerning which last my companion's knowledge seemed profound; we spoke but little of books, of which he seemed amazingly ignorant—in fine, we exchanged thoughts and reflections on any and everything except ourselves. And thus, as evening drew nigh, we came to the top of a hill. Here he stopped all at once and taking off his dilapidated hat, pointed with it up at the thing that rose above us, looming against the sunset-glory, beam, cross-bar and chain.

"Look at that!" quoth he, staring up at something hideously warped and weather-beaten and clasped round with iron bands,—an awful shape that dangled from rusting chain. "But for my light heels—I might have come to that—and yet why not—his troubles are over. So in a year—six months—who knows,—there hang I—"

"God forbid, Anthony?" cried I.

Now at this he whirled round and, clapping his two hands upon my shoulders, burst forth into vehement oaths to my deep amazement until I saw the tears in his haggard eyes.

"....Curse and confound it!" he ended. "Why must you call me Anthony!"

"Because it is the only name I know you by, for one thing."

"Well!" said he, blinking and scowling savagely.

"And because I like the name of Anthony."

"Oh! egad do you? Well, I like the name Peregrine."

"Good!" said I, and we walked on down the hill together. "My other name is Vereker," I volunteered, seeing he was silent.

"Vereker?" he repeated and stopped to stare at me. "No relation to Sir Jervas Vereker?"

"His nephew!"

"The devil you are!" And here he stood looking down at me from his superior height, rasping his fingers up and down his thin, unshaven cheek like one quite dumbfounded.

"Do you happen to know my uncle?"

"I do—or rather I did, humbly and at a distance, for Sir Jervas is, and always will be, magnificently aloof from all and sundry—but you know this, of course?"

"On the contrary, though I have seen him frequently, I know him not in the least."

"My dear Vereker—who does?"

"My name is Peregrine!" said I, whereupon came that impulsive hand to rest lightly upon my shoulder again for a moment.

"My dear Peregrine, your uncle is unique; there never was any one quite like him unless it were Sir Maurice Vibart, the famous Buck, though your uncle, perhaps, is not quite so coldly devilish; still, he's sufficiently remarkable."

"How so?"

"Well, he has fought three duels to my knowledge, won a point-to-point steeplechase not so long ago and a fortune with it—came down at the first jump and rode with a broken arm though nobody knew until he fainted. Youthful despite years, quick of eye, hand and tongue, correct in himself and all that pertains to him, one who must be sought—even by Royalty, it seems—who might have married among the fairest and lives solitary except for his man John. Sir Jervas Vereker is—Sir Jervas."

"You seem to know my uncle rather well."

"I did—for my name besides Anthony is Vere-Manville!" Here he paused as expecting some comment but finding me silent, continued: "My father was killed with Sir John Moore, at Corunna, and I was brought up by a curmudgeonly uncle, the most preposterous unavuncular uncle that ever bullied a defenceless nephew to the dogs. Well, I grew up and was a moderately happy man despite my uncle, until I took to my bosom a friend who deceived me and a mistress who broke my heart."

"Oh," said I, not a little touched by this gloomy and romantic tale, "then this explains your—your—"

"My present misery, Peregrine? Not altogether. Had I been a philosopher and bent to the storm, I might perchance have gone my solitary way a broken and embittered man, but philosophy and bending to storms is not in me, unhappily, for chancing to encounter my faithless friend, I twisted his nose to such a tune that he demanded satisfaction which resulted in my wounding him; after which I consigned my perjured mistress to perdition; after which again, purely because she happened to be a wealthy heiress, my curmudgeonly uncle cast me adrift, cut me off and consigned me to the devil."

"Here is a very moving story!" said I.

"It is, Peregrine, it is, egad—and consequently I have been moving ever since and going to the devil as fast as I can, though sadly hampered by lack of funds."

"What do you mean by 'going to the devil?'"

"Why, there are many ways, Peregrine, as of course you know, but mine would be ale, beer, wine, brandy—had I the necessary money."

"Are you determined on it?"

"Absolutely!" said he, taking off his battered hat to scowl at it and clap it on again. "Absolutely, Peregrine—I am firmly determined to drink myself to the final exodus."

"How much money should you require, Anthony?"

At this he turned to stare with an expression of whimsical dubiety and thereafter fell to rubbing his unshaven chin as rather at a loss.

"Let us say fifty guineas—no, we'll make it a hundred while we're about it—a hundred guineas would do the thing admirably—though to be sure much might be done with less."

"I have only eighteen pounds," said I, thrusting hand into pocket; "which will leave nine for you—"

"Hey!" he exclaimed, stopping in his sudden fashion. "What's this—what the devil—I say, curse and confound everything, man, what d'ye mean?"

"Being both solitary wanderers, we will share equally so far as we may—"

"No—not to be thought of—preposterous—"

"So I ask you to honour me by accepting these nine pounds—"

"I'll be shot if I do!"

"They may help you to—"

"To my drunken dissolution? Ridiculous! Nine pounds' worth would never do it, I'm so infernally healthy and strong! Nine accursed, miserable pounds—what use to a drinker such as I?"

"Many, Anthony, and I think I can guess one of the first—"

"And that?"

"To procure yourself a shave!"

"Egad!" cried he with a sudden, merry look, "I believe you're in the right of it! A stubbly chin makes a man feel such a pernicious, scoundrelly, hangdog walking misery."

"Precisely!" said I, holding out the nine pounds. "So take your money, Anthony."

"Positively no!" said he, scowling down at the coins. "I thieve occasionally, but I don't beg—yet, and be damned t' you!" And thrusting hands into pockets, he went on again. So I put up the money and we walked on, but in silence now, while the shadows deepened about us. And thus we went for a great while until with every stride this silence became painfully irksome—at least, to me. All at once his arm was about my shoulders, a long, nervous arm drawing me to him, then he had freed me and we stood facing each other in the gathering dusk.

"Perry!" said he, in strange, shaken voice. "Dear fellow, will you forgive a graceless dog? You meant kindly, but I couldn't—I should despise myself more than I do—so—Oh, curse and confound it—what about it?"

For answer I reached out and took his hand; so we stood for a long moment speaking never a word. And presently we went on down the darkling road together.

CHAPTER VI

DESCRIBES CERTAIN LIVELY HAPPENINGS AT THE "JOLLY WAGGONER" INN

We had gone thus no great distance when we heard a sound of hoofs and wheels and perceived an open travelling chaise coming up behind us. The lane was narrow and rutted and thus the vehicle was progressing at an inconsiderable pace, and as it passed us where we stood in the hedge, I saw it contained a man and a woman. This man was richly dressed, and handsome in a big, plethoric fashion, but beholding his face, the small eyes, heavy jowls and fleshy nose, I took an instant aversion to him.

"Did you notice that fellow?" I enquired, brushing the dust from me.

"Did you see—her?" exclaimed Anthony.

"A fleshly brute if ever there was one!" said I.

"Such glorious eyes and hair—a sweet angelic creature, Perry. Her eyes seemed so big and appealing. Oh, curse it, why must women have such eyes. Damn everything!"

"It will be a beautiful night!" said I, staring up at the purple vault where stars began to wink.

"She looked—miserable—almost like one afraid."

"I wonder where we shall sleep, Anthony?"

"Oh, anywhere, in some barn, under a hedge, in a rick—what matter?
Why should she look afraid, I wonder?"

I made no answer, for truth to tell my mind yearned and my body hungered for the sweet, cool luxury of lavender sheets; the thought of a draughty barn or comfortless ditch appalled me, but I held my peace, only I scanned the dim road before me with eager eyes for some sign of tavern or inn.

And presently from the loom of trees I espied a twinkling light that upon our nearer approach I saw proceeded from a wayside inn with a great trough of water before it and a signboard whereon, though evening was falling apace, I could make out the legend—

THE JOLLY WAGGONER

and above this the dim semblance of a man in gaiters and smock, bearing a whip in one hand while in the other he upheld a foaming beaker—but never in nature did ale or beer ever so foam, froth, bubble and seethe as did this painted waggoner's painted beer.

"What now?" enquired my companion, for I had halted. "What is it, Peregrine?"

"The beer!" said I.

"Where, man, where?"

"Yonder!" and I pointed to the sign. "Did ever eyes behold beer so preternaturally frothy?"

"Of course not, Perry my lad, because reality is never so perfect as the dream! The cove who painted that was damnably dry, perishing of a noble thirst, not a doubt of it, and being a true artist he painted it all in—egad, there's thirst in every inch of that foam—it's a masterpiece!"

"It's a daub—and a bad one!" said I. "Indeed, on closer inspection the foam looks very like cheese!"

"Excellent—the poor painting-cove was hungry also, and there you are! I'd hang that thing in my dining room (supposing I had one) to get me an appetite—it's made me hungry already and as for the thirst—Oh, confound it—come on—"

"By no means!" said I resolutely. "Here is a cosy inn; here will we eat and sleep—"

"At your expense? Curse me, no, Peregrine."

"Damme, yes, Anthony."

"I say positively I'll not—"

"Look at that cheese-like foam, Anthony!"

"Curse your pitiful eighteen pounds!"

"A dinner, a glass and a downy bed with sheets, Anthony!"

"Remember I'm a man of astonishing determination, Peregrine!"

"Forget your ridiculous pride, Anthony!"

"Ha—ridiculous, d'ye say, sir?"

"And utterly preposterous, sir!"

"Preposterous! By heaven!" he exclaimed, cocking the battered hat very ferociously over one eye. "Were you a little nearer my weight and size, sir—"

"Sir," quoth I, nettled by the allusion, "does my size offend you—"

"Rather say lack of size, sir—"

"Sir?"

"Sir!"

Now while we stood glaring upon each other in this very ridiculous manner, we were startled by a clatter of hoofs from the inn yard, and the snorting squeal of a horse in pain.

"By heaven, Perry!" he exclaimed, forgetting his ferocity and settling his hat more firmly with a blow of his fist, "I believe some damned scoundrel is kicking a horse!" And away he strode forthwith and I hastened after him. Reaching the yard behind the inn we perceived an ostler and a postboy who cherished a trembling horse between them, talking together in hushed but sullen tones.

"Who's been savaging the horse, my lads?" demanded Anthony, running a hand over the sweating animal with the caressing touch of a true horseman. "Come, speak up and no mumbling!"

"'T were the genelman in the blue spencer as druv up 'ere a while ago cursing 'orrid, an' 'im wi' a young fe-male. A bad 'un by 'is looks an' ways, I think, an' I don't care if 'e 'ears me say it."

"Ah—with a lady, was he?"

"'E were!"

"A very beautiful lady—young, with hair—eyes—"

"W'y, she may 'ave 'ad heyes an' she might 'ave 'ad 'air—likewise she may not—she may ha' been as bald as a coot an' as blind as a mole for all I see—"

"That'll do, my lad, that'll do! But she was young, wasn't she?"

"'Ow should I know?" exclaimed the ostler, his manner losing all respect as he observed Anthony's general down-at-heel appearance. "I didn't think to open 'er mouth nor yet ob-serve 'er teeth—"

"That'll do, my lad, that'll do—"

"Oh, will it an' all—why then, git out o' this yere yard. Who are you t' ax questions—out wi' ye an' quick's the word!" Saying which, the tall ostler approached in a very dangerous and threatening fashion; but even as he moved, so moved Anthony, only infinitely quicker, and lo! in place of large, scowling visage were two large hobnailed shoes that wavered uncertainly aloft in air while their owner rolled upon a pile of stable sweepings.

"That was what Natty Bell would call 'one to go on with!'"

"Lorramity!" gasped the ostler, sitting up and glancing about in dazed fashion. "Lorramity—that's done it, that 'as!"

"If it hasn't, we'll try another!" suggested Anthony in cheery tone.

"By cripes!" exclaimed the ostler, taking up a handful of stable sweepings in an aimless sort of manner. "That was a one-er, that was!"

"I believe you!" quoth the postboy. "It were a leveller as you was a fair askin' an' a-pleading for, an' you got it!"

"Is the lady stopping here to-night?" enquired Anthony.

"She are, sir!" answered the postboy.

"She am, sir!" answered the other, "an' because why, sir—I'll tell ye true, if you won't go a-landin' me no more o' them one-er's—"

"Because 'is near 'orse cast a shoe, sir," explained the postboy.

"An' no smith nigher than Sevenoaks, which is seven miles away."

"Peregrine," said my companion, turning towards the inn, "remembering the foam and your magnanimous offer we will reconsider our decision. This way!" And pushing open a door, we found ourselves in a comfortable chamber, half bar, half kitchen, where was a woman of large and heroic proportions who, beholding Anthony's draggled exterior, frowned, but the sight of my silver buttons and tasseled Hessians seemed to reassure her, for she smiled and bobbed a curtsey to them and asked my pleasure. At my suggestion of supper and beds for two, she turned to frown at Anthony's attire again and called, "Susie!"

In answer to which summons presently appeared a trim maid who, at her mistress's bidding, forthwith brought us to a small chamber none too comfortable, and there left us to kick our heels.

"As lovely a pair of eyes that ever eyes looked into, Perry!"

"Why, she's a fine, plump, buxom kind of creature," said I, "but I think she squints a little—"

"Squints!" cried Anthony, turning with a kind of leap—"I'll be damned if she does—"

"Well, then, take notice when she comes to lay the table—"

"What table? Who?"

"Why, the maid—"

"Ass! I meant the Lady of the Chaise! And she was frightened, Perry—and no wonder—a man who would kick a horse would savage a woman—by heaven, there are times when murder is a virtue!" Here he rose suddenly as a heavy, trampling footstep shook the ceiling above us. "Peregrine," said he, tossing his hat into a corner, "while you remain here to observe the squint-eyed maid, I will forthwith investigate."

Left alone, I sat impatiently enough, twiddling my thumbs; but as time passed and brought neither Anthony nor the maid with supper, my impatience redoubled, so that I rose and, opening a door, found myself in a passage wherein were other doors, from behind one of which came the dull, low sound of a woman's passionate weeping. Inexpressibly moved by this, I hastened forward impulsively and, opening this door, stepped into the room beyond.

She was crouching at the table, a slender, desolate figure, her face hidden in her arms, but hearing my footstep, she lifted her head with a weary gesture and, looking into the beauty of this pale, tear-wet face, I read there a hopeless terror that went far beyond fear.

At sight of me she half rose, then sank down again, as from an inner chamber strode a tall, heavily built man in whom I instantly recognised the gentleman of the chaise. Beholding me, he halted suddenly and stood a minute like one utterly amazed, then his face was convulsed with sudden fury, his full lips curled back from strong, white teeth, and uttering a snarling, inarticulate sound, he caught up a heavy walking cane and strode towards me, whereupon I retreated so precipitately that my heel catching in the worn floor-covering, I tripped and fell; then, or ever I could rise, he stooped and catching me in merciless hands, shook me like the savage monster he was and dragging me across the floor, hurled me into the passage; lying breathless and half-stunned, I heard the slam of the door, the rattle of a bolt and thereafter the sound of his voice, hoarse and muffled and very evil to be heard. I was upon my knees and groping for my hat when powerful arms caught me and lifted me to my feet.

"Why, Perry—curse and confound it!" exclaimed Anthony. "What in the name of—"

He broke off suddenly and I felt the arm about me grow tense and rigid as from beyond the bolted door the harsh voice reached us, fiercer, louder than before.

"Let you go back—and be laughed at for a fool? Not I! Little fool…. No, by God … weep your eyes out … we're as good as married … to-morrow morning … come here … obey me—"

"God!" exclaimed Anthony between shut teeth.

"And the door is bolted!" said I.

"No matter! Out o' my way!"

I saw him leap, saw his foot shoot out, heard a rending crash and next moment he was in the room and I behind him. The man in the blue spencer was in the act of locking the door of the inner room and stood, his hand upon the key, glaring at us beneath drawn brows.

"What the devil!" quoth he, and snatching the stick where it lay on the table, turned upon Anthony with the weapon quivering in his big fist. "Out of this!" he snarled. "Back to the mud that bred you—d'ye hear!"

"One moment!" said Anthony, his grey eyes very wide and bright. "There is a lady in the room yonder and the doors are devilish flimsy, otherwise I should endeavour to describe the kind of thing you are—I intend very shortly to tread on you, but first—"

I saw the heavy stick whirl high, to fall whistling on empty air as Anthony, timing the blow, sprang lightly aside, then leapt heavily in with stiffened arm and fist that smote the scowling face reeling back to the wall. And now rose sounds evil to hear, fierce-panted oaths, the trampling of quick, purposeful feet, and a dust wherein they swayed and smote each other in desperate, murderous fashion; sickened by this beastly spectacle I shrank away, then ran to catch up the flickering lamp and with this grasped in tremulous hands, waited for the end. They were down at last, rolling upon the floor; then I saw the shabby, weather-beaten figure was uppermost, saw this figure reach for and grasp the heavy cane, saw the long arm rise and fall, heard a muffled groan, a sharp cry, a shout of agony; but the long arm rose and fell untiring, merciless, until all sounds were hushed save for a dull moaning and the monotonous sound of blows.

"Anthony—for God's sake—don't kill him!" I cried.

"Murder—sometimes—virtue!" he gasped. At this I set down the lamp in a safe place and, running in, caught that merciless arm, commanding and beseeching in turn. "Right, Peregrine—loose my arm—he's had about—enough—besides, I'm devilish blown!"

So I loosed him and, standing back, saw beyond the door a throng of pale, fearful faces, that parted suddenly to make way for a short, squat man who carried a blunderbuss. Anthony saw him too, for in a moment he was up and, thrusting hand into his bosom, drew thence a small pistol.

"Put down that blunderbuss!" he commanded; whereupon, after a momentary hesitation, the squat fellow stepped forward and laid it sulkily upon the table. "Here, Peregrine," said Anthony, "take this pistol and keep 'em quiet while I walk on this scoundrel a little!" Unwillingly enough, I took the weapon, while Anthony forthwith stood upon his prostrate antagonist and proceeded very deliberately to wipe his villainous-looking boots upon the gentleman's fine blue spencer; this done, he stepped down and beckoned the squat man to approach, who came in, though very unwillingly, and closely followed by the ostler and postillion.

"'Ave ye killed the pore soul?" questioned the squat fellow, eyeing the prostrate man very much askance.

"Alas, no—so I will ask you and these good fellows to carry him out and lay him in the horse-trough—"

"'Orse-trough?" exclaimed the landlord.

"Horse-trough!" nodded Anthony.

"Not us!" answered the landlord.

"Think again!" said Anthony, taking up the blunderbuss.

"Ye mean t' say—" began the landlord.

"Horse-trough!" said Anthony, levelling the ungainly weapon.

"Come on, master," quoth the ostler, "'e du be a mortal desp'rit cove for sure! An' what's a little water; 't will du un good!" So in the end they raised the groaning man and bore him forth, followed by Anthony with the blunderbuss across his arm. And presently from without came a splash, a fierce sputtering and a furious torrent of gasping oaths, which last sound greatly relieved me; and now, what with this and the excitement of the whole affair, I sank down in a chair, trembling from head to foot and my head bowed upon my hands. But hearing a light footstep, I looked up to behold the lady, a bewitching vision despite red eyes and pallid cheeks, where she stood surveying me—then all at once she came forward, impetuous, her hands clasped.

"Oh, sir, how can I ever thank you—and my nose so red and my eyes so dreadfully bleared!"

And in the extremity of her gratitude I believe this beautiful young creature would have knelt to me but that I caught and held her hands in mine; and it was at this moment that Anthony strode in, still a little breathless by reason of his late exertions.

"Oh, Peregrine—" he began and stopped, for at sight of him the lady shrank closer to me, viewing him with terrified eyes, as indeed well she might, for now, in addition to the woeful misery of his garments and stubble of beard, his wild and desperate appearance was heightened by a smear of blood across his pallid cheek. "Ah!" said he, beholding her instinctive gesture of aversion. "Pray assure madam that in spite of my looks she has nothing to fear!" and with one of his grand obeisances he turned to go, but in that moment I had him by the sleeve.

"Madam," said I, bowing to her as she stood viewing us with startled eyes, "I have the honour to present your deliverer and my friend, Mr. Anthony Vere-Manville!" And now I saw that her eyes indeed were very beautiful. So I turned away and left them together.

CHAPTER VII

WHITE MAGIC

Reaching the other room I found the squint-eyed maid had set forth our supper—a goodly joint of cold beef flanked by a loaf, cheese and a jug of ale. A mere glance at this simple fare reminded me how extraordinary was my hunger which I was greatly tempted to satisfy then and there, but checked the impulse resolutely and sat down to wait for Anthony. Nevertheless my gaze must needs wander from crusty loaf to mellow cheese and thence to juicy beef so that I was greatly tempted to begin there and then but schooled my appetite to patience. At last in strode Anthony who, seizing my hand, shook it heartily.

"Peregrine," said he, staring very hard at the beef, "what perfectly glorious hair—"

"Hair?" said I.

"So silky, Peregrine, and—ripply."

"Ah!" said I, glancing from the beef to his ecstatic face. "You mean—"

"To be sure I do!" said he, and shook my hand again.

"And her eyes—you must have observed her eyes?"

"Somewhat red and swollen—"

"Tush!" said he, and catching my hand again, led me to a small and dingy mirror against the wall.

"An ill-looking scoundrel!" he exclaimed, pointing to his reflection. "A miserable wretch, a friendless dog, and Peregrine, I tell you she stooped to trust this scoundrel, to touch this wretch's hand, to speak gentle words to this homeless dog. She's a saint, begad—a positive angel and—oh, stab my vitals—she's hungry and I forgot it—"

"So am I, Anthony—so are you—and here's supper—"

"Where?" he enquired, still lost in contemplation of his villainous reflection.

"On the table, of course."

"Dammit, what a repulsive object I look!" he groaned. "And yet, what matter? Yes—it's just as well she should have seen me at my very worst! And yet—these cursed bristles! I tell you she's an angel, Perry!"

"And hungry, Anthony."

"So she is, sweet soul!" he exclaimed and was gone as he spoke, to reappear in another moment ushering in our fair guest, whose mere presence and dainty grace seemed to make the dingy chamber more sweet and homelike.

"Madam," said I, taking up the carving-knife and bowing as she seated herself between us, "I fear we can offer you but the very simplest of fare, but if you are hungry—"

"Ravenous, sir!" said she, with a little upward motion of the eyes that I thought very engaging. "I have eaten nothing since I ran away this morning—"

"And this beef cuts very well!" said I. And so we began to eat forthwith, speaking but seldom (and Anthony not at all) until our hunger was somewhat appeased.

More than once I had noticed her bright eyes flit from the elegance of my garments to the ruin of Anthony's; at last she spoke:

"And you are—two friends, I understand?" she questioned.

"Yes, madam," answered Anthony, "of about six hours standing. My friend Mr. Vereker found me upon the road and took pity on my destitution. It is to Peregrine we are indebted for the food we eat—"

"And to Anthony for your safety. As to friendship," I pursued, "it is a gift of heaven, greater than time and born in a moment—and this I hope may endure as long as time, because Anthony is the only friend I possess."

Now at this she leaned back and glanced at us beneath wrinkled brows for a moment, then suddenly and with sweet impulse she reached out a hand to each of us.

"Then let us all be friends," said she, "for I am lonely too!"

So for a long moment we sat thus, hand in hand, and neither speaking. "And now," said she at last, "since we are friends, I want you to know how I came to run such risks. I am Barbara Knollys, and my father wishes me to marry a man I hate, so I determined to run away to my aunt Aspasia, because, though I fear my father, my father fears aunt Aspasia more. Captain Danby offered to escort me to aunt's house at Sevenoaks, but once I was in his chaise I grew afraid of him and instead of following the high road he drove by desolate lanes and—oh, he was hateful and so at last we came here. And now you say that Captain Danby has gone?" she enquired of Anthony.

"Quite!" said he a little grimly. "He is, I believe, snug in bed."

"I trust, sir, you—didn't—hurt him—more than was—necessary?"

"Rest assured of it, madam."

"Heaven is very kind to have brought me out of such danger and set me safe in the care of—gentlemen," said she, glancing from one to other of us.

"Rest assured of this also, madam!" said I, while Anthony looked from her to me with shining eyes. At this moment we started, all three, as borne to our ears came the distant rumble of thunder, followed by a fierce wind-gust that rattled crazy door and lattice and, dying in a dismal wail, left behind the mournful sound of pattering rain.

"O heavens!" exclaimed our companion, clasping slender hands. "A storm—and I am terrified of thunder—"

"It will soon pass!" said I.

"But I must start at once!" she faltered. "I must reach my aunt's house to-night."

"There is the chaise!" suggested Anthony.

"Ah, no, no—impossible!" she cried. "The chaise was engaged by Captain Danby and the postillion is in his pay—"

"The chaise shall be ready whenever you desire," said Anthony, rising, "and the postillion shall drive you wherever you appoint if—if you can trust yourself to the care of such a—a down-at-heels rogue as—myself."

"Mr. Anthony," said she, very gravely, "this morning I was a foolish girl—to-night I am a woman—my adventure has taught me much—and a woman always knows whom she may trust. And you are a friend and a gentleman, and one I can trust and so I accept your offer most thankfully." Saying which, she reached out her hand to him and with such a look as made me half wish myself in Anthony's place. So he took her hand, made as though to raise it to his lips, then loosed it and stood with bowed head, seemingly lost in contemplation of his broken boots.

"Thanks!" he mumbled. "I—I—thank you!"

"Now I must prepare for the road!" said she and sped away with never so much as a glance at me, leaving Anthony staring after her like one in a dream, and I saw his eyes bright with unshed tears.

"Perry!" he exclaimed, "O Perry—did you hear her?" And crossing to the little mirror he stood to behold his reflection again. "She has given me back my self-respect!" said he. And then, "Oh, for a barber!" he groaned. "Damn this stubble. I look like an accursed gooseberry! And now for the chaise, she must be safe with her aunt to-night, sweet soul. And she trusts me, Perry—me!" Here he turned to scowl at his reflection again. "An angel!" he murmured.

"But Anthony, if one of the horses has cast a shoe—"

"Shoe?" he repeated dreamily. "The prettiest, daintiest shoe in all Christendom. I noticed it particularly as she stood there—on that old, worn mat—"

Seeing him so lost, I ventured to shake his arm and repeat my query, whereupon he roused and nodded.

"To be sure. Perry, to be sure! We must persuade our ostler and postboy to find us another—let us see to it forthwith!" So saying, he picked up Captain Danby's heavy cane and with it gripped in purposeful hand, led the way from the room.

CHAPTER VIII

I AM LEFT FORLORN

At the extreme end of a narrow and somewhat dingy passage we came on a door, from behind which proceeded a din of voices in loud confabulation, together with much jingling of glasses, so that I judged the worthies we sought were engaged upon what I believe is known as "making a night of it."

This hoarse babel ended suddenly as, opening the door, Anthony strode in, his whole person and attitude suggestive of that air I have already mentioned as one of polite ferocity.

"Aha!" said he, feet wide-planted, Captain Danby's stout cane bending in his powerful hands. "How far is it to Sevenoaks, pray?"

"Better nor seven mile!" answered the surly landlord, setting down his spirit-glass.

"Ah, all o' that!" nodded the ostler over his tankard.

"Every bit!" added the postboy.

"An' 'oo might you be?" demanded an individual in top-boots, a large man chiefly remarkable for a pair of fierce, black whiskers and a truculent eye.

"Seven miles!" exclaimed Anthony, unheeding his interrupter. "I had feared it shorter—oh, excellent! Now my lads, we require the chaise—up with you, set to the horses and be ready to start in ten minutes at most. Come—bustle!"

"Lord!" exclaimed Black Whiskers, "You'd think 'e was a nearl or a jook to 'ear un—'oo is 'e?"

"Why, it's 'im as we was tellin' you of, Mr. Vokes!" quoth the landlord.

"'Is werry own selluf!" nodded the postboy.

"The desp'rit cove as gie me the one-er!" added the ostler.

"Aye, Mr. Vokes," continued the landlord with unction, "this is 'im as committed the 'ssault an' battery on 'is betters."

"Oh, is it?" said Mr. Vokes, nodding in highly menacing fashion.

"Ah!" nodded the landlord. "An' then goes for to make us go for to nigh drownd the pore, unfort'nate genelman in my own 'oss-trough, an' 'im now a-sneezin' an' a-groanin' an' a-swearin' in bed fit to break your 'eart. 'Ere be the desp'rit rogue as done the deed!"

"Oh, is it!" repeated Black Whiskers, scowling. "Why, very well, then—'ere's to show 'im 'oo's 'oo!" and he reached for a heavy riding-whip that lay on the floor beside him.

"Sit still, Mr. Vokes—remain seated, lest I pink you!" commanded Anthony, saluting him with the Captain's cane as if it had been a sword. The man Vokes stared, swore and rose up, whip in hand, whereupon Anthony lunged gracefully, thrusting the cane so extremely accurately into the middle of Mr. Vokes' waistcoat that he doubled up with marked suddenness and fell back helpless in his chair, groaning and gasping painfully.

"Now, my lads," quoth Anthony cheerily, as he picked up the whip, "the word is 'horses'! Come, bustle now!" and he cracked the whip like a pistol shot.

"Lord love me!" exclaimed the landlord, retreating precipitately. "I never see no thin' like this 'ere—no, never!"

"That'll do, my lad, that'll do!" said Anthony, flourishing the whip. "In six minutes or so I expect the chaise at the door."

"But I can't drive a hoss wot's cast a shoe, can I, sir?" whined the postillion, his eye on the whip.

"You can get another, my lad."

"Theer ain't no other 'oss nowhere, except Mr. Vokes' mare!" quoth the ostler.

"Then of course Mr. Vokes will be glad to lend us his mare, I'm sure."

But here Black Whiskers found voice and breath for a very decided negative, with divers gasping allusions to Anthony's eyes and limbs. Hereupon Anthony betook him again to his posture of *escrime*, the cane-point levelled threateningly within a foot of Mr. Vokes' already outraged person.

"Fellow," said he, "next time address me as 'sir'—and say 'yes'!"

For a moment the flinching Mr. Yokes paused to eye the levelled cane, the ready hand and fierce grey eyes behind it, then spoke the desired words in voice scarcely audible by reason of pain and passion; but they sufficed, the cane was lowered, the whip cracked, and forthwith into the yard filed landlord, ostler and postillion with us at their heels. And here by aid of flickering lanthorns, amid wind and rain, the horses were harnessed and put to, the chaise brought to the door where stood one cloaked and hooded who, with Anthony's ready assistance, climbed nimbly into the chaise.

"Anthony—your pistol!" and I handed it to him. "Take care," said I, as he thrust it carelessly into his bosom.

"Tush!" he laughed, "had it been loaded I should have blown out what brains I have days ago!"

"Good-bye, Anthony!" said I, and, or ever he could prevent, thrust a guinea into his hand. For a moment I thought he would toss it in my face, then he thrust it into his pocket.

"Egad, Perry!" said he, seizing my hand in his vital clasp. "You are a devilish—likeable fellow and—d'ye see—what I mean is—oh, dammit! Look for me at Tonbridge." Having said which, he sprang down the steps, entered the chaise and banged to the door. But now at the open window was a lovely face. "Good-bye—Peregrine," and with the word she reached out her hand to me.

"Good-bye," said I.

"Barbara," she suggested.

"Good-bye, Barbara!" said I, and lifted the hand to my lips.

"At Tonbridge, Perry!" repeated Anthony.

"At Tonbridge!" said I, whereupon the postillion vituperated the rain and wind, chirruped to his horses, and the chaise rolled away into the tempestuous dark.

For them, rain and wind and darkness, for me such comfort as the inn afforded, but of the three it was I who was desolate and forlorn.

CHAPTER IX

DESCRIBES THE WOES OF GALLOPING JERRY, A NOTORIOUS HIGHWAYMAN

"An' now—wot about my door?" demanded a gruff voice. Starting, I turned to find the landlord at my elbow and immediately my forlornness grew intensified. I felt miserably helpless and at a loss, for the man's sullen face seemed to hold positive menace and I yearned mightily for Anthony's masterful presence beside me or a little of his polite ferocity.

"Come—wot about my door?" demanded the landlord, more threatening than ever. "Ten shillin' won't mend my door—"

"What door?" I questioned, fronting his insolent look with as much resolution as I could summon.

"The door as you an' that desp'rit villain broke betwixt ye—fifteen shillin'—ah, a pound won't pay for the mendin' o' my door—wot about it—come!" Here he lurched towards me, shoulders hunched, chin brutally out-thrust so that I shrank instinctively from him, perceiving which, he grew the more aggressive.

"That will do!" said I in woefully feeble imitation of Anthony's masterful manner. "That will do—and what is more—"

"Oh, will it do? Wot about my door?"

"You may charge it in your bill—"

"Not me, by goles! 'T is money as I wants—thirty shillin'—in my 'and—this 'ere very moment."

"I intend to stay the night, so will you please have a fire lighted in your best—"

"Thirty-five shillin's the word—in my 'and—this moment—my fine little gent—that's wot!"

Feeling myself quite powerless to cope with this drunken creature, I shrank before him, trembling with mingled rage and disgust; perceiving which, he scowled the fiercer and thrust a hairy fist into my face. Threatened thus with bodily harm, I glanced hastily over my shoulder with some wild notion of ignominious flight, but dignity forbidding, I stood my ground sick with apprehension and with my sweating hands tight-clenched.

"Smell it!" quoth the landlord, setting his fist under my nose. "Which is it t' be,—forty shillin' or this?"

I was groping for my purse when over my shoulder came a large, plump, red hand that took my scowling aggressor by an ear and tweaked it till he writhed, and turning, I beheld the large, plump woman who, putting me aside, interposed her comfortable bulk before me.

"Oh, Sammy," sighed she reproachfully. "You been a-drinkin' again—shame on ye to go a-frightin' an' a-scarin' this poor child. Go an' put your wicked 'ead under the pump this instant, you bad boy. As for you, my pore lamb, never 'eed 'im; 'e bean't so bad when 'e's sober. Come your ways along o' me, dearie." And folding me within one robust arm she brought me into that room that was half bar and half kitchen.

"There!" she exclaimed, leading me to the great settle beside the fire. "Sit ye there, my lamb, and never mind nobody. Lor'! You be a-shiverin' an' shakin' like a little asp, I declare. Poor child!" sighed she, gustily commiserate, and patting my head with her great plump hand. "Pore little soul—never mind, then!"

"Madam," said I, somewhat overwhelmed by her solicitude, "I am not so very—so extreme youthful as you deem me."

"Ain't you, lovey?"

"Indeed, no! I am nineteen."

"Nineteen, dearie—lor', an' you s' small an' all—"

"I am five feet three—almost!"

"Are ye, dearie—lor! But then I'm s' big, most other folks seems small to me—'specially men—men is all children—'specially my man. Which do mind me. Sammy," she called, "go into the wash'us an' let Susie pump on ye. Susie, jest you pump water on your master's 'ead—this moment."

"Yes, ma'm!" And presently sure enough, from somewhere adjacent rose the clank of a pump to the accompaniment of much splashing and gasping.

"That'll do, Susie!"

"Yes, ma'm."

"Now you, Sammy, go an' lie down—this moment. 'E'll be all right arter this, dearie. Susie!"

"Yes, ma'm."

"Go light a fire for this young genelman in Number Four. This moment."

"Yes, ma'm."

"The best chamber but one, dearie. And a feather bed!" All this as she bustled to and fro, and very quietly despite her size, while I sat gazing into the fire and hearkening to the patter of rain on the windows and the wind that howled dismally without and rumbled in the wide chimney so that I must needs wonder how it fared with the travellers and if I should ever see either of them again.

"You look very lonesome, dearie!" remarked the landlady at last, with a large wooden spoon in her hand. "Can I get ye anythink? A drop o' kind rum or nice brandy—or say a glass o' purl—a drop o' purl took warm would be very comfortin' for your little inside."

"Thank you—no!" said I, a little shortly. "But if you could oblige me with pen, ink and paper, I should be grateful."

"Why, for sure, though I'm afraid the pen's broke."

"I'll cut another."

"Ye see there ain't much writin' done 'ere, 'cept by me with my B-e-t-y for Betty and S-a-m-i-e for Samuel." So saying, she presently set out the articles in question; then, having made shift to cut and trim a new point to the quill, I wrote as follows:

NOBLEST AND BEST OF AUNTS: It is now an eternity of twenty-four hours since I left the secure haven of your loving care. Within this space I have found the world more wonderful than my dreams and man more varied than a book. I have also learned to know myself for no poet—it remains for me to convince myself that I am truly a man.

As to my sudden departure, I do beg you to banish from your mind any doubt of my deep love and everlasting gratitude to you, the noblest of women, believe rather I was actuated by motives as unselfish as sincere. Writing this, I pray that though this separation pain you as it does me, it may yet serve to bring to you sooner or late a deeper happiness than your great unselfish heart has ever known. In which sincere hope I rest ever your grateful, loving PEREGRINE.

P.S. I shall write you of my further adventures from time to time.

I was in the act of folding my epistle when I started, for above the lash of rain and buffeting wind, it seemed that some one was hailing from the road. Presently, as I listened, I heard a mutter of rough voices without, a tramp of feet, and the door swung suddenly open to admit two men, or rather three, for between them they dragged one, a short, squat fellow in riding boots and horseman's coat, but all so torn and bedraggled, so foul of blood and mire, as to seem scarce human. His hat was gone and his long, rain-soaked hair clung in black tangles about his bruised face and as he stood, swaying in his bonds, I thought him the very figure of misery.

"House!" roared one of his captors. "House—ho!" In response the landlady entered, followed by her sullen spouse (somewhat sobered by his late ablutions) and the man Vokes.

"Lor'!" exclaimed the landlord, plump fists on plump hips and eyeing the newcomers very much askance. "An' what might all this be?"

"Thieves, missus—a murderin' 'ighwayman—Galloping Jerry 'isself—a bloody rogue—"

"'E looks it!" nodded the landlady. "Bleedin' all over my clean kitchen, 'e be. Take 'im out t' barn—"

"Not us, ma'm, not us—'e's nigh give us the slip once a'ready, dang 'im!" Saying which, the speaker kicked the poor wretch so that he would have fallen but for the wall, whereupon the man Vokes laughed and nodded.

"Ecod!" quoth he. "I'm minded to try my boots on 'im myself."

"Not you, Mr. Vokes!" said the landlady. "No one ain't a-goin' t' kick nobody in my kitchen, and no more I don't want no murderin' 'ighwaymen neither—so out ye go."

"Not us, missus, not us! We be officers—Bow Street officers—wi' a werry dangerous criminal took red 'anded an' a fifty-pound reward good as in our pockets—so 'ere we be, an' 'ere we bide till mornin'. Lay down, you!" Saying which he fetched the wretched captive a buffet that tumbled him into a corner where he lay, his muddy back supported in the angle. And lying thus, it chanced that his eye met mine, a bright eye, very piercing and keen. Now beholding him thus in his helplessness and misery, I will confess that my very natural and proper repugnance for him and his past desperate crimes was greatly modified by pity for his present deplorable situation, the which it seemed he was quick to notice, for with his keen gaze yet holding mine, he spoke, albeit mumbling and somewhat indistinct by reason of his swollen lips:

"Oh, brother, I'm parched wi' thirst—a drink o' water—"

"Stow ye gab!" growled the man Tom. "Gi'e him one for 'is nob, Jimmy."

But as his nearer captor raised his cudgel, I sprang to my feet.

"That'll do!" I cried so imperatively that the fellow stayed his blow and turned to stare, as did the others. "You've maltreated him enough," said I, quite beside myself; "if he desires a little water where's the harm; he will find few enough comforts where he is going?" And taking up a jug of water that chanced to be near I approached the poor wretch, but ere I could reach him, the man Tom interposed, yet as he eyed me over, from rumpled cravat to dusty Hessians, his manner underwent a subtle change.

"No, no, young sir—can't be—I knows a genelman when I sees one, but it's no go—Jerry's a rare desperate cove an' oncommon sly—"

"Then give him the water yourself—"

"Not me, sir!"

"I tell you the man is faint with thirst and ill-usage—"

"Then let 'im faint. A young gent like you don't want nothin' to do wi' th' likes o' 'im—let 'im faint—"

At this I set down the jug and taking out my purse, extracted a guinea.

"Landlord," said I, tossing the coin upon the table, "a bottle of your best rum for the officers—a bowl of punch would do none of us any harm, I think."

26

"Lor'!" exclaimed the landlady, sitting down heavily.

"By goles!" quoth the landlord, reaching for the guinea.

"Allus know a genelman when I sees one!" said the man Tom, making a leg to me and knuckling shaggy eyebrow. So they suffered me to take the water to their prisoner, who drank avidly, his eyes upraised to mine in speechless gratitude.

"Don't believe 'em, brother," he whispered under cover of the talk where the others clustered around the hearth watching the preparations for the punch; "don't believe 'em, friend—I'm no murderer an' my pore old stricken mother on 'er knees for me this night, an' my sweet wife an' babbies weepin' their pretty eyes out, an' all for me. I'm a pore lame dog, brother, an' here's a stile as be 'ard to come over; howsomever, whether 'tis sweet wind an' open road for me by an' by, or Tyburn Tree—why God love ye for this, brother!"

Here he closed his eyes and bowed his head as one in prayer, for I saw his swollen lips moving painfully, then glancing up, beheld the man Jimmy watching us.

"Wot's Jerry a-sayin' of, sir?" he questioned.

"Praying, I believe."

"More like cursing. Jerry's a-flamming o' ye, young sir. An' the punch is ready at last." So while the storm raged outside, we sat down at the table beside the hearth where glasses were filled from a great bowl of steaming brew and forthwith emptied to my very good health. And now to the accompaniment of howling wind and lashing rain, the Bow Street officers recounted the history of Galloping Jerry's capture.

"'T were this evenin' as ever was just about dark, on the 'ill yonder. About 'arf way up there's a biggish tree, an' we was a-layin' for 'im there, Jimmy an' me, wi' our barkers ready, 'avin' been given the office. Presently we 'ears the sound o' hoofs an' down 'ill easy-like comes a mounted cove. It's 'im!' says I. 'Sure?' says Jimmy. 'Sartin,' says I, 'I knows 'im by 'is 'at!' 'Werry good!' says Jimmy, an' lets fly an' down comes the 'oss 'eadfirst, squealin' like a stuck pig, an' away down 'ill shoots Jerry, rollin' over an' over, an' then we was on 'im wi' our truncheons an' we give 'im wot for—eh, Jimmy?"

"Ar!" quoth Jimmy. "We did!"

"And a werry pretty little job it were—eh, Jimmy?"

"Ar!" quoth Jimmy. "It were!"

"Considerin' 'im such a werry desp'rit cove an' all—an' a pair o' popps in 'is 'olsters as long as your arm—they're in the pockets o' my greatcoat yonder—you can see 'em stickin' out. Yes, a sweet, pretty bit o' work as ever we done, eh, Jimmy?"

"Ar—though 'e floored you once."

"Aye—that was when 'e slipped off the darbies—Oh, a desp'rit cove an' the more credit to us! A desp'rit villain—slipped th' darbies, 'e did, an' us was forced to truss 'im wi' rope."

Here every one vied in expressions of acclaim and all eyes turned to that shadowy corner where the prisoner sat crouched in the same posture, bloody head bowed feebly on bowed breast. And now, as the glasses emptied and were refilled (with the exception of mine), we hearkened to tales of horrid murders and ghastly suicides, of gruesome deeds and bloody affrays of hunters and hunted until the landlady gasped and, calling the maid for company, went off to bed, while the men turned to stare uneasily behind them and I myself felt my flesh creep. But as the great bowl emptied, tongues began to stutter, and in the midst of a somewhat incoherent reminiscence of Tom's, the man Vokes snored loudly, whereupon Tom blinked and pillowing his bullet head on the table, promptly snored also; and glancing drowsily around upon the others, I saw they slumbered every one. Hereupon I rose, minded to seek my chamber, but before I reached the door I was arrested by a hoarse whisper:

"Brother—for th' love o' God!"

Peering towards the captive, I saw him upon his back, his face ghastly in the shadow. "Oh, brother," he whispered faintly, "I think I'm a-dyin'! Show kindness to a dyin' man an' ease my poor arms a bit." Moved by pity for his misery and seeing how cruelly he was bound, I contrived, with no small ado, to loosen his bonds somewhat, whereupon he blessed me faintly and closed his eyes. "If ye could bring me a drop more water, death 'ud come easier," he whispered.

So I rose and, coming to the table, found the jug empty, therefore out I went to the place beyond where I judged was the pump, and here found a bucket brimming with water wherewith I filled the jug. Creeping back to the kitchen, I stopped at once, my heart thumping, for to my wonder and dismay I beheld the prisoner on his feet, free of his bonds and rubbing and chafing his wrists and hands and arms. Then all at once this pitiful creature leapt to swift and terrible action, for at one bound, as it seemed, he had reached the chair where hung the officer's greatcoat, whipped forth and cocked the pistols and with these murderous things levelled in his hands, crept upon the sleepers. The jug slipped from my nerveless hold and, roused by the crash of its fall, the man Tom lifted his head only to stare dazedly into the nearest pistol muzzle and the awful scowling face behind it; while the highwayman, reaching out his second pistol, awoke Mr. Vokes with a smart rap on the crown, whereupon, cursing drowsily, he sat up, clasping his hurt and immediately sank cowering in his chair, which action roused the landlord who stared, gasped a feeble "Lorramighty!" and sat motionless.

"Norra word!" quoth the highwayman. "Let a man s' much as whisper an' I blow that man's face off. Ah, an' by hookey, I would, whether or no, if I was th' bloody rogue ye tell me for, 'stead of an 'ighly respectable genelman o' the road with a eye to business. So now turn out your pockets all—an' quick about it."

It was strange to see with what apparent eagerness each man stripped himself of such valuables as he possessed, all of which the highwayman appraised with expert eye.

"Young master," quoth he, beckoning to me with a flourish of his nearest pistol, "come you here!" Trembling I obeyed and at his command transferred the spoil to the capacious pockets of his muddy coat—in I thrust them with unsteady fingers,—rings, purses, a couple of watches, silver snuff and tobacco boxes, etc.: which done, he bade me fetch the ropes that had bound him.

27

"Now you," quoth he, tapping the flinching Tom's bristly cheek with his pistol barrel, "you're a likely cove at tying knots—get to work, my lad, and sharp it is!"

So under his watchful eye, Tom proceeded to bind his companions very securely to their chairs, which done, the highwayman again summoned me and commanding Tom to remove his belt, constrained me to bind the officer's arms behind him therewith and scarce knowing what I did, I lashed the man Tom fast to his chair. This done, the highwayman showed me how I must gag them and when this had been done to his satisfaction, he nodded:

"And now," quoth the highwayman, his battered features twisted in a wry smile as they sat thus gagged and helpless, "hearken all. If I was the murderous cove you name me, I might cut your throats as ye sit, which would be a j'y, or I might shoot ye or set the place afire an' roast ye, 'stead o' which I spits on an' leaves ye. An' now, young master, for your own sake—come along o' me; they'll likely be arter you too for this as a accomplice o' the fact. So come along o' Jerry an' damn their eyes an' limbs, say I!" With which, having stayed to kick Mr. Vokes and the two Bow Street officers, he thrust pistols into pockets and seizing me in powerful grip, hurried me away.

CHAPTER X

THE PHILOSOPHY OF THE SAME

The storm had passed and I remember the moon was shining as, turning our backs upon the silent inn of the "Jolly Waggoner," we made off along the road at a good, sharp pace. And now, what with the stillness of the night and the strange happenings of the last few hours and the wild figure of the highwayman who seemed even more grim and terrifying by moonlight, my overwrought emotions brought on me a nausea of horror and faintness so that I stumbled more than once, whereupon my companion, tightening his grip, dragged me on, cursing me heartily; so that, contrasting his brutality with my aunt Julia's tender, loving care and my desperate plight with the luxurious security of home, I felt all at once the hot smart of tears and so fell to a silent passion of grief and yearning.

Thus we tramped on some while, the highwayman and I, until, having mastered this weakness somewhat, I ventured to steal a glance at him and immediately forgot my own grief in stark wonder and amaze to behold him weeping also, for upon his scarred cheek the moon showed me the gleam of tears, and even as I stared he rubbed at his eyes with hairy knuckle, sniffed and cursed softly. So great was my astonishment that I stopped to stare at him, whereupon he stopped to scowl at me.

"Well?" he enquired gruffly. "An' what now?"

"You—can shed tears also, then?" said I.

"Well, an' why not?" he demanded. "Can't a cove grieve now an' then if he's a mind to?"

"But you're a highwayman!"

"Which seein' you say so, I'll not deny," said he. "So I'll trouble you for your purse an' also your ticker—an' sharp's the word!" And speaking, he whipped a pistol beneath my chin, whereupon I delivered up the articles named as quickly as my consternation would allow. "And now," said he, pocketing my erstwhile property and seizing my arm again, "come on, friend, an' let this be a warnin' never to disturb a 'ighwayman wot grieves."

"Why do you grieve?"

"For my Chloe!"

"Your wife?"

"Wife—no! Never 'ad a wife—never shall. There's no woman breathin' could ekal my Chloe for love an' faithfulness—used to nibble my 'air, she did, poor lass!"

"Nibble your hair?" I repeated. "Pray who was she?"

"My mare, for sure—my pretty mare as 'adn't 'er ekal for speed nor wind—my mare as they Bow Street dogs shot an' left to bleed 'er life out in the mud an' be damned to 'em."

"Then the tale of your wife and babies weeping for you was untrue?"

"Every word of it, friend. An' what then? A man's apt to say anything to save 'is neck—now ain't 'e? Wouldn't you?"

Now at this I was silent and we walked for a while with never a word.

"And your mother?" I questioned at last. "Your mother praying for you—was that also untrue?"

"My mother," said he, lifting his face to the radiant moon, "my mother died three years ago—on her knees—prayin' for me—an' it's like enough she's on 'er knees afore th' Throne a-prayin' for me this werry minute."

"And yet you are a—highwayman?"

"Why, friend, 'tis in the family, y' see. My father was one afore me an' uncommon successful—much looked up to in 'is perfession, though a little too quick o' th' trigger finger—but 'e was took at last, 'ung at Tyburn an' gibbeted on Blackheath. They took me to see 'im in 'is chains, an' bein' only a little lad, I cried all the way back 'ome to my mother an' found 'er a-cryin' too. But because 'e'd been so famous in 'is perfession they gibbeted 'im very 'igh, an' so, as folk 'ad looked up to 'im in life they did the same in death."

"Yours is a very evil, dangerous life," said I, after a while.

"Evil?" he repeated. "Well, life mostly is evil if ye come to think on it. An' as for danger—'t's so-so—three times shot, six times in jail an' many a rousin' gallop wi' the hue an' cry behind. But arter all 'tis my perfession an' there's worse, so what I am I'll be."

"And will you let your mother pray in vain?"

"In vain," he repeated, "in vain? Why, blast the Pope, hasn't she saved me from bein' scragged many a time—didn't she save me t'night?"

"Doesn't she pray rather that you may turn honest?"

"Honest!" quoth he, spitting. "Let them be honest as can! An' look 'ee, my lad, I'll tell ye what—you leave my dead mother alone or 't will be the worse for ye."

Having uttered which threat he strode on, scowling and snorting, now and then, in a very disturbing manner, so that I ventured no further remark and we walked a great way in silence until, suddenly venting a snort fiercer and louder then ever, he spoke:

"Honest!" he ejaculated. "Honest—why, curse your carkis, who are you to talk o' honesty? d'ye know as you're liable to be took by any o' these honest uns—took an' appre'ended as my accomplice afore an' arter the fact—d'ye know that?"

"God help me!" I ejaculated, in agonised dismay. "Oh, heaven help me!"

"Let's 'ope so!" he nodded grimly. "Meantime, I intend to do a bit for ye that way meself—seein' as you 'elped me t'night wi' that cursed knot. I'd managed 'em all but one an' that were out o' reach—so because o' that theer knot an' my good mother, I'm a-goin' to—do the best I can for ye."

"How—when—what do you mean?" I questioned eagerly.

"Never you mind, only I am—an' no man can say honester or fairer, an' I'm a-goin' t' do my best for ye because, bein' the son o' my blessed mother, I'm that tender-'earted that, though I'm th' son o' my feyther I've knowed myself to drop a tear in the very act o' business. She were an' old lady in a pair-'oss phaeton wi' plenty o' sparklers an' nice white hair: a rosy old creetur, comfortably plump and round—'specially in front. 'O Mr. 'ighwayman!' says she, weepin' doleful as she tipped me 'er purse an' the shiners, "ow could ye do it?' 'Ma'm,' I says, wipin' my eyes wi' my pistol—and—'ma'm, I don't know—but do it I must!' An' I rode away quite down-'earted." Here he turned to regard me with his wry smile.

Thus we held on, by field paths and narrow muddy tracks until the moon was down and I was stumbling with weariness. At last, my strength almost spent, we entered a wood, a dismal place where a mournful wind stirred, where trees dripped upon me and wet leaves brushed my face like ghostly fingers, while rain-sodden underbrush and bracken clung about my wearied limbs. Through this clammy dreariness I followed my tireless companion until suddenly his dim form vanished and I was groping amid damp leaves; but through this dense thicket came his hand to seize and drag me on until I found myself in a place of utter darkness.

"Stand still!" he commanded.

A moment after I heard him strike flint and steel and presently he lighted a candle-end by whose welcome beam I saw we stood in a roomy cave. And an evil place I thought it, full of unexpected corners, littered with all manner of odds and ends and divers misshapen bundles. Having set down the candle, the highwayman drew a dingy blanket before the cave mouth and turned to scowl at me, eyeing my shrinking person over from dripping hat to sodden boots; and well might I shrink, for surely few waking eyes have beheld such a wild and terrifying vision as he presented, his battered face, his garments mired and torn, his hands hidden in the pockets of his riding-coat.

"Tyburn Tree!" said he suddenly. "The nubbing cheat! 'Tis there I'm like to go one o' these days an' all along o' my kind 'eart—with a curse on't. There were only three men in this 'ard world as knew o' this 'ere refuge, an' Ben Purvis was shot three year ago an' poor Nick Scrope swings a-top o' River Hill—which left only me. An' now 'ere's you—curse on my kind 'eart, says I!"

"Indeed—oh, indeed you may trust me—"

"W'y, there it is—I must trust you, blast my kind 'eart, I says! But look now, my cove, this here cave being as ye might say the secoor 'aven of a pore soul as the world don't love—if you should ever peach to a nark or speak a word of it to the queer coves, why then this pore soul will come a-seekin' till you're found an' blow your danged face off."

Hereupon I broke into such fervent protestations of secrecy as seemed to satisfy him, for he turned, and from a roughly constructed cupboard took a black bottle and two mugs; having filled the mugs he passed one to me and, raising the other to his lips, nodded:

"Happy days, pal!" said he; and so we drank together. The potent spirit warmed and comforted me despite the misery of wet boots and damp clothes, and seated on a box I was already half-asleep when his grip on my shoulder roused me and, starting up, I saw he had undone one of the bundles and spread the contents before me on the floor, namely: a rough jacket, cord breeches, woollen stockings and a pair of stout, clumsy shoes. "Get 'em on!" he commanded. So because I needs must, I obeyed; and though these rough garments fitted me but ill, I found them warm and comfortable enough.

"You'll do!" he nodded. "Roll ye'self in the mud an' your own mother'll never know ye. An' now—off wi' you!"

"Do you mean—I must go?" said I, aghast and shivering at the recollection of the dreary wilderness outside.

"Aye, I do so!" quoth he, seating himself on the small barrel that served him as a chair.

"And will you send me away destitute—without a penny?"

At this he was silent awhile, head bowed as one in profound thought, then groping in his capacious pocket, he at last drew forth my purse, stared at it, weighed it on his palm and suddenly thrust it into my hand; then as I stood amazed beyond speech, he took out my watch.

"Gold!" he muttered, as if to himself. "A gold tattler as would bring me—take it an' be damned!" saying which he thrust it savagely upon me.

"This—this is generous—" I began.

"Norra word!" he growled. "They said my feyther was a rogue an' hanged him according, but my mother was a saint as went back to heaven, so if you must thank anybody, thank 'er memory. An' now off wi' ye, lest minding my feyther, I take 'em back again."

Hereupon I made haste to be gone, but reaching the blanket at the cave mouth, I turned and came back again.

"Good-bye, Galloping Jerry!" said I, and held out my hand.

Now at this he drew in his breath sharply and sat scowling at my outstretched hand as though it had been something very rare and curious; at last he raised his keen eyes to my face in quick, strange scrutiny.

"Why, Lord love my eyes!" he exclaimed, like one greatly amazed, "Lord love my eyes and limbs!" Then, all at once, he took my hand, gripping it very hard, and held it thus a long moment, loosing it as suddenly; and so I turned and, lifting the blanket, went out into the dreary desolation of the wood.

On the misery of this night's wanderings I will not dwell; let it suffice to say that, sick and reeling with weariness and lack of sleep, I came at sunrise upon a barn into which I crept and here, with no better couch than a pile of hay, I was thankful to stretch my aching body, and so fell into a deep and dreamless slumber.

CHAPTER XI

WHICH PROVES BEYOND ALL ARGUMENT THAT CLOTHES MAKE THE MAN

I awoke very stiff and sore and full of a black, oppressive melancholy despite the bright sunshine that poured in at every crack and crevice of the old barn. To this depression was added sudden dread as I recalled the incidents of last night and how (albeit unwittingly) I had favoured the escape of a desperate outlaw, thus placing myself in danger of arrest and possible imprisonment.

At this horrid thought I started up in great perturbation until observing thus my clumsy shoes, thick stockings and other garments of my rustical disguise, my apprehensions abated somewhat and I sat down again to ponder gloomily on my future course.

And now leapt Memory to tempt me, for I must needs think of my aunt who, viewed from my present deep of misery and loneliness, seemed like some goddess very high and remote. I yearned bitterly for that passionate, if somewhat tyrannic, devotion to my every need and comfort, and for the serene, untroubled haven her love and mere presence had ever afforded me.

With the money in my possession I had but to charter a horse or vehicle and in a few hours should be with her again, safe from all fears and dangers, secure from all further hardships. Moved by this thought, I rose to eager feet, but remembering the keen, critical eyes and aggressive chin of my uncle Jervas, I sat down again.

I remained thus some considerable time, torn between these conflicting emotions until at last, clenching my hands, I determined I would go on and persevere in the adventure at all hazards; though I must confess I came to this final decision more from pride and fear of ridicule than strength of character.

I remember I had just arrived at this conclusion that was to so vitally affect and change my after life, when the door of the barn creaked suddenly open and a man appeared who, espying me where I sat crouched among the hay, stooped to view me over. For a moment I blinked, dazzled by the sun-glare, then I saw him for a tall, bony man with a long nose and a ferrety eye.

"Come out o' that!" quoth he, fondling the lash of an ugly-looking whip he carried. "Who give you leave to snore in my barn? Come out of it!"

"Sir," said I, rising and saluting him with a somewhat haughty bow, "I regret to have trespassed upon your property, but when I remind you of last night's dreadful storm and further inform you that I was lost, you will, I am sure—"

"Come out of it—d'ye hear!" he repeated more angrily then before. "And don't try coming any o' your imperence wi' me, my lad—come, out ye go!"

"Willingly!" said I disdainfully. "Permit me first to assure you that if my sheltering in this barn has caused any damage to your property, I will reimburse you to any reasonable—"

"Get out—ye damned young thieving gipsy!" he roared, and cut at me fiercely with his whip; whereupon, forgetting dignity and all else in the sharp, unaccustomed pain, I took to my heels nor did I stop until I was safe beyond pursuit and out of sight of the scene of my humiliation.

This incident (though I could have wept for very indignation) served but to make me the more fixed in my resolution to follow the course I had marked out for myself, come what might.

My present worldly possessions amounted to some fourteen pounds and a valuable gold watch, thanks to the highwayman's gratitude; moreover I remembered Anthony's promise to meet me at Tonbridge and this cheered me greatly. To Tonbridge I would go and there await his coming.

Musing thus, I was aroused by the hoof strokes of a horse and, glancing up, beheld a plump man on plump steed ambling towards me down the lane. Waiting until he was sufficiently near, I stepped into the road and saluted him.

"Good-day, sir!" said I. "Pray pardon my detaining you, but this neighbourhood is strange to me. Will you therefore have the kindness to direct me to Tonbridge?"

The plump man eyed me over, damned my impudence, and rode off with never another word, leaving me to stare after him mute with indignation and surprise; and so to plod on, racking my brain to discover in what particular I could have offended.

I was yet busied on this perplexing problem when I espied a pleasant-faced fellow leaning over a gate; him I accosted thus:

"Sir, I am a stranger hereabouts and should esteem it a kindness if you would direct me to Tonbridge." The man stared, open-mouthed, and hardly had I finished speaking than he threw back his head and laughed loudly.

"Sir, why do you laugh?" I demanded, a little stiffly.

"Good lad!" he grinned. "Ye be a play-actor, for sure?"

"Certainly I am—not! Pray how may I get to Tonbridge?"

"Why, like Gammer Perkins' old sow," he grinned, "one leg afore t' other! I bean't sich a green 'un as ye think."

"Thank you for nothing!" said I sharply.

"Oh, ye can't make a fule of I!" quoth he, grinning.

"No," I retorted, "Nature has done so already!"

This seemed to tickle him mightily for some reason.

"By gum, but you be a rare un, ecod!" he cried, slapping his leg. "Gi'e us some more, lad—I'd rayther laugh than eat any day—sing us a song—step us a jig, will 'ee? Come, I don't mind payin' for 't. I du love a good laugh an' I'll pay. I don't mind spendin' a penny—no b' gum, 'ere's a groat—there y' are! Now tip us a song or jig—come!" Saying which, he tossed the four-penny piece into the road at my feet. Now at this I grew angry beyond words, but he was a large man, so I turned on indignant heel and left him leaning over the gate to stare from me to the despised coin and back again in open-mouthed wonderment.

And now, as I trudged on, my mind was exercised on the question as to whether this part of the world was peopled only by ill-tempered bullies, surly wretches, or bovine fools. So came I to a place where the ways divided and I was deliberating which to follow when I heard a shrill whistling and glancing about, beheld a large woman who talked very fast and angrily to a small man, who whistled extremely loud and shrill, heeding her not in the least. Being come to where I stood, the man paused and stopped his whistling.

"O laddie," quoth he, jerking grimy thumb at his companion, "will ye 'ark to this brimstone witch—been clackin' away all along from Sevenoaks, she 'ave! Gimme a tanner an' she's yourn—say thrippence—say a penny!" At this the woman started to berate him again and he to whistling.

"Pardon me," said I, when at last I might make myself heard, "will you be so obliging as to tell me the way to Tonbridge?"

"Look at 'im, Neddy, look at 'im!" cried the virago, stabbing bony finger at me. "Tell 'im t' close 'is trap or it's twist 'is yeres I will. Tell 'im 'e can't make fun o' we—"

"Make fun of you!" exclaimed I, falling back a pace, aghast at the suggestion. "Indeed nothing was further from my intent! Believe me, my good woman, I—"

"Don't ye dare go callin' me ye 'good woman' in them breeches an' ye shirt all tore! An' look at ye 'at—I seen better on a scarecrow, I 'ave! You're trash apeing y'r betters—poor trash, that's wot you are! Good woman indeed! You tell 'im wot we think of 'im, Neddy—tell 'im plain an' p'inted!" Instantly the little man set thumb to nose and, spreading his fingers, wagged them at me in a highly offensive manner, at the same time ejaculating the one word:

"Walker!"

Which done, he nodded, the woman scowled, and so they left me.

So here it was, then, the answer to this perplexing riddle—my clothes! Mechanically I took off my hat and examined it as I had not troubled to do hitherto and saw it for a shapeless monstrosity faded to the colour of dust and with more than one hole in crown and brim. Truly I (like the woman) had seen better on many a scarecrow. I now stooped to survey as much of my person as possible—my thick and clumsy shoes, my rough stockings, the old, cord breeches that disfigured me, hideous in themselves and rendered more so by numerous darns and ill-contrived patches. Here then, as it seemed, was the explanation for the brutality, surliness and odious familiarity I had been subjected to; for my voice and manner being out of all keeping with my appearance, I must naturally become an object of suspicion, coarse merriment, or aversion.

Here I must needs begin to realise and justly appreciate how very much I had owed in the past to the excellence of my tailor, for, clothed in the dignity of broadcloth and fine linen I had unconsciously lived up to them and walked serene, accustomed to such deference as they inspired and accepting it as my due; but stripped of these sartorial aids and embellishings, who was to recognise the aristocrat? Nay, his very airs of birth and breeding, his customary dignity of manner would be of themselves but matter for laughter. To strive for dignity in such a hat was to be ridiculous and peering down at the cord breeches, stockings and shoes, I knew that these henceforth must govern my behaviour. But how adapt myself to these debasing atrocities? This question proving unanswerable, I determined to buy other clothes at the first opportunity.

On I tramped, rejoicing in the peaceful solitude of these leafy byways though, as the day advanced, conscious of a growing thirst and prodigious hunger. At last I espied an inn before me and hurried forward; but an inn meant people, folk who would talk and stare—remembering which, I paused, despite my hunger, and half-fearing to enter the place by reason of my clothes. As I stood thus, viewing the inn shyly and askance, a man stepped from the open doorway and came striding towards me, a jovial-faced, full-bodied man who, catching my eye, nodded good-humouredly, whereupon I ventured to address him.

"If you please, sir," said I, touching my hat respectfully (as such a hat should be touched), "can you tell me the way to Tonbridge?"

"I can, my lad, I can!" quoth he, crossing muscular hands on the handle of the thick stick he carried. "But Tonbridge is a goodish step from here and you look tired, my lad, peaked and pale about the gills. Are ye hungry?"

"Yes, sir!"

"Ha, thought so! Must eat beef—beef's the thing! d'ye like beef, hey?"

"Yes, sir!"

"How about pudding-steak and kidney pudding—d'ye like that?"

"Yes, sir!"

"Good lad! So do I! Just had some in the 'Artichoke' yonder—all hot! Go and do likewise, my poor lad! Say Squire sent ye—and eat hearty!" As he spoke he reached into a pocket of his smallclothes, took out a shilling, pressed it into my hand, nodded and strode away.

31

CHAPTER XII

THE PRICE OF A GODDESS

Stomach is and ever has been a mighty factor in the affairs of mankind: the proud and lowly, the fool and sage, all alike are slaves to its imperious dictates. Let it go empty, and it is a curse, breeding cowardice, gloomy suspicions, unreasonableness, angers and a thousand evils and dissensions; fill it and it is a comfort, promoting good-fellowship, kindliness and abounding virtue. Hence, instead of saying of a man—"He has a good heart"—should not the dictum be rather—"He is the happy possessor of an excellent stomach regularly and adequately filled?" For truly how many actions, evil and good, may be directly traced to the influence of this most important organ! Thus, to your true Philosopher, "the Stomach is the thing," and so long as his own be comfortable he may philosophise with stoical fortitude upon other people's woes (and occasionally his own) more or less agreeably; but starve him and our Philosopher will grieve for himself as miserably as I—or even you. The Tooth of Remorse may be sharp but the Fangs of Hunger bite deeper still, and who shall cherish beauty in his soul or who find patience to rhapsodise on a sunset when his stomach is empty as a drum? Thus, alas, Soul goes shackled by, and Intellect is the slave of, Stomach!

All of the which foregoing points to the fact that the steak and kidney pudding had been excellent, even as my benefactor had said; wherefore, drowsing in somnolent content, I sat amid leaves beside a prattling rill musing comfortably as a well-fed young philosopher may, when these reflections were banished in sudden alarm, for upon the drowsy afternoon stillness rose a stir of leaves, a snapping of twigs, the sounds of one who burst through all obstacles in desperate flight. Starting to an elbow I gazed wildly about and thus espied a girl who, breaking through the bushes that crowned the bank above, came bounding down the steep. At sight of me she checked her wild career and turned to stare back whence she had come, catching her breath in great, sobbing gasps very distressing to hear.

I remember the round, full column of her throat as she stood thus, her long, night-black hair a troubled torrent stirring in the gentle wind. Then she swung about to face me, one hand upon her quick-moving bosom, the other grasping a small, evil-looking knife.

"Young man," she panted, "young man—help me—!"

As she uttered the words, two men appeared on the bank above us, tall, dark-complexioned fellows who scowled down on me in manner I found exceedingly disturbing. "Oh, young man," cried the girl, flourishing her knife and frowning up at her pursuers, "young man, if you've any manhood in ye—stand up and help me!"

And now the two men began to descend into the little dell with a certain deliberation very discomforting to witness, and I arose, greatly at a loss and looking from one to other of them in growing apprehension.

"Young man," demanded the girl in scornful undertones, "why do ye tremble?"

At this moment (and to my inexpressible relief) from the leafy tangles adjacent rose a voice, shrill and imperious:

"Jochabed—Bennigo!"

The men halted and, following their gaze, I beheld a woman, ancient and bowed with years yet apparently wonderfully active none the less, a strange, wrinkled old creature extremely neat of person, with keen, bright eyes and a portentous chin. Having descended the bank, she stood leaning on the staff she carried, her quick glance darting from the men to the girl, and the girl to me, many times over.

"Oho—aha!" she ejaculated at last. "Scant o' breath be I, tur'ble scant, being s' very old—aha—but age be wise!"

And now she turned to address the woman, though in language quite beyond my comprehension, stabbing her staff at us all four in turn.

"No, gammer—no!" cried the girl passionately, but at the ancient woman's commanding gesture she fell mute, though she scowled in sullen defiance and I saw the knife glitter where she gripped it, half concealed by a fold of her petticoat. Here one of the men muttered some unintelligible word and pointed scornfully at me, whereupon the old woman rapped him smartly over the knuckles and fixed her uncomfortably shrewd gaze on my person, scanning me over very keenly, more especially my face and hands.

"Well, my pretty young gorgio," said she, "there be horses a-sweating along o' you, eyes a-looking and hearts a-grieving all along o' you—though you ain't much to look at—so—I guess you be better than ye look. Now here be a maid—a regular dimber-damber dell as looketh better than she be, for her's a gnashing, tearing shrew wi' no kindness in her. But she be handsome—as ye may see—and courted by many, whereby hath been overmuch ill-feeling, fighting and bloodshed among our young men—so wed this day she shall be for peace and quiet's sake! Him as can show most o' the pretty gold taketh her for good, and all according to our laws and ways."

Scarcely had she done speaking than the two young fellows hastened to count over to her such monies as they possessed, while the girl watched sullen and defiant.

"Aie—aie!" quoth the old woman suddenly. "Bennigo, you have but three to Jochabed's eight, so Jochabed taketh her—unless the nice, kind, young gorgio will give more—the fine young gorgio as my wisdom telleth me is other than he do seem—aha! What of it, young master—aie—aie?"

"Young man," whispered the girl, grasping my arm in strong, compelling fingers and staring at me with eyes big and desperate, "young man, if you would not see bloody work—turn out your pockets!"

Moved by her wild looks, I obeyed almost involuntarily, but hardly was my purse out of my pocket than she snatched and tossed it to the old woman.

"Count, grannam, count!" she cried imperiously, "and if't is not enough I've my little *churi* for the first as dare touch me!"

The old woman opened my purse, told over its contents very deliberately, nodded and, thrusting it into her bosom, spoke with the fierce-eyed men in her strange dialect, tapped each with her staff and motioned them to be gone; hereupon, and to my unutterable wonder, they obeyed her and slunk off without a word.

"Fourteen guineas!" said she. "Fourteen guineas be more than eight—fourteen guineas, a florin, one groat and three pennies! Aha, 't is more than she be worth, I think, by reason of her shrewish tongue and unkindly ways, and if only a *hindity mengro* and no true *Camlo* yet she be's a *rinkinni fakement* to look at, but then a bargain is a bargain—an' I wishes ye j'y o' her, my young rye!" Which said, she reached out her staff and touched first me and then the girl lightly on head and breast, muttering a farrago of strange words while her bright glance flashed from one to other of us; then she turned and, bowed upon her staff, climbed the ferny steep nimble and sure-footed despite her years and left us staring after her, the girl frowning and sullen as ever, I full of chagrined surprise and a growing uneasiness.

CHAPTER XIII

WHICH TELLS SOMEWHAT OF MY DEPLORABLE SITUATION

And after we had stood thus some while my companion spoke, though without troubling to turn her head or so much as glance towards me:

"Young man, what now?"

"Why, now," I answered, taking off my hat and bowing, "I have the honour to bid you good-bye!"

At this she wheeled quickly and stood viewing me over with a bold, unwavering gaze that it seemed nothing might abash; and though her eyes were large and well-shaped, yet I remember thinking them excessively unfeminine, the eyes rather of an ill-natured, pugnacious boy; and now, because of the hard coldness of her look, the unmaidenly, calculating intensity of her regard, I grew very conscious of my disfiguring garments and felt myself quite out of countenance.

"Why d'ye blush, young man?"

"Because you don't!"

"And why should I blush?"

"It would be more maidenly—?"

"Maidenly?" she repeated, and broke into such a mockery of laughter that I felt my cheeks indeed burn with a painful effusion and turning abruptly, I walked away in high dudgeon.

"Come back!" she commanded, but I went only the faster and being very earnest to rid myself of her, was even meditating ignominious flight, when I heard the leap of her feet in pursuit, felt her grip upon my arm and was checked thus so violently that I was amazed at the strength of her.

"Don't come your fine airs over me, young man," she panted in hot anger, her full, red lips tight-drawn, her great eyes dark and passionate. "Don't do it!" she repeated. "Don't ye dare!"

"Most decidedly not!" I answered, retreating before her threatening mien; and thus, not caring to turn my back on this young virago, I fronted her fierce scrutiny with what resolution I could, while devoutly wishing myself anywhere else in the world. And it was now that I realised she was taller than myself by fully an inch—indeed, perhaps a little more.

"Why does ye stare so?" she demanded.

I craved her forgiveness and lifted my offending gaze to the leaves above her head and maintained a dignified silence; whereupon she questioned me breathlessly,

"Now what are ye thinking?"

"That the ancient person spoke truly."

"You means as I'm a shrew?"

"Pray remember it was not I said so."

"But you means so! Come, does ye or don't ye?"

"Madam," I began, very conscious of the evil glitter of her knife, "if you will permit me to—"

"Don't 'madame' me, young man! I don't like it and I won't be madamed by you or any other—so don't dare—"

"Certainly not!" said I, fixing my gaze on the leaves again. "And may I suggest that we might converse more easily if you would have the kindness to put away your knife?"

"My little *churi*, d'ye mean? Not I, young man, not I! 'T is my best friend as saves from evil more than once! And how do I know as you won't come any games?"

"Games?" I repeated, shaking my head in mystification. "The sports of youth never interested me—indeed, I never play games—"

"No," cried she, with sudden, shrill laugh, "I don't think you do!" Here (to my startled amazement) she whipped short petticoats above her knee and thrust the knife into her garter. Now though my gaze was immediately abased to earth I none the less had a memory of an exceedingly well-turned and shapely limb.

"And so you thinks I'm a shrew, does ye?" she demanded, head aslant, and hands on shapely hips.

"I think you might perhaps be just a little more gentle."

"Tush, young man, gentleness don't serve a maid among the Folk!"

"What folk?"

"The Romans."

"Romans?" said I, puzzled.

"Aye, Romans. The Romany, gipsies, the poor folk."

"Are you a gipsy, then?"

33

"I guess so! Though old Azor, of the Romany *rawni Camlo*, do ever tell I'm no true Roman. So mayhap I'm not. However, when I grows up I takes to my little knife—by reason of the *chals*—aye, and uses it too, otherwise I might ha' been tamed by now instead o' being free to choose. Ah, yes, I might ha' been creeping the ways wi' some man's brat on my shoulders, to work while he slept, go hungry till he'd ate his fill and slave for him—ah, I hate men!" And she spat in contempt and very coarsely. Yet I could not but notice how perfectly shaped was this vivid, scornful mouth.

"So you don't like me, young man, and I do not like you, which is a pity, seeing you buys me out o' the tribe and—"

"Bought you!" I exclaimed, utterly aghast.

"Indeed and to be sure you did. Which is what many a man has wished to do ere this. However, according to the law of our tribe we are mates—"

"Great heaven!" I exclaimed in such unfeigned consternation that she knit her black brows at me. "Impossible!" quoth I. "Ridiculous—absolutely preposterous! There is no bond between us—you are free, quite free—nay, I'll go—now—"

"Are ye a man?" cried she between snapping white teeth. "If so, you'll be the first as runs away from me. And why? Is it that I'm not good enough—fine enough—handsome enough—"

"My good girl, pray be reasonable—" I pleaded, which seemed only to enrage her the more until, finding me mute and so helpless against the torrent of her wrath, she checked upon a word, her red lips curved to sudden smile, and her voice grew singularly and sweetly soft.

"Poor young man, sit down and let us talk," said she, as if we hadn't uttered a word hitherto. So willy-nilly down I sat facing her amid the fern and very ill at ease. "Poor young man," said she again, "don't go for to look so downcast over so small a matter. Here's you and here's me; what's done is done! Treat me fair and you'll find me faithful, quick with my needle, a good hand at cooking and not so unkind as they tell o' me. Your life shall be my life and mine yours. Where you go I'll follow and belike it is we shall get along without overmuch fighting and bloodshed."

"But," said I, my brain whirling, "I had no idea—I—I—never imagined anything of this sort—the whole situation is—impossible!"

"You bought me, remember!"

"Did I?"

"Of course you did!" said she, looking at me great-eyed and I saw her lips quivering. "You pays over to old Azor fourteen guineas, a florin, one groat and three pennies."

"The act was slightly involuntary, as I remember!" said I.

"Talk plain, young man, talk plain! You buys me, and what's more, old Azor weds us and makes me your mort according to the law o' the Folk."

"But not according to the laws of the English Church," said I, "and I am not one of the Folk. So you are quite free: the words of old Azor cannot bind me—"

"But they do bind me, young man, now and hereafter. Besides, you have bought me away from the tribe and I may never go back and you can never leave me solitary."

Here I groaned and she sighed, but with that quiver of red lips that might mean tears or laughter.

"A truly terrible situation!" said I.

"It is, young man, it is! Though it might ha' been worse."

"How so?"

"Well, though I have no liking for you, neither your looks, nor your ways, nor your talk, you are better than Bennigo and Jochabed that are very brute beasts."

Now at this I leapt to my feet and, turning on indignant heel, strode off, but soon she was up with me and together we presently came out into the high road. And now as she went beside me I saw with added misgiving that the sun was already westering.

CHAPTER XIV

IN WHICH I SATISFY MYSELF OF MY COWARDICE

After we had walked thus in silence for may be a mile or more, she spoke.

"Where are you taking me?" she demanded.

"Why do you follow me?" I retorted.

"Because I must—also it is my whim—and you so wishful to be rid o' me! And why?" she demanded sullenly.

"I prefer solitude."

"That's a pity!"

"Under the circumstances, it is!" I agreed.

"You haven't said what you mean to do wi' me!"

"Nothing!"

"Or where you takes me to?"

"I don't know."

"You must be a fool, young man. Where shall ye stay the night?"

"I don't know this either!"

"Lord, young man, you *are* a fool!"

"I begin to suspect I am!" said I bitterly. "However, I wish you would not call me 'young man.'"

"Why not, young man?"

"Because I resent the appellation."

"Talk plain, young man. You do what?"

"I strongly object to the term 'young man.'"

"But you are a man, ain't you—or something like one? And then you're young—very young, I can see that."

"I am nineteen!"

"And I am eighteen and years older than you! But if you don't like 'young man' what must I call ye?"

"Whatever you please," said I stiffly.

"I called ye 'fool' just now, but that won't do, seeing there's s' many about, so I think you shall be 'Tom'—"

"My name is Peregrine!" said I in sudden wrath. For a moment she viewed me with her direct, half-sullen gaze, then drooping dark lashes, laughed with a flash of strong white teeth.

"Hoity-toity! Don't be angry, Joe!" she mocked; and then: "Peregrine," said she, as if trying the sound of it. "'Peregrine' sounds very fine but then it don't agree wi' your looks—yes, I thinks Tom will suit ye better—or Sam, p'raps."

To this I deigned no answer but trudged on in moody silence, endeavouring to formulate some method of escape from this outrageous creature and so absorbed that I paid not the least heed to her foolish chatter until suddenly and most unpleasantly roused by the touch of her fingers on my ear which she tweaked none too gently. This extraordinary familiarity bred in me such indignant disgust that I sprang from her touch to stand dumb and trembling with fury.

"What," cried she, wilfully mistaking these tremors, "did I fright him then! Lord, how he do tremble! Oh, young man, you be a poor sort, I think!"

"Poor indeed!" cried I passionately. "Poorer even than you judge me, for I haven't a penny in the world! But here is my watch—all I have left—take it—take it, for God's sake, and let me go!" Saying which I drew forth my gold repeater and would have forced it into her hand, but now she sprang back in her turn and, bowing her head, fronted me with both arms rigidly out-thrust.

"Lord God!" she muttered. "D'ye think 'tis your money I want—your dirty money!"

"What matter my thoughts?" I cried. "Here is my watch; pray take it and let us say good-bye!"

Now here, to my unutterable amazement, she flung herself down, and crouched against the high, grassy bank, burst into a tempestuous weeping while I stood gaping and infinitely distressed.

"I—I beg your pardon!" said I at last and then, struck by the inadequacy of these trite words, drew a pace nearer. "Oh, pray—pray don't weep!" I pleaded. "If I have hurt you, I crave your forgiveness!" Here she sobbed but the fiercer. "But indeed—indeed," I stammered, "I thought—that is, I did not think, I—I mean I could not leave you destitute and having no money to bestow, I—"

"Money!" cried she bitterly. "Money!" And here, checking her sobs, added very unreasonably, "I hates you!"

"Please," said I, "oh, pray believe I meant only kindness! I thought you were—"

"A girl o' the road, a creeper o' ditches and byways—well, I'm not, I tell ye—I'm not! And I only followed ye because you were so wishful to be rid o' me and because you were so silly and young and strange I couldn't understand ye. But I do now, and I'm done wi' you! Go away—go away; I hates you more than Bennigo or Jochabed—go away, I hates you!"

"Blind me, and no wonder!" chuckled a hoarse voice behind me with such startling suddenness as for a moment bereft me of speech or motion; then, wheeling about, I came face to face with a rough-clad, villainous-looking man who stood, powerful legs apart, hairy fists grasping a short, heavy stick or bludgeon, and evil head out-thrust to stare beyond me at the prostrate form of my companion who had merely lifted her head to watch us through her tumbled hair.

"What d' you want?" I questioned the fellow, breathlessly.

"Never you mind, my chick," he growled, leering upon the girl's shapeliness with evil eyes. "I know what she wants—and it ain't you, so cut your stick and leave 'er to the man who can comfort a fine, 'andsome lass."

Though addressing me, his eyes were for my companion, his loathsome gaze never swerving from her prostrate form; very slowly and deliberately he began to approach her, and now in the man himself, in his every look and gesture there was an indescribable beastliness that turned me physically sick. But none the less, though my soul shrank within me, I ventured to grasp him by the sleeve.

"Let her alone—let her alone!" I gasped, dry-mouthed.

At this he turned on me, his evil face convulsed with a look of such brutish ferocity as appalled me, yet I only tightened my grip more desperately and repeated my passionate cry:

"Let her alone, I say; let her alone!"

Snarling inarticulately he leapt, striking at me with his bludgeon, a cruel blow that staggered and dazed me, sapping alike my strength and fortitude for, beholding the murderous glare of his eyes as he made to smite again, blind panic seized me and, reeling aside, I sped away on stumbling feet, my head throbbing with the blow,—deafened, sick and half-blind. But all at once I stopped, suddenly oblivious of self as, louder than the buzzing torment of my wounded head, rose a distressful cry and the more hateful sound of desperate struggling. Round I turned and, peering, saw them locked in close grapple, and her slender body bent and swaying in his merciless clutch: at which sight my pain and sickness and selfish fear were all forgotten and in their stead sprang a passionate desire to kill and be done with this evil thing that defiled the earth in man's shape. So back again sped I, and with every step this murderous desire grew until my mind held no other purpose. I remember snatching up the bludgeon he had let fall, whirling it aloft in both hands and striking for his bullet head, but in that instant (and well for him) he espied his danger and, loosing the girl, stooped and taking the blow across the broad of his back was beaten to his knees; but, as I swung again, he sprang in beneath my lifted arms. I felt the sickening impact of a blow and the bludgeon flew from my hold; then he was upon me, belabouring me with both fists, but twining my legs in his, I clung to those merciless arms, while above his fierce snarling and the painful shock of his blows, I heard the girl calling out to me:

"Fight him—fight! Don't cling like a woman—stand away—hit him back—fight!"

But though spent and faint with my hurts, I clung the more tenaciously, my face buried in his foul-smelling jacket, but at last he wrenched one arm from my desperate embrace; there was a sudden blinding shock that hurled me backward into the road: lying thus helpless, my antagonist leapt to kick the life out of my defenceless body, but I saw him reel suddenly and whirl about, grasping at an arm that spouted blood between his hairy fingers, while he stared at the girl crouched for another spring, the knife glittering in her hand.

"Go—go, filthy beast!" she panted. "Go, or I'll be the death o' ye!" And speaking, she began to creep towards me. The fellow gave back, staring from this deadly knife to her fierce eyes and reading there the truth of her words, he turned and made off, spattering blood as he went.

Relieved of his evil presence, I closed my eyes awhile feeling myself very faint and sick; when I opened them again I saw her standing above me, knife in hand, looking down on me with her sombre gaze.

"Kick me if you will!" I groaned.

"Why should I kick you?"

"Because I am a coward!" I mumbled, covering my bruised face. "I ran away—and left you—"

"Still, I don't think I'll kick you," said she in a soft, grave voice, "because although you runs away like a coward, you comes back again. Though to be sure I didn't need you—"

"But," said I, keeping my face hidden, "I heard you cry out—"

"That was because I wished you to come back, though having my little *churi*, I didn't need you; I've managed worse than him before now! However, you did come back—which was more than I expected. But I'll never call you 'young man' any more because you ain't a real man, are you?"

"God help me!" I groaned, for added to my shame the pain of my hurts was more than I could well bear, "O God help me!" And now indeed it seemed that in some measure He answered my prayer, for, as I strove to rise, the faintness seized me again and I sank to a blessed unconsciousness.

CHAPTER XV

PROVING THAT A GODDESS IS WHOLLY FEMININE

I was lying beneath a tree, my head softly pillowed and wet with cool water that refreshed me wonderfully; thus I presently turned my head and glanced up into eyes that gazed down upon me, very beautiful eyes these seemed, being soft and tender and darkly grey.

"Are ye better?" she questioned. Now at this I wondered, for the voice matched the eyes for gentleness.

"Thank you, much better."

"He hurt you more than I thought."

"It was the blow on the head—slight concussion, I think."

"And you stands up to him like—"

"You mean I ran away like a coward."

"He was twice as big as you—"

"No matter! Cowardice is always despicable, more especially in defence of one of the weaker sex," said I dismally.

"But you saves me, to be sure!"

At this I strove to rise in sheer amazement and thus found my head pillowed in her lap.

"How did I save you?" I demanded bitterly. "I that am a craven!"

"By giving me the chance to reach my little *churi*. However, I was never once afraid of the beast."

"I was!" I confessed miserably. "Afraid beyond words!"

"But you comes running back, and very fierce too!"

"I meant to kill him!"

"Why trouble to kill him?"

"I could not bear he should foul you in his brutal arms!"

Here came her hand to touch my aching brow and I closed my eyes again.

"Does your head ache very much?" she enquired.

"A little!" I groaned.

"Can ye walk?" she enquired. "'Tis goin' to storm and rain on us soon,
I think—can ye walk a small ways?"

For answer I got to my knees and, with her ready assistance, to my feet, but found myself very faint and sick and with my head throbbing as though it would burst.

"Come!" said she, taking my hand in her warm, strong, clasp. "There's rain in this wind—come! I knows a fair, likely place—"

"No, no!" cried I. "Please leave me, I shall be very well here—the rain will do me good, perhaps—besides, I have no money to pay for a night's lodging—"

"But I have!"

"No matter, I cannot live on your money."

"Aye, but you can, for this money is yourn as much as mine, seeing as I prigs it."

"What do you mean?"

"Lord, what should I mean except as I takes it, nabs it—steals it from yon dirty beast while he struggled wi' me. Look!" And taking out a ragged belcher neckerchief she unknotted one corner and showed me three bright, new guineas.

"Ah, throw them away!" I cried. "The man was so vile—"

"He was!" she nodded. "But his money is clean enough and will be useful to us—"

"But you are—a thief!" I exclaimed, aghast.

"And you are a fool!" she retorted, thrusting the money into a small leathern bag she carried at her girdle. "And he was a dirty rogue and his money shall feed us until I can earn more. And now let us hurry afore the storm ketches us."

"Where to?"

"There's a place I know where we can be warm and sheltered and nothing to pay."

And so, because of her persistence and my sickness, I suffered her to lead me where she would, though more than once I tripped and should have fallen but for her ready arm. Presently turning out of the road we came to a meadow and here, half-blinded by the pain of my head and scarcely able to drag one foot after the other, I earnestly besought her to leave me, storm or no storm; to which she merely bade me not to be a fool, with the further assurance that she would leave me when she wished and not before.

I remember stumbling down a grassy slope and through a tangle of bushes and dense-growing trees, amid whose whispering leafage shadows were deepening, and so at last to a half-ruined barn, very remote and desolate, into which she conducted me.

Here, from amid a pile of mouldy hay, she dragged a ladder which she reared to a small hatch or trap in the floor above and bade me mount. This I did, though very clumsily and presently found myself in an upper chamber or loft, illuminated by a small, unglazed window that opened beneath the eaves at one end. Scarcely was I here than she was beside me and brought me to an adjacent corner where was a great pile of hay that made the place sweet with its fragrance, whereon, at her behest, I sank down and would have expressed my gratitude, but she checked me, frowning.

"Are ye hungry?" she demanded ungraciously.

"Indeed, no, I thank you," I answered, lying back upon my fragrant couch.

"Well, I am!" she retorted sullenly. "And you will be, sooner or later, so I'll go afore the storm ketches me."

"Go where, and for what?"

"To buy supper with money as I stole, for you an' me to eat—"

"I'd rather starve!" quoth I, sitting up the better to say it.

"Starve!" she repeated, with a scornful flash of her great eyes. "You? d'ye know what starvation means? Ha' you ever tried it?"

"No," I admitted, "but none the less—"

"Then don't talk foolishness!" said she disdainfully. "You'll be glad t' eat an' ask no questions when you're hungry enough! And don't go pitying yourself and grieving over your bruises. If your eyes are bulged and blacked a bit—what of it? Lord! I've seen men get it worse than you an' come up smiling, but then to be sure they were men and stronger than you. However, you'll be better to-morrow! So now go to sleep and forget all about yourself if ye can—sleep till supper's ready and when I say eat—eat."

"Many thanks, but I do not desire any supper."

"Wait till you smell it!"

"I shall neither smell it nor eat it," I answered, frowning, "because I propose to rid you of my presence almost immediately."

"Meaning as you will cut your stick?"

"Certainly not! I mean that I shall take my departure just so soon as I find myself sufficiently recovered."

"Why, then," said she, compressing her lips and jutting her round chin at me in highly unfeminine fashion, "you'll have to jump or fly."

"What do you mean?"

"I shall take away the ladder!"

"You would never do such a thing!" quoth I, starting.

"Tush!" she retorted and, turning from me with a disdainful swirl of her short petticoat, began to descend into the depths below, seeing which, I scrambled to my feet and crossed to the trap, only to behold her standing beneath me, the ladder dragged quite out of my reach.

"Fly down, little bird!" she cried insolently. "Jump, Jack—jump!" and snapping finger and thumb at me, was gone before my anger might find vent in words.

Trapped and imprisoned thus, I presently came wandering disconsolately back to the hay-pile and lying there began to ponder upon the extreme unlovely deportment of this strange creature whose almost every speech and look and gesture outraged all my preconceived ideas of "the sex", and bitterly to deplore my present situation.

Evening was falling apace but there was still sufficient light to show me something of the place wherein I lay and the orderly disorder that surrounded me. In one corner, upon a rough board that served for a shelf, stood six battered volumes flanked by divers pots and pans; against the wall near by hung a small, cracked mirror, while dangling from nails driven into the warped and twisted timbering of roof and walls hung a great variety of baskets, large and small and variously shaped, of rush or bent withies, many of which seemed in course of manufacture. These and many other objects I took casual heed of as I lay, but often my gaze would rove back to the six books standing so orderly amid the pots and pans; indeed, these so stirred my interest that I began to wonder what manner of books these might be and what should bring them in such a strange and desolate place, so that despite my aches and pains I felt much disposed to rise and investigate them, but in the end was content to lie and stare at them while the light failed and shadows deepened until, my eyes little serving me, I closed them and fell fast asleep.

CHAPTER XVI

IN WHICH I BEGIN TO APPRECIATE THE VIRTUES OF THE CHASTE GODDESS

Assuredly never were the nostrils of mortal youth saluted with odour more inspiring and altogether more delectable than that which, wooing me from the drowsy arms of Morpheus, awoke me to growing consciousness of three several things, namely: light, movement and an extraordinarily poignant hunger.

Being awake, I firstly sniffed of this most appetising aroma, then lifting my head espied the girl busily combing her long hair before that small mirror I have mentioned. Now although the place was illumined by no more than a farthing dip, yet this was sufficient to wake many fugitive gleams and coppery lights in these long, rippling tresses, so that I lay for some time content to watch as she combed with smooth-sweeping motions of arm and wrist; but suddenly this arm grew still and I knew that she was viewing me through this silky curtain as it hung.

"Well?" she demanded suddenly, and putting back the hair from her face, stood looking down at me with her sombre, half-sullen gaze.

"Well?" said I, sitting up. And now, beholding her face framed thus in her glossy tresses, the wide, low brow, the deep eyes, the delicate modelling of nose and chin, the vivid lips, I realised that she was beautiful—beautiful as any fabled goddess or dryad; and what with this, the rippling splendour of her hair that covered her like a garment, the deep silence of this remote solitude, there rushed upon me a sense of such intimacy that I caught my breath and averted my gaze instinctively, awed by, yet delighting in, this sudden consciousness of her beauty.

"Well," said she again, "d'ye smell it?"

Starting, I glanced up, to find her busied with the comb again and immediately recognised that here was neither goddess nor dryad but merely a well-shaped, comely young woman with extraordinarily long hair; which fact established, my hunger (momentarily forgotten) returned with keener pang than ever.

"Are ye going to sleep again?" she enquired, finding me silent.

"No!"

"Well, don't you smell it?"

"Pray what is it?"

"A duck as I be roasting to our supper."

"Duck!" I repeated, mouth watering. "I have breathed its enticement ever since I awoke."

"Wi' plenty o' sage and onion, a new loaf, and cheese!" she added, with a nod of her shapely head at each item, "unless," said she, eyeing me askance, "you're minded to starve—as you said?"

At this I grew very despondent and, sighing, watched her twist her glossy hair into two long braids and tie up the ends with small ribbands which I thought a very quaint and pretty fashion.

She now bade me help her to set up the supper table, which proved to be a weather-beaten half-door propped upon baskets. This done, she took the candle and descended below, I following; and here, within an old cauldron pierced with many holes, burned a fire, above which was a covered pot whence emanated that fragrance I have already mentioned, but stronger and more savoury than ever now, so that my hunger was wrought to a passionate yearning, more especially when, having removed the pot from the fire, she lifted the cover. Ascending to the loft she pronounced supper all ready and bade me sit down and eat. But this I could not do for my pride's sake as I freely confessed, which seemed to surprise her not a little.

"Well then," said she, perceiving me thus determined, "you may eat if you are truly hungry, because none o' the money I prigs pays for this duck."

So down I sat forthwith and never in all my life enjoyed any meal quite so much, as I told her.

"Well, then, eat it!" said she in her ungracious, half-sullen manner.

"I mean to," I retorted, "though I must say you are a wonderful cook." At this she merely scowled at me and I did not venture another remark until the sharper pangs of hunger were appeased, then, sighing, I spoke again. "Yes, I repeat you are a wonderful cook! But then everything seems so wonderful to me—this place, for instance—so strange and so solitary!"

"It is!" she answered, leaning her chin on her hands and staring at me across the table. "That's why I runs away here to hide from the *chals* or when in any trouble wi' old Azor—yes, 'tis a very lonely place, which do make me wonder if you be afeard o' ghosts?"

"No—that is, I don't think so—if such things do really exist. But why do you ask?"

"A woman was murdered here once an' they say her spirit walks, so there's few people dare venter here by day an' never a one by night, an' that's why 'tis so lonely an' that's why I loves the place."

"Then you don't believe in ghosts?"

"Well I sees strange things among the Romans; there's the *dukkerin* and *dukkeripen*, an' the Walkers o' the Heath. They're a strange folk, the Romans—'specially old Azor!"

"But you are not afraid—never have been?"

"No," she answered, shaking her head slowly, "I've never been afeard of anything or any one yet—except old Azor." And beholding her as she said this, observing the proud cast of her features, the lofty carriage of her head, her compelling eyes, resolute chin and the noble lines of her form, I knew she spoke truth and began to doubt if she were no more than a mere comely, well-shaped young female, after all.

"Pray, what is your name?" I enquired.

"Anna."

"Indeed it is a pretty name, though you are more like my conception of
Diana."

"Who's she?"

"She was a young goddess."

"A goddess?" repeated my companion in her deep, soft voice, "that don't sound much like me."

"A goddess, very brave and strong, who despised all men and feared none!"

"That does sound more like me! Though I thought all goddesses were beautiful?" she added wistfully.

"So they were," I nodded, "but how do you know this?"

"From Jerry Jarvis—"

"What, the Tinker?" I exclaimed. "Do you mean the tinker who calls himself a 'literary cove'—the wonderful tinker who writes excellent poetry and travels about with a pony named Diogenes?"

"Yes, there be only one Jerry Jarvis," answered my companion. "'Twas Jerry taught me to write and lent me books to read. I've known him since I can remember and he was always kind. Jerry's a good man!"

"And writes real poetry!" I nodded. "At least I think so. I should like to meet him again."

"Well, he'll be Tonbridge way about now. I knows all his rounds an' he's reg'lar as a clock."

"Do you know the way to Tonbridge?"

"Of course!"

"Yes, I'll go to Tonbridge to-morrow; you shall tell me the best way to get there, if you will."

"'Tis very sure you are better of your beating."

"Yes, thank God!" I answered.

"Though your eyes will be black to-morrow."

"Which will serve me right and properly for my cowardice."

"But you're not afeard o' ghosts!"

"Heaven knows," quoth I bitterly, "I might be if I saw one. And as for solitude, I don't think I should care to stay here alone night after night and day after day as you seem to have done."

"Oh, you gets used to it."

"But how do you pass your time in this solitude?"

"Reads mostly, and makes my baskets; there be few can ekal me at rush or willow. And there's good money in baskets!"

"What books have you read?"

"Not so many as I'd like."

"Tell me some of them."

"Well there's the 'Castle of Otranto' and Virgil and 'Peregrine
Pickle' and the Psalms, and 'Tom Jones' and John Milton's Poems,
'Tristram Shandy.' Dryden, Plutarch's lives—oh, and a lot beside—"

"And which do you like best?"

For answer she reached the six volumes from amongst her pots and pans and these I found to be: Shakespeare, 'Tristram Shandy,' the Bible, Anson's Voyages and 'Robinson Crusoe.'

"You have shown most excellent judgment and a most catholic taste!" said I.

"You loves books, too!" she nodded. "I sees that by the way you handles 'em. And I keeps these six here because I can read them over and over and never tires, though there's a lot I don't understand."

"That," said I, looking upon my companion with new vision, "that is because each of these books shrines some part of undying Truth which can never weary and never die. I think," said I, setting the books back in their accustomed place, "I think I will call you Diana, if I may?"

"Very well."

"And my name is Peregrine."

"You seemed to like your supper," said she, beginning to clear away the platters.

"More than words can express!"

39

"So did I," she nodded, "and that was worth a little risk."

"What risk, Diana?"

"Well, I tells you the duck was not bought with any of the beast's money, didn't I?"

"Yes. Pray, how did you come by it?"

"Prigged it!"

"Great heaven! You mean that you—"

"Yes. I goes to a farmhouse as I knows of to get some milk an' eggs, an' spies four ducks on the kitchen table, trussed an' stuffed all ready for the oven, so I brings one away—only one, though I might ha' nabbed two just as easy—"

"But this was burglary!" I gasped.

"But 'twas a dainty supper!"

"This is frightful!" I exclaimed.

"But the duck was very tender—you said so."

"Oh, girl," I cried, "don't you know it is very wicked to steal? Are you aware you have broken one of God's commandments, contravened the law and made yourself liable to arrest and imprisonment—indeed, people have been hanged for less! O Diana, how could you do a thing so shameful, so unworthy your womanhood—how could you—how could you?"

But instead of answering or paying the least heed to this so earnest appeal, she continued her business of clearing away supper things and table, and thereafter begun to make herself a couch of hay in the corner remotest from mine, and all without so much as a glance in my direction.

"And now," said she at last, "if you're quite ready, I'll blow out the candle."

"Whenever you will," I answered, stretching myself upon my hay-pile. Almost as I spoke the light vanished, and in the pitchy gloom my hearing seemed to grow the more acute; I heard her light, assured tread, the fall of her shoes as she kicked them off, the rustle of the hay that was her bed, a long-drawn, sleepy sigh. These sounds at last subsiding, I spoke:

"Have I angered you, Diana?" Here I paused for answer but getting none continued, "Though indeed my strictures were all well-meant, for I cannot bear that you should do anything unworthy—" Here, though she uttered no word, I distinguished a sudden, petulant rustle of hay as if she had kicked viciously. "And so, Diana," I continued, "I want you to promise that henceforth you will so govern your conduct, so order your life that you may become a woman, gentle and sweet and good, in whose presence no evil thing may exist, one who is herself an inspiration to good and noble things, a woman whose friendship is a privilege and whose—whose love would be a crowning glory. Do you understand, Diana?"

"Hold your tongue!" she cried very suddenly. "Hold y'r tongue an' go to sleep—do!"

In the fervour of my exordium I had assumed a sitting posture but at her coarse rejoinder I fell back, inexpressibly shocked, and lay staring upon the dark, tingling with mortification that I should have wasted myself in such vain appeal and been thus callously repulsed by one who was no more than an ignorant gipsy-wench, prone to coarse expressions and small larcenies, a creature knowing little difference between good and evil and caring less. But now, remembering her rough upbringing and the wild folk who had fostered her, my anger gave place to commiseration, for how could she, under such circumstances, be other than what she seemed? And yet—was she in herself good or evil? This doubt troubled me so much that I turned to stare towards that dark corner where she lay; and listening to her gentle and regular breathing, I judged that she slept already, though more than once I heard the hay rustle as she stirred, sighing plaintively. But sleep was not for me, my mind being greatly troubled by this same unanswerable question: Was she a Diana indeed, dowered with the virtues of that chaste goddess, or only a poor, small-souled creature debased by the circumstances of her lawless origin?

Now as I lay thus wakeful, vainly seeking an answer to this most distressing question, I became aware that the place was no longer dark; instead was a soft glow, an ever-increasing radiance, and lifting my eyes to the unglazed window I beheld the moon,—Dian's fair self, throned in splendour, queen of this midsummer night, serene and infinitely remote, who yet sent down a kindly beam, that, darting athwart the gloom, fell in a glory upon that other Diana where she lay outstretched in peaceful slumber. And gazing upon this face, softened and beautified by gentle sleep—the wide, low brow, these tender lips, this firm and resolute chin, I thought to read therein a sweet nobility, purity and strength; and, like the darkness, my doubts and trouble were quite banished.

Therefore, lifting my gaze once more to Dian's placid loveliness, I breathed her a sigh of gratitude, for it seemed that she had shown me the answer to my question. And thus, my mind at rest, I presently fell asleep.

CHAPTER XVII

HOW WE SET OUT FOR TONBRIDGE

"Oho—hey—hallo!"

Starting up, I opened sleepy eyes to be dazzled by a glory of early sunshine, and creeping from the hay wherein I lay half-buried, I came blinking to the open trapdoor and beheld Diana standing below, flourishing a long-handled fork at me.

"Kooshti divvus," said she.

"Good morning!" said I.

"It is!" she nodded. "That's what I said! And the less reason to sleep—here's me been up an hour an' more."

"You should have waked me, Diana."

"I was too busy. But if you are awake, come down and wash."

"Wash what?"

"Yourself—Lord, you needs it bad enough by your looks! And 'cleanliness is next to godliness'—they says. So go an' wash!"

"Certainly!" said I, a little haughtily. "Though permit me to assure you that I am not in the habit of neglecting so healthful and necessary—"

"Soap an' towel—in th' basket—corner yonder!" said she, kneeling to puff the fire to a blaze as I descended the ladder.

"Thank you, and where shall I find the necessary water?"

"Outside—in the brook—enough to drown'd you! And take your time, make a good job of it—a clean body makes a clean mind—sometimes. So scrub hard!" At this I came where she must meet my look.

"And pray, madam," I demanded, head aloft and arms folded, "do you thus suggest that my mind is so very unclean?"

"O la!" cried she, waving the fork at me with a pettish gesture. "Don't try to come your fine airs over me in such breeches and your eyes black and face all smutty—go an' get washed first!"

At this I turned and marched out of the barn, quite forgetting soap and towel until she came running to thrust them upon me, willy-nilly.

"There's ham an' eggs for breakfast!" she volunteered.

"Then I trust you will enjoy them," said I stiffly, "but as regards myself I most certainly shall not—"

"Don't frown," she admonished, "for with your face so bruised and swollen it do make you look that comical!" And laughing, she sped away, leaving me to scowl upon the empty air.

But the morning was glorious; I stood in a dew-spangled world radiant with sunshine while all about me the feathered host, that choir invisible, poured forth a song of universal praise to greet this new-born day. With this joyful clamour in my ears, this fresh, green world before my eyes, I grew joyful too, and hasted towards the brook, my foolish petulance quite forgotten.

Following these murmurous, sun-kissed waters, I came where they widened suddenly into a dark and silent pool; and here, well-screened by bending willows, I ventured to bathe and found in the cool, sweet water such gasping delight that I could have sung and shouted for pure joy of it. Greatly invigorated and prodigiously hungry, I donned my unlovely garments happily enough but stooping above this watery mirror to comb my damp locks into such order as my fingers might compass, I beheld my face, its features bruised and distorted out of all shape; and remembering Diana had laughed at and made mock of these disfigurements, I sat down, not troubling about my hair, and began to muse upon her heartlessness, contrasting this with my aunt Julia's unfailing sympathy and tender, loving care, and immediately felt myself woefully solitary, miserably cold and desperately hungry. The world, despite sunshine and bird-song, was a dark and evil place wherein I stood desolate and forlorn; here, bowing my head between my hands, I began to despair of myself and the future. But now, and all at once, what must obtrude upon these gloomy thoughts but a vision of ham and eggs, a tantalisation that would not be banished.

"Perry—green!" I lifted my head to listen intently; and presently heard it again, a voice rich and full and smooth as note of blackbird, calling upon my name: "Perry—green! Breakfast's ready—ham an' eggs! Perry—green!" Snatching soap and towel I rose, my gloomy thoughts forgotten again, and hasted whither this voice summoned me.

"Are ye washed?" she enquired, dexterously skewering a large ham rasher upon the iron fork and transferring it to a platter.

"I am!"

"And hungry?"

"Extremely!"

"Then you may eat! Here's breakfast—only don't go asking how I got it—nor yet where!"

So we ate, scarce speaking; I, for one, seldom lifting my gaze from the platter balanced upon my knees. I ate, I say, each mouthful a joy, ham that was a melting ecstasy and eggs of such delicate flavour as I had never tasted till now, it seemed.

"Diana," I sighed at last, "you are a truly wonderful cook!"

"No," she answered; "you are hungry, that's all. 'T is a good thing to be hungry—sometimes!"

O gentle and perspicacious reader! You, madam, who being so daintily feminine, cannot be supposed to revel in the joys of hog-flesh, flesh of ox, sheep, bird or fish, no matter how excellent well cooked; and you, honourable sir, who, being comfortably replete of such, seated before your groaning board at duly frequent and regular intervals, masticate in duty to yourself and digestion, but with none of that fine fervour of enthusiasm which true hunger may bestow—I cry ye mercy! For your author, tramping the roads, weary yet aglow with exercise, hath met and had familiar fellowship with lusty Hunger, and learned that eating, though a base necessity, may also be a joy. If therefore your author forgetteth soul awhile to something describe and mayhap dilate upon such material things as food and drink and their due assimilation, here and now he doth most humbly crave your patient forbearance.

"It is a good thing to be hungry—sometimes!" said Diana.

"If one may assuage that hunger with such ham and eggs!" I added.
"Though I greatly fear I shall never taste their like again."

"Anything'll taste good," quoth she, rising, "if you're hungry enough!"

"Diana," said I, watching her as she flitted lightly to and fro, engaged on what she called "tidying up." "Diana, what are we going to do?"

"I thought we were going to Tonbridge?"

"I am."

"Well then, the sooner we starts the better."

"But," I demurred, rubbing my chin and staring hard at the toe of my clumsy shoe, "don't you think it a little unwise—very extraordinary and—yes, extremely irregular for—for two people of opposite sexes to consort thus? Are not folk apt to misjudge our intimacy?"

"What folk?"

41

"Well, I mean the world."

"Lord, Peregrine, who's us for the world to trouble about?"

"I merely mention this because I dread lest I compromise you."

"What's compromise?"

"Well," I explained, lifting my gaze to the time-worn timbering above my head, "people seeing us together might suppose we—we were—lovers—"

"But we ain't!" she retorted, turning to look at me. "And never shall be—shall we?"

"No!" said I with my gaze still turned upward. "Of course not! But none the less people might think we were—were living together!"

"Well, so we are, ain't we?" she demanded.

"But," said I, staring at my shoe again, "suppose they imagine—"

"What, Peregrine?"

"Evil of us?"

"What matter, s' long as we knows different?"

"But I cannot bear that any should speak or even think evil of you, Diana—"

"Never mind about me—though it's kind of you!" she added in that suddenly soft, half-shy tone that I have before attempted to describe. "Y' see," she continued, "nobody ever troubled themselves about me all my life, except Jerry—or them as I keeps my little knife for. And you ain't that sort, so we'll go on together until I feels like leaving you, an' then I'll go—"

"Go where, Diana?"

"Back to the lonely places—"

"What do you mean?"

"Nothing!" she answered, shaking her head. "You wouldn't never understand. But I'll go along wi' you to Tonbridge."

"Very well!" said I. "And on the way, if you'll allow me, I'll teach you to speak more correctly and to behave with a—a little more—feminine restraint—"

"Oh—and why should I?" she demanded, cheeks flushed and proud head aloft.

"Because," I answered, struck anew by her beauty, "though you look like a goddess you speak and act like a—like—"

"A what? And—be careful!" she warned.

"I don't know."

"Come, speak out!"

"Indeed, I can think of no just parallel; you are like no one I ever saw or heard. But your speech and actions often do not match your looks."

"And your looks don't match your words or actions!" she retorted, "you speak s' very grand and look s' very—s' very—"

"What?" I questioned anxiously.

"I don't know. 'T isn't a scarecrow—scarecrow's clothes fits better—but you looks an' acts like nobody as ever I see afore."

"At the very first opportunity I will certainly purchase better garments!" quoth I, scowling down at the noxious things that covered me.

"With no money?" she scoffed.

"I have my watch!" quoth I.

"They'll think as you prigs it and hand you over to the narks an' queer cuffins—"

"That sounds very terrible; what do you mean?"

"I means the *plastramengroes*."

"What in the world is that?" said I.

"Oh, *Kooshti duvvel*!" she exclaimed. "You don't know nothin'; you're what they calls a *rye*, ain't you?"

"Pray, what is a rye?" I enquired, a little diffidently.

"A *gorgio* gentleman," she explained patiently.

"What should give you that impression?"

"You're s' different to the 'Folk'—or any of the padding kind."

"Yes, I suppose I am—despite my clothes!"

"Your speech is soft an' your ways are softer, but you have a high an' mighty look about ye at times—although you're so precious green."

"Green?"

"As grass!" she nodded, "Very green—like your name."

"My name is Peregrine, as you know."

"But t' other suits ye best!"

"You grow more unkind, Diana!"

"You're a scholar too, o' course?"

"I have received a somewhat careful education."

"What d'ye know?"

"Well, I am fairly conversant with Greek and Latin, though a trifle shaky on the higher mathematics, I fear."

"You've read lots an' lots o' books?"

"I have."

"And you're nineteen years old?"

"True!"

"And such a very poor, helpless thing!" said she in lofty scorn. "Oh, you may be able to teach me how t' speak an' how t' behave, but 'tis me as could teach ye how to live without friends or money! You may know how to use words but ye can't use your hands! You can talk but ye can't 'do'—you don't know how to help yourself nor nobody else! You're a poor creature as would creep into a wet ditch an' perish o' want an' misery—an' all because you're so full o' Greek an' Latin an' fine airs that you can't even tell how many beans make five!" Having said which, all in a breath, she turned and, mounting the ladder, left me staring vacantly at the crumbling wall and greatly humbled since all these indictments I knew for very truth. Sitting thus, I heard her descend the ladder, felt her hand upon my bowed shoulder and glancing up, saw her eyes big and soft and tender.

"Come, Peregrine," said she in her gentle voice, "let us go, and while we walk you shall give me my first lesson how to talk—and behave, if you will."

"No," said I, rising, "first you shall teach me how to be a little less of a fool. Pray—how many beans do make five?"

"Why, four an' a little one, o' course," she answered, with a tremulous laugh.

"Diana," said I, clasping her hands in mine, "you were exactly right; considering all my advantages, I am indeed a poor, helpless sort of thing! You shall teach me how to become a little wiser, if possible. So let us try to help each other like friends, Diana, like true friends."

"Yes," said she, "like true friends, Peregrine."

Then, having hidden the ladder among the hay, we went forth from the barn into the sunshine together.

CHAPTER XVIII

CONCERNING THE GRAMMAR OF A GODDESS

A broad, white road led between grassy banks topped by hedgerows and trees whose wide-flung, rusting leafage cast a pleasant shade, while high in the sunny air a lark carolled faint and sweet against the blue. From the distant woods stole a wind languorous and fragrant of dewy earth, of herb and flower, a wind soft as a caress yet vital and full of promise (as it were) so that as I breathed of it, hope and strength were renewed in me with an assurance of future achievement. Filled thus with an ecstasy unknown till now, I stopped suddenly to look above and round about, glad-eyed; and thus presently my eager gaze came upon my companion who had paused also, her eyes upraised to watch the flight of a mounting lark. Beholding her in this graceful posture, so vivid with life and youthful strength, all slim shapeliness from wind-kissed hair to buckled shoe, she seemed the spirit, nay the very embodiment, of this fair midsummer morning.

"O Diana!" I exclaimed. "Is it not good to be alive?"

"The lark seems to think so," she answered, her gaze still uplifted. "Yet I wonder if he is truly happy, or sings only because 'tis his nature?"

"Because he's happy, of course!" I answered. "Who wouldn't be happy on such a morning?"

"Well, I ain't, for one!"

"Not happy, Diana—but why?"

"Because!"

"Because of what?"

"Oh, never mind! Let's go on."

"Won't you tell me?"

"No. Let's go on."

"May I not share your sorrows, Diana?" I enquired, and laid my hand on her arm; but she shook me off, though not before I had seen her eyes were suffused with tears. Therefore I caught and held her hand so that she stopped, facing me, and thus I saw her tears were falling and she not troubling to hide or wipe them away.

"Can't you let me alone?" she sobbed.

"Why, Diana!" I exclaimed. "O child, don't weep; true friends must share sorrow as well as joy! So, if we are to be friends, tell me what is troubling you."

"Yonder!" said she, pointing to the blue distance before us. "'Tis the beyond—'tis the Future as do fright me."

"But I thought you feared nothing, Diana?"

"Only myself!" she cried, throwing out her arms in a sudden wild gesture. "There be a devil inside o' me sometimes—a devil as even old Azor was afeard of an' most o' the men—"

"Then I think this must be rather a good devil, Diana."

"Ah no—no!" she cried. "'Tis a devil as drives me to wild thoughts an' ways—things as do shame me. 'Tis very fierce and strong!"

"Still, I do not think I fear this devil—or ever should, Diana."

"You? But you calls yourself a coward!"

"To be sure I did, and very properly, because I was greatly afraid of a ruffian with a bludgeon and fled accordingly. But I do not fear devils in the least."

"Because you don't know—"

"There you are quite wrong!" said I, patting the hand I still held and noting its strength and shapeliness. "For, and apprehend me, Diana, we all, each one of us, possess a devil large or small, and my own is uncomfortably big and strong occasionally, and very difficult to overcome. But this is what devils are for—"

"You're flamming me!" she cried angrily and snatched her hand away.

"A very unpleasing word! Pray what does it signify?"

"You're gammoning—"

"That is rather worse—"

"You're making game o' me!"

"On the contrary, I'm very serious! Don't you see, Diana, that all demons and devils are a means to our ultimate good?"

"No, I don't! How can they be?"

"In this manner: every devil, be he an evil thought, passion, hate or revenge, a desire to do harm, to lie, to steal, to kill or to run away like a coward—these are all demons to be fought with and overcome, and the oftener we vanquish them, the stronger and better we grow, until at last you—or I—may become something very near an angel."

"I could never be an angel!" she retorted sullenly. "And what's more, I don't want—"

"You do," said I, "indeed you do, I'm sure, or why should you so hate this devil of yours and fear the beyond? And there is an angel inside you, Diana; I have seen it peep at me through your eyes—"

"Now I think you're talking foolish!" said she petulantly.

"Perhaps so," I nodded, "but 'foolish' is an adjective which in this instance should be an adverb and which we will proceed to make so by the suffix 'ly.' Thus instead of saying, I talk 'foolish,' you must say I talk 'foolishly'—"

"So you do!" quoth she.

"Then I will talk grammar instead, Diana. Pray give me your most careful attention. Yonder is a tree, which is a noun common; the tree is shady, which is an adjective qualifying the noun 'tree,' and casts its shade obliquely, which is an adverb governing the qualifying verb 'casts.'" Thus, as we walked, I proceeded to give her a definition of the various parts of speech with their relation one to another, and found her to be, on the whole, very quick and of a retentive memory. Encouraged thus, I plunged into my subject whole-heartedly and was discussing the difference between transitive and intransitive verbs when she checked me in full career by asking:

"Have you a father and mother?"

"Good heaven!" I exclaimed. "What has this to do with grammar?"

"Well, but have you?" she persisted.

"No," answered I; "they died before I can remember."

"So did mine!" she nodded. "But you have friends?"

"Yes."

"Many?"

"Three," I answered. "To be particular, one aunt and two uncles."

"Rich folk, ain't they?"

"Well, yes, I suppose they are. And allow me to point out that the word 'ain't' is becoming obsolete in polite conversation, giving place to 'are not' or to 'is not' as the case may be. Now, returning to our grammar—" And forthwith I began to decline for her benefit verbs regular and irregular, together with their tenses; I parsed and analysed simple sentences, explaining the just relation of Subject, Object and Predicate, while she watched me grave-eyed and listened to my grammatical *dicta* with an attention that I found highly gratifying. Thus I dilated upon the beauties of our language, its wealth of metaphor and adjectival possibilities, its intricacies and pitfalls, until the sun was high and my throat parched.

"There, Diana," I concluded, "here endeth our first lesson for the present. I trust you have not found me too discursive?"

"Well," said she, knitting her black brows thoughtfully, "I'm not sure. It all sounds very—wonderful, but I don't understand a word of it."

"Great heaven!" I ejaculated. "Why could you not say so before?"

"I didn't like to interrupt you."

"Here I have been talking for a good hour—"

"Two hours," she nodded; "indeed, you're a wonderful talker!"

"But all to no purpose it seems!" said I ruefully.

"No," she answered, "it has helped to pass the time and I knows that a noun is a tree."

"Oh, indeed!" quoth I. "And what more have you learned?"

"That if you add to a verb it's an adverb, though both are much of a muchness, and an adjective is not like either, though they all has summat to do with a tree we passed a long time ago."

At this I gasped and sinking down in a shady spot, fanned myself feebly with my hat.

"My poor child," said I mournfully, "my poor—"

"I'm not your child!" she retorted. "And as for poor—what o' this?" and she shook the bag at her girdle until the coins within it chinked.

"This is most distressing!" said I, shaking my head.

"What is?"

"A noun is not a tree—"

"You says it was—"

"I told you a tree was a noun—which is a very different thing."

"If a tree's a noun, a noun's a tree—or should be, and if 'tain't, then grammar's foolish and I don't want none of it—"

"That sentence is execrable grammar, Diana, because two negatives make a positive hence when you say 'you don't want none,' it really means that you do want some—"

"I don't care!" she said in her sullen fashion.

"But you must—"

"Well, I shan't!"

"Don't be a naughty child, Diana! Please come and sit down."

"I hates your grammar—"

"The sun is very hot, Diana, so come and sit down here by me and let us talk like the true friends I hope we are."

With a petulant gesture she obeyed; so there we sat side by side, our backs to the broad bole of the great tree, a branch of which, drooping low, made for us a green bower, as it were. And here, sitting thus side by side, we continued our discussion on this wise:

DIANA (sullenly). However, I don't want any more o' your grammar; I gets along well enough without it—

MYSELF (interrupting). But then I want you to do much more than just get along, Diana.

DIANA. How much more?

MYSELF. Well, I want you to live to the utmost of your capacity, to make the very best of yourself and your life, to become the wonderful woman you may be if only you will. And this you can never do without a knowledge of grammar and deportment.

DIANA. And why d'ye want me to do—to be all this?

MYSELF. Because it is a duty you owe to the world and your own womanhood. If we all strove to do our best, the world would become a better place for everybody, at once.

DIANA (passionately). Oh, 'tis easy for you to talk so fine; you've got friends—rich friends t' help you! But who have I got—

MYSELF. Well, Diana, his name, as I told you before, is Peregrine.

DIANA. You?

MYSELF. Precisely—

DIANA. d'ye mean—what do you mean?

MYSELF. That I will be your true friend always—to help you so long as you need—if you will have me. My friends shall be your friends—especially my aunt Julia, who is the noblest and best of women—

DIANA (ungraciously). A *Kooshti para rati*—a true *rawni*—a grand lady, I s'pose?

MYSELF. She is a truly great lady.

DIANA. And wears silk gowns that rustle, I s'pose?

MYSELF (mystified). I believe her gowns do rustle—but what in the world—?

DIANA. Then I should hate her!

MYSELF. But why? In the name of reason why under heaven should—?

DIANA. Just because!

MYSELF. Pray be more explicit. Why should you hate one whom—?

DIANA. Because she'd rustle her fine silks at me and look through me and try to make me feel I was only small beer.

MYSELF. 'Small beer' is an extremely unpleasing phrase, Diana.

DIANA. But it tells ye what I mean. I sees grand ladies afore to-day and I don't want any of 'em to rustle at me! I won't have their pity and I don't want their help—I likes the silent places and my little *churi* best.

MYSELF. My aunt Julia is a very noble woman, as good as she is beautiful, a woman whom all respect and honour—

DIANA. Well, I hates her already.

MYSELF. That is exceedingly unreasonable! How can you hate one you have never seen?

DIANA. Easily.

MYSELF. But in heaven's name, why?

DIANA. Because I do!

MYSELF. That is no answer! (Here she scowled at me.) Pray be sensible, Diana! (Here she kicked viciously at a tuft of grass.) Indeed you make it very difficult for me to help you.

"I don't want your help either!" she retorted angrily.

"No matter!" quoth I, folding my arms. "My mind is quite made up."

"So is mine!" and speaking, she would have risen, but I caught a fold of her petticoat. "Let go!" she cried.

"Sit still, Diana, and listen to me!"

"Let me go!"

"Not until you have heard all I wish to say—" As I spoke, with a movement incredibly quick, she flashed out her knife.

"What, Diana," said I, staring into her fierce eyes, "do you think that is necessary with me? Would you harm your friend, child?" The fierce eyes drooped and, averting her head, she sat mute and still. "I am going to help you," I continued, "because in spite of any or every demon, I know you are sweet and pure and good."

"How—d'ye know this?" she questioned.

"I know it, I am sure of it—oh, well—because!"

"That's no answer!" said she in her turn.

"Still, I think you know what I mean. But, and this is very sure, Diana, because I respect you, I would have the world respect you. And therefore I am going to help you however I may. So that is settled once for all."

"Suppose I—runs away?"

"I shall have to find you, of course."

"Then you—don't want to be rid o' me—so much?"

"Certainly not!"

"But you offered me your gold watch to—"

"True!" I admitted, a little put out. "But I—I did not know or understand you—then."

"And do you now?"

"I think so—or at least enough to know that you can also help me if you will—"

"How could I help you?" she questioned wistfully.

"You might perhaps teach me to be—less of a coward—more like yourself—"

"Like me?" she repeated, wondering.

"You are so strong, Diana, so brave and fearless and I—ran away like the coward I am—left you alone to face—"

Here, once more overcome by memory of my shame, I covered my face; but now, all at once, perceiving my abasement and bitter remorse, moved by a sweet impulse she clasped her arm about my stooping shoulders and sought earnestly to comfort me.

"There, there," she murmured, her voice very soft and sweet, "never grieve so, Peregrine—you're no coward! When a coward runs away, he keeps running in the same direction; a coward don't come back to be beaten black and blue—see your poor face!"

"You laughed at it this morning!" said I, striving to steady my voice.

"Yes, I know I did, but only—only because!" she answered gently. "But you ain't—I mean are not—a coward; you fought your best—"

"But to no purpose!" I added bitterly. "Nature has shaped me in such puny mould, I'm so miserably weak—" Here the arm tightened and, conscious thus of all the throbbing strength and vitality of her, I felt my own weakness the more. "Oh, I'm a miserable, undersized rat!" I groaned.

"Hush!" she whispered, as if I had shocked her. "'Tisn't size or strength as wins a fight, Peregrine; 'tis quickness an' knowing how—but most of all being game-plucked. The next time a man hits ye, stand away and hit back; there's nothing will keep a man from hitting you like hitting him often and hard."

"It seems that my uncles were right, after all!" said I. "Hard knocks are sometimes more efficacious than the best-reasoned arguments. You have seen many fights, I suppose, Diana?"

"Lots!"

"I wish you could teach me how it is done!"

"Why, so I will, Peregrine—stand up! Now," she admonished, as we faced each other, "put up your hands—so!" Hereupon I imitated her posture. "Now," she continued, "I'm going to hit you in the face!" which she immediately did, though lightly and with her open hand. "Now hit me if you can, Peregrine."

But though I tried my best, she was so wonderfully quick and light upon her feet that I smote but empty air or my blows were parried, while her hands flashed, now here, now there, to pat and tap my face as often as she would. So we sparred together until, flushed and laughing and breathless, we paused by common consent.

And thus I had my first lesson in the Noble Art.

"You do be very light o' your feet!" said she as we sat side by side beneath the tree again, "and much quicker than I thought, Peregrine!"

"I—I'm glad—very glad you think so!" I answered vastly elated by this praise.

"Yes, if you had proper teaching, you might be able to take your part against most o' them."

Now at this I became filled with such a glow of pleasure as amazed me by its intensity, such indeed as no praise from tutors or even my loved aunt Julia had ever inspired.

"Though to be sure," she added, "'t would all depend on whether you was game-plucked. No, size don't always count; why, Jessamy Todd ain't—is not—much bigger than you."

"And who is he?"

"Lord, haven't you heard? Why, Jessamy was one of the greatest, fiercest fighters that ever was, they say! But he had the ill-luck to kill a man and turned religious."

46

"Do you know him?"

"Very well. I've heard him preach often."

"Preach?" said I.

"Yes, Jessamy never fights now—unless he has to—goes about preaching. And he preaches as well as he used to fight, and sings as well as he preaches."

"I should like to meet Jessamy Todd," said I.

"Well, so you will, if you pad the hoof long enough. But now, what o'clock is it?"

"Half-past twelve," I answered, consulting my watch. "Yet surely it can't be so late?"

"But it is—look at the sun! And don't you feel 't is dinner time? There's a little tavern down the lane yonder—let's go and eat."

"Not unless I pay for it—"

"With no money?"

"Here is my watch!"

"Don't be foolish!" she exclaimed, springing to her feet. "Get up and come along, do! No, stay where you are; things will taste sweeter out here—they always do. Only don't go trying to run off or any such foolishness—just stay where you are an' wait for me."

"But—"

"I won't be long—so promise!"

"I promise!"

Waiting for no more, she sped away all lithe and vigorous grace; when she was out of sight, I lay upon my and, staring up at the rustling canopy above, became lost in thought, wondering, among other things, if I could ever possibly attain unto that mysterious virtue she had called 'game-plucked' and just precisely what it might be.

CHAPTER XIX

HOW AND WHY I FOUGHT WITH ONE GABBING DICK, A PEDDLER

"You won't be wantin' ever a broom, now?"

Starting up in no little amazement, I beheld a man who bore a bundle of brooms upon his shoulder and a pack upon his back, while round his neck dangled ribbands and laces of many colours and varieties; a smallish, grizzled, plump man with an ill-natured face.

"You won't be wantin' ever a broom?" he repeated.

"No, thank you," I answered; "though indeed I should think it was sufficiently obvious."

"Nor yet a mop?"

"No!"

"Why then, a belt? 'Ow about a fine, leather belt wi' a good steel buckle made in Brummagem?"

"I couldn't buy anything of you if I wished," I explained, "because I have no money."

"Eh—no money?" said the man, turning to spit into the road. "No money—eh? Then wot about 'er, the Eve as you was a kissy-cuddlin'—"

"I was not!"

"Oh!" he exclaimed, "then if not, why not? Yah, ye can't gammon me! She's a Eve, ain't she, an' all Eves loves a bit o' kissy-cuddly. An' she looks a nice warm armful, so why not try? Better soon nor late!"

"What d' you mean?" I demanded, trembling with indignation.

"I mean as she's a Eve, an' all Eves loves a bit o' kissy-cuddly an'—"

"That will do!" cried I, clenching my fists. "I've told you I can purchase none of your wares, so pray have the goodness to cease your importunities and go."

"Go?" said the Peddler. "An' why should I go? I ain't a-trespassin' on your private property, am I? No, because 'tis a public 'ighway. Very good! An' England's a free country, ain't it? It is! Very good again! I ain't a-goin' to go until I wants to go; you can't make me go nor nobody else. So 'ere I waits till your Eve comes back. An' why? 'Cause if you ain't got no money—she 'as, I'll lay, an' I've ribbands an' laces, rings an' garters as no Eve can say 'No' to. Besides, she looks a fine gal as Eves go, an' there's enough o' the old Adam inside o' me to—"

"Are you going?" I demanded.

"Not me!" he answered, turning to spit at a butterfly that hovered near. "I'm a free-born Briton, I am, as scorns the furrin' yoke!"

Hereupon I rose, that is to say, I forced my unwilling body upon my shaking legs and faced him.

"Then I must do my best to make you!" said I, with as much stern resolution in voice and look as I could summon.

"What—you?" exclaimed the Peddler, regarding me with eye of scorn. "You—eh?" he repeated. "Well, burn my neck, there's imperence for ye!"

"Put up your hands!" said I.

"What—fight, is it?"

"It is!" said I. "Unless you prefer to depart immediately."

"Well, twist my innards!" exclaimed the Peddler, laying aside his brooms. "The owdacious young willin'! Wants t' fight! An' 'im sich a young whipper-snapper!"

He was a middle-aged man, squat of figure with short, plump legs, but I thought him formidable enough and felt the old nauseating fear growing upon me as I watched the determined manner in which he prepared for the approaching combat. Having removed his pack and the multifarious articles that draped his person, he took off his coat, folded it neatly and laid it by, which done, he slowly rolled up his shirt sleeves, eyeing me fiercely and scowling portentously the while. Now as I watched him, my sweating palms tight-clenched, my jaws hard-locked to prevent my teeth from chattering, the thought occurred to me that the hurts I was about to endure and endeavour to inflict should not only save Diana from evil, but might also prove to her (and myself) if I were indeed possessed of that thing she called 'game-pluck.'

At this moment my opponent rapped himself soundly upon the chest and nodded fiercely; quoth he:

"I'm a-goin' t' gi'e ye two more black heyes to start wi', and 'aving draw'd your claret an' knocked out a tusk or so, I'll finish the job by leatherin' ye wi' one o' my best leather belts wi' a fine, steel buckle made in Brum—"

But here I launched myself at him and, forgetting all caution in my trembling eagerness, beset the fellow with a wild hurly-burly of random blows, one or two of which found their mark, judging by his grunts; then his fist crashed into my ribs, driving me reeling back so that I should have fallen but for the friendly tree. This steadied me (in more senses than one) for in this moment I remembered Diana's admonition, and, seeing him rush in to finish me, I stepped aside and as his fist shot by my ear, I smote him flush upon the side of his bristly chin; and lo, to my wonder and fearful joy, he spun round and came violently to earth in a sitting posture! For a moment he sat thus, staring wide-eyed at nothing in particular; then I stepped forward and tendered him my hand.

"What now?" he gasped.

"Let me help you up!" I panted.

"Whaffor?" he demanded.

"That I may—knock you down again—as speedily as possible," I answered.

"Not me!" he answered, feeling his chin in gentle, tentative fashion. "I'm jolted sufficient an' the ground's danged 'ard 'ereabouts! An' wot's more—why, burn my neck—it's Anna!" he broke off and pointed with stubby finger. Turning about, I beheld Diana on the other side of the hedge. And she was looking at me!

"Ha, well done, Peregrine!" she exclaimed; at which, and because of the expression in her eyes, I felt again that strange sense of joyous exhilaration which had thrilled me once before, insomuch that I felt almost sorry the combat was ended so soon. Then, before I might aid her, she was through the hedge and shaking my hand as a man might have done.

"Lord love me!" ejaculated the Peddler, scrambling to his feet. "So you've turned into a Eve at last, 'ave yer, Anna? You as couldn't abide a man! An' 'ere you be in a nice little garden o' Eden along o' your Adam, eh? Found yourself a lad at last for kissy-cuddly, eh? You as was so prim! What'll folks say when I tell 'em?"

"That you'm a liar, Gabbing Dick, as big a liar as ever you was."

"When I tells folk as Anna's took up wi' a lad at last—an' 'im such a whipper-snapper! When I tell 'em as 'ow you—"

"That's enough!" cried I passionately. "Take your things and go before I endeavour to kill you—"

"Lord, Peregrine!" said Diana, viewing me in big-eyed wonder. "'T is only Gabbing Dick, and he must talk dirt, but nobody minds."

"Well, I do, and if he doesn't depart immediately—"

"Depart's th' word!" nodded the Peddler, and taking up his pack he adjusted it, shouldered his brooms and then paused to spit thoughtfully. "What'll folk say when I tell 'em as I see you kissy-cuddlin' a whipper-snapper—"

Clenching my fists I took a step towards him; saw him shrink away, staring, not at me, but the knife in Diana's hand.

"Hop, Dick, hop!" said she, making the blade flash and glitter evilly, whereupon the fellow, clutching his wares, made off with sudden alacrity; but being at a distance he stopped and turned.

"I 'opes," he cried, "I do 'ope as your Adam tires o' ye an' leaves ye despairin'—danged soon, an' that's for you, Anna! An' I 'opes as she pokes out both your eyes for ye—both on 'em, mind—an' that's for you, young whipper-snapper!"

Then he spat towards us, nodded, and hasted off along the road.

"And now, let's have dinner!" said Diana.

"Dinner?" I repeated, frowning after my late antagonist.

"Beef, Peregrine!"

CHAPTER XX

OF THE TONGUE OF A WOMAN AND THE FEET OF A GODDESS

Roast beef is now, has been, and probably will be, long acclaimed and proclaimed by every true-born Englishman as his own peculiar diet; *vide* the old song:

"When mighty Roast Beef was the Englishman's food
It ennobled our hearts and enriched our blood.
O the Roast Beef of Old England
And O for old England's Roast Beef!"

By long association and assimilation it has become, as it were, a national asset, a very part and parcel of the British constitution.

From ages dim and remote it has gone to the building of a sturdy race which, by dint of hard knocks and harder heads, has won for itself a mighty Empire. Our Saxon ancestors devoured it; our Norman conquerors scorned, tasted and—ate of it; our stout yeomen throve on it; our squires and gentry hunt, fight, make speeches and laws upon it; and doubtless future generations shall do the like.

As for myself, I have frequently eaten of it, though never, I fear, with either that awe or appetite which such noble fare justly demands. But to-day within this green bower, blessed by a gentle wind that rustled the leaves about me and stirred Diana's glossy tresses where she sat beside me, I ate of beef, cold, and set between slices of new bread,—ate with a reverent joy as any healthy young Briton should. And presently, meeting the bright glance of my companion, I sighed.

"Diana," said I, "heaven sends dew for the flower, honey for the bee and butterfly, the worm for the bird, and beef for the Briton. Let us then be duly thankful that we are neither flower, butterfly nor bird."

"It would be worse to be the worm, I think," she answered.

Alas! It seemed we were not to be long unmolested for, roused by a shuffling step, I glanced hastily up and beheld an old woman hobbling towards us bent upon a stick, a miserably ragged, furtive, hag-like creature who nodded and leered upon us as she came.

"Lor', Ann!" she cried in queer, piping tones. "Lorramity, Ann—so you've fell in love at last, 'ave ye, dearie? And why not, my pretty, why not? There's nowt like a bit o' love—'cept it be a bit o' beef! O Ann, gi'es a bite o' the good meat—a mouthful for poor old Moll, do 'ee now—do!"

"Why, for sure!" answered Diana. "You can eat and welcome, Moll; sit ye down here by me and rest your old bones. And I ain't fallen in love wi' no one, Moll."

"Ain't you, Ann; lor', dearie, ain't you!" piped the old creature, snatching the food Diana offered. "But what about your nice young pal 'ere? Is 'e for comp'ny's sake—jest to keep away the solitood, eh, dearie?"

"We're padding it to Tonbridge, Moll."

"Tonbridge—hey!" gabbled this fearsome old woman, clawing at the meat with her bony, talon-like fingers in a highly offensive manner. "Tonbridge, hey, dearie?" she mumbled, stuffing the meat into her mouth until I wondered she did not choke to death outright. "'T is a goodish step from 'ere, dearie," she gasped, when at last she could speak, "a goodish bit an' love may ketch ye afore ye get there—eh, dearie, eh? I 'ope's it do, for love's a pretty thing when you're young—I know, for I was young once—aye an' 'ansome too, I was—"

"I don't love anybody, Moll, and never shall."

"Don't say that, dearie, oh, don't say that! Some man'll win an' tame ye yet, for all your proud, wild ways an' little knife—'e will, dearie—'e will; maids is for men an' men—"

"Never think it, Moll!" said Diana, shaking her head. "As for men, I hates 'em and always shall—"

"What d'ye say t' that, my fine, nice laddie—eh, eh?" piped the old, witch-like creature, leering at me hideously. "Ann's a beauty, ain't she? Made to be kissed an' all, ain't she, eh? If I was you, I'd kiss 'er afore ye reached the next milestone an' that ain't fur—kiss 'er afore she knowed, I would, an' if she takes it unkind, never trouble, jest you wait till she's asleep—steal 'er little knife an'—"

"Let us go!" said I hastily, getting to my feet.

"That's th' sperrit, laddie, that's th' sperrit!" croaked the old woman. "Afore th' next milestone—on th' lips! All maids love it an' so'll she, 'spite all 'er skittish ways—on 'er mouth, mind!"

But I hasted away, nor paused until I was some distance down the road, then glancing back, I saw Diana bestow on this frightful old creature all that remained of our dinner, and money besides.

"A truly dreadful old person, Diana!" said I, as she joined me. "I wonder you can stop to consort or speak with such—"

"She's a woman, after all, Peregrine, very old and worn and generally hungry. And how can it harm me to be a little kind to her?"

"She suggests vile things!"

"What o' that, if she don't do 'em, or make others do 'em?"

"A horrible creature!" I repeated.

"Without a friend in the world, Peregrine."

"Do you happen to be acquainted with every discreditable vagabond hereabouts, Diana?"

"I knows most o' th' padding kind, trampers and sech. There'll be many going Tonbridge way to-day and tomorrow, because o' the fair."

"Then cannot we reach Tonbridge by ways unfrequented?"

"There's the field-paths, though 'twill take us a day longer—maybe two—"

"No matter, let us go by the field-paths, Diana."

So we presently struck off from the great, dusty high-road and went by ways pleasantly sequestered. By shady copse and rustling cornfield; past lonely farms and rick-yards; past placid cows that chewed, somnolent, in the shade of trees or stood knee-deep in stilly pools; past hop-gardens from whose long, green alleys stole a fragrance warm and acridly sweet; past rippling streams that murmured drowsily, sparkling amid mossy boulders or over pebbly beds; past rustics stooped to their leisured toil who straightened bowed backs to peer after us under sunburned hands; wheresoever I looked, I found some new matter for delight.

The afternoon was very hot for the wind had fallen, and, being somewhat distressed and weary with travel, I was greatly tempted to propose a halt that I might rest and feast my sight upon the many and varied beauties of this Kentish countryside, but seeing Diana walk with the same smooth, tireless stride, I forbore for very shame.

The stream we were following presently brought us to a wood where leaves rustled lazily, birds chirped drowsily and the brook whispered slumberously; a shady wood where wearied travellers might rest awhile, and, their troubles lulled to sleep, dream of journeys ended and happiness to be.

Here my companion paused; and watching her as she stood to stare down into the stream that widened hereabouts to a placid pool, it seemed to me more than ever that she was akin to the beauties around us, herself the spirit of these solitudes.

"O Diana!" I exclaimed, beholding her rapt expression. "Do you see it—feel it too—all the unending wonder of it?"

"Well, Peregrine," she answered, her gaze still bent upon the pool, "I be wondering where we shall eat and sleep to-night, for we're miles away from Brasted—"

"Heavens, child!" I exclaimed, seating myself beside the stream. "Have you no soul? Cannot you soar above such base material wants? Listen to the voice of this brook; has it no message for you?"

"It sounds cool, Peregrine, so while you rest, I'll bathe my feet."
And sitting down, off came her shoes and stockings forthwith.

Now though, after my first startled glance, I kept my eyes averted, I could not help being very conscious of these white feet as they splashed and dabbled beside me and of their slim shapeliness.

"Diana, have you indeed no soul?" I repeated.

"If I have, it don't trouble me much!" she answered. "Why don't you dabble your feet; 'tis better than drinking?"

"O girl," I sighed, "have you no thought beyond your immediate bodily needs, no dreams of the greater—"

"Dreams?" she exclaimed bitterly. "It don't do for the likes o' me to go a-dreaming! Let them dream as can afford."

"But even the poorest, humblest of us may have our dreams, Diana, visions of a greater self and nobler living. Dreams are the soul's relaxation and inspire us to higher purpose. I think it is this faculty that lifts us above the brute creation."

Here, finding my companion silent, I glanced up to behold her watching a man who was approaching astride of a shaggy, bare-backed pony, a dark-complexioned, impudent-looking fellow with bright eyes and a wide mouth. At sight of us, he checked his steed with a jerk of the halter, smote his boot with the stout ash stick he carried, and burst into a shout of laughter. Here again I became extremely conscious of Diana's pretty, naked feet; but the fellow never even so much as glanced towards them.

"Aha, Anna!" he cried. "Whose mother's j'y ha' ye got theer?" and he pointed at me. At this she turned and spoke angrily in that unknown speech she had used with old Azor and in which he answered her. Thus they talked awhile, Diana scowling and fierce, he grinning and impudent.

"Hey, my buck!" he cried suddenly, tossing the ash stick to me. "You can tak' it; aye, tak' it—'t will be more use to you nor me—her'll need it more nor my pony, aye, that 'er will. Don't stand none o' her tricks, pal, though her'll take a lot o' taming, an' you ain't no match for 'er by your looks, but lay into 'er wi' yon stick an' do your best—" Having said which, he laughed again and, turning his pony, trotted off. Outraged by his insolence, I caught up the stick with some notion of running after him, but Diana checked me.

"Not him!" she said. "He ain't—isn't like Gabbing Dick; he's a fighting man and dangerous."

"Who is he?" I demanded.

"A Romany."

"And what did the fellow say to you?"

"Nothing to harm."

"Did he suggest—the—the same as the Peddler and that hateful old hag?"

"Lord—and what if he did?"

"Why, then," I answered, "for your sake there is but one of two courses that I can honourably adopt. I must either leave you at once or marry you at the—the first opportunity."

"Marry me!" she breathed. "Marry—me?"

"Exactly!" said I, folding my arms and staring down into the stream in a very determined fashion. At this, she sat so very still and silent that at last I ventured to glance up, to find her regarding me great-eyed. Then, all at once, to my indignant surprise, she began to laugh, but ceased as suddenly, and I wondered to see her eyes brimming with tears.

"But I—don't love you, and you don't love me—and never can!" said she at last.

"No!" I answered. "Nevertheless, my honour demands it!"

"What is honour?" she questioned wistfully.

"It is another name for duty!" I answered. "And my duty is to guard you from all evil or suspicion of evil."

"What evil, Peregrine?"

"The evil of vile tongues."

"But they can't make us evil, whatever they say of us."

"But what of your maidenly reputation?" I demanded. "That hateful peddler-fellow and vile old hag will make your name a byword—O, decidedly I must marry you!"

"Because of your duty?"

"And because it will resolve all my other difficulties with regard to your education; for instance, I will send you to the best and most select young ladies' academy—"

"What sort of a thing is that, Peregrine?"

"A place where ladies are educated in all the higher branches and taught deportment and all the refinements and usages of polite society."

"O!" exclaimed Diana, and sent up a sparkling shower of water with a flirt of her white foot.

"Furthermore," I continued, wiping my cheek—for some of this water had splashed me, "furthermore, Diana, you need never fear the future any longer, because as my—my wife, you would of course lack for nothing."

"Meaning as you'd find me plenty to eat and drink, Peregrine?"

"Heavens, yes, child!" I exclaimed. "You would be a lady of some position in society."

"A lady—O!" she exclaimed, and flirted her foot again.

"I beg you won't do that!" said I, wiping my face.

"But I like to, Peregrine."

"Why, pray?"

"Because you are such—oh, such a Peregrine!"

"That sounds ridiculous, Diana!"

"But means a lot, Peregrine. But tell me, if you can make your wife a real lady, you must be a gentleman and rich—are you?"

"I shall have a sufficiently comfortable fortune when I come of age."

"You will be rich and grand—like your aunt?"

"I suppose so."

"Without working for it?"

"Of course; I shall inherit it from my father."

"Any one could get rich that way, couldn't they? And when will you get your money, Peregrine?"

"In two years' time. Meanwhile, by writing to my uncles, I can procure all the money I need."

"Why don't you?"

"I propose doing so at the very earliest opportunity." At this she turned and looked at me with her direct, unswerving gaze, so that I grew suddenly uncomfortable. "You don't doubt my word, do you, Diana?" I questioned, glancing down at my grotesque attire.

"No, Peregrine, I don't think you could deceive any one. Only I was wondering what brings the like o' you padding the roads dressed like—like you are."

Hereupon, sitting down beside her, I told my story at large, much as I have written it here, to all of which she listened with such deep interest and grave attention as gratified me not a little. When at last I had ended my narrative, she sat, chin in hand, staring down at the rippling waters so long that I must needs ask what she was thinking.

"That 't is no wonder you are so soft!" said she.

"Soft?" I repeated indignantly.

"Yes, soft, Peregrine, and so green—so precious green! You've never had a chance."

"Of what?"

"Of living. And your Aunt Julia's a fool!"

"Diana—!" I exclaimed, inexpressibly shocked.

"Such a fool, Peregrine, that I'm greatly minded to let you marry me just to see my lady's face when I take ye back and say, 'Ma'm, here's your precious Peregrine married to a girl o' the roads, ma'm, and a-going to be a man in spite o' you, ma'm!' Oh, tush! And now let's go on—unless you'm minded to sleep in the wood yonder and no supper."

"As you will!" said I stiffly.

And so, when she had donned her stockings and shoes, we continued our way together, though in silence now.

CHAPTER XXI

IN WHICH I LEARNED THAT I AM LESS OF A COWARD THAN I HAD SUPPOSED

There is, I think, a wistful sadness in the fall of evening, a vague regret for the fading glories of the day which, passing out of our lives for ever, leaves us so much the richer or poorer, the nobler or more unworthy, according to the use we have made of the opportunities it has offered us for the doing of good or evil.

Thus I walked pensive through the solemn evening stillness, watching the shadows gathering and the sky slowly deepen to a glimmering dusk, wherein the first faint stars peeped.

Suddenly, from the mysteries of sombre trees hard by, stole the plaintive notes of a blackbird singing, as it were, in poignant, sweet farewell:

'This day, with its joys and sorrows, its pain and travail, its possibilities for works good or evil, is passed away. O ye that grieve for chances lost or wasted, that sorrow for wrongs done or good undone, be comforted. Sleep ye in the sure hope that God of His mercy shall renew your hope for better things with to-morrow's dawn. So comfort ye!'

As I stood, the better to hear, my mind busied with some such thought as this conjured up of the bird's evening hymn, Diana's hand met mine in sudden, warm clasp.

"O Peregrine," she murmured, "so you love the silent places too?"

51

"Yes!" said I. "Yes! It is in such places that angels walk."

"Angels, Peregrine?"

"Great and noble thoughts, Diana. These are truly God's angels, I think, since they are the inspiration to all great and good works."

"It is in the silent places I am happiest, Peregrine."

"Because you have a soul, thank God!"

"What do you mean by a 'soul,' Peregrine?"

"I mean that part of us which cannot perish because it is part of God Himself. I mean that part of us whereby, in spite of this fleshly body, we may rise above fleshly desires and gain some perception of the Infinite Truth—which is God. Do you understand, Diana?"

"No, I'm afraid I don't," she answered wistfully, "but you won't lose patience wi' me, Peregrine?"

"Never, Diana. How could I when I don't understand myself. Who does? The wisest philosophers of all ages have been puzzling over their souls and never understood the wonder of it. Who shall describe the soul and its ultimate end?"

"Well," said she diffidently, "there's Jerry Jarvis—"

"What, the Tinker?" I exclaimed.

"Yes. He made a verse about the soul—I mean this one—

"'And when my time shall come to die
I care not where my flesh may lie
Because I know my soul shall fly
    Back to the stars!'"

"Ah, yes, the stars!" said I, lifting my gaze to the spangled firmament above us. "This is a great thought—who knows?"

And presently as we went on together, hand in hand, came night very still and silent and full of a splendour of stars that made a soft twilight about us, very wonderful to behold.

"Now, why do that?" I demanded suddenly, for she had slipped her hand from mine.

"Because!" she retorted.

"Because of what?"

"Just because!"

"Does it impede you to hold my hand?"

"Of course not."

"My hand is neither unpleasantly clammy nor particularly dirty, is it?"

"No, Peregrine."

"Then why not hold it?"

"Because!"

"Upon my word!" I exclaimed, "you are very provoking!"

"Am I, Peregrine?"

"Extremely so! Why won't you hold my hand? And pray answer intelligibly."

"Because I don't want to!"

"Oh, very well!" said I, greatly huffed. "Then you shall decline the verb 'To be' instead."

"I do, Peregrine."

"Do what?"

"Decline any more of your verbs."

"Ha, then you don't wish to learn—?"

"I do, Peregrine, I do! But I'm sure I shall learn quicker if you'll let me try to talk like you; I've learned a bit already only you never notice—"

"Oh, yes, I do—God in heaven!" I gasped, my heart leaping in sudden sickening dread. "What is that?" My flesh chilled with horror as from the gloomy depths of the wood upon our left rose a sound evil beyond description, an awful scuffling intermingled with gasps and sighs very terrible to hear.

Spellbound by this dreadful, hushed clamour, I stood rigidly, staring into those dense shadows whence it came; then joyed to the warm, strong clasp of her fingers on mine and, in this awful moment, wondered to feel her hand so steady.

"Are you afraid, Peregrine?" she whispered.

"Yes!" I mumbled. "Yes!"

"But are you brave enough to go and see what it is? Dare you go—alone?"

"No!" I gasped. "No—I should—die—" My teeth snapped shut upon the word and I began to creep forward, the ash stick clutched in shaking hand, my eyes glaring in horrified expectancy. Foot by foot I forced my shivering body forward into the denser shadows of the underbrush, on and on in such agony of fear that the sweat poured from me, for now this frightful struggling was louder and more menacing; therefore, lest I should blench and turn back, I ran wildly forward until, all at once, I stopped at sight of a shapeless something, a dim horror that started and wallowed, gasping, upon the ground before me; then, as I stared, the thing bleated feebly, and I knew it for a sheep and, coming nearer, saw the poor animal lay upon its back, kicking and struggling vainly to regain its feet.

My revulsion of feeling was so great that a faintness seized me and I leaned half-swooning against a tree. And in this moment Diana's arm was about me and her voice in my ear.

"Oh, but that was brave, Peregrine—I never thought you'd go! Now help me to get the poor thing to her feet." So between us we contrived to set the sheep upon its legs and watched it amble feebly away. Then, side by side, we came out of the wood where we might behold the stars.

"Diana," said I, with my gaze uplifted to their glory, "did you know it was only a sheep?"

"Of course!"

"And I am a little braver than you expected?"

"Yes, Peregrine."

"Then—suppose you take my hand again!"

CHAPTER XXII

DESCRIBING THE HOSPITALITY OF ONE JERRY JARVIS A TINKER

We stood upon a hill beneath an orbed moon whose splendour dimmed the stars; below us lay a mystery of sombre woods with a prospect of hill and dale beyond, and never a sound to disturb the all-pervading stillness save the soft, bubbling notes of a nightjar and the distant murmur of the brook that flowed in the valley at our feet, here leaping in glory, there gliding,—a smooth and placid mirror to Dian's beauty, a brook that wound amid light and shadow until it lost itself in the gloom of trees thick-clustered about a little hamlet that slept in the shadow of hoary church tower.

Thus as we descended the hill, I walked reverently, my soul upraised in chaste and fervent ecstasy. However, this fine, poetical rhapsody was banished, suddenly and most unpleasantly, by my companion who, setting fingers to mouth, emitted a shrill whistle,—three ear-piercing blasts that shattered the night's holy calm and startled me to indignant protest.

"Heavens, Diana!" I exclaimed, "why do that? It was desecration!"

"You'll know if you listen, Peregrine!" As she spoke there came an answering whistle from the woods before us. "It's Jerry!" she nodded. "It's Jerry Jarvis—hark, he be coming to meet me!"

"Then he knows it is you?"

"Of course! He learned me to whistle for him so when I was a little child and—" She turned suddenly, and with a little, glad cry of "O Jerry!" ran forward into the shadows and was clasped and hugged in a pair of dim arms.

"Why, Ann—why, Anna, dear child—have ye come a-seeking your old Jeremy? What is it this time, dear lass; tell your trouble to your old pal—"

"O Jerry, I'm free, I'm free of 'em at last!"

"Free o' the Folk, lass? Lord, here's j'y! But what of old Azor—that witch o' darkness?"

"Her too, Jerry."

"How, lass, how so?" Here Diana reached her hand to me and I stepped into the Tinker's purview.

"He did it for me, Jerry."

"Lord!" exclaimed the Tinker, falling back a step. "Lord love me—a boy! A lad at last! Well, well, 't is nat'ral, I suppose, though what I can see of him bean't much to look at, Ann—but no more am I, for that matter! And he ain't exactly a Goliath of Gath—though no more am I again. But then I've noticed that great men be generally of a comfortable, middling size. And if he be your *chal*, my dear—"

"Have you forgotten me so soon, Mr. Jarvis?" said I at this juncture, whereupon he turned to peer into my face, then caught and wrung my hand.

"Strike me blue!" he exclaimed. "It's the bang-up young gent in the jerry 'at 'as left a home luxoorious to see the world and l'arn to be a man!"

"That very same!" said I.

"Why, then, Lord love me, here's j'y again!" cried he, grasping my hand with a heartiness there was no mistaking. "But how come you hereabouts and along of Anna, too? And how comes Anna free o' the Folk at last and along wi' a young *gorgio* gent wi' nothing flash about him? And what's come o' your bang-up duds? And I'd like to know—but wait a bit! Are ye hungry?"

"We are!" answered Diana.

"Good!" exclaimed the Tinker. "Then come your ways to my fire, children; I've a couple o' rabbits in the pot wi' a lump o' pork and an onion or so for comp'ny, which is a supper fit for any king."

"You are very kind, Mr. Jarvis," said I, a little awkwardly, "but I ought to tell you that I am as poor as I look—I haven't one penny—"

"Well, that don't make me speechless wi' surprise, young sir; money has a habit o' going, 'specially when you're young, but a full stomach's better than a full purse, I think."

"But," said I, "having no money, how may I repay your hospitality?"

"By eating hearty! And as for money, Lord love my eyes and limbs—who wants your money?"

"There, there, Jerry—don't get peppery!" said Diana soothingly. "Peregrine don't understand the likes of us, yet."

53

"Why no, Ann, I was forgetting the poor, misfort'nate young gent has never known the blessings of hardship, never suffered, never lacked for anything all his days and consequently knows nothing o' true hospitality or the brotherhood o' the roadside—how should he?"

"Then you shall teach me, if you will, Mr. Jarvis," said I, humbly.

"Then, sir—come and eat," he answered, "and don't go 'mistering' me; I'm Tinker Jarvis and Jerry to my friends."

"Then please don't call me 'sir'—my name is Peregrine."

"Then it's a bargain, friend Peregrine!" said he, and led us into the deeps of the wood where was a small clearing well shut in by bush and thicket; and here burned a fire that crackled cheerily beneath a bubbling pot, a fire whose dancing light showed me the three-legged stool, the dingy tent and Diogenes the pony tethered near by, who, having lifted shaggy head to snuff towards us enquiringly, fell to cropping the grass again. And beholding all this, the Tinker's shrewd and kindly face and Diana smiling at me across the fire, I felt a sense of rest and companionship vastly comforting.

CHAPTER XXIII

DISCUSSES THE VIRTUES OP THE ONION

"There's nothing like an onion!" said the Tinker, lifting pot-lid to lunge at the bubbling contents with an inquisitorial fork. "An onion is the king o' vegetables! Eat it raw and it's good; b'ile it and it's better; fry it and it can't be ekalled; stoo it wi' a rabbit and you've got a stoo as savoury an' full o' flavour—smells all right, don't it, Ann?" he enquired suddenly and a little anxiously, for Diana had possessed herself of the fork and was investigating the pot's bubbling contents with that deft and capable assurance that is wholly feminine. "Smells savoury, don't it, Ann?" he questioned again, noting her puckered brow.

"Very!" said I.

"Did ye put in any salt or pepper, Jerry?" she demanded.

"Drat my whiskers, never a shake nor pinch!" he exclaimed, whereupon Diana sighed, shook her head in silent reprobation and vanished into the dingy tent as one acquainted with its mysteries, leaving the Tinker gazing at the pot quite crestfallen.

"A man can't always be for ever a-remembering everything, Ann!" said he, as she reappeared. "An' besides, now I come to think on it, I aren't so partial to pepper an' salt—"

"A stew should never boil, Jerry!" she admonished.

"Why, that's a matter o' taste," he retorted. "I always b'ile my stoos and uncommon tasty I find 'em—"

"And a little thickening will improve it more," she continued serenely. "And if you had cut the rabbits a little smaller, it would ha' been better, Jerry. Still, I daresay I can make it eatable, so go an' talk to Peregrine and leave me to do it."

Obediently the Tinker came and seated himself beside me.

"Friend Peregrine," said he, jerking his thumb to the busy figure at the fire, "I stooed rabbits afore she was born—ah, hundreds on 'em!"

"And boiled 'em hard as stones!" she added.

"I've throve on b'iled rabbits, Peregrine friend, rabbits and other things cooked by these two hands, lived and throve on 'em these fifty-odd years—and you see me today a man hale and hearty—"

"Which is a wonder!" interpolated Diana without glancing up from her labour.

"Pray," said I, seeing him at loss for an answer, "what did you mean by the 'Brotherhood of the Roadside'?"

"I meant the Comradeship o' Poverty, friend, the Fellowship o' the Friendless, the Hospitality o' the Homeless. The poor folk on the padding-lay, such as live on the road and by the road, help one another when needful—which is frequent. Those as have little give freely to them as have none—I to-day, you to-morrow. The world would be a poor place else, 'specially for the likes o' we."

"Do you mean that all who tramp the road know each other?"

"Well, 'ardly that, brother. To be sure, I know most o' the reg'lar padding-coves, but you don't have to know a man to help him."

"Are you acquainted with a peddler called Gabbing Dick?"

"Aye, poor soul. Dick's father was hung for a crime he didn't commit, just afore Dick was born, which drove his poor mother mad, which is apt to make a child grow up a little queer, d'ye see?"

"And old Moll?" said I, with growing diffidence.

"Aye, a fine figure of a woman she was once, I mind. But her man was pressed aboard ship and killed, and she starved along of her babby, though she did all she could to live for the child's sake and when it died, she—well, look at her now, poor soul!"

"The world would seem a very hard and cruel place!" I exclaimed.

"Sometimes, brother—'specially for the poor and friendless. But if there's shadow there's sun, and if there's darkness there's always the dawn. But what o' yourself, friend; you've been fighting I think, judging by your looks?"

"Yes, and—I ran away!" I confessed miserably.

"Humph!" said the Tinker. "That don't sound very hee-roic!"

"But he came back, Jerry!" said Diana in her gentlest voice.

"Ha!" exclaimed the Tinker, looking from her to me and back again, keenly. "Then he is hee-roic!"

"No!" said I, "No, I'm not—and never can be!"

"Oh," said the Tinker. "And why?"

"Because I'm not brave enough, strong enough, big enough—"

"Lord, young friend, don't be so down-hearted and confounded humble; it aren't nat'ral in one so young! What do you think, Ann?"

"That he's hungry," she answered.

"Aye, to be sure!" chuckled the Tinker. "And I reckon no hero can feel properly hee-roic when his innards be cold and empty—"

"But I'm not hungry," I sighed, "at least—not very. But the longer I live the more I know myself for a hopeless incompetent—lately, at least—a poor, helpless do-nothing—"

"Lord love ye, lad," quoth the Tinker, laying his hand upon my bowed shoulder, "if you've learned so much, take comfort, for to know ourselves and our failings is surely the beginning o' wisdom. But if you can't be a conquering hero all at once, don't grieve—you ain't cut out for a fighter—"

"He beat Gabbing Dick, anyway," said Diana suddenly, whereat I lifted drooping head and looked towards her gratefully, only to see her vanishing into the dingy little tent again.

"Well, but—" said the Tinker as she reappeared, "Gabbing Dick ain't a fighter like Jem Belcher or Gentleman Jack Barty or Jessamy Todd. Dick's a poorish creetur'—"

"He's twice as big and heavy as Peregrine!" she retorted.

"True!" said he. "And yet friend Peregrine ain't exactly—"

"Supper's ready!" she cried.

"Good!" exclaimed the Tinker, rising, but his sharp eyes seemed keener than ever as he glanced from Diana's lovely, flushed face to me and back again. Then down we sat to supper as savoury as mortal palate could desire; the Tinker, having tasted, sighed and winked his approbation at me, forgetful of Diana's bright and watchful eyes.

"Well, Jerry," she demanded, "how is it?"

"'Twill do, lass, 'twill do," he answered; "though you've come it a leetle too strong o' the pepper and salt, to my thinking, still—it'll do. And now, friend Peregrine, I'm consarned to know what's become of all your money—"

"He buys me with it," answered Diana.

"Eh—bought you?"

"For fourteen guineas, a florin, one groat and three pennies, Jerry!"

The Tinker gulped and stared.

"Lord love you, gal—what d'ye mean?" he questioned.

"'T was all old Azor's doing, Jerry. She gives me to her grandson Joseph for his *mort,* but I gives Joseph a touch of my little *churi* and runs away and happens on Peregrine. But she follows me with Jochabed and Bennigo, that I hates more than Joseph, and she was for going to force me to take him could give most money, and Peregrine has most, so she weds me to Peregrine."

"Wed you?" exclaimed the Tinker, blinking.

"Aye, according to the ways o' the Folk—she weds us and leaves us. Then while I was considering about running off from Peregrine and where I should go, Peregrine goes for to run off from me, so then I followed him, of course—and here we are!"

"Lord!" exclaimed the Tinker. "Lord love my eyes an' limbs—here's a pretty kettle o' fish!"

"It is!" nodded Diana. "For now Peregrine wants to marry me according to the ways o' the Church!"

"Hum!" said the Tinker, staring very hard at a piece of pork impaled upon his knife-point. "Ha—marriage, hey, friend Peregrine? Marriage is an oncommon serious business and you are a—leetle young for it, ain't you?"

"I'm nineteen turned!" said I.

"And I'm fifty and more, young friend, and never found courage for it yet—and never shall now!" Here the morsel of pork vanished and he masticated thoughtfully. "And I suppose," said he, his keen eyes flashing from me to Diana, "I suppose you'll be tellin' me as you're in love and a-dyin' for each other—"

"No!" said Diana sharply.

"Of course not!" said I, imitating her tone.

"And never could be!" she added, frowning at the fire.

"Utterly impossible!" I added, frowning at her.

"Strike me pink!" ejaculated the Tinker, scratching chin with knife-handle and staring at us in ever-deepening perplexity. "Then why want to marry?"

"I don't!" said Diana, with the same unnecessary vehemence.

"Nor I either!" I added. "But my honour and—circumstances would seem to demand it."

"What circumstances, young sir?" demanded the Tinker, his features distorted by a sudden fierce scowl. "Ha, d'ye mean as you've taken advantage of—"

"Don't be foolish, Jerry!" said Diana serenely. "Does he look as if he would take advantage of any one? d'ye think he could take advantage o' me? Can't you see he ain't—is not th' kind I keeps my little knife for? Don't be foolish, Jerry; he's never even tried to kiss me—nor wanted to—"

"How do you know that?" I demanded impulsively. Now at this she turned and looked at me, red lips parted in speechless surprise.

55

"How do you know?" I repeated. "How can you be so sure?"

"Be-cause!" she murmured and then, all at once, from throat to brow crept a wave of hot colour, her long lashes drooped and she turned away with a strange, new shyness; and in this moment I saw she was altogether more lovely than I had ever imagined her.

"Why, Diana!" I said. "Child, you need never trouble to take your knife to me; the respect I have for your goodness is enough—"

"Ah, Peregrine," she whispered fiercely, without turning her head, "I am only good because I have seen enough of evil to hate it!"

"And it is just because I would shield you from all and every evil that I would marry you, Diana."

"Ha!" exclaimed the Tinker, so suddenly that I started, having clean forgotten his existence. "Ha!" said he. "You're quite sure as you don't love each other, then?"

"Quite!" said Diana.

"Absolutely!" said I.

"Oh!" said the Tinker, wiping his knife upon his breeches. "Well, considering you was both so hungry, you ain't neither of you eaten dooly of this stoo as was fit for any king. And talkin' o' wed-lock, if you ain't in love with each other—yet, I should wait until you are, which," said he, glancing up at the leaves above his head, "which judging by the look o' things, I should say might 'appen at any moment 'twixt now and Christmas. Meantime, what are ye going' to do?"

At this, being somewhat at a loss, I looked at Diana and she at the fire again.

"Now if," pursued the Tinker, "if you'm minded, both on ye, for to j'ine comp'ny and travel the country awhile along o' Diogenes an' me—say the word, an' I'll be the j'y-fullest tinker 'twixt here an' John o' Groat's!" As he ended, Diana reached out suddenly and, catching his hand, fondled those work-roughened fingers against her soft cheek.

"O Jerry," she sighed, "you were always s' good and wise!"

"Then, dear lass, you'll come?"

"Of course I will. I'll weave baskets—"

"And I'll mend kettles, if you'll teach me, friend Jerry," said I, grasping his other hand.

"Why, children!" said he, looking upon us gentle-eyed, "Lord love ye now—you make me as proud as if I was a dook 'stead of only a travelling tinker!"

"It were best of all to be a poet, I think!" said I. "Have you written any more verses lately?"

"Well—I have!" he confessed, with a look that was almost guilty. "I'm always at it when there's time—I must. There was an idee as came to me this very evening an' I had to write it down. 'T was that as made me forget the salt an' pepper—"

"Is it about the Silent Places, Jerry?" questioned Diana eagerly. "Or a lonely star, or the sound of a brook at night—?"

"It's got a bit of all on 'em," said the Tinker.

"I should very much like to hear it," said I.

"Honest an' true?" he enquired a little diffidently.

"Honest and true!" I answered, as I had done upon a former occasion.

"Then so ye shall, though it ain't finished, or rather it ain't begun, as ye might say, for I can't find a good opening verse. I want to say that if a man don't happen to be blest wi' riches there's better things for him if he's only got eyes to see 'em." Saying which (and after no little rummaging) the Tinker drew a crumpled paper from capacious pocket and, bending to the fire, read as follows:

"'Instead of riches give to me
Eyes, the great, good things to see
The golden earth, the jewelled sky
The best that in all hearts doth lie.

Give me this: when day's begun
A woodland glade, a ray of sun
Falling where the dewdrops lie
Give me this, and rich am I.

Give me this: the song of bird
In lonely wood at sunset heard
Piping of his evening hymn
'Mid a leafy twilight dim.

Give me this: a stream that wendeth,
Where the sighing willow bendeth,
Singing through the woodland ways
Never-ending songs of praise.

Give me these, with eyes to see
And richer than a king I'll be.'"

"D'ye like it, Peregrine?" he enquired, anxious and diffident.

"So much that I wish I had written it."

"Jerry writes verses like birds sing and the wind blows, just because he must," said Diana gravely. "All that is best happens so, I think. Are you for Tonbridge tomorrow, Jerry?"

"Aye, I am, lass, 'cording to custom. Maybe I'll pick up plenty to do at the fair."

"And maybe you'll find your friend, Peregrine," said she, rising.

"What friend?"

"Him you was to meet, of course."

"Why, to be sure—Anthony! I'd clean forgotten him."

"That's strange," said she, "seeing you were so anxious to find him."

"It is," said I, "I wonder what should have put it out of my head?"

"Ah—I wonder!" said the Tinker. "What, goin' to bed, lass? Tent soot ye?"

"Yes—I laid your blankets under the tree yonder—Good night!" And with a wave of the hand she was gone.

Then, having made up the fire, we presently rolled ourselves in our blankets and lay down where we might behold the stars. And after some while the Tinker spoke drowsily:

"I'm glad—very glad, friend Peregrine, as I've met you again, not only because you like my verses but because I like your ways. But I'm sorry—aye, very sorry, as you should ha' fallen in wi' Diana—"

"And why, pray?" I demanded, a little sharply.

"Because if you should happen to fall in love wi' her and really want to marry her, which I don't suppose—and she was foolish enough to let you—which I'm pretty sure she wouldn't, being of a proud temper and mighty independent—'t would be a very bad thing for you and a terrible shock to that fine aunt and those rich uncles o' yours as you told me of—"

"And why should it be?"

"Because Anna ain't of your world and not being born wi' drawing-room manners she'd shock you twenty times a day, throw your fine aunt into a fit and give your uncles paralytic strokes—Anna's all right in her way but—"

"She's a very beautiful girl!" said I hotly. "And good as she's beautiful!"

"She is!" said the Tinker heartily. "Sweet an' good still, in spite of everything, an' I know—I've watched her grow up—"

"And taken care of her," I added, "like the good friend you are."

"I've done what I could, when I could, but she's mostly had to take care of herself and done it well, too—for she's as brave as—"

"As Diana—as beautiful and as chaste!" said I.

"Quite sure as you ain't fallen in love—or falling, friend
Peregrine?"

"Of course—quite."

"To—be—sure!" murmured the Tinker drowsily. "But though your pockets be empty, you ain't in any violent hurry to get back to your luxoorious home, are ye?"

"No!" said I.

"By reason of Anna?"

"By reason that, like her, I have learned to love the Silent Places."

"Ah, yes, lad, I know—for I love 'em too. But you're young and in the
Silent Places one may meet wi' demons an' devils."

"Maybe!" I answered.

"Or walk with God!" said the Tinker.

CHAPTER XXIV

HOW I MET ONE JESSAMY TODD, A SNATCHER OF SOULS

Diogenes the sturdy pony trotted at such good pace that where the ways were rough the Tinker's light cart creaked and lurched until the tins wherewith it was festooned rattled and clinked and I, perched precariously on the tailboard, legs a-swing, was fain to hold on lest I be precipitated into the ditch, yet felt myself ridiculously happy notwithstanding.

Thus we bumped and jingled through shady lanes and pleasant byways, I for one, seldom speaking, content to watch tree and hedge flit by and the ever-changing prospect beyond, though often turning to glimpse Diana's shapely back where she sat on the driving seat beside the Tinker; and at such times often it would happen she would glance round also, and thus our glances would meet and as we gazed, slowly but surely the colour would deepen in her cheek, her long lashes would flicker and droop, and she would turn away and I full of wonder and an infinite joy, marvelling that I could ever have thought such eyes hard, bold and unfeminine. Thus, albeit perched so precariously on the swaying tailboard I was none the less marvellously content.

O Diogenes of the plodding hoofs! O creaking wheels, O tinkling pots and pans, had I but possessed the wisdom to understand your oft-repeated message, how much of doubt, of grief and pain I might have spared myself.

Suddenly Diana hailed and waved her hand, the Tinker checked Diogenes in full career, and with a jingling clank the cart pulled up as a man sprang lightly forth of the dry ditch wherein he had been sitting, a man of no great stature but clean-limbed and shapely, despite rough and dusty clothes,—a keen-eyed, short-nosed, square-jawed fellow whose mouth had a humorous twist.

"Why, Jessamy," said Diana, leaning down to give him her hand, "'t is good t' see you!"

"And so it is, lad!" nodded the Tinker. "How goeth the good work?"

"Fairish, Jeremy, fairish!" answered Jessamy, in a sweet voice peculiarly rich and mellow. "Old Nick's a toughish customer d'ye see, and a glutton for punishment; wind him, cross-buttock him or floor him wi' a leveller amidships, but he'll come up smiling next round, ready and willin' for more, an' fight back at you 'ard as ever, alas!"

Here I got down from the cart that I might better behold the speaker, who now turned to glance at me with a pair of the kindliest blue eyes I had ever seen.

"Jessamy," said Diana, "this is my—my friend Peregrine as do want you to teach him the game."

"The game," repeated Jessamy, shaking his head a little ruefully, "the game's all vanity and vexation o' spirit! Besides, your young friend don't look cut out for the ring—"

"Lord, Jess, he don't want to be a fighter! Peregrine only wants to know how—"

"Why, that's different," sighed the ex-pugilistic champion, "though I ain't got the heart nor yet the time to teach any one—"

"But I want you to, Jessamy," said Diana imperiously.

"Why, that's different again, Anna, and so I don't mind showing him a thing or two if time and opportoonity offer."

"Are ye for Tonbridge Fair, Jessamy?" enquired the Tinker.

"I am so, Jerry. I'm a-marching, comrade, wi' royals and studden-sails set, messmate, and all for the glory o' the Lord, brother."

"Then if you'm be minded for a lift, Jessamy, there be room for ye alongside Peregrine!" Up we mounted forthwith, the Tinker gave Diogenes his head, and we bumped and jingled on our way.

"Pray, Mr. Todd," I gasped, as we clutched and swayed together, "may I enquire if you have been a soldier or a sailor?"

"Both, brother," he answered, "I was a powder-boy aboard the old *Bully-Sawyer*—a powder-monkey and sat on my tub?"

"But why on a tub?"

"In case o' sparks from the guns—broadside agin' the wind—"

"What—have you been in action?"

"For sure, brother—"

"Ah!" I exclaimed eagerly. "Tell me about it."

"I can't, brother—all as I remember is sparks and flame—the roar of the guns—screams and cries—blood and—things as no eyes should see and bad to think on—and me squatting on my tub amidst it all—wanting my mother. Later on I turned soldier and didn't find that life a bed o' roses either; to-day I'm a soldier o' the Lord ready to fight, sing and preach to His glory, and ever ready to cheat Old Nick o' what don't belong to him—"

"What do you mean?"

"Souls, brother. I plucks brands from the burning with j'y and gather sheaves with gratitood. You've 'eard o' body-snatchers, I suppose?"

"I have."

"Well, I'm a soul-snatcher. I snatches 'em to the Lord whensoever and wheresoever I can, brother."

"But surely," I demurred, "the soul, which is an abstraction, a part of the Infinite and thus of God Himself, is therefore imperishable. Socrates taught this, Pantheism is based on this, the arguments of the Peripatetic Philosophers all trend to this belief, and Christ preached the Soul's immortality and life after death. Thus, if the Soul is immortal and cannot perish, how may it be saved?"

"By the Blood o' the Lamb, brother; otherwise ye shall be cast into outer darkness to weep and gnash."

"But why?"

"For sins, committed in the flesh and unrepented."

"Supposing a man sins daily for threescore years and ten and dies unrepentant, must he go down to hell and be tormented for ever and ever for so short a time of sinning?"

"He must, brother, alas!"

"Horrible!" I cried. "Horrible, and most unjust."

"Why, it do seem a bit 'ard to the likes o' we, brother, but then we only see as through a glass darkly. God is a just God, a jealous God and a God o' Vengeance; 't is in the Book—"

"Then this is not Christ's Heavenly Father, but Jehovah, the blood-spattered deity of the Jews, a God of battles, of sacrifices and death, a God pitiless and without mercy. But man's soul, being conceived of the Infinite Mind, may never utterly perish even though corrupt with sin or debased by ignorance, for even then that divine Spark which is the very life of the soul shall sooner or later grow to a flame, burning up the evil, lighting the gloom of ignorance until in course of time, years, ages, or aeons, the soul purified and perfected shall win back to the God whence it came!"

For a full minute after I had ended Jessamy Todd was silent, staring from me to the cloudless sky and back again with a look of growing perplexity; at length he spoke:

"You've seen better days, brother, I'm thinking."

"No, indeed," I answered, "never so good as these."

"I'm likewise thinkin' as your speech and talk don't rightly match your rig-out, brother."

"Which, on the whole, is just as well," I answered.

"And you've read and learned a lot from books, brother."

"But you have read a better book, friend Todd, and much more of it."

"Ah, you mean this, brother?" said he, taking out a small, well-worn Bible.

"I mean the Book of Life," I answered; "you have lived while I have only dreamed, so far."

"Why, to be sure, I've seen a good deal o' life and something o' death, one way or another. I've known friendship and loneliness, plenty and poverty, been hooted and cheered and had a prince shake my fist—"

"What for?"

"'T was arter I'd beat the Chelsea Snob, him as licked the Bristol Slasher; they thought the Snob would eat me but—ah, well these were days o' vanity, brother, and no grace about me—no, not a ha'porth."

"Please tell me of it."

"Well, I was fighting for Sir Jervas then, him they call 'The Firebrand'—"

"Do you mean Sir Jervas Vereker?"

"Aye, I do—one o' the bang-up nobs, a tip o' the tippies, but the best sportsman and truest friend ever man fought for—"

"Good!" quoth I.

"D'ye happen to know him, brother?" enquired Jessamy, with another look of mild surprise.

"I begin to think I do not," I answered. "Pray, why is he called 'The Firebrand'?"

"Because he's allus so precious cool, I reckon."

"Well, pray continue," I urged.

But at this moment we became aware of a confused uproar, a ribaldry of laughter and shouting. Round I started, to see we were approaching a small inn, with a sign bearing the legend "The Ring o' Bells," before which inn stood a number of vehicles and a rough crowd of merrymakers who danced and sang and flourished ale-pots. Beholding this unholy company, my alarm grew, for it seemed their vociferations were directed at us.

"Pull up, Tinker—pull up and drink wi' us!" roared one.

"Aye—a drink, a drink, come down an' drink!" cried another.

"And bring the gal along wi' ye!" cried a third.

Suddenly, seeing Jeremy heeded them no whit, a big, swaggering fellow stepped forward, a flashily dressed herculean figure in tops and cords, his high-collared, brass-buttoned coat moulding a mighty chest and spread of shoulder; which formidable person now advanced upon us flourishing a quart pot and with divers of the riotous company at his heels. No honest, sun-burned rustics these, but pallid, narrow-eyed folk whose half-furtive, half-hectoring air gave me a sense of evil streets, of dark alleys and dens where iniquity lurked, and my alarm and abhorrence waxed acute, finding vent in words:

"What vile wretches!"

"Not so, brother!" answered Jessamy, viewing them with his kindly eyes where they had halted across the road, barring our advance. "No, brother, these are all souls to be snatched to the Lord, one way or t' other, brands to be plucked from the—"

"Pull up, Tinker!" roared the big fellow threateningly. "You've got a lass there as I likes the looks on; pull up, d'ye hear! Look at the shape of 'er!" quoth he, pointing out Diana to his companions. "A tidy piece—eh, my bucks an' pippins?"

Here rose an answering chorus of laughing profanity and worse, amongst which I caught the words, "Pretty filly!" "A dainty tit!" "A kiss all round, Tom! Share an' share, Tom!" "Oho, Tinker, pull an' be damned t' ye!"

Instead of complying, Jeremy touched the pony to faster pace and with a jingling clash of tinware we bore down upon this lewd-tongued company which, howling obscenity, scattered promptly right and left—all except the big man Tom who, with a dexterous leap, caught the rein, jerking and wrenching at the bit with hand so cruelly strong that the poor animal reared up, snorting with fright and pain and the cart came to a lurching standstill.

"Didn't ye hear me tell ye to pull up?" demanded the man Tom, scowling. "When I says a thing, I means it. And now, first of all I wants a kiss from the gal an' then—"

"Stand off, ye vermin!" quoth Jeremy and, reaching down beneath the seat, whipped out a long-barrelled pistol and levelled it full into Tom's big, evil face, whereupon my trembling hand loosed the saucepan I had clutched as a weapon and I stared from the tense features of the two men to the calm, coldly contemptuous face of Diana. Then spake Jessamy Todd:

"All right, Jerry! Put up your barker; here's where I climb into the ring for a round wi' Old Nick," and taking off his frayed hat he sent it spinning through the air to the big man's feet, who promptly kicked it into the ditch.

"Open your trap an' I'll serve ye the same!" snarled the fellow.

"Good!" answered Jessamy cheerily, and alighting from the cart he walked slowly towards the speaker, viewing the big man over with kindly eyes, though his square chin jutted somewhat.

"Friends and brothers," quoth he, throwing out his arms, "I'm a man o' peace as cometh afore you wi' peace in his heart and the Word o' the Lord upon his tongue—" Now at this, some laughed, some cursed blasphemously, and one began a song so unspeakably vile that my ears tingled, and hot with shame I stole a glance at Diana, who sat watching Jessamy's good-tempered face, calmly serene and apparently utterly unconscious.

"And I love ye, friends and brothers," continued Jessamy, "because you be all tabernacles o' the Lord, 'spite o' your beastly ways, and formed in His image, for all your ugly mugs. Why therefore will ye desecrate the tabernacle and debase His image—"

59

The cheery, musical voice was drowned by shouts and obscene objurgations, while the big fellow, seeing the Tinker had laid by his pistol, clenched brawny fists, shot out brutal jaw and glared at Jessamy in murderous fashion, whereupon the excited crowd, swollen now considerably, hooted and clamoured, pushed and jostled all about us in a very threatening manner, so that my hand instinctively clenched itself on the saucepan again and I crept nearer to Diana.

"Set about 'im, Tom! Ah, break 'is nob, lad!" bellowed the swaying crowd. "Show 'im 'ow you laid out the 'North-country Collier,' Tom. Knock out 'is ivories—choke 'im wi' your famble!"

"Hark 'ee, friend Tom," said Jessamy, apparently quite unmoved by the growing hostility of the rabble, "I love ye, Tom! And I love ye, first because you're a child o' God, though to be sure ye don't look it, Tom!" Here Tom unbuttoned and tossed aside his tight-fitting coat. "And secondly," pursued Jessamy, "I love ye because somewhere inside o' ye you've got an immortal soul—of a kind, Tom, that the Lord holdeth precious and beyond rubies—though only the Lord knoweth why, Tom." Here the big man tightened his belt and proceeded to roll up his sleeves. "Therefore, Tom," continued Jessamy, watching these preparations with kindly interest, "therefore, 't is your soul as I'm after and the souls of all these pals o' yours—these poor lost lambs as look so uncommonly like wolves, Tom. Howbeit—"

Uttering a scornful oath, Tom snatched an ale mug from one near by and dashed its contents into Jessamy's face, whereupon rose a yell of fierce laughter and acclaim.

"And now, Tom lad," sighed Jessamy, his blue eyes mild as ever, while the liquid dripped from the great jut of his chin, "now, dear friend, let's you an' me pray together!" Then, lifting his face to the cloudless sky, Jessamy began thus, while Tom and his fellows stared mute with amazement or perhaps awed by something in that shapely, patient, yet grimly alert figure:

"O Lord who looketh into all hearts and in every heart can find something good among the evil—aye, Lord, even in this Tom's heart, since he is child o' Thine—grant that I, Thy humble instrument, may rouse the good within Thy Tom's heart one way or t' other, either by reason and gentleness or force and—"

I uttered a gasping, inarticulate cry of warning but in that instant Jessamy moved his head an inch or so and the heavy pewter tankard that should have brained him flew harmlessly by and rolled clattering a good twenty paces behind him.

"Ah, Peregrine," said Diana in sighing whisper, "O Peregrine—watch Jessamy—watch!" And as she spoke the big fellow rushed. On he came, head lowered, mighty fists whirling, to butt and smite, but Jessamy moved also, slightly, but enough, and as his terrible assailant blundered past, smote him lightly on the crown with open palm.

"Lord, Tom lad," he admonished in his clear, ringing tones, "that's a fool's way to set about harming your brother. Give over, Tom, give over and let's pray instead." Uttering a furious oath, Tom swung about and smote fiercely with right and left. But ducking the blows, Jessamy slipped nimbly aside, shaking his head in mild reproof.

"Come, come, Tom," said he; "can't ye see you're as harmless as a bleatin' lamb or cooin' dove? I've no wish to hurt ye, so let's ha' done and get on with our prayers—"

"Fight!" roared Tom, beside himself with fury. "Stand up an' fight, you—" and here followed a torrent of foulest invective and abuse.

"So be it!" said Jessamy. "Though I warned ye, and Lord knows I've been patient. But if ye will, ye will, so, being a man o' peace, I'll finish ye comfortable and quick—come on, my poor lad!"

Tom came; with a rush that it seemed nothing might withstand, he hurled himself upon that quiet figure, mighty shoulders hunched, huge body quivering, eager for the fray; ensued a quick, brief trample of feet, the swift play of merciless arms, of mighty fists that smote the air, and then I saw the upward flash of Jessamy's left, heard the impact of a dreadful blow, and as Tom's head and shoulders jerked violently up, I saw the flash of Jessamy's right and the great body of his assailant, rocked and shaken by these two unerring, terrible blows, shrank horribly upon itself, rolled a limp and twisted heap in the dust, and lay still, with Jessamy poised above him, his kindly features transfigured with a wild and terrible joy. For a long, breathless moment Jessamy stood thus above the great, huddled form of his insensible antagonist, and for that moment no one moved, it seemed, and never a word spoken; then Jessamy sighed, shook his head, clasped his hands and looking up to heaven, prayed thus, none daring to interrupt:

"Lord, seeing force and conflict was needful, let it not be in vain but forgive, I beseech Thee, my unholy joy therein. As Thy servant's fist smote this Thy son's flesh, so may Thy Truth smite his heart and he come to Thy grace thereby!"

This supplication ended, he turned to a pale-faced, gaping individual who stood near by, a slopping tankard grasped in nerveless hand.

"Friend," says Jessamy, "I'll trouble you for your ale." The man gave it eagerly:

"Lord, sir," said he, grinning ingratiatingly, "you did Tom up in proper style and no mistake." Stern-faced, Jessamy turned, and, stooping above his prostrate and still unconscious antagonist, dashed the ale into his bloody face, whereupon Tom groaned and stirred feebly.

"Ale be good stuff—sometimes, took externally, which is a Latin word meaning not in the stomach!" said Jessamy, and setting an arm beneath Tom's battered head, lifted him to a sitting posture. "How are ye now, Tom?" he enquired.

"Bad, damned bad!" groaned Tom. "To hit a man—wi' a brick—ain't the Christian way to fight; it ain't Johnny Bull."

"Here's your brick, friend Tom," said Jessamy, showing his brawny fist.

"Why, then—who—who are ye?" stammered Tom.

"I'm Jessamy Todd, preacher, man o' peace—and your friend, if you'll ha' me, Tom."

"Jessamy—Jessamy Todd? You? O Lord, I'm bit! Jessamy Todd—why, then, no wonder."

And now the crowd caught up the name, speeding it from lip to lip.

"Jessamy Todd! It be Jessamy Todd!"

60

"Can ye walk, friend Tom?"

"I think so."

"Then up wi' you and along o' me into the 'Ring o' Bells'; I'll soon make ye comfortable, an' then you an' me will pray together, shall us, friend?"

"As ye will!" mumbled Tom. So, having aided his late antagonist to rise, Jessamy turned to nod and smile at us.

"Drive on, brothers," said he, "I must bide here awhile on the Lord's business, so drive on. I'll look for ye at the fair."

My stiffened fingers loosed the saucepan handle, for now all about us were faces that smiled and nodded cheerily, and as we jingled on our way again, the fickle crowd, their animosity quite forgotten, saluted us with ringing cheer.

CHAPTER XXV

TELLS OF MY ADVENTURES AT THE FAIR

A hoarse clamour upon the air, shouts, laughter, the bray of horns, throbbing of drums, clashing of cymbals and tinkling of bells: a pandemonium that deafened me, a blatant uproar that shocked and distressed me as I stood, amid the hurly-burly of the fair—in it, not of it—staring about me for some glimpse of Diana or the Tinker who had vanished amid the surging crowd hours ago, it seemed, and whom I had sought vainly ever since.

Thus I wandered, lost and none too happy, amid a jumble of carts and waggons, carriages and country wains, of booths and stalls and tents; amid a restless, seething crowd of people who pushed and strove more or less good-naturedly. Among all these unfamiliar sights and sounds I ranged disconsolate, awed by the vast concourse, deafened by the universal uproar, and not a little disgusted by the coarse humour and rough horse-play of this truly motley throng.

On I went, a lost soul, pushed and jostled; past rows of gaudy tents and shows, each with its platform before it, where men and women, in outlandish livery and spangled tights, danced and sang, cracked broad jokes, beat drums, blew horns, or strove to out-roar each other in crying up their respective wares and wonders. One in especial drew my notice,—a stout, bull-necked Stentor in mighty cocked hat, whose brassy voice boomed and bellowed high above the din, so that I paused to observe him in wondering disgust.

"In meat alone—in meat alone!" he roared. "Will eat 'is weight in meat alone! The famous and fab'lous Franko o' Florence, the fire-eatin', flame-swallerin', fat feller as weighs thirty-two stone if a hounce—seein's believin'—and all for a tanner—a tanner! Sixpence an' no more! Come and see Franko the fattest feller o' Florence as will eat fire, devour glass and swaller swords, and all for sixpence—for sixpence! See Franko as will dance ye a hornpipe, breakdown or double-shuffle wi' helegance and hease, bein' nippy, neat and nimble though weighin' thirty-two stone, seein's believin'—and all for a tanner—a tanner! Walk up, ladies and gents, an' don't be shy; walk up an' shake 'ands wi' Franko the fab'lous fat feller as can sing ye, dance ye, tell fortun's, forecast the future, cast 'orrer-scopes, strike na-tivities or stand on 'is 'ead—and all for sixpence—for sixpence!"

In this fashion, or much like it, he held forth tirelessly until, chancing to meet my wide-eyed gaze, he immediately singled me out for his remarks thus:

"Wot O, my Lord, wot O! You in the nobby 'at an' patched unmentionables—wot O! Walk up, Tom-noddy, my lord, walk up and spend a tanner; never mind your breeches, walk up an' see the stoopendious fat feller as could swaller ye, breeches, patches, 'at an' all, an' never blink a heyelid—a man as can swaller 'is wight in meat alone—in meat alone!

Walk up, my lord, an' see Franko
Breeches or no, my lord, breeches or no!"

This sorry and meaningless jingle set the immediate crowd in a roar. I became an object for ribald laughter and cheers; I was pushed and hustled, albeit good-naturedly enough, but none the less to my great annoyance, so that I made all haste to wriggle away and, espying a narrow lane between these canvas booths and tents, I slipped into it, took to my heels and turning a sharp corner in full career, came thus upon an ancient man who sat upon a box, puffing serenely at a long pipe and who, despite my so sudden appearance, merely glanced at me with a pair of keen, bright eyes and wished me "Good-day." Hereupon I stopped and, because I had very nearly upset him, took off my hat, bowed, and humbly craved his pardon; at this he gave me a second and keener glance and uncovering his white head, returned my salute with grave punctilio.

He was a slight, spare old man habited in shabby garments of a quaint, old-world fashion, but in his upright carriage was an impressive dignity, in his vigorous gestures, quick eyes and strongly marked, resolute features an air of command, a latent power very arresting.

"I fear I startled you, sir!" said I.

"I am not readily startled," he answered, "though indeed this very afternoon I was beset by gipsy rogues hereabouts and rescued from their clutches by a young Amazon of a remarkable beauty and a rare intelligence. Youth is ever impetuous, though I trust your so passionate speed does not argue depredations upon your neighbour's goods; you are not a runaway pickpocket, I hope?"

"Indeed, no, sir!" I answered, and briefly narrated the reason of my flight.

"Hum!" ejaculated the aged person and sat puffing his pipe and regarding me with such close scrutiny that I grew a little uneasy.

"I trust that you believe me, sir?" said I.

"Entirely, sir!" he answered with a quick, decisive nod. "For I perceive that you are a gentleman. Therefore, if you have the time and inclination, pray sit down and let us talk awhile."

"Willingly, sir," said I, seating myself upon the grass, "for it is at least quieter here, and I will confess the crowd with its tumultuous turmoil and sordid vulgarity offends me greatly."

"Indeed, sir!" said my companion. "And yet it is simply to listen to what you term offensive and vulgar turmoil that I am here. For, sir, yonder clamour, being inarticulate, may speak infinitely to such as hearken understandingly, being one of Nature's awful voices, a very symphony of Life. Heard separately, each sound is an offence, I admit, but blent thus together they become akin to the incessant surge of ocean, the roar of foaming cataracts, the voice of some rushing, mighty wind, and these are the elemental music of God."

"Indeed, sir," said I, "sitting here with you sufficiently remote from the crowd's too-familiar contact, I can begin to appreciate the wisdom of your remarks."

"Yet you speak a little disdainfully, I think, sir! But what is there more proper to the contemplation of a philosopher than a concourse of human beings? How compelling its interest, how infinite its variety! The good rub shoulders with the evil, the merry with the sad, the murderer with his victim, each formed alike yet each different—"

All at once as I listened, my attention was distracted by a face that projected itself suddenly through the canvas of an adjacent tent, an evil, stealthy face with narrowed eyes that watched us furtively a while and was suddenly gone; my companion espied it also, it seemed, for he sighed a little impatiently. "Tush, young sir!" said he. "Will you allow the face of a peeping rogue to alienate your mind from a conversation that promises to become interesting?"

"But sir," said I, rising somewhat hurriedly, "this place is suggestively lonely; I think we were wiser to retire—"

"Go if you will, young sir," broke in my strange companion a little grimly, "hasten away by all means, but I remain here."

"As you will, sir," I answered and sat down again, though careful to keep my eyes in the one direction.

"Sir," continued the aged person, "I have seen much of men and cities, I have journeyed in the desolate places of the world, but—"

Uttering a warning cry, I sprang to my feet as three men appeared, desperate-seeming fellows who approached us with a very evident intention: but suddenly, as I watched them in sweating panic, I heard a sharp click behind me, and immediately they halted all three, their ferocious looks smitten to surprised dismay—and glancing over my shoulder I beheld the aged person still puffing serenely at his pipe but with his slender right hand grasping a small, silver-mounted pistol levelled at our would-be aggressors across his knee. And there was something very terrible, I thought, in his imperturbable serenity.

"Rogues! Rascals!" sighed he. "To rob is sinful, to disturb the excogitations of philosophers is blasphemous. I found it necessary to shoot one of your sort recently—and why not again?"

At this the three began to whine while the ancient person hearkened and puffed his pipe, viewing them with eyes of scorn.

"Oh, begone!" said he. "See you do not trouble me again, lest I prove better citizen next time and rid the country of you once and for all." Scarcely had the words left his lips than the cowed ruffians made off so hastily that they might have vanished into thin air.

"And now, sir," said my companion, carefully uncocking the pistol ere he pocketed it, "let us continue our so agreeable conversation. A crowd of humans, sir, to my mind is a mystery deep as ocean, sublime as the starry firmament, for who shall divine the thoughts, hopes, passions and desires animating its many various and component entities? Moreover, though composed of many different souls, it may yet possess but one in common, to be swayed to mirth and anger, lifted to a reverent ecstasy or fired to bloody vengeance and merciless destruction. What is there can give any just conception of a mystery so complex?"

"Surely nothing, sir," said I.

"Nay, young sir, therein I venture to think you are wrong, for we possess a divine joy, a soul medium, a very gift of God and we call it,—music, sir. To such as have ears, music is the speech of Gods, of the Infinite, soaring far above mere words, revealing the unconceived, speaking forth the unthinkable."

"And what, sir, is the unthinkable?" I questioned.

"That which flashes upon a man's consciousness without the labour of thought, an intimate cognizance of—What the devil is it now, Atkinson?" he broke off so suddenly that I started and, glancing up, beheld an extremely neat, grave, sedate personage who removed his hat to bow, and advancing deferentially, stooped sleek head to murmur discreetly in my aged companion's ear.

"Tell 'em I'm engaged; bid 'em be hanged—no, say I'll come!" The grave personage bowed again and moved sedately off.

"Young sir," sighed my companion, rising, "I have found you particularly interesting, your arguments well-founded, your views on music particularly arresting. It grieves me, therefore, to depart, but duty calls. Pray oblige me with your arm, for I am a little lame. A bullet, sir!" he volunteered as he limped beside me. "A shattered knee-cap to remind me of my vivid youth, an awkward limp to keep in my mind the lovely cause—aha, she was all clinging tenderness and plump as a partridge then. I was her Eugenio and she my Sacharissa—a withered crone to-day, sir, and, alas, most inelegantly slim, I hear—bones, a temper, an eagle's beak and nut-cracker chin! Aye, me—what changes time doth ring—*eheu! fugaces!*"

"And what of—him, sir, your opponent?" I ventured to ask.

"Was necessitated to buy himself a new hat, seeing I'd peppered the one he wore, young sir."

Now at this moment, my gaze chancing to be turned earthwards, I espied a pair of elegant though very dirty boots that strode us-wards, jingling their spurs in oddly familiar manner; therefore I glanced up, beholding in turn white buckskin breeches, flowered waistcoat, bottle-green coat with twinkling silver buttons, the frill of an ample shirt-front and above, the square, dimpled chin, shapely nose and resolute blue eyes of my uncle George who, flourishing off his hat, advanced towards us, his handsome face beaming in cheery welcome.

"Well met, my Lord!" he exclaimed, grasping the ancient person's hand. "You've heard the fight's off?"

"Is it, George? I grieve!"

"Yes, it seems Jerningham's man Croxton—The 'Thunderbolt'—fell foul of a harmless-looking customer on his way here, and who should it be but Jessamy himself. So they fought there instead of here, and The 'Thunderbolt's' bolt is shot, sir—and that's the dooce of it—the whole thing's a bite!"

"Bite indeed, George!" agreed his lordship, shaking white head until his shabby hat toppled. "Though, to be sure, my money is on Jessamy. But indeed the affair slipped my memory—old age, George! However, Fortune was so kind as to send me this young gentleman, a youth of remarkably sound ideas, Sir George; his conception of the ethics of music, for instance—"

My uncle George glanced at me, stared, uttered an unintelligible sound and fell back, gaping.

"How are you, Uncle George!" said I, and removing my shapeless hat, I bowed.

"Ha?" exclaimed his lordship. "You would seem to be acquainted with each other! Pray, George, have the goodness to introduce us."

"My lord, this—this is my nephew, Peregrine—young dog—"

"What, poor Jack's boy?"

"The same, sir. Peregrine, his lordship, the Earl of Wyvelstoke. Nephew Peregrine took it into his head to see the world, sir—and this is how he does it!"

"Admirable!" exclaimed his lordship. "Indeed, Mr. Vereker, should you protract your stay in these parts, I shall hope to repeat the pleasure of this afternoon and hear more of your musical concepts. Good-bye t' ye, George!"

And limping to a light carriage that stood adjacent, the slender, shabby figure climbed in with the aid of the assiduous Atkinson, and drove away.

"Well, upon my soul, Peregrine," exclaimed my uncle, removing his hat to ruffle his brown curls, "a precious pickle you look, b'gad! Where in the world—what under heaven—your breeches, Perry—that unspeakable—if only Julia could see you now. Oh, the dooce!"

Such were his more or less coherent expressions as his astonished gaze took in the various items of my appearance. Then all at once he laughed and down came his great hands upon my shoulders. "B'gad, Perry, I love ye for 'em, lad; dooce take me if I don't!" he exclaimed. "Those breeches now—where did you find 'em?"

"Sir, they were bestowed by one Galloping Jerry, a highwayman."

My words produced all the effect I had anticipated; the hat fell from his lax grasp and lay unheeded, while my uncle stared at me in speechless surprise. "These garments, sir," I continued, lowering my voice mysteriously, "are merely a disguise, for it seems there was a possibility of my being apprehended as Galloping Jerry's accomplice. Allow me to return your hat, sir."

My uncle George clutched it and made a kind of gurgling sound in his throat.

"However," I continued, "I am anxious to exchange these things for others less conspicuously hideous and should esteem it a kindness if you would advance the necessary money for it, for sir, I am penniless."

"Ha—your highwayman cove robbed you, of course!"

"He did, Uncle, but had the extraordinary magnanimity to restore all he'd taken. My money, sir, went in the—the purchase of a gipsy maiden—"

"Hey—gipsy—a woman—d'ye mean—you—"

"A young gipsy girl, Uncle."

"Good God!" he ejaculated faintly and, sinking upon the shaft of the empty cart behind him, he fanned himself feebly with his hat. "Peregrine," said he, shaking grave head at me, "your aunt Julia is right—a wonderful woman! Poetry is your line, after all—books—romances, lad—imagination—"

"You think I am romancing, sir?"

"Aye, though I call it 'gammoning.'"

"Sir, you affront me!"

"No offence, Perry," said he kindly. "You just can't help it—comes natural to you—like a gamecock fights. What other marvels have you seen?"

"A tinker, Uncle."

"Hum! Anything else?"

"I saw Jessamy Todd fight the big fellow at the 'Ring o' Bells' this morning and—"

"What?" cried my uncle, on his feet in a moment. "You saw Jessamy fight? Oh, begad, Perry—why couldn't you say so before?"

"You believe this, then, sir?"

"I do. Tell me all about it. I've heard rumours—they say it was a clean knockout—"

"The big man was indeed rendered quite unconscious, Uncle—"

"And you saw? Out with it, Perry lad!"

"But sir," I enquired, a little disdainfully, "why all this stir about a vulgar brawl?"

"Vulgar brawl, begad—"

"Well, a brutal bout at fisticuffs with a ruffian—"

"Heavens and earth, boy," exclaimed my uncle, in growing indignation, "don't ye know you were privileged to see one of the very greatest fighters of any time, school or—oh, b'gad—"

"You mean Jessamy Todd, sir?"

"Of course I do. And what's more—Tom Croxton, The 'Thunderbolt'—the man who forced Jessamy to fight—was a plant—"

63

"Now pray, Uncle George, how may a great, hulking ruffian even faintly resemble any such thing?"

At this my uncle gasped, stared, shook his head, jingled his spurs and finally spoke:

"In Heaven's name, don't pretend you're so infernal green, Perry! The 'Thunderbolt' is a fighting man from Lambeth, a tough customer who's won a fight or so lately and thought he could beat anything on two pins. So we were bringing him down here, hoping to match him with Jessamy, or, failing him, some other good man. But the fool, not knowing Jessamy, get's himself thrashed, and the whole thing's a flam."

"Jessamy has given up the game, Uncle."

"I know, but he loves it still. And you saw the fight! Tell me of it—no, wait—the others must hear." So saying, my uncle George hooked his powerful arm in mine and led me whither he would. By devious ways we went, to avoid the crowd; dodging behind empty caravans and waggons, skirting booths and tents until we came on one greater than all the rest, a huge canvas structure into which he brought me forthwith. The place was empty except for some scant few persons grouped about a stage whereon two fellows, naked to the waist, their fists swathed in what I believe are termed 'muffles', dodged and ducked, feinted or smote each other with great spirit and gusto until one of them, reeling from a flush hit, sat down with sudden violence and remained in this posture to blink and get his breath.

"Dooce—take me—Tom!" exclaimed this individual, in breathless reproach. "Your—infernal mug's—hard as—iron!"

"Craggy, my lord!" answered the other hoarsely. "Cragg by name an'
Craggy by natur', my lord!"

Thither my uncle George led me, his spurs jingling, whereupon the spectators turned to salute him and stare at me, among whom I recognised my uncle Jervas.

"What, George," enquired one, "ha' you found Jessamy?"

"No!" answered my uncle, slapping me on the shoulder. "But the next best thing, Devenham—"

"And a demned queer-looking thing it is, George!" added the recumbent gentleman, viewing me with a pair of blue eyes, one of which exhibited signs of recent punishment.

"None the less, Jerny," answered uncle George, "it is my nephew. Gentlemen, I have the honour to present Mr. Peregrine Vereker! Nephew, in the floored Corinthian with the damaged ogle, you will remark Richard, Marquis of Jerningham; on my right, Viscount Devenham; on my left, Sir Peregrine Beverley; before you Major Dashwood, Mr. Wemyss and your affectionate uncle Jervas. And now, gentlemen all, my nephew will tell you that he comes fresh from witnessing the defeat of Jerningham's unfortunate champion The 'Thunderbolt' at the hands of the unconquerable Jessamy Todd!"

"Aha!" cried the Marquis, springing lightly to his feet and muffling naked torso in gaudy dressing-gown; and next moment he and the others were thronged about me vociferous for knowledge.

For a moment I stood looking round upon the ring of clean-cut, eager faces, tongue-tied and somewhat non-plussed; but seeing with what unaffected and hearty good will they greeted me, nor heeded my disfiguring attire, I made my bow and plunged into a full and particular relation of Jessamy Todd's encounter with the man Tom. As my narrative progressed, the interest of my audience waxed, and I was gratified and stimulated by a ripple of excitement and hushed exclamations which, as I ended, swelled to a ringing cheer for Jessamy Todd. Thereafter my hand was shaken heartily by one and all, with many laudations on my descriptive powers, in the midst of which my uncle Jervas touched me on the shoulder and, bowing my adieux, I took my departure and thus presently found myself in the open air walking, rather sheepishly, between my two relatives.

Once beyond eyeshot of the curious, my uncle Jervas paused and fell back a step, the better to behold me, peering through his glass at each individual article of my attire and murmuring such ejaculations as:

"Astounding! Astonishing! Amazing!"

"Tells me he had 'em of a highwayman, Jervas!" volunteered uncle
George.

"A most distressing vision!" sighed my uncle Jervas. "A positive walking disgust! And yet—hum!"

"And a very creditable pair o' black eyes, Jervas."

"True, George! Our youth has been observing life at close quarters, it seems."

"B'gad—he has so, brother!" chuckled uncle George.

"Tells me he's spent all his money on women!"

My uncle Jervas very nearly dropped his eyeglass.

"Now—'pon my everlasting—" his voice failed and he gazed at me quite dumbfounded for once.

"Think o' Julia!" said uncle George, with a kind of groan. "Think of—'Ode to a Throstle'—poor Julia—sweet soul!" My two uncles turned from my indignant form to regard each other; then, all at once, the grim lips of my uncle Jervas twitched, quivered to a flash of white teeth, but his laughter was drowned by uncle George's cachinnations where he stood on one leg, slapping at the other brawny thigh until the dust flew.

"Sirs," said I, folding my arms and glancing from one to other disdainfully, "your mirth is as unwarranted as unseemly! The money in question was expended in the service of—of one who—whose need was instant and great. I have the honour to bid you good-bye!"

But, as I turned, my uncle Jervas laid his hand on my arm, a white, elegant hand strangely out of place on my rough and weather-beaten coat-sleeve.

"Pray accept our sincerest apologies, Peregrine," said he. Now at this I glanced up in wondering surprise, for in the touch of this slim hand, in voice and look, I had an indefinable sense of comradeship that thrilled me with sudden pride.

"My dear Uncle," I exclaimed, grasping his hand, "pray trust me always to remember that I am a Vereker also."

"B'gad, and there ye have it, Jervas; couldn't ha' put it better yourself!"

"And pray, sirs, how is my dear and best of aunts?"

At this question my uncle Jervas pursed his lips in a soundless whistle and smoothed snowy shirt-frill with caressing fingers.

"Perry," said uncle George, removing his hat to ruffle his curls, "you've heard of bears robbed of cubs, of the Hyr—what's-a-name tiger—"

"Hyrcanian, George!" murmured uncle Jervas.

"Well, they're playful pets in comparison. How is your aunt? B'gad, Perry, my lad, that's precisely the dooce of it, d'ye see!"

"She—she is very well, I hope?" faltered I.

"Assuredly!" answered my uncle Jervas. "But being the—ah—truly feminine creature she is, your remarkable aunt, with more or less reason, has leapt to the conclusion that we are the cause of what she terms your 'desertion', and is a little incensed against us—"

"Incensed, d'ye call it, Jervas?" exclaimed uncle George. "A little incensed is it—oh, b'gad!"

"And declines to see or hold communications with us—"

"And when she does, she—she don't!" added uncle George. "Last time I ventured to call, she looked over me, and under me, and round me, and through me but never—at me. Dooced trying y' know, Perry!"

"And most disappointing!" said I. "My dream that you—one of you might comfort her—"

"Was a damned piece of impertinence!" murmured my uncle Jervas, his aesthetically pallid cheek tinged with unusual colour. "Your aunt knows her own mind and has grieved, raged, wept, languished and advertised for you in her thorough fashion—"

"Offers five hundred pounds for your recovery, lad!" added uncle George.

"Which," continued uncle Jervas, "is a fair sum of money, the natural consequence being that the poor, sweet soul has been plagued by all manner of people, day and night, eagerly endeavouring to restore waifs and strays of both sexes and all ages, so much so that your uncle and I were compelled to call in and suppress such notices as had appeared—here is one!" From his pocket uncle Jervas took a handbill which he unfolded and passed to me; whereon I read this:

L500. LOST. REWARD. MR. PEREGRINE VEREKER AGED 19.

Here followed a most minute and painfully accurate description of my garments and person; and below, these words:

WHEREAS: my loved nephew, PEREGRINE VEREKER, acting upon the PERNICIOUS & EVIL COUNSEL of certain CRUEL and HEARTLESS advisers, fled from home and his only TRUE FRIEND on the night of the 10th. inst: the above L500 will be paid to such person or persons who shall return him safe and unharmed or give such information as shall lead to his happy recovery and restoration to the loving care of JULIA CONROY.

"Great heaven!" I exclaimed, crumpling the document angrily. "It reads as if I were some pet animal!"

"Precisely!" murmured my uncle Jervas. "As you seemed likely to become, nephew. None the less, the document evinces something of your aunt's desire for your return, and it is easy to imagine her gratitude when I shall restore you to her arms—"

"Hold hard, Jervas!" exclaimed my uncle George, clutching my left arm. "'Twas I found him!"

"But consider, my dear George," sighed my uncle Jervas, laying elegant hand upon my right shoulder, "I bear the brunt of her blame, as usual—"

"But damme, Jervas—"

"But pray reflect further, dear George; I am, alas, slightly your senior and, as such, claim the right—"

"But my dear uncles," I interrupted at this juncture, "pray remark that I have no intention of returning home for some time."

"Oh, indeed, nephew?" sighed my uncle Jervas, his slim hand tightening a little. "May one venture to ask why?"

"I know!" sighed uncle George. "Women, Jervas—feminine spells, poor lad!"

"For one thing," I answered patiently, "because I have decided to become a tinker for a while."

"Hum!" murmured my uncle Jervas. "A useful trade, but scarcely one I should have chosen for you—still—"

"And there he is, at last!" exclaimed uncle George suddenly, and beckoned with imperious hand; thus, glancing whither he looked, I espied Jessamy Todd and, with a sudden twist, I broke away and ran to meet her who walked at Jessamy's side.

"O Diana!" I exclaimed, "I have been looking for you all afternoon. Come!" And taking her hand, I led her up to my astonished uncles.

"Sirs," said I, "it is my privilege to introduce my friend Diana, whom I hope to marry as soon as possible."

For a long moment after I had spoken, Diana stood, shapely head aloft, fronting their amazed scrutiny in proud and sullen defiance; when at last she spoke, her voice sounded all untroubled and serene.

"I know," said she, nodding, "I know what's in your minds—you'm thinking as I ain't fit for him! Well, my fine gentlemen, he shouldn't marry me, even if he loved me—which he don't, or I loved him—which I don't and never shall!" Then without so much as a glance in my direction, she turned and sped away.

But I was not to be left thus, for, escaping uncle George's restraining clutch, I followed her; glancing back, I saw my uncle Jervas, white, impressive hand on Jessamy's shoulder, speaking very earnestly to him and with his keen gaze fixed on myself.

It was amid the jostling traffic of the booths that I found her; she was standing before a stall devoted to the sale of gauds and finery, but espying me she made off and I, intent on pursuit, was wriggling my way through the crowd when rose a sudden cry of "Thieves! Robbery! Stop thief!" Rough hands seized me and, checked thus rudely in full career, I was swung around to confront a small, fierce-eyed fellow who cursed and swore, hopped and flourished his fists under my nose in very threatening and unpleasant manner.

"V'ere is it, ye young wagabone?" he demanded in shrill accents. "V'ere is it? As fine a lady's lookin'-glass as ever vas, a genuine hantique framed in solid silver an' worth its weight in gold. V'at ha' ye done wi' it, you desp'rit, thievin' young willin', you?"

Now it was upon my lips to indignantly deny so vile an accusation, but the words were arrested by a sudden, horrid thought, a dreadful suspicion, for in this moment I remembered Diana had passed this way very recently and, calling to mind the unfortunate predilection for appropriating the goods of others which she had termed "prigging," I knew a sudden shame on her account and therewith a sick fear lest she be caught with the damning evidence of guilt upon her.

Thus, despite the fierce hands that grasped me and the bony knuckles that obtruded themselves painfully into the nape of my neck, I stood mute, profoundly unheedful of the little man's excited capering, whirling fists and threats of condign punishment.

By reason of the little man's excited antics and high-pitched threats and wailings, we were very soon the centre of a pushing, inquisitive throng; faces peered at me, fists were shaken and voices reviled me, in especial one, that of an evil-faced man whose narrow eyes seemed vaguely familiar. Every moment the hostile demonstrations of the crowd grew more threatening until suddenly, and to my inexpressible comfort, above the angry clamour arose a voice peculiarly rich and musical.

"Give way, friends, give way—yon lad's a friend o' mine—give way!" The ring about me was split apart by the forward thrust of a sinewy shoulder, and Jessamy appeared with Diana close beside him. "Why, what's the trouble, brother?" he enquired.

"Thievin'—robbery, that's what!" cried the little man, capering higher than ever. "Stole me silver-framed mirror, 'e 'as, the young wagabone—a genuine hantique worth its weight in hemeralds—stole me mirror and don't deny it, neither—!"

"Who says he stole it?" demanded Jessamy. "Did any o' ye see him commit the fact?" At this the small man blinked, and the two that held me stared upon each other a little at a loss.

"Who says my friend stole your vallybles—come!" demanded Jessamy.

"Why, we all says so!" cried the little man. "An' he can't deny it—and no more 'e don't, neither!"

"However," said Jessamy, "my friend ain't stole your mirror, friend."

"Then 'oo 'as?" demanded the little man, capering again.

"Why—him, for sure!" said Diana suddenly, pointing at the narrow-eyed fellow who, blenching before her fierce look, turned to flee. "It's Hooky Sam!" she cried, and in that moment leapt upon him. Ensued a moment's scuffling and Diana sprang away, the stolen mirror in her hand. "Here's your trinket!" she cried, tossing it to its gaping owner. "Next time it's stole, don't go blaming the wrong one."

Hereupon my captors loosed me and turned to seize the real culprit but, profiting by the momentary confusion, he ducked and squirmed, wriggled and dived under and between such arms and hands as made to stay him and, breaking free, took to his heels, and the crowd, losing all interest in us, betook itself to the chase, shouting and hallooing in joyous pursuit.

"And now, friend," said Jessamy, addressing the small man, who danced and capered no more but stood somewhat crestfallen, "'twould be well done, I think, to ask my young friend's pardon." The which he did and I little heeding, all my looks being for Diana, who stared back at me; and meeting her clear-eyed scrutiny, I felt my cheeks flushing guiltily and turned to grip Jessamy's hand and to thank him for his trust and friendship.

"But why," demanded Diana, "why did you let 'em think it was you?"

Now here, having no answer ready, I adopted her own method.

"Just because!" said I.

CHAPTER XXVI

THE ETHICS OF PRIGGING

Evening was at hand, lights began to wink and flare among booths and shows, and the crowd seemed to be growing even more riotous; thus I, for one, was profoundly thankful to leave behind its roaring clamour and seek those quiet, leafy shades where the Tinker had appointed us to meet with him.

"And to think," said Jessamy, as we walked on side by side, "to think as 'Firebrand Vereker' is your uncle—not to mention Sir George, as once fou't ten rounds wi' 'Buck Vibart'! To think—"

"Mighty fine gentlemen, ain't they, Jess?" enquired Diana, with a toss of her shapely head.

"Of the finest, Ann! Honoured by all, from the Prince down. And to think as Mr. Vereker here—"

"My name is Peregrine;" said I, "indeed, I would rather you called me Perry, it is shorter."

"As Mr. Perry, here—"

"Perry!" I admonished.

"As—Perry is their own nevvy—"

"Though he don't look like it!" added Diana.

"Why, that's true, Ann, that's true; but his clothes can be changed—"

"But his face can't, Jess!"

"Lord bless me, Ann, what's wrong wi' his face?"

"Only everything!" she answered, with another disdainful gesture of her head.

"I am extremely sorry that my face displeases you, Diana," said I.

"So'm I!" she nodded. "Though it ain't your fault, I s'pose."

"If you allude to my bruises and black eyes—"

"They're nearly well," said Jessamy.

"I don't!" said Diana.

"Then pray what particularly displeases you in my face this evening?" I enquired.

"All of it! You! Your ways! Makin' a fool o' me afore your fine uncles and them staring their proud eyes out! As if I'd ever marry—you!" At this Jessamy opened his eyes rather wide and I fancy his lips quivered slightly.

"Ah, but you will, Diana!" said I. "My mind is made up."

"What's that matter?"

"A great deal! The whole affair is settled definitely." Here she turned on me in such flaming anger that I fell back a step in utter amazement, and Jessamy, murmuring something about "seeing if supper was ready" quickened his stride and left us together.

"Why did ye do it?" she panted. "Why did ye let 'em think 't was you stole that looking-glass?"

"Because it was my whim!"

"Oh, I know—I know!" she cried, positively gnashing her teeth at me.

"Then why trouble to ask?"

"You thought 'twas me!" she cried. "You dared to think I'd stolen it. You did—you did! Ah, you're afraid to own it!"

"And if I did," cried I, angered at last, "hadn't I reason enough, remembering your—your propensities—"

"What d'ye mean? What's propensities?"

"Well, your predilections—"

"Ah, talk plain!"

"Well, then, remembering those three guineas and the duck you filched, I naturally supposed—"

Uttering a sobbing cry she leapt, striking at me wildly, but ducking in under the blow, I caught her in my arms. For a moment she struggled fiercely, then her writhing body grew soft and yielding in my clasp, and she burst into a passion of tears.

Now as she drooped thus in my embrace, her slender form shaken by sobs, I leant nearer and, moved by a sudden impulse, kissed her hair, her eyes, her parted lips, lips that quivered under mine for a breathless moment; then, loosing her, I stepped back to see her staring at me through her tears with a look of speechless amaze. Suddenly her glance fell and she covered her burning cheeks; and, glancing up from earth to sky, I felt a vague wonder to see them all unchanged.

"O Diana," said I, a little breathlessly. "O Diana, don't cry! And forgive me for misjudging you, I—I was ashamed, but I would have gone to prison for you gladly just the same. I'm—humbly sorry; you see, it was—that duck and the man's three guineas. Only don't—don't sob so bitterly, Diana, or I shall have to—kiss you again."

At this, she walked on once more, though she kept her gaze averted.

Far before us strode Jessamy who, reaching a five-barred gate, took a run and cleared it with a graceful ease that filled me with envious admiration. Reaching this same gate in due course, I clambered over and, from the other side, proffered Diana my assistance, but she merely scowled and setting hand to the top bar, over she came with a vision of shapely limbs and flutter of petticoats.

"You have very pretty ankles!" said I impulsively.

"Don't be foolish!" she retorted, with a petulant fling of her shoulder; and after a moment, "what are my ankles to you?" she demanded sullenly.

"A great deal, seeing they will belong to me some day."

"Never—oh, never!" she cried, between clenched teeth. "I'm done wi' you, young man."

"Folly!" I retorted. "Don't be silly, young woman."

"I'll—I'll run away—"

"Very well," said I, nodding, "then I'll find you again if it costs me every penny of my heritage!" At this she turned with clenched fists, but seeing me stand prepared, walked on again.

"I hate you!" she exclaimed vehemently.

"No matter!" said I.

"You're a—a coward!"

"I know it!" I sighed.

"A fool wi' no manliness in you!"

"Agreed!" quoth I. "You shall teach me better—"

"I'm done wi' you—finished, d'ye hear?"

67

"Also, I begin to suspect that you are really a little annoyed with me, Diana; pray, why?"

"Ah! You know why!"

"Then be generous and try to forgive me!"

By this time we had reached a little wood where flowed a stream, its murmurous waters brimful of sunset glory; and here, as by common consent, we paused a while to look down at this reflected splendour, and when at last she spoke, her voice was gentle, almost pleading.

"The duck was—only a duck, Peregrine."

"Yes!" said I.

"And we were hungry—you know you were?"

"Very hungry, Diana."

"And the—the three guineas as I—finds in—that beast's pocket did us more good than it could ha' done him?"

"True, Diana."

"And I only took it because it—it was there to take—and might be useful. But now we—we don't need it any more—I don't, so—there it goes!" And with a sudden gesture she cast into the brook a handful of coins, among which I caught the sheen of gold and silver. "But I—I ain't a thief—I'm not!" she cried passionately. "I never stole anything all my days; I—I only—prig—" Here, acting on sudden impulse, I caught her hand to my lips.

"O Diana," said I, "dear child, it is in my mind you will never prig again, either—"

"But I shall—I know I shall!" she cried, a little wildly, but yielding her hand to my lips. "Yes, I know—I'm sure I shall, Peregrine, and what should you do then?"

"Grieve, child!"

"Look!" she whispered suddenly, bending to stare down into the glory of the brook, "O Peregrine—do you see it?" From the stream she pointed upward to the radiant heaven where, immediately above us, sailed a small, curiously-shaped cloud. "Do you see it, Peregrine?"

"Only a little, golden cloud, Diana."

"It is—the 'Hand of Glory,'" she whispered.

"What is it—what does it mean?"

"It means, Peregrine, it means that you—that I—oh, you must find out!" And snatching her hand from mine, she fled from me into the wood.

CHAPTER XXVII

JUNO VERSUS DIANA

I was busily engaged blowing the bellows of the Tinker's small, portable forge; besides the making and mending of kettles, pots, pans and the like, it seems he was a skilful smith also, able to turn his hand from shoeing a horse to fashioning such diverse implements as the rustic community had need of, for beside the forge lay a pile of billhooks, axe-heads, sickle-blades and the like, finished or in the making.

So I blew the fire, wielded the heavy sledge-hammer or stood absorbed to watch the deft strokes of his hammer draw out, bend and shape the glowing steel, though turning very often to behold Diana sitting near by, her quick hands busied upon the construction of her baskets of rush or peeled willow: thus despite the heat of the fire, the sulphurous flames and the smoke-grime that besmirched me, I laboured joyously and swung the ponderous sledge more vigorously for the knowledge that her bright eyes were often raised to watch me at my work.

Thus bellows roared and hammers rang until the sun was high and the Tinker, returning the half-forged billhook to the fire, straightened his back and wiped the sweat from sooty brow with sooty hand.

"We shall make a tidy smith of him yet, eh Anna?"

"In time—with patience!" she nodded.

"The question is—wages. What ought us to pay him, Ann?"

"Nothing!" said I.

"Five shillings," said Diana.

"Good, we'll make it seven shillings a week to begin wi'," quoth the Tinker, and whipping the glowing bill from the fire, he clapped it on the anvil and at sign from him I whirled up the sledge and brought it down with resounding clank, which he followed with two blows from his lighter hammer, and we fell to it merrily, thus: Clang—chink, chink! Clang—chink, chink! While with every stroke the bill took on form and semblance, growing more and more into what a billhook should be.

"A good thick steak, I think you said, Anna?" enquired the Tinker, while I blew the fire for the next heat.

"And fried onions, Jerry."

"Steak an' onions!" he exclaimed, rolling his eyes ecstatically. "Did ye hear that, Perry? And to make good vittles better, there's nowt like smithing! The only thing agin' steak an' onions is that there's never enough onions!"

"There will be this time!" said Diana, with another nod.

"D'ye hear that, Perry? Lord, I am that ravenous!"

"But 'tis scarce twelve o'clock yet, Jerry."

"Are you hungry, friend Peregrine?"

"I always am, lately."

"Poor Perry's hungry likewise, Ann! Come, what of it?"

"You must wait till dinner time."

"Which is when a man's hungry—or should be. Come, lass, famishin' an' faintin' away we be!"

Laughing, Diana rose and crossed the glade to where, screened among leafy thickets, stood cart and tent.

"Now as regards paying me wages, Jerry," I began, then stopped and caught my breath suddenly, for Diana was singing.

Yet could this indeed be Diana's voice—these soft, sweet, rippling notes mounting in silvery trills so purely sweet, swelling gloriously until the whole wood seemed full of the wonder of it, and I spellbound by this simple, oft-heard air, but which, sung thus and thus glorified, touched me to awed delight.

"Aha!" exclaimed the Tinker, as the liquid notes died away. "She can sing when she's happy. Jessamy says there's a fortun' in her voice—" But I was off and across the glade and next moment standing before her.

"Why—Diana!" I exclaimed. "O Diana!"

"What is it?" she demanded, glancing up from the onion she was peeling.

"Why have I never heard you sing before? Why do you sing so seldom?"

"Because I only sing when—when I feel like it and to please myself."

"Your voice is wonderful!" I exclaimed. "We will have it cultivated; you shall be one of the world's great singers, you shall—"

"Don't be silly!" she exclaimed, flushing.

"But I tell you your voice is one in ten thousand!"

"And this onion is one of six, so take a knife and help me with 'em, 'stead of talking foolish—only go wash first; you're black as a sweep."

"Gladly," said I, "if you will sing again."

"Nobody can sing and peel onions—they make your eyes run."

"Why, then, let me—"

"Hush!" she exclaimed suddenly.

"What is it?"

"Strangers coming—listen!" And presently I heard it too, a rustle of leaves, crackling of twigs, voices and jingling spurs, coming nearer. Then as I rose with a premonition of approaching fate, forth into the clearing stepped my uncle George, my uncle Jervas and my aunt Julia. She was dressed for riding and carried the skirt of her close-fitting habit across her arm, and never had she looked handsomer nor more magnificently statuesque as she stood, her noble figure proudly erect, all potent femininity from feathered hat to dainty, firm-planted riding boots.

My lips were opening in glad welcome, I had taken a quick step forward, when her words arrested me.

"George Vereker!" she exclaimed, with a waft of her jewelled riding switch towards Diana and myself, "O Sir Jervas, is it with such dreadful creatures as these that you have doomed my poor, delicately nurtured Peregrine to consort? Aye, well may you grow purple, George, and you turn your back in shame, Jervas, to behold thus the degrading company—"

But here, waiting for no more, I started forward, and halting within a yard of my aunt, I laid grimy hand upon grimy shirt-bosom and bowed.

"Dear Aunt Julia, I rejoice to see you!" said I.

For a long moment my aunt gazed on me with eyes of horrified bewilderment then, all at once, she dropped her riding-switch and, gasping my name, sank into the ready arms of my uncle George, who promptly began to fan her vigorously with his hat, while my uncle Jervas, lounging gracefully against a tree, surveyed me through his single glass and I saw his grim lips twitch.

"Tell me I dream, George!" wailed aunt Julia. "Say it is a horrid vision and make me happy."

"It is, Julia, it is!" said my uncle Jervas. "And yet, upon me soul, 'tis a vision that grows upon me; observe the set of the shoulders, the haughty cock o' the head, the determined jut of the chin; yes, Julia, despite rags and dirt, I recognise Peregrine as a true Vereker for the first time." Saying which, my uncle Jervas very deliberately drew on his riding glove and stepping up to me, caught and shook my hand or ever I guessed his intention.

"Uncle—O Uncle Jervas!" I exclaimed and stooped my head lest he should see the tears in my eyes.

"By Gad, Julia—sweet soul," exclaimed my uncle George. "Jervas is exactly right, d'ye see? Perry may look a—a what's-a-name vision, but he's a Vereker for all that—lad o' spirit—beautiful pair o' black eyes, though you can't see 'em for dirt—"

My aunt moaned feebly.

"But dirt, my dear soul, dirt won't harm him, nor black eyes—do him good, d'ye see, do him a world o' good, doing him good every minute—"

"Enough, George Vereker!" exclaimed my aunt in her terrible voice, and freed herself from his hold like an offended goddess. "O heaven, I might have known that you, George, would have abetted my poor, wilful boy in his dirt and bodily viciousness, and that you, Jervas, would have condoned his turpitude and moral degradation. None the less, though you both desert me in this dreadful hour, shirking your duty thus shamelessly, this woman's hand shall pluck my dear, loved nephew from the abyss, this hand—" Here, turning to behold me, my poor aunt shivered, gasped and setting dainty handkerchief to her eyes, bowed noble head and wept grandly as a grieving goddess might have done.

69

"O Peregrine," she moaned from this dainty mystery, "O rash boy—to have sunk to this—sordid misery—rags—dirt! You that were wont to shudder at a splash of mud and now—O kind heaven—grimed like a dreadful collier and I think—yes, O shameless youth, actually smiling through it—"

"And why not, m'dear creature?" sighed uncle Jervas. "Dirt is of many kinds and Peregrine's is at least honest and healthy—"

"Cease, Sir Jervas, I pray!" cried my aunt with a flash of her fine black eyes. "Nevermore will I heed your perfidious counsels, nor the fatuous maunderings of graceless George. There stands my poor, misguided Peregrine—an object for angels to weep over, an innocent but a little while since—but now—now, alas—and you—both of you his undoing!"

"Pardon me, dear Aunt," said I hastily, "but there you are in error and do a monstrous injustice to my two generous uncles. Allow me to reiterate the statement I set down in my letter, that I left Merivale and you of my own accord; indeed my uncles would have stayed me, but I was determined to be gone for your sake, their sake and my own. Indeed, Aunt, so deep is my affection that I would see you truly happy, and knowing the deep and—and honourable sentiments my uncles have for you, I—I dreamed that they—that you—that one of them might have won your hand and—and you find that happiness which you have denied yourself on my account."

"Misguided boy!" murmured my aunt, lovely eyes abased, "Come, dear Peregrine, doubtless one of your uncles can find you a cloak to—to veil you from the curious vulgar—only let us be going, pray."

"Dear Aunt—where?"

"Back to Merivale, to your books, your paintings and my loving care."

"Not yet, Aunt. Ah, pray do not misunderstand me, but when I set out, it was with the purpose of doing better things than penning indifferent verse, or painting futile pictures—"

"Peregrine—nephew—do I hear aright?"

"You do, Aunt. I came out into the world to open the greatest book of all—the book of Life—to try to meet and know men and learn some day, perhaps, to be a man also and one you can honour. Instead of reading the actions of others, I intend to act a little myself—"

"Peregrine—cease!"

"And so, dear Aunt, here I stay until I can return to you feeling that I have achieved something worthy my sex and name."

"Peregrine, come with me—I command you!"

"Then, dearest Aunt, with all the humility possible, I fear I must disobey you."

My aunt Julia drew herself to her stately height, setting her indomitable chin at me, and into her eyes came that coercive expression which resurrected the memory of childish sins of omission and commission, an expression before which my new-found hardihood wilted and drooped; but in this desperate moment I glanced at Diana, and, meeting the calm serenity of her untroubled gaze, I folded my arms and, bowing my head, awaited the deluge with what fortitude I might and, in the awful stillness, heard uncle George's spurs jingle distressfully.

"You mean that—you—will—not—come?" she demanded.

"I do, dear Aunt."

"That you actually—disobey me?"

"Dear Aunt—I do!"

"Pray, who is the young person I notice behind you?"

"Person, Aunt?"

"The young woman—the wild, gipsy-looking creature."

"Ah, pray forgive me—I should have introduced you before. Diana, this is my aunt, Lady Julia Conroy—Aunt, this is my friend Diana."

"And pray what is she doing here?"

"She is about to cook a steak and onions—"

"Do you mean—O pitiful heaven—that she is—living here with—"

"With Jeremy Jarvis, a tinker, Jessamy Todd, a champion pugilist, and myself."

"Shocking!" exclaimed my aunt, sweeping Diana with the fire of her disparaging regard.

"Moreover, dear Aunt," I continued, stung by something in her attitude, "it is my hope to make myself sufficiently worthy to win Diana in—in marriage!"

"Marriage?" repeated my aunt in a hoarse whisper. "I dream! Marriage? With a wild woman! George! Jervas!" she gasped in strange, breathless fashion. "Our poor boy is either mad—or worse, and whichever it prove, it is all your doing! I hope, I sincerely hope, you are satisfied with your handiwork! As for you, you poor young woman," she continued, turning on Diana in passionate appeal, "if my nephew is mad, be you sane enough to know that such a marriage would drag him to perdition and bring you only misery and shame in the long run. Give up my poor, distracted nephew and I will be your friend. If it is money you require—"

Diana laughed:

"My lady, an' if you please, ma'm," said she, curtseying, finger beneath dimpled chin, "I ain't your young woman an' by your leave, ma'm, never could be, because, though I don't love Mr. Peregrine, I can't abide you, ma'm. When I wants money, being only a gipsy mort, I works for it or prigs it. So I don't want your money, thanking you kindly, ma'm, and I don't want your nephew, so you may take him and willing. An' I don't want your friendship or help, because I likes loneliness and the Silent Places better. So take your precious nephew, ma'm, and when you get him safe home, wash him an' keep him in a glass case; 'tis what he's best fitted for. But watch him, lady, lock him up secure, because I think—I know—I could whistle him away from you whenever I would—back, ma'm, back to me and the Silent Places. And so good-day, ma'm, my best respects!" Saying which, Diana curtseyed again and turned away.

"The creature!" exclaimed my aunt. "The minx! The insolent baggage!" And she stepped proudly forward, an angry goddess, the jewelled switch quivering.

"Stop, lady!" said Diana, throwing out a shapely arm with gesture so imperious that my aunt stood staring and amazed. "Stop, ma'm—don't forget as you're a great lady and I'm only a gipsy mort as could tear you in pieces for all your size! To spoil them fine eyes would be pity, to pull that long hair out would be shame, so don't use your whip, lady—don't!" Having said which, she turned and walked serenely away.

"A most dreadful young person!" exclaimed my aunt. "See from what calamitous evils I have snatched you, dear Peregrine. Come, let us be going. I have William with your mare, but seeing you cannot ride as you are, we will take a chaise."

But folding my arms, I shook my head.

"What—O boy, what does this mean?"

"It means, dear Aunt, that I love the Silent Places too!"

"But Peregrine, you will not desert me now—now that I have found you—you will not—cannot! Ah, come back, Peregrine!" she cried, deep bosom resurgent, arms outstretched and eyes dim with unshed tears.

"Dear Aunt, it is impossible!" I mumbled. "Loving you as I do, yet must I leave you a while, foregoing the tender shelter of your love for—for—"

"Dirt and misery!" she broke in. "The shameful allurement of a sly minx, an unspeakable—"

"Madam!" I cried, "have done! You shame yourself and me! It has been my good fortune to have fallen in with honest people with whom I shall remain awhile, enduring their lot, living their life and by their brave patience learn fortitude, and their proud humility shall in time, I hope, teach me the duties of a gentleman—"

"My poor, distraught Peregrine!" she sighed. "My poor, poor boy. So thus I leave you because I must. But some day, when your stubborn will is broken, when your proud head is bowed with grief and shame, come back, dear prodigal, come back, and you shall find these arms outstretched in eager welcome, this solitary heart still open to shelter and protect. Farewell, my Peregrine—I go to weep and pray for you in the night silences. George—Jervas, lead me hence!"

Now as I stood, my eyes smarting with tears evoked by her last words, my uncles tendered their arms with grave and ready courtesy, but in that moment as I watched in a silent grief conjured up by my aunt's last words, the keen glance of uncle Jervas met mine for one brief moment and, in that space, his right eyelid flickered unmistakably; then uncle George coughed explosively and at the same instant tossed something to the foot of a tree; coming thither, I took up a well-filled leathern wallet and a heavy purse; with these, my uncles' parting benefactions in my hands, what wonder that I saw their retreating forms through a mist of tears.

CHAPTER XXVIII

EXEMPLIFYING THAT CLOTHES DO MAKE THE MAN

"The Rubicon," said the Tinker, "the Rubicon is a river as no Roman ever crossed without doo thought. 'The die,' as Julius Caesar remarked when he crossed it, 'the die is cast!' Friend Peregrine, you ha' sent away your lady aunt a-grieving, poor ma'm, and your fine gentlemen uncles likewise, and consequently what I asks is—what now?"

"Clothes!" said I. "This afternoon let us drive into Tonbridge, find a tailor, get rid of these atrocities and afterwards sup at some cosy inn."

"Your gentlefolk brought you money then?"

"They did," said I, and laying by my platter, I drew from my breeches pockets the wallet of my uncle Jervas and uncle George's purse.

"Ha!" exclaimed the Tinker, rubbing his long chin with the haft of his knife. "How much?"

"We will investigate," said I, and opening the wallet, I discovered the sum of thirty pounds in gold and notes and a carefully folded missive with these words:

'If you wish to tinker, Peregrine, tinker like a gentleman. If you must make love, do it like a Vereker, that is to say, a man of honour.'

"My soul!" exclaimed the Tinker, round of eye.

In uncle George's purse were twenty guineas with a crumpled paper bearing this scrawl,

'More when you want it, Perry lad.'

"Lord love me!" exclaimed the Tinker, staring at the money I had placed on the grass between us. "It's a fine thing to have uncles—rich 'uns. What d' you think, Ann?"

"That you'd better eat your dinner while it's hot."

"But—fifty pound, Ann! Never saw so much money all at once in my life—an' all gold an' bank notes, nothing s' common as silver or copper—Lord! Fifty pound!"

"Divided by four is exactly twelve pounds ten shillings," said I, and counting out this sum, I thrust it into the Tinker's hand.

"Eh—what—why, why, what's this?" he demanded.

"Your share," I answered.

"But why—what for?"

"Because we are friends and comrades, I hope, and according to the rules of the Brotherhood of the Roadside as expounded by you, 'those that have, give to those that haven't—it would be a poor world else.'"

"No, no!" he exclaimed, "no, no, can't be done—I think ye mean kindly, but it won't do."

"But why not?" I demanded.

"Because no man as is a man takes money unless he's earned it or lent it, or happens to be starving—"

"Nor woman either!" said Diana.

"Very well!" quoth I, a little ruefully, cramming the money back into my pockets. "Then perhaps you will come to Tonbridge and help me to spend it?"

"I would wi' j'y, but there's my work—ask Ann, she'll go wi' you."

"I'm busy, too!" said she, whereupon I turned and strode off in high dudgeon. But presently she overtook me, "Don't you think you'd better wash first?" she enquired. At this I stopped, for I had clean forgotten my grime.

"Why should I trouble to wash? How can it matter to you?"

"Not much, Peregrine, but you look a little better with a clean face and we shall likely meet plenty o' folk—"

"Do you mean you will come with me?"

"Yes, Peregrine."

"Then I'll wash."

"Yes, I brought you the soap and towel." So we came to the brook where she sat to watch while I performed my so necessary ablutions.

"I have no wish to hinder your work," said I, towelling vigorously.

"No, Peregrine."

"And I am quite able to find my way to Tonbridge alone."

"Yes, Peregrine."

"And it is a goodish distance, so if you would rather not come, pray do not trouble."

"No, Peregrine."

"Heavens, girl!" I cried. "Cannot you say more than 'yes and no, Peregrine'?"

"Aye, I could!" she nodded. "I could say you are a fool and a sight too cocksure—and, oh, a lot more—but I won't!" with which she rose and left me. My toilet achieved, I returned to find Jerry busy harnessing Diogenes, the pony.

"For if you'm a-going, Peregrine, you may as well do the marketing, and there's a mort o' stores to bring back. Besides, Anna can take her baskets t' sell, d'ye see."

So in a while, behold Diana throned on the driving seat, reins in hand, while I led Diogenes up the winding, grassy slope to the high road; this done, I climbed aboard and off we swung for Tonbridge town.

Diogenes pounded along merrily, the wheels creaked and rattled cheerily, a soaring lark carolled joyously somewhere in the sunny air above us; but Diana drove in sullen silence, her face averted pertinaciously, wherefore I scowled before me and kept silence also; thus Diogenes, wheels and lark had it all to themselves. And when we had driven thus some distance I spoke:

"You are a very bright and cheery companion this afternoon!"

At this she jerked her shoulder at me with a petulant gesture.

"Indeed," said I, "it is a great wonder that you troubled to come with me—"

"I've my baskets to sell!" she retorted in her most ungracious manner.

"Why are you so changed to me?" I questioned. "Are you still angry about that unfortunate business of the mirror, or is it because I kissed you, or—"

"Ah—don't talk of it!" she cried fiercely. "No man's ever kissed me so before—on the mouth—"

"Thank heaven!" said I.

"I hate ye for it and her most of all!"

"'Her', Diana? Whom do you mean?"

"Your fine lady aunt!"

"But, good heaven! What had my aunt Julia to do with it?"

"I don't care! I hate her—with her great, proud eyes and haughty ways—and offering me money an' all—"

"Yes," said I, "it was wrong of her to attempt to bribe you—"

"You did as much once—only it was your watch, so don't you talk! I suppose my lady thinks I'm after you for your money. Oh, I wish t' God I'd never seen you! And I shan't much longer—"

"Ah, do you mean that you will attempt to run away?" I demanded. But Diana merely stared sullenly at the road before us. "This would be very, very wrong, Diana, very cruel and very wicked because, according to the laws of the Folk, you are already my wife."

"But not according to the Church. You said so—an' you ain't of the Folk!"

"But I might turn gipsy—others have done so."

"Aye, but not your kind; you're best wi' your fine aunt to coddle you—go back to your grand house an' servants, young man, and stay there!"

"Some day, but not yet," I answered. "And when I go—you will go with me."

"Oh, shall I!" she exclaimed scornfully. "You're precious sure of yourself, ain't you?"

"I am!" I nodded, folding my arms. "And of one other thing!"

"What?"

"That you will make a very ill-tempered wife!"

"Oh, shall I!"

"You will."

"Not your'n, anyway. You ain't man enough."

"We shall see!" said I between shut teeth.

"Aha, now you're angry!" she laughed gleefully, and with some little malice.

"You are enough to enrage a saint!" I retorted, and turning my back, I bore with her gibes and fleerings as patiently as I might nor deigned her further notice, so that in a little she became mute also; and thus at last we reached Tonbridge. Scarcely were we in the High Street than, not waiting for Diana to draw rein, I leapt from the cart with such precipitation that I tripped awkwardly and rolled, grovelling, in the dust. Scrambling hastily to my feet, I saw she had pulled up and was eyeing me a little anxiously, but her voice was sullen as ever when she spoke.

"Are ye hurt?" she questioned ungraciously.

"Thank you—no!" I answered, brushing the dust from my bruised knees.

"All right!" she nodded, "I'll meet ye in the yard at 'The Chequers'—half-past four!" and away she drove without so much as one backward glance.

The place was busy by reason of the fair, the wide roadway thronged with vehicles, and as I edged my way along the narrow, crowded pavements gay with chintz and muslin gowns, polished boots, flowered waistcoats and the rest of it, I felt myself a blot and blemish, a thing to be viewed askance by this cheery crowd in its holiday attire. A short-legged man in a white hat roared at me to hold his horse; a plump and benevolent old lady earnestly sought to bestow upon me twopence in charity, but I paid no heed and began to seek eagerly for a tailor where I might exchange my sorry garments for things less poverty-stricken.

And presently, to my great relief, I beheld a shop above whose crystal window panes was a sign with this inscription:

VAUGHAN
TAILOR & SARTORIAL ARTIST
To The
NOBILITY & GENTRY

In this window was displayed cloth of every kind and colour, together with framed pictures of stiff-limbed young gentlemen in most trying and uncomfortable postures and clad in garments innocent of crease or wrinkle.

Incontinent I lifted the latch and entered the shop to behold a stout young gentleman contorting himself horribly in a vain endeavour to regard the small of his back.

"There!" he gasped. "The breeches! Told you they were too tight—I heard 'em crack—they're too infernal tight, I tell ye!"

"Oh, dear me, impossible, sir!" sighed a pale, long-visaged person, flourishing a tape-measure. "A gent's breeches can't be too tight; the tighter they are the more *ton*! Indeed, tight breeches, sir, are—What's for you, my lad?" he enquired, catching sight of me.

"I desire to purchase a suit of clothes."

"Oh, dear me—no, no!" sighed the long-visaged person. "Not here, lad, not here! We build garments for gentlemen only, no ready-made goods here; we deal strictly with the nobility and gentry of the county—go away, lad, go away!" Here he flapped his tape-measure at me, the stout gentleman stared at me, and I crept forth into the street again among the dainty, sprigged gowns and high-collared coats amid which I wandered somewhat disconsolate until by chance my wandering gaze lighted upon a small, dingy shop in whose narrow window squatted a small, humpbacked, bespectacled man plying needle and thread with remarkable speed and dexterity. It was a small shop but so stuffed and crammed with garments of all kinds that they had overflowed into the street, for the narrow doorway was draped, choked and festooned with coats, breeches, pantaloons, shirts, waistcoats, stockings, boots, shoes, a riotous and apparently inextricable tangle.

Into this small and stuffy shop I forced myself a passage, whereupon its small, busy proprietor glanced up at me over the rim of his large spectacles.

"Well, son, what d'ye lack?" he demanded.

"Clothes, if you please," said I humbly.

"And that's no lie, neether—so ye do, by James!" he nodded.

"Can I purchase some?"

"If you've enough o' the rhino, son."

For answer I drew a bank note from my pocket at random and laid it upon the small counter.

"You have, b' James!" quoth the little man, "a fi'-pun note!" And thrusting needle into the garment he was making he rose with brisk alacrity. "What d'ye want in my way, son?"

"Everything!" said I.

"And here's the place t' get it, b' James! I've everything in clothes from the cradle to the grave—infant, child, youth and man, births, marriages or deaths, 'igh-days or 'olydays—I can fit ye with any style, any size and for any age, occasion or re-quirement."

So saying, he ushered me into a small room behind the shop where he proceeded to whisk forth a bewildering array of garments for my inspection, until table and chairs were piled high and myself dazed with their infinite variety.

"B' James!" cried the little man, blinking, "I'll turn ye out as nobby a little spark as ever cocked a neye at a sighin' young fe-male. Look at this coat, the roll o' this collar up to your ears, and as for buttons—well, look at 'em—see 'em flash! As for weskits, see 'ere, son, climbin' roses worked into true-lover's knots and all pure silk! Then 'ere's a pair o' pantaloons as no blushin' nymp' could resist—an' you shall 'ave the lot—ah, an' I'll throw in a ruffled shirt—for four-pun' ten—take 'em or leave 'em!"

"Thank you, I think I'll leave them," said I. "My desire is for things a little less ostentatious—"

"Os-ten—ha, certainly! Say no more, son, look around an' take y'r choice—"

At last, and almost in spite of the small tailor, I selected a suit a little less offensive than most, the which I donned forthwith and found it fit me none so ill; shirt, shoes, stockings and a hat completed my equipment, and though the garments were anything but elegant, yet my appearance, so much as I could see of it in the small, cracked mirror, was, on the whole, not displeasing, I thought. At the tailor's suggestion I purchased three extra shirts, as many cravats, stockings and a neckcloth.

"And now," said I, as he tied up the somewhat unwieldy parcel, "what do I owe you?"

"Well, son—I mean, sir," he answered, peering at me over his spectacles, "them beautiful clothes has turned you from nobody as matters into somebody as do; your credit is rose five hundred, ah, a thousand per cent and I ought to charge ye a couple o' hundred guineas, say—but seein' as you're you an' I'm me—let's call it fi'-pun!"

So having paid the tailor, I bade him good afternoon and strode forth into the street and, though a little conscious of my new clothes and somewhat hampered by the bulbous parcel beneath my arm, felt myself no longer in danger of being roared at to hold horses or proffered alms by kindly old ladies. I strolled along at leisurely pace, casting oblique and surreptitious glances at my reflection in shop windows, whereby I observed that my new garments fitted me better than I had supposed, though it seemed the hair curled beneath my hat brim in too generous luxuriance; so perceiving a barber's adjacent, I entered and gave my head to the ministrations of a chatty soul whose tongue wagged faster than his snipping scissors. Shorn of my superabundant locks, I sallied forth, and chancing upon a jeweller's shop, I entered and purchased a silver watch for the Tinker, another for Jessamy Todd, and lastly a gold locket and chain for Diana.

CHAPTER XXIX

TELLS OF AN OMINOUS MEETING

Precisely upon the stroke of half-past four I turned under the arch of the "Chequers" inn and, coming into the yard, looked about for Diana. The place was fairly a-throng with vehicles, farmers' gigs, carts, curricles and the like; in one corner of the long penthouse I espied the Tinker's cart with Diogenes champing philosophically at a truss of hay, but Diana herself was nowhere to be seen. Therefore, having deposited my parcel in the cart among divers other packages (which I took to be the stores Jeremy had mentioned), I seated myself in a remote and shady corner and glanced around. Horses munched and snorted all about me, unseen hostlers hissed and whistled, and a man in a smart livery hung upon the bridles of two horses harnessed to a handsome closed travelling carriage, blood-horses that tossed proud heads and stamped impatient hoofs, insomuch that the groom alternately cursed and coaxed them, turning his head ever and anon to glance towards a certain back door of the inn with impatient expectancy. And thus it befell that I began to watch this door also and as the moments elapsed there waked within me a strange and bodeful trembling eagerness, a growing anxiety to behold what manner of person that door would soon open for. So altogether unaccountable and disquieting was this feeling that I rose to my feet and in this moment the door swung wide and a man appeared.

He was tall and slim and superlatively well clad, his garments of that quiet elegance which is the mark of exceeding good taste; but it was his face that drew and held my gaze, a handsome face, paler by contrast with the raven blackness of flowing, curled hair, a delicate-nostrilled, aquiline nose, a thin-lipped mouth and smooth jut of pointed chin. All this I saw as he stood as if awaiting some one, half-turned upon the steps, a magnificent and shapely figure, tapping impatiently at glittering, be-tasselled boot with slender, gold-mounted cane. And then—Diana appeared and paused in the doorway to stare up at him while he smiled down on her, and I saw his smiling lips move in soft speech as, with a hateful and assured deliberation, his white fingers closed upon her round, sunburned arm and he gestured gracefully towards the carriage with his cane.

"Ah, damn you—stand off!" I cried, and clenching my fists I sprang forward, raging. As I came he swung about to meet me, the slender cane quivering in his grip, and thus for a moment we faced each other. And now I saw he was older than I had thought and, meeting the intensity of these smouldering eyes, beholding quivering nostrils and relentless mouth and chin, my flesh crept with a fierce and unaccountable loathing of the man and, unheeding the threat of the cane, I leapt on him like a mad creature. I felt the sharp pain of a blow as the cane snapped asunder on my body and I was upon him, pounding and smiting with murder in my heart. Then the long white hand seized my collar and whirled me aside with such incredible strength that I fell and lay for a moment half-stunned as, without a glance towards me, he opened the carriage door and imperiously motioned Diana to enter.

"Come, my goddess, let us fly!" said he, soft-voiced and smiling. But as he approached her, she tossed aside her basket, stooped, and I saw the evil glitter of her little knife; the gentleman merely laughed softly and made deliberately towards her; then, as she crouched to spring, I scrambled to my feet.

"Don't!" I cried. "Don't! Not you, Diana! Throw me your knife—leave him to me—"

At this the gentleman paused to glance from Diana to me and back again.

"Aha, Diana, is it?" said he. "You'll be worth the taming—another time, chaste goddess! Venus give you to my arms some day! Here's for your torn coat, my sorry Endymion!" Saying which, he tossed a guinea to me and, stepping into the carriage, closed the door. The staring groom mounted, the horses pranced, but, as the carriage moved off, I snatched up the coin and, leaping forward, hurled it through the open window into the gentleman's pale, smiling face.

"Damn you!" I panted. "God's curse on you—I'll see you dead—some day!" And then the carriage was gone and I, gasping and trembling, stood appalled at the wild passion of murderous hate that surged within me. And in this awful moment, sick with horrified amaze since I knew myself a murderer in my soul, I was aware that Diana had picked up my new hat whence it had fallen and was tenderly wiping the dust from it.

"Why, Peregrine," sighed she reproachfully, "you've had all your curls cut off!"

"To the devil with my curls! Come, let us go!" And snatching my hat I clapped it on and led the way across the yard and, heedless of the spectators who gaped and nudged each other, we got into the cart, paid our dues, and drove out into the High Street, nor did we exchange a word until we had left the town behind us; then:

"Why are you so frightful angry, Peregrine?"

"Ah, why?" I groaned. "What madness was it that would have driven me to murder? Had you but thrown me your knife I should have stabbed him—killed him where he stood—and loved the doing of it. Oh, horrible!"

"No, wonderful!" sighed she, laying her hand on my drooping shoulder. "I—I liked you for it! You weren't afraid this time. Did he hurt you?"

"Not much."

"And he tore your fine new coat—the beast! Never mind, I'll mend it for you to-night, if you like."

"I can buy another," said I gloomily.

"No, that would be wicked, wasteful extravagance, Peregrine, and I can mend it beautifully."

"Very well!" I sighed.

"That's three times you fights for me, Peregrine."

"And been worsted on each occasion!" said I.

"No, you beats Gabbing Dick, remember," said she consolingly, her hand on my shoulder again. "And I—I likes you in your new clothes, though I wish you had your curls back again because—"

"How came you at the inn with that man?" I demanded suddenly.

"I had been selling my last few baskets."

"And he saw you?"

"Yes."

"And spoke to you?"

"Yes."

"And he—tried to—kiss you, I suppose?"

"Yes—but what's it matter; don't let's talk of it any more, Peregrine."

"And did he kiss you—did he?" At this she began to frown. "Did he kiss you, Diana—answer me?"

"I'll not!" said she, setting her chin.

"Ah, but you shall!"

"Oh, but I won't! Who are you to question me so?"

"Tell me, or by God I'll make you!"

"Ah, don't talk, you couldn't—no, not if—" I seized her, wrenched and swung her down across my knees (careless alike in my sudden frenzy of fallen reins, of danger or death itself) and having her thus helpless, set my hand about her soft, round throat.

"By God!" I gasped, "but you shall tell me, Diana; you shall tell me if he dared sully you with his vile touch—speak—speak!"

And now as I glared down at her I saw her eyes grow wide and suddenly fearful.

"Oh, Peregrine," she whispered. "Don't—don't look at me so—as if you hated me—don't, ah, don't!" And then, oh, wonder of wonders! Her arms were about my neck, drawing me lower and lower until her soft cheek met mine and, clasping me thus, she spoke under her breath:

"He didn't. Peregrine—he didn't! No man shall ever kiss me in line except—just—one!"

"Who?" I questioned, grasping her to me. "Who is that one?"

"Loose me, now," she pleaded. "You'll make me cry in a minute, and I hates to cry." So I obeyed her and sitting up, saw that Diogenes, like the four-footed philosopher he was, had come to a halt and was serenely cropping the grass by the roadside. And so we presently drove on again, but though Diana frowned no more, she persistently avoided my glance.

"Diana," said I at last, vainly endeavouring to meet her gaze, "who is the—one man?"

"Him as I shall marry, of course—if I ever do!" she answered.

"Then that man is myself, of course!"

"You are a sight too cocksure!"

"Am I?"

"Yes, and—very rough, I think."

"Oh, forgive me—did I hurt you—just now, when I—"

"You did!"

"Where?"

"Here, on the throat, Peregrine."

75

"Let me look," said I, peering. Then, "The wound is not apparent, Diana, unless it is—here!" and leaning closer, I touched her soft neck with my lips. "Did I hurt you anywhere else?"

"No!" said she hastily and with sudden shy look.

"I could almost regret my gentleness!" I sighed. After this we drove in silence awhile; that is to say Diogenes ambled along at his own leisurely gait, as if he very well knew that 'time was made for slaves'.

So I looked at Diana, drinking in this new, shy beauty of her, and she looked at earth and sky, at hedgerow and rolling meadow but with never a glance at me.

"It was wrong of you to think the gentleman kissed me!" said she suddenly, beginning to frown.

"It was!" I admitted. "Very wrong indeed!"

"Then why did you?"

"Because I was a fool!"

"Well, I don't like fools!"

"Then I will endeavour to be wiser."

"'T will need a lot o' trying, I think," said she, scowling.

"Good heavens!" said I. "Are *you* angry now?"

"Yes, I can be angry as well as you, I s'pose?"

"Of course!" said I. "You have contrived to be very ill-tempered lately."

"Oh, have I?"

"You have! And very slipshod in your speech—indeed, your diction is worse than ever—"

"Oh, stow your gab!"

"Now you are coarse and vulgar in the extreme!"

"Well, that's better than pretending to be what I ain't. And if you don't like my talk—hold your tongue and I'll hold mine!"

"I will!" said I.

"Do!" she snapped. And so was silence again, wherein the birds seemed to sing quite out of tune and Diogenes a lazy quadruped very much needing the whip.

"Cannot you drive a little faster?" I suggested.

For answer she lashed Diogenes to a gallop so that the cart lurched and swayed in highly unpleasant fashion; but presently, this speed abating somewhat, I ventured to loose my grip of the seat and thrusting hands into pockets, felt the case containing the locket and chain.

"Are you any better tempered yet?" I enquired.

"No—nor like to be—"

"That's a pity!"

"Oh—why?"

"Because you look prettier when you don't frown—"

"Oh tush!"

"Though you're handsome always. And besides I—I brought you a small present—"

"Well, you can keep it—"

"You haven't looked at it yet!"

"Don't want to!"

"Here it is," said I, opening the case. "Do you like it?"

"No!"

"Won't you accept it?"

"No, I won't!"

"Why, very well!" said I, and shutting the case I threw it into the road.

"Ah, don't! How could you!" she cried and reined Diogenes to abrupt standstill. "Go and pick it up—this instant!"

"If you don't want it—I won't!" said I, folding my arms.

"I didn't say I didn't want it—"

"But you wouldn't accept it—"

"No more I will—yet—"

"Now of all the ridiculous, unreasonable creatures—"

"So please go an' pick it up, Peregrine."

"If I do, will you let me put it round your neck?"

"Wait till—till I feels a little kinder to you!"

"That will be a unique occasion and one to remember!" said I bitterly, and springing from the cart, I went and took up my despised gift, though with very ill grace. "And pray, madam," I enquired, thrusting the case into my pocket and frowning up at her where she leaned, chin on fist, viewing me with her sombre gaze, "when are you likely to feel any kinder?"

"How should I know—and you look s' strange and different in your new clo'es—"

"It is to be hoped so!" said I.

"And your curls all cut off!"

"I never thought you'd notice—"

"And you seem more cocksure than ever—"

"Cocksure is an ugly word, Diana."

"So I think I liked you better as you were."

"Good!" said I, climbing back into the cart. "It remains for me to make you like me best—as I am."

"How?"

"By marrying you."

"But you don't—we ain't in love with each other or any such silliness," said she, flicking idly at the hedge with the whip.

"I'm not so sure, Diana. Indeed, I begin to think I do—love you in a way—or may do soon."

"Oh, do you?"

"I do!"

"Have you ever been in love?"

"Never."

"Then you don't know nothin' about it."

"Do you?" I questioned.

"More than you!" she nodded.

"Ah, do you mean that you have loved—some man—"

"Of course not, silly!"

"Good!" said I. "And you have promised faithfully never to kiss any other man but me—"

"I said the man I married—"

"Well, that *is* me."

"Oh, is it?"

"Of course!"

CHAPTER XXX

OF A TRULY MEMORABLE OCCASION

The silence was broken only by the plodding hoofs of Diogenes, the creak of harness and rattle of wheels, while Diana grew lost in thought and I in contemplation of Diana; the stately grace of her slender, shapely form, the curve of her vivid lips, the droop of her long, down-swept lashes, her resolute chin and her indefinable air of native pride and power. All at once her sombre look gave place to a smile, her slender hand tightened upon the reins, and glancing up I saw that we had reached a place where four roads met, and here, seated beneath the finger-post was a solitary, shabbily dressed old man absorbed in a book; roused by the sound of our approach, he glanced up and I recognised the ancient person, Lord Wyvelstoke.

"It's my old man!" said Diana, and waved her hand in joyous greeting, whereupon he arose and doffing his weather-beaten hat, bowed white head in stately greeting.

"Surely it is my pleasure to behold my courageous young Amazon," said he, limping forward. "Greetings, fair Penthesilea!" and taking the hand she reached out to him, he kissed it gallantly.

"And you are still alone!" said she, smiling down at him as she had never smiled at me. "Are you always alone?"

"Always!" he answered, sighing. "Though I have my books—and an old man's dreams. But, God bless you, child, how radiant you look; you seem the soul incarnate of this glorious day."

"And this is Peregrine," said she a little hastily, with a wave of her hand in my direction.

"Sir, I trust I see you well!" said I, bareheaded and bowing, and his lordship, glancing at me for the first time, recognised me despite my altered appearance.

"Mr. Vereker," quoth he, with another bow, "this is a twofold pleasure! So you are acquainted with my Penthesilea?"

"Yes, sir, though I know her as Diana!"

"But my real name's Anna, sir—as I tells you at the fair," she added.

"Yes," answered his lordship, "and you called me your old pal, I remember. Yet Mr. Vereker is indubitably right, for Diana you surely are, as fair as the chaste goddess, as brave and—"

"As nobly good!" said I.

"Assuredly, sir!" he nodded, in the quick, decisive way I remembered. "The eyes of Age are as quick to recognise purity as the eyes of Love, and a great deal less prejudiced."

77

"If you're saying all this about me—don't!" quoth Diana. "Because I ain't a goddess and don't want to be. And now, old gentleman, it's gettin' lateish and I've supper to cook, so if you'm going our way let me give you a lift; there's plenty o' room for you 'twixt Peregrine an' me."

"No, no," sighed his lordship with a somewhat sad and wistful smile. "You have each other, and I am old and wise enough to know that age is no fit companion for youth and beauty—"

"But I like old folks," said Diana in her direct fashion. "I like you, your voice and grand manners; it's plain you was a fine gentleman once—though your coat wants mendin'."

"Indeed, I fear it is almost beyond mending," answered his lordship; "but it is a favourite, and old like myself, though I am glad you can find it in your heart to be kind to an old fellow in a shabby coat—"

"What's a coat matter?" smiled Diana. "Peregrine's was worse than yours."

"Yes," nodded his lordship. "I fancy it was, and I'm glad—very glad that you like me also, Diana; it does me good, child."

"Why, then, come on up," she commanded, reaching out her hand to him in her imperious manner.

"Pray do, sir," said I. "It would be an honour and pleasure."

"It'll save your poor, old, stiff leg, sir!" added Diana.

"Ah, Diana, fair goddess," said he in his placid, stately manner, "when you put my disturbers to such ignominious flight at the fair, you graciously unbent enough to address me as 'your old pal'—"

"You seemed s' very lonely!" she explained.

"Child," he sighed, "I am lonely still!"

"Why, then," said she in her gentlest voice, smiling down into his wistful face, "come on up, old pal, an' forget your loneliness awhile."

And now his lordship smiled also, and having pocketed his book, climbed into the cart with our assistance and seated himself between us.

"This," sighed he, as Diogenes ambled on again, "is exceedingly kind in you, to burden yourselves thus with a solitary and garrulous old man—"

"What's garrulous?" demanded Diana.

"Talkative, my child, excessive verbosity—Mr. Vereker will doubtless remember our conversation on music," said he, with a whimsical glance at me.

"Indeed, yes, sir," I answered. "I was greatly interested."

"Well, I like to hear you talk, too," said Diana, "you speaks like Peregrine does, only he says such silly things, and he's a great deal too cocksure of himself into the bargain!"

"Concerning which," said his lordship gently, "you may have remarked that Mr. Vereker possesses a chin."

"What's his chin to do with it? You've got one—so have I for that matter."

"True, child, we all three possess chins that typify dogged resolution to a remarkable degree—"

"Peregrine's hatefully dogged; I know that!" sighed Diana.

"Excellent youth!" nodded our aged companion, regarding me with twinkling eyes.

"And Diana is excessively and unreasonably illogical!" I retorted.

"Adorable maiden!" sighed his lordship, glancing at Diana.

"Lord, Peregrine, how can you say such things!" she exclaimed indignantly. "He only says it because he wants to marry me!" she explained into our companion's right ear. "If I don't tell you he will in a minute; he tells it to every one."

"Perspicacious youth!" nodded his lordship.

"And Diana very foolishly attempts to deny me, for no just or adequate reason," I explained into his left ear.

"Extremely natural and feminine!" nodded his lordship.

"Because of his grand aunt and fine uncles for one thing," said Diana.

"And for what other reason?" I demanded.

"Just because!"

"Because of what?"

"Never mind!"

"And there you have it, sir!" I exclaimed. "Did you ever hear such futile answers?"

"Often, and generally from the loveliest lips, Mr. Vereker—"

"Pray, sir, call me Peregrine if you will: and, sir," said I, grasping his worn left sleeve, "I beg you to advise me in this matter, for you are so wise—"

"Never heed him, old pal!" cried Diana, grasping his right sleeve. "Peregrine only thinks he ought to marry me because he bought me and folks talk and—"

"Pardon me, dear child, but how and where may one purchase a goddess?" his lordship enquired. "You said 'bought', I think?"

"Yes, he bought me for fourteen guineas, a florin, one groat and three pennies!" and in two breaths, or thereabouts, she had recounted the whole incident.

"Admirable!" exclaimed his lordship, glancing from one to other of us with shining eyes. "Ridiculous! Magnificent!"

"And that's the only reason he wants to marry me—"

"There you are wrong, Diana, and most unjust!" said I indignantly. "You know my chief purpose in wedding you is to take you from this wandering life and shield you from all hardship and coarseness."

"And what of love, Peregrine?" enquired his lordship, gently. At this I hesitated, glanced down at the gleaming buckles of my new shoes, glanced up at the blue serenity of heaven, and finally looked at Diana, to find her watching me beneath scowling brows.

"And there you have it!" said she in disdainful mimicry, "he—he don't know!"

The Ancient Person smiled and laid his small, white hand upon Diana's brown fingers.

"But then, dear child with the wise, woman's eyes—you have seen and surely know." Now at this Diana glanced swiftly from him to me and then, to my amazement, flushed hotly and drooped her head. "Ah, yes," sighed his lordship, "I see you know, child, so what matter?"

"Sir," said I, "what do you mean?"

"Peregrine, I touch upon an abstract theme and therefore one better sensed than described, so I will not attempt it." Here, to my further surprise, Diana nestled closer to him and whispered something in his ear.

"I believe," said the Ancient Person, after Diogenes had plodded some little distance, "I believe you are camping with Jessamy Todd?"

"Yes, sir, but pray, how did you learn this?"

"Well, I know the redoubtable Jessamy rather well."

"We'm settled in the wood beyond Wyvelstoke Park," added Diana, "along by the stream."

"I know it," nodded his lordship, "I have killed many a fine trout along that same stream. I shall do myself the pleasure of finding you one of these days, if I may?"

"Pray do sir," said I eagerly, "you will find Jeremy Jarvis the most wonderful tinker in the world and one who writes poetry besides mending kettles and shoeing horses."

"This has been a truly memorable occasion," said his lordship, "I feel myself honoured by your confidence, it has given me a new interest in my solitary life."

"And why are you so solitary?" questioned Diana.

"Because old age is usually solitary, and because in my youth, when Love came to me, I was a coward, by reason of worldly considerations, and let it plead in vain, alas! And thus, although my friends were many in those days, my empty heart was always solitary, and now—my friends are mostly dead, and I am—a childless, lonely old man!"

The white head drooped disconsolate, the slender, delicate hands wrung each other, and then about these bowed and aged shoulders Diana clasped protecting arm and stooped soft cheek to his.

"Ah, poor old soul, don't grieve!" she murmured. "Here's Peregrine and me will be your friends and pals, if you'll have us, and if you're ever very lonely or in want, come to us—wait!" Then, opening her gipsire, and before I could prevent, into those slender fingers she thrust a bright, new guinea; for a long moment his lordship stared down at the coin while I grew alternately hot and cold. When at last he lifted his white head I saw his keen eyes dimmed with unshed tears.

"Why, child?" he murmured. "Generous girl—"

"No, don't!" she smiled. "Don't say anything! Only let me be your friend to cheer your loneliness an' help you now an' then."

Lord Wyvelstoke stared at the coin in his palm as if it had been a very rare and curious object, then, having deposited it carefully within an inner pocket, he bared his head in his courtly fashion.

"Diana," said he, "sweet friend, you have given me something precious as my vanished youth and more lasting; accept a once solitary old man's gratitude. Mr. Vereker—Peregrine, you who stand perhaps where I stood years ago with the best of all things in your reach—grasp it, boy, follow heart rather than head, and may you find those blessings I have never known. Here, I think, is the advice you sought of me—for the rest, you are a Vereker, sir, and carry honour in your name. And now is good-bye for a time; my way lies yonder," said he, pointing towards a by-lane. So here we stopped and down sprang I to aid our Ancient Person to alight.

"You'll come soon and let me patch your coat?" said Diana, giving him her hand.

"Assuredly!" he answered, with his quick, decisive nod. "Meantime, God be kind to you both, your friendship has lifted much of the heaviness of years from my heart and I shall walk the lighter henceforth!" So saying, he bent and kissed Diana's hand, shook mine vigorously and limped away.

"A dear old man!" said Diana, looking after him gentle-eyed.

"I wonder," said I, "I wonder what he meant by that talk regarding my 'head and heart'—"

"How should I know?"

"But what do you think?"

"That you'd better get in if you're goin' to!" Obediently I clambered into the cart, whereupon Diana prodded the somnolent Diogenes into motion.

"Where did you meet his l—that Ancient Person, Diana?"

"At the fair. Hooky Sam and two pals tried to rob him, an' him such a poor, lonely old soul, only I stood 'em off, made 'em cut their stick, I did."

"But he had a pistol—"

"What—him? Well if so, he didn't have t' use it, my little *churi* was enough."

"Indeed, you are far braver than I was, Diana—"

79

"Tush! There's few men as won't cut and run from a female if she's got a knife—an' means t' use it."

"This was why he named you Penthesilea."

"Who's she?"

"She was a Queen of the Amazons and fought at Troy—"

"What's Amazons?"

"Fierce, terrible women who hated men and loved to fight."

"Well, I hates a fight, so don't you go calling me Penthe—whatever her name was."

"No, Diana, I would have you her very opposite, if possible."

"How d'ye mean?"

"I'd have you a lady, sweet-mannered, soft-voiced, tender and gentle—"

"Like your aunt? But she ain't exactly a pet lamb, Peregrine, nor yet a cooin' dove—now, is she? And as for me I'm just—"

"My goddess Diana!"

"Was the real goddess a lady?"

"Well, I—I suppose so—but I want to ask you—"

"No, tell me about her—the goddess Diana."

"Well, besides Diana, she was called Cynthia, Delia, Ancia, Orthia and several other names—"

"And all of 'em pretty, too!"

"And she was passionately fond of hunting."

"And didn't like men overmuch, did she?"

"Well, it appears not. She changed Actaeon into a stag and had him devoured by her dogs—"

"Which wasn't very ladylike, Peregrine—that was coming it a bit too strong, I think! Why did she do it? Poor young man!"

"Because he spied upon her—at her toilet."

"Was that all? d'ye mean he catches her undoin' her curl papers?"

"She was—bathing!"

"Oh!" said Diana. "Well, poor young man! She'd got modesty pretty bad, I think, and if all goddesses are like her—"

"They were not."

"Oh, well, let's talk o' something more human-like—"

"Ourselves!" I suggested.

"Well, I sold every one o' my baskets and earned fifty-six shillings. How much money did you spend, Peregrine?"

"I'm not sure, but about twenty-seven pounds, I fancy."

"Pounds?" she cried so suddenly that Diogenes pricked his ears. "For them noo duds—"

"Horrible!" I exclaimed.

"It is!" said she. "It's wicked robbery—"

"I mean your grammar, Diana, and the word 'duds', whatever it may mean, sounds atrocious, especially on your lips—"

"Oh, tush! d'ye mean as they charges you all that money for them new—"

"Those!" I corrected.

"Things you're wearing—"

"You forget the despised locket and chain," said I reproachfully, "and I also purchased two silver watches—"

"Watches? Two on 'em? What for?"

"One for our Tinker and one for Jessamy," I explained.

"Foolishness!" she exclaimed.

"Indeed, madam?"

"It's wicked waste o' money—an' don't call me 'madam'!"

"I suppose I may be permitted to spend my money to please myself, girl?"

"I s'pose so, boy! Easy come, easy go! You can get more any time ye want, just for the askin', can't you? But you wouldn't spend s' gay an' careless if you had to earn your money, to slave an' sweat for it—not you!"

"How do you know?" I demanded in towering anger.

"Just because!"

"I consider you are very—exceedingly—" I checked the word upon my lips and scowled.

"Well? Very exceedingly—what?" she demanded.

"Never mind!"

"I don't!" she retorted, and flicked Diogenes to speedier gait, for evening was beginning to fall.

CHAPTER XXXI

A VEREKER'S ADVICE TO A VEREKER

Diogenes, perceiving he was permitted to loiter no more, philosophically betook himself to his heels, or rather hoofs, and trotted briskly supper-wards, up hill and down, until suddenly, above the rattle and grind of the wheels, I was aware of a man's voice, peculiarly sonorous and sweet, upraised in joyful singing.

"Praise God from whom all blessings flow
Praise Him all creatures here below—"

The single voice was joined by others that swelled in jubilant chorus:

"Praise Him above, ye Heavenly Host
Praise Father, Son and Holy Ghost."

Reaching the top of a hill I looked down upon a little hamlet shady with trees, a cluster of thatched, flower-girt cottages, a hoary church, an ancient inn before which last stood Jessamy Todd and a group of rustic folk, men in smocked frocks or shirt sleeves, bare-armed women in aprons or print gowns, children tousled and round of eye, and all, for the most part, very silent, with heads reverently bowed, for Jessamy was praying:

"—so Heavenly Father here we be, Thy children all, weary with another day's labour, grant us this night Thy peace, each one. If any there be that grieve, O Father, comfort 'em; if any there be in pain, O Father, pity an' cherish 'em; if any do bear ill-will agin his brother, O Father, turn his anger to love that love may come thereby. Oh, make us strong against all temptations, that when we come to our last, long sleep we may rest with Thee for ever. Amen.

And good-night, friends and brothers."

Hereupon Jessamy put on his hat, paused to grasp the horny hands extended to him, then lifted a large canvas bag to his shoulder, but at my shout he turned and flourished his hat in salutation as we drove up.

"Why, Jessamy," exclaimed Diana, as he placed the bag in the cart, "what's come t' your face?" And now I saw his comely features were disfigured by an ugly blue weal.

"Oh, nothin' much, Ann," he exclaimed, smiling a little sheepishly.
"Only a whip—"

"Lord, Jess—whose?"

"I come on a fine gentleman thrashing of a little lad, whereupon I ventured a word of remonstrance as in dooty bound and turned to look to the lad as lay a-weepin', whereupon the gentleman took occasion to gi'e me this here—ye see he didn't 'appen to know me, poor soul!"

"Well, I hope you gave the 'poor soul' all he needed!" cried Diana, cracking the whip so loudly that Diogenes pricked startled ears.

"I'm afraid I did, Ann, God forgive me. The Old Adam's very strong in me."

"And how's the poor boy?"

"Why, the gentleman wore ridin' boots, d'ye see—"

"Ah!" exclaimed Diana between white teeth. "And what's become o' the gentleman—"

"They—put him to bed," confessed Jessamy guiltily, "but he's nice an' comfortable, Ann, an'll be right as nine pence in th' morning."

"What sort of a person was he?" I enquired.

"A biggish chap, a bit too round an' wi' too much neck."

"How often did ye hit him, Jess?"

"Four times, Ann! Four times, an' one would ha' been plenty. Four times an' me preachin' forgiveness an' brotherly love—"

"Brotherly love's no good agin' that kind o' beast, a good strong fist's the thing, or better still a little, sharp *churi*—like mine!"

"Ah, but when I hit him," sighed Jessamy, "I went on hitting him—not for the good of his soul but because—I—I j'yed in it—"

"Well, it did him just as much good, anyhow!" said Diana whereupon Jessamy sighed again and shook his head in self-reproof. Seeing him thus downcast, I laid a hand on his arm and with the other felt in my pocket.

"Do you happen to possess a watch, Jessamy?" I enquired.

"Aye, for sure," he nodded, "that is, I did, an' a rare good 'un too, but it don't go these days by reason of a brick as was hove at me by a riotous fe-male."

"Good heavens!" I exclaimed. "Why?"

"The poor creetur' being in liquor didn't take kindly to my method o' prayer, so she let fly a brick as took me in the watch, bein' fortunate for me but bad for my watch—a good, silver watch, too, as was given me by my old dad just afore he died. An' so I ain't had the 'eart to buy another."

"Then will you please accept this?" said I a little diffidently, aware of Diana's sharp eyes, and I thrust the timepiece into his hand.

"Why—but—how can I—Lord bless me!" stammered Jessamy, glancing from the watch to me and back again irresolutely.

"You'd better put it into your pocket, Jess, quick, or he'll throw it into the ditch!" nodded Diana. "So put it into your pocket and thank the pretty gentleman." This Jessamy did, after no little demur and with reiterated expressions of thanks.

"Which do remind me, sir, as I have a letter for you," said he.

81

"And my name is Peregrine," I nodded.

"A letter, Peregrine, as was give to me for you by your uncle, Sir Jervas." And presently, having felt through his numerous pockets, he brought forth the letter in question, which, with due apology, I proceeded to open and read; here it is:

"MY DEAR PEREGRINE: Apropos of your forthcoming marriage (at this I started) be guided by your own discretion in the matter, since Marriage is one of the few serious dangers to be feared in an otherwise somewhat vapid tedium we call life. Be yourself to yourself, guide, philosopher and friend, since you are likely to heed the wisdom of such more than that of any other friend, for I judge that being a Vereker, no Vereker (or any other lesser human) can stay you from your fixed purpose. So (writing as a relation who has developed an unexpected regard for you) my serious advice is—act upon your own advice. Your beautiful gipsy is a magnificent creature with a mind and will of her own, the dignified unrestraint of a dryad and the deplorable diction of a wandering gipsy wench. She would be excellent as a picture, entertaining as a companion and execrable as a wife. This of course is merely the opinion of a Vereker which to another Vereker is of not the slightest consideration. None the less, being somewhat your senior in years, I would venture to point out what I have learned by bitter experience, to wit, nephew, viz: that which is delightful for an hour may disgust in a week and become intolerable within a month.

    In which certainty
  I subscribe myself,
    Most humbly your uncle,
      Jervas Vereker.

P.S. If you care to designate such address as will find you, your allowance shall be forwarded either by week or month as you shall determine."

Scarcely had I finished the perusal of this characteristic missive than we turned from the road and jolted down the grassy slope towards the little wood from whose rustling shadow came the blithe thump and ring of the Tinker's busy hammer, which merry clamour ceased suddenly; and forth to welcome us came Jerry, sooty and grimed as Vulcan himself and smiling in cheery greeting. And glancing from his honest face, with its wise and kindly eyes, over the quiet peace of this sheltered wood and smiling countryside, to Diana's proud and vital beauty, I knew indeed that no Vereker or any other human could stay me from my purpose.

"Jeremy," said I, plunging hand into pocket, "I don't know if you possess a watch or want a watch, but I've bought you one; pray accept it in memory of our friendship and as a very small mark of my esteem."

"Lord love me—a silver watch!" exclaimed the Tinker for about the tenth time, clapping the same to his ear.

"Two on 'em, brother!" said Jessamy, doing the same by his.

"My soul!" exclaimed the Tinker. "Fortune ain't in the habit o' showering brand-noo silver watches about me like this an' it's apt to ketch me unprepared with words to soot the occasion—"

"True, brother, when Peregrine stuck mine into my fist it was like a roaster in the short ribs, low, brother, low—I was floored, taken aback, an' nat'rally broached to an' come to a dead halt—"

"Wicked extravagance, I call it!" exclaimed Diana, glancing up from the potatoes she was peeling. "Though if he wants to waste his money, he couldn't ha' wasted it better!"

"For that," said I, seating myself beside her, "I will help you with those things if you'll show me how!" At this she glanced swiftly at me without lifting her head and in her eyes was an indescribable kindliness and her vivid lips were curved to smile so tender that I stared in joyful bewilderment and forgot all else in the world until roused by the Tinker's voice:

"And exactly what o'clock might it be by your chronometer, Jessamy?"

"Precisely fifteen minutes an' three quarters past seven, brother."

"Then, according to mine, you're precisely three quarters of a minute fast, Jessamy, my lad."

"Why, as to that, friend," answered Jessamy, "it's in my mind that you're just about that much slow, comrade."

And so, reaching a knife, I began to help Diana in the peeling of potatoes and, though finding it a somewhat trying business, yet contrived ever and anon to steal surreptitious glances at her downbent face and to surprise more than once that new soft and shy-sweet wonder in her glance.

"You'll cut yourself if you aren't more careful!" she admonished, and the kindness it seemed had somehow got into her voice.

"What matter?" said I. "What does anything matter except—"

"What?" she questioned softly.

"You, Diana—you and only you—"

"Don't be silly!" said she, but in the same gentle voice and though she stooped her head a little lower, I thought the colour was deepened in her cheek.

"Should you think me silly, Diana, if I told you—"

"Yes, I should!" she answered so suddenly that I started and the wet potato shot from my grasp.

"I fancy it'll rain to-night, Jessamy," said the Tinker, glancing up at the heavens.

"Brother, I'm pretty sure of it," answered Jessamy, "I noticed the clouds bankin' up to wind'ard. We'd best rig up t' other tent—"

"Why, Peregrine," exclaimed the Tinker, as I stooped to recover the elusive vegetable, "who's been sp'iling of your noo coat, your collar's all ripped, lad?"

"A black scoundrel who insulted Diana," I exclaimed, clenching my fists.

"A gentleman as spoke to me, you mean!"

"The damned rogue tried to kiss you—"

"Well, what of it—I didn't let him, did I?"

"You have no business to run such risks," said I angrily, my gorge rising at memory of the fellow, "a tavern is no place for a girl—"

"Well, I can't live under a glass case!" she retorted. "And, anyway, I can take care of myself—better than you can!"

"Yes," I answered humbly, "I fear I am not a very terrible champion—Jessamy, O Jessamy, teach me how to fight!"

For answer Jessamy rose and opening his canvas bag reached thence four of those padded gloves termed 'mufflers.'

"With your uncle George's compliments!" said he, glancing at me with twinkling eyes. "And now, seeing the light's good, if you'm minded to try a round or so afore supper, why cheerily it is, messmate!"

Then, tossing aside the half-peeled potato I stripped off my coat.

CHAPTER XXXII

HOW I MADE A SURPRISING DISCOVERY, WHICH, HOWEVER, MAY NOT SURPRISE THE READER IN THE LEAST

From brake and thicket gemmed with a myriad sparkling dewdrops, birds were singing a jubilant paean, as well indeed they might upon so fair a morning; yet these were but a chorus to the singer down by the brook whose glorious voice soared in swelling ecstasy and sank in plaintive sweetness only to rise again, so high and clear and ineffably sweet as seemed verily to inspire the birds to an eager and joyful emulation.

So they sang together thus in pretty rivalry, the birds and Diana, until, her song ended, I went my way and presently found her beside the bubbling rill, combing out her shining hair. At sight of me she laughed and, tossing back her tresses, flourished her comb in a sweep that took in radiant sky, earth and sparkling brook.

"O Peregrine, ain't it glorious!" she cried.

"It is!" said I, staring at her loveliness, whereupon she flushed and recommenced combing her hair.

"Thought you was asleep an' snoring," said she in her most ungracious manner.

"Well, you see I'm not, and besides I don't snore!"

"Tush, how can you know?"

"I don't think I do—and for heaven's sake why talk of such things on such a morning, Diana?"

"Because!" she answered, turning away.

"Because of what?" I demanded, grasping a silky handful of her glossy hair. "Why are you so ungracious to me lately; why do you do and say things that you imagine will make me think you hard and unlovely; why do you try to shock me so often?"

"I don't! How?"

"By pretending to be trivial and shallow and commonplace."

"Because I am!"

"Don't blaspheme, Diana. How could you be shallow or commonplace, you who taught me to love the Silent Places? So why attempt things so impossible, dear child?" And taking hold of her smooth, round chin I turned her head that she must look at me. "Why, Diana, why?" I repeated. For a moment she met my look, then her lids fluttered and fell. Yet she stood before me strangely docile.

"Because," said she at last, "you looks at me lately as—as you are doing now, as if—as though—"

"I had only just found out how beautiful you are, Diana? And don't you know why?"

"Yes," she murmured, "but—you don't."

"I have discovered the reason this morning," said I, drawing her a little nearer, "I love you, Diana, I know it at last. Why, good heaven, I must have loved you for days!"

"You have!" she nodded, without looking at me.

"You—you knew it, then?"

"Of course!" she nodded again. "So did Jerry—so did Jessamy, so did your tall uncle—and your aunt, I think, and—and everybody else in all the world—except yourself, Peregrine."

"Blind fool that I was—"

"No, Peregrine, it was because you never guessed, that I didn't run away—"

"And you never will now, Diana, because you are mine, But I loved the sweet, pure soul of you first and so, my Diana, although I am longing—longing to kiss you—those dear gentle eyes, your red lips—I never will until you give them, because my love, being very great, is very humble, like—like this!" And sinking to my knees, I would have kissed the hem of her gown, but with a soft, sweet cry of reproach, she slipped to her knees also and swaying to me, hid her face in my breast.

"O Peregrine," she murmured, looking up at me through a mist of tears, "it is a wonderful thing to be loved by a gentleman—"

"Then God keep me so!" I whispered.

"He will, Peregrine, so long as you are Peregrine—kiss me!" And so for a deathless moment I held her close, to kiss her tumbled hair, her tearful eyes, the tremor of her sweet mouth.

"Peregrine—dear," she sighed, "at first I hated love and when it came it frighted me and then, when it came to you and you not knowing, I knew love could only be a dream 'twixt you and me and so I—I tried to make you hate me—I talked and acted rough—as much as I could, or—or very nearly—but I couldn't keep it up all the time, it hurt me so—"

"Then," cried I, "why then, you do love me, heart and soul, Diana?"

"Ah—don't you know—even yet?" said she passionately. "You are so different, so gentle—oh, you're—just Peregrine! Ah, it isn't your money I want, or to be a fine lady like your aunt wi' horses and carriages and servants; ah, not dear Peregrine, no—it's just you and me together in the Silent Places—"

"And so we will be," I cried, "together in life and death—"

"O Peregrine, it isn't a dream is it—a dream that can't come true. You'll—make me marry you, won't you?"

"Ah, by God I will—whenever you are ready, for you are mine!"

"Yes, yours," she whispered, "for ever and always! You ha' no doubts o' the future, have ye, Peregrine?"

"None!" said I, arrogant in my happiness.

"When I called you cocksure I—loved you for it!"

Thus sat we, embracing and embraced, beside this prattling stream, looking upon the glory of this midsummer morning and each other to find all things ever more beautiful, and knowing a happiness that went far beyond mere speech.

Birds have sung as blithely—perhaps; the sun may have beamed as kindly and brooks have laughed as joyously as this chattering rill of ours, but as for me, I soberly doubt it.

"Peregrine," said she at last, "where is my locket?"

"Here!" said I, reaching the case from my pocket. "When your singing woke me to this wonderful, glorious morning, I brought it to find you."

"How pretty it is!" she sighed happily, touching it tenderly with the extreme tip of one slender finger.

"It isn't anything near good enough," said I, viewing it a little gloomily, "I will get you one infinitely better—"

"No!" said she. "This is what I shall always love best," and stooping, she touched the trinket with the heaven of her mouth. Then, being upon our knees, she stooped her head that I might set it about her throat, but what with her nearness and the touch of her velvety neck, I bungled the business sadly, so that she lifted her two hands to aid me and her lips being so near, how could I help but kiss her.

"Now this, Peregrine!" she commanded, drawing my mouth to the locket where it hung. And so I kissed the locket and chain and throat and neck until she laughed, a little tremulously, and slipping from my hold, sprang to her feet and fled away.

And now, being upon my knees, I bowed my head and passionately besought a blessing on this sweet-souled Diana, this woman of mine, and upon our love and the years that were to be. My supplication ended, I remembered that this was the first prayer I had uttered since faring out into the world. And as I arose, came Jessamy, rubbing sleep from his eyes.

"Lord bless us, Perry, what a morning—the j'y of it, brother! List to the birds and hark—ah, do but hark how Ann do be singing; never 'eard her voice sound so wonderful afore, Perry."

"Nor I, Jessamy," said I, as the golden notes died away; "but then there never was quite such another morning as this."

CHAPTER XXXIII

OF TWO INCOMPARABLE THINGS. THE VOICE OF DIANA AND JESSAMY'S "RIGHT"

Exuberant, with blood a-dance and nerves braced and tingling from the sparkling water, we faced each other upon the grassy level, Jessamy and I, stripped to the waist and with muffled fists and I very conscious of the keen eyes that appraised my slender arms, and the muscles of what uncle George would have called my 'torso.'

"I'm afraid I am—hatefully puny!" I exclaimed, casting a disparaging glance at my proportions.

"Smallish," nodded Jessamy, "smallish, but that ain't a matter to weep over, brother. Small muscles is quicker than big. Moreover, the Lord has given you a sound and healthy body and left you to develop an' do the best wi' it. Fresh air an' exercise, sledge 'ammer an' bellers'll work wonders in a week or so, mark my words. Now come on an' keep your weather peeper on my right, for look'ee your left is a feeler, good to keep your man away, to jolt him now an' then an' to feint him to an opening, then it's in wi' your right an' all o' you behind it—that's my way and I've found it a pretty good way."

"You've always won your fights, haven't you, Jessamy?"

"Pretty often—though 'tis all vanity, lad, arter all—"

"And why did you win—and often against bigger and stronger men?"

"Well, p'raps because I eat little an' drink less, or p'raps because I meant to win, or p'raps again because I knew how. However, the fightin' game is all vanity an' vexation an' keep your ogles on my right! Now, into me, lad, an' hit hard—that's your fashion—try for my chin but don't forget my right! Swing in for my ribs, Perry—and heartily! Steady boy—on your toes now!"

Such were his expressions as we danced and ducked, feinted and smote, and as often as he bade me watch his right, that same right smacked home upon my ribs or face while I wasted myself in futile yet exceedingly earnest efforts to smite in turn his ever-moving body or elusive, wagging head, what time over and under and through my guard shot his terrible fists, to tap me lightly here, to pat me there until my breath grew short. And now, while I stood to get my wind, he explained how it was done, showing me sudden volts and turns and shifts which he termed foot-work. He showed me how to drive in short-arm blows, swinging from the hips, and how to evade them; how, when occasion favoured, to hit from the shoulder with all my strength and weight behind the blow, and how to meet a ducking head with what he called an uppercut, just such a terrible stroke as had caused the downfall of the big man Tom.

Thus Jessamy alternately smote and lectured me until, warned by Diana's clear call, we donned shirts and waistcoats and strode away to breakfast.

"And how's he shaping, Jessamy?" enquired the Tinker, serving out ham, pink and savoury, from the hissing frying pan, while Diana poured out the coffee.

"None s' bad," answered Jessamy; "he's quick an' willing an' don't mind bein' knocked down now and then, which is a good thing—you went down pretty frequent that last round, brother!" Here Diana, noting my battered dishevelment, scowled at Jessamy adorably.

"It ain't—isn't needful to hit quite so hard, is it, Jessamy?" she enquired.

"Why, yes, Ann. Peregrine wants me to teach him to fight an' you can't teach that to any man by tapping him, d'ye see."

"But, then, Jessamy," said the Tinker, with his twinkling, bright eyes on Diana, "Peregrine ain't exactly a Milo o' Crete as had a habit o' slayin' oxen wi' a blow of his fist; Peregrine's delicate frame could never endoor real good, hard knocks—"

"But it could, Jerry!" exclaimed Diana. "Nobody could hit him harder than I've seen him hit, except Jessamy, p'raps." Now at this I was seized of such a yearning to kiss her that I bent lower over my platter lest the impulse prove ungovernable.

"It ain't size as counts, brother," added Jessamy, "no—not once in a thousand; an' as for this cove Milo, big an' heavy an' slow as a waggon o' bricks, I could eat him alive any day. Though to be sure 't would only be vanity an' vexation arter all," he added mournfully, "so let's talk o' better things."

"Why, then, Jessamy," said the Tinker, his eyes twinkling more than usual, "what might be the pre-cise time by your chronometer?"

"It is now," replied Jessamy, solemnly consulting his watch, "exactly five an' three quarter minutes to seven, Jerry."

"Then I take leave to tell ye, you're exactly two minutes an' a half slow," retorted the Tinker, glancing at his own.

"You're very silent, Peregrine; does aught grieve ye?" enquired the Tinker.

"Did I shake ye up a bit too much, brother?" enquired Jessamy anxiously.

"No, no, indeed," I answered, "it is only that I am a—a little thoughtful this morning."

And so, in a while, breakfast being done, Jessamy rose.

"An' now for another go at Old Nick!" quoth he.

"Where are ye for to-day?" questioned the Tinker.

"Tonbridge—'tis market day an' Nick'll be busy in every tavern an' inn, as usual. What'll I bring back for supper?"

"Well, a chicken's tasty," mused the Tinker, "but then so's lamb, or there's liver an' bacon—"

"A shin o' beef!" said Diana in voice of finality.

"Stooed!" nodded the Tinker. "Stooed wi' plenty o' vegetables. A shin o' beef or say a couple—oh, prime! An' it's my turn to pay, Jessamy."

"No, it's mine!" quoth Diana.

"Pray allow me!" said I, reaching for my purse.

"Lord bless us, we're all that rich!" laughed Jessamy. "Come, let's toss for it." The which we did and the lot fell to Jessamy. "A couple o' shins o' beef, loaves an' what vegetables?"

"Get some of all sorts!" nodded the Tinker.

"We've plenty o' potatoes an' onions!" said Diana. "And bring 'em as early as possible, Jess; a shin o' beef ought to simmer for hours."

"Cheerily it is, Ann!" and catching up the canvas bag, Jessamy flourished his hat and strode off.

"How does Jessamy contrive to live?" I enquired.

"Lord, Peregrine," answered the Tinker, "Jessamy's rich—or was—made a fortun' wi' his fists, though I reckon he's give most of it away, like the tender-hearted cove he is."

And now, while Diana busied herself in matters culinary, Jeremy and I lighted the forge and got us to work. And very often above the ring and clamour of our hammers would rise the wonder of her voice singing some wild air of the Zingari or plaintive old ballad; so often and so gloriously she sang that at last, as I blew the fire for another heat, Jeremy bade me hush, and silent thus we stood to hearken.

"Peregrine," said he at last, "I knew Ann's voice was a wonder, but I never heard her sing so blithe an' happy-'earted. I wonder why?"

"Perhaps it is this wonderful morning," said I, watching the flutter of her gown amid the thickets across the little glade.

"Aye, most likely, for 't is surely a day o' glory, lad, a glory as is a-shining at me this moment out o' your eyes, Peregrine, singing in your voice—"

"Jeremy," said I, reaching out to grasp his grimy hand, "O Jeremy, you are right. Love found me in the dawn and this morning Diana promised to be my—wife. God make me worthy!"

"Amen, lad, amen!" said the Tinker.

And then from the shade of the willows that bordered the stream limped the small and shabby yet stately form of Lord Wyvelstoke.

CHAPTER XXXIV

THE NOBLE ART OF ORGAN-PLAYING

Catching sight of me as I hurried towards him, Lord Wyvelstoke advanced, a vigorous man despite his lameness and silvery hair.

"Peregrine—who was it?" he enquired, slipping his hand within my arm and glancing round the glade. "Who was it sang so divinely—can it be, is it—our Diana? But of course it is—"

"Yes, sir," said I, wondering at his eagerness.

"She has a peerless, a wonderful voice, but more—she sings with that divine intuition that is genius. I must speak with her—meantime, pray present your friend."

"This, sir, is my good and kind friend, Jeremy Jarvis; Jerry, his
Lordship, the Earl of Wyvelstoke."

The Earl bowed to the Tinker with his usual grave courtesy, and the Tinker (albeit a little disquieted) knuckled sooty eyebrow and bobbed tousled head to the Earl, humbly respectful yet with a simple dignity all his own.

"You seem very happily situated here," said his lordship, sweeping the shady dingle with his keen gaze.

"Why, as to that, sir—my lord," said Jeremy with unwonted diffidence, "I fear we'm a-trespassing on your land, but my friend Todd—Jessamy assured me—"

"Rest assured, friend Jarvis! None of my keepers shall disturb you—"

"Peregrine—O Jerry, dinner! Come while it's hot and come quick!" called Diana from those boskages that screened our little camp.

"It's liver and bacon," said she, busy at the fire, but beholding our companion, she set down the frying pan and hastened to welcome him with both hands outstretched.

"Why, 't is my old pal!" she cried, whereupon Jeremy blinked and seemed to swallow hard.

"You're just in time for a bit o' liver an' bacon. Bring another plate, Jerry."

"But, Ann," said he, hesitating and much at a loss, "p'raps his lordship won't care t' eat off a tin plate an'—"

"Who?" demanded Diana, turning, with the frying pan in her hand.

"His lordship! What, don't ye know this gentleman's the Earl o' Wyvelstoke?" Diana set down the frying pan and turned upon his lordship with a frown.

"Is this true?" she demanded. "Are you a lord?"

"I am, Diana."

"An earl?"

"I confess it. But always your pal, I trust, notwithstanding—"

"Why, then you own Wyvelstoke Park?"

"I do."

"And—this wood?"

"Yes, Diana."

"An' horses an' carriages an' houses, I suppose?"

"Yes, child."

"Why, then, you're rich! And you let me give you a guinea!"

"A treasure dearer to me than all the rest!" he answered gently; and taking out the coin he looked down at it, smiling wistfully.

"And I thought you were such a poor, lonely old soul—"

"So I was, Diana, and so I should be without your friendship."

"I s'pose you don't want any liver an' bacon, do you, lord?"

"Why not, goddess?"

"Because lords an' earls don't eat liver an' bacon off tin plates, do they?"

"You behold one who would if you will so far honour him," answered the
Earl with one of his stately obeisances.

"You might have told me, all the same!" said Diana, pouting a little.

"Dear child, had I done so would you have called me your old pal? It is a title dearer to me than any other." Hereupon she brought him the three-legged stool which, despite his protestations, she forced him to take. And so we began dinner, though often the Tinker would pause, food-laden jackknife in mid-air, to steal amazed and surreptitious glances at his lordship, sitting serenely, the tin plate balanced on his knees, eating with remarkable appetite and gusto.

"D'ye like it, old pal?" questioned Diana suddenly.

"Diana," answered the Ancient Person with his whimsical look, "words are sometimes poor and inadequate—I like it beyond expression."

"That's because it's strange to you an' in the open air—"

"Nay, child, I have eaten strange meals amid strange people in strange, wild places of the earth, but never such a meal as this."

"D'ye mean foreign places—across the sea?" questioned Diana eagerly.

"Yes, I have seen much of the wonders and glories of the world, vasty deserts, trackless forests, stupendous mountains, mighty rivers, and yet—and yet what more wonderful than this little island of ours, what more tenderly beautiful than our green, English countryside? The thunderous roar of plunging cataracts, the cloud-capped pinnacles of mighty mountains may fill the soul with awed and speechless wonder, but for pure joy give me an English coppice of a summer evening when blackbird and thrush are calling, or to sit and hearken to the immemorial music of a brook—Friend Jarvis, you write verses, I believe?"

"Lord, sir—my lord," answered Jeremy, his bronzed cheek flushing, "how should you know that?"

"I learned the fact from Peregrine who spoke of them in such high praise that I should much like to read some of them if you would suffer me—"

"Why, sir," stammered Jeremy, "they're wrote on such scraps an' bits o' paper, I only write 'em to please myself an'—an'—"

"Because he must!" added Diana. "You see, old pal, Jerry writes poetry like the birds sing and brooks flow, just because 't is his nature. I know lots of his verses by heart an' I love all of 'em, but I like this about the Silent Places best; listen:

"'He that the great, good thing would know
Must to the Silent Places go,
Leaving wealth and state behind
Who the great good thing would find.
Glories, honours, these will fade,
Life itself's a phantom shade;
But the soul of man—who knoweth
Whence it came and where it goeth.
So, God of Life, I pray of Thee
Ears to hear and eyes to see.
In bubbling brooks, in whispering wind
He who hath ears shall voices find,
Telling the wonder of the earth:
The awful miracle of birth;
Of love and joy, of Life and Death,
Of things that were ere we had breath;
Of man's soul through the ages growing,
Whence it comes or whither going,
That soul of God, a deathless spark
Unquenched through ages wild and dark,
Up-struggling through the age-long night
Through glooms and sorrows, to the light.
The soul that marches, age to age,
On slow and painful pilgrimage
Till man through tears and strife and pain
Shall thus his Godhead find again.
Of such, the wind in lonely tree
The murmurous brook, doth tell to me.
These are the wonders ye may know
Who to the Silent Places go;
Who these with reverent foot hath trod
May meet his soul and walk with God.'"

"Friend Jarvis," said the Ancient Person, setting down his empty platter and beginning to fill his pipe, "Peregrine was exactly right; you are a most astonishing tinker. You, sir, are a poet as I am a musician,—by a natural predisposition; and your poetry is true as is my music because it is simple; for what is Truth but Simplicity, that which touches the soul, the heart, the emotions rather than the cold, reasoning intellect, since poetry, but more especially music, is a direct appeal to and expression of, the emotion? Do you agree?"

"Why, sir," answered the Tinker, shaking his head a little sadly, "I don't know aught about music, d'ye see—"

"Fiddlestick, man! You are full of music. Who has not heard leaves rustle in the wind, or listened to the babble of a brook; yet to the majority they are no more than what they seem—rustling leaves, a babbling brook—but to you and me these are an inspiration, voices of Nature, of God, of the Infinite, urging us to an attempt to express the inexpressible—is it not so?"

"Why, my lord," quoth the Tinker, chafing blue chin with knife-handle, "since you put it that way I—I fancy—"

"Of course you do!" nodded his lordship. "Take yonder stream: to you it finds a voice to speak of the immemorial past; to me it is the elemental music of God. As it sings to-day so has it sung to countless generations and mayhap, in earth's dim days, taught some wild man-monster to echo something of its melody and thus perchance came our first music. What do you think?"

"'Tis a wonderful thought, sir, but I should think birds would be easier to imitate than a brook—"

"Possibly, yes. But man's first lyrical music was undoubtedly an imitation of the voices of nature. And what is music after all but an infinite speech unbounded by fettering words, an auricular presentment of the otherwise indescribable, for what words may fully reveal all the wonder of Life, the awful majesty of Death? But music can and does. By music we may hold converse with the Infinite. Out of the dust came man, out of suffering his soul and from his soul—music. You apprehend me, friend Jarvis?"

"Here an' there, my lord. I—I mean," stammered the Tinker, a little at a loss, "I understand enough to wish I could hear some real music—but music ain't much in a tinker's line—"

"You shall!" exclaimed his lordship, rising suddenly. "I will play to you, and after, Diana shall bless us with the glory of her voice if she will. Your arm, Tinker. Leave your irons and hammers awhile and come with me—let us go. Your arm, friend Jarvis!"

"But, sir—my clothes, my lord!" gasped Jeremy. "I ain't fit—"

"A fiddlestick!" quoth his lordship. "Give me your arm, pray." So limping thus beside the Tinker, the Earl of Wyvelstoke led us along beside the brook until we presently reached a grassy ride. Here he paused and, taking a small gold whistle that hung about his neck, blew a shrill blast, whereupon ensued the sound of wheels and creaking harness, and a phaeton appeared driven by a man in handsome livery who, touching smart hat to his shabby master, brought the vehicle to a halt, into which we mounted forthwith and away we drove. Soon before us rose stately parapet, battlement and turret above the green of trees ancient like itself, a mighty structure, its frowning grimness softened by years. Diana viewed massive wall and tower with eyes of delighted wonder, then suddenly turned to clasp the hand of the slender, shabby figure beside her.

"Poor old soul, no wonder you were lonely!" she sighed, whereupon the Earl smiled a little wistfully and stooped to kiss her sunburnt fingers in his stately fashion.

The carriage stopping, behold the sedate Atkinson (who manifested not the least surprise at our incongruous appearance) a square-shouldered, square-faced person he, whose features wore an air of resolution, notwithstanding his soft voice and deferential ways.

At a word from the Earl he ushered us in by a side entrance, through a long and noble gallery, where stood many effigies in bright armour, backed by pictures of bewigged gentlemen who smirked or scowled upon us, and fair dames in ruff and farthingale who smiled, or ladies bare-bosomed who ogled through artful ringlets; across panelled rooms and arras-hung chambers, to lofty and spacious hall, with a great, many-piped organ at one end. Here his lordship made us welcome with a simple and easy courtesy, himself setting chairs for Diana and the Tinker.

"Sit ye, friend Jarvis," said he, "and if you care to smoke, pray do so, you will find tobacco in the jar on the cabinet yonder. As for you, my goddess of the Silent Places, yonder comes my admirable valet with fruit and sweetmeats for your delectation; you, Peregrine, have Diana beside you. Listen now, and you shall hear the joy of Life and Youth and Self-sacrifice. Blow, Atkinson!" So saying, he crossed the wide hall and seated himself at the great instrument.

I saw his white fingers busy among the many stops, then his slim hands fell upon the keys and forth gushed a torrent of sweet sound, a peal of triumphant joy that thrilled me; great, rolling chords beneath and through which rippled an ecstasy of silvery notes, whose magic conjured to my imagination a dew-spangled morning joyous with sun and thrilling with the glad song of birds new-waked,—a green and golden world wherein one sped to meet me, white arms outstretched in love, one herself as fresh and sweet as the morning.

But now the organ notes changed, the pealing rapture sank into a sighing melody inexpressibly sweet and softly tender, my vision's smiling lips quivered to drooping sadness, the bright eyes grew dimmed with tears; and hearkening to the tender passion of this melody, full of poignant yearning and fond regret, I knew that here was parting and farewell. And lo! She, my Spirit of Love, was gone, and I alone in a desolate wilderness to grieve and wait, to strive and hope through weary length of days. And listening to these soft, plaintive notes, I bowed my head with eyes brimful of burning tears and heart full of sudden, chilling dread of the future, and glancing furtively towards Diana's beautiful, enraptured face, I clenched my fists and prayed desperate, wordless supplications against any such parting or farewell. And then, in this moment, grief and fear and heart-break were lost, forgotten, swept utterly away as the wailing, tender notes were 'whelmed in the triumphant melody that pealed forth, louder, more sublimely joyous than ever. She was back, within my arms, upon my heart, but a greater, nobler She, mine for ever and the world all glorious about us.

The rapture ended suddenly on a note of triumph, and Diana, leaning to me, was looking at me through glistening tears, our hands met and clung and never a word between us; then we glanced up to meet the Ancient Person's keen, smiling glance and his voice was gentle when he spoke.

"God bless you, children! Then hearing, you saw and understood? No true love can be that knows nothing of pain, for pain ennobles love and teaches self-sacrifice and this surely is the noblest good of all. And now, friend Jarvis, I will endeavour to show you something of the soul's upward pilgrimage, the working out of man's salvation as pictured in your verse."

He turned back to the organ and from its quivering pipes rose a series of noble chords, stately and solemn, a hymn-like measure, rolling in awful majesty, shattered all at once by a wild confusion of screaming discords that yet gradually resolved into a wailing melody of passionate despair beneath which I seemed to hear the relentless tramp of countless marching feet with, ever and anon, a far, faint echo of that first grand and stately motive.

And as I listened it seemed I watched the age-old struggle between might and right, the horrors of man's persecution of man, the agonies of flaming cities, of Death and Shame, of dungeon and torment. I seemed to hear the thunder of conflicting hosts, the groans of dying martyrs, to sense all the sweat and blood, the agony and travail of these long and bitter years wherein man wrought and strove through tears and tribulation, onward and up to nobler ideals, working out his own salvation and redemption from his baser self. Suddenly, above this wild and rushing melody, rose a single dulcet voice, soft yet patiently insistent, oft repeated with many variations, like some angel singing a promise of better things to come,—a voice which, as the wailing tumult died, swelled to a chorus of rejoicing, louder and louder, resolving back into that majestic hymn-like measure, but soaring now in joyous triumph, rising, deepening to an ecstasy of praise.

And then I was staring at the slender, shabby figure who sat, hands on knees, glancing down into the Tinker's awed face.

"Well, friend Jarvis?" he questioned, with his kindly smile.

"Ah, sir!" cried the Tinker. "Music can surely say more than words ever will."

"O Peregrine!" sighed Diana under her breath, "has it told you how I love you—all those things that I can never tell you?" And then she was away, to seat herself upon the organ-bench beside our host, while he explained something of the wonders of the noble instrument, its pedals, stops and triple rank of keys.

"Lord, Peregrine!" said the Tinker in my ear. "This is a day to remember, this is a—my soul!" he exclaimed and fell suddenly mute as a gorgeous person in powder and silk stockings entered, bearing tea upon a silver tray; a somewhat nervous and high-strung person he seemed, for catching sudden vision of the grimy Tinker's shock head and my shirt sleeves, his protuberant eyes took on a glassy look, he gulped audibly, his knees bent and he set down his burden with a jingling crash.

The Earl turned sharply; the footman began setting out the tea things.

"I've never seen an organ close to before," said Diana, "though I've often stopped outside a church to listen."

The footman's hands grew vague, his glassy eyes turned themselves upon Jeremy in fascinated horror, beneath which disdainful scrutiny Jeremy flushed, uneasily conscious of work-grimed hands and clothes.

"Of course I shan't mind singing to you," said Diana, "because you are my old pal."

The footman dropped a plate; stooping for this, he brought down three or four spoons and forks in his agitation.

"Atkinson!"

"My lord!" answered Atkinson, appearing suddenly.

"What is this?" demanded his lordship, fixing the gorgeous person with terrible eye.

"The third footman, I believe, my lord."

"Send him out—he annoys me."

The gorgeous person having taken himself off, Jeremy sighed in huge relief but glanced furtively askance from dainty china and snowy linen to his own grimy hands and smirched garments; perceiving which embarrassment the Earl hastened to set him at his ease:

"John Bunyan was a tinker also, friend Jarvis," said he, as we drew to the table. And a cheery meal we made of it, for what with his lordship's tactful, easy courtesy and Diana's serene unconsciousness, who could worry over such trifles as grimy hands or shirt sleeves; and if the Tinker be-jammed his fingers or Diana drank from her saucer, she did it with such assured grace as charmed me, and when his lordship followed her example, I loved him for the courtly gentleman he was.

"You have studied and thought deeply, I think, friend Jarvis?" said his lordship. "You reverence books?"

"Aye, sir—my lord. I used to peddle 'em once, but I read more than I ever sold."

"Ah, yes," said Diana; "'t was our good, kind Jerry taught me how to read and write when I lived wi' the Folk."

"And what of your parents, child?"

"I only remember old Azor."

"But you are not of the Zingari, I think?"

"I don't know, old pal—and what's it matter—O Jerry, the shin o' beef!" she exclaimed, clasping her hands. "Jessamy's back by this and it ought to be in the pot. So if you want me to sing—"

"We do!" said his lordship, and rising he brought her to the organ; there, standing beside him while he played a hushed accompaniment, she sang, at my suggestion, that same wild gipsy air which had so stirred me once before in the wood. But to-day, confined within these surrounding walls, her voice seemed to me even more glorious, so softly pure and plaintively sweet, anon soaring in trilling ecstasy—until the swelling glory sank, languished to a sigh and was gone; and I for one lost in awed wonder and delight. For to-day she sang with all that tender, unaffected sweetness, all that passionate intensity that was part of her strange self.

"Diana," said his lordship gravely, "God has entrusted you with a great and beneficent power; you have a rare and wonderful voice such as might stir mankind to loftier thought and nobler ideal and thus make the world a better place. Child, how will you acquit yourself of this responsibility? Will you make the most of your great gift, using it for the benefit of countless others, or let it atrophy and perish unheard—?"

"Perish?" exclaimed Diana, opening her eyes very wide. "Old pal, what do you mean?"

"I mean, Diana, that every one of the gifts that nature has lavished upon us—speech, sight, thought, motion—would all become atrophied and fail us utterly without use. The more we think and the more varied our thoughts, the greater our intellect; he that would win a race must exercise his muscles constantly, and this is especially true in regard to singing. Have you no thought, no will to become a great singer, Diana?"

"Yes," she answered softly, "I might ha' liked it once, but—not now—because, you see, I've found a—better thing, old pal, and nothing else matters!"

"Child," he questioned gently, "may I be privileged to know what this better thing may be?"

"Yes—yes!" she answered, stooping to catch his hand in her sweet, impulsive way and fondle it to her soft check.

"Love has come to us—Peregrine and me, he—knows at last, though I think you had guessed already because you played our love into your music, better—oh, better than I can ever tell it. Only it's here in my heart and in the sunshine; the birds sing of it and—and—oh, how can I think of anything else?"

The Ancient Person laid gentle hand upon her glossy hair. "Wait, dear child, and Love, I think, shall open to you a nobler living, shall give you pinions to soar awhile—"

"How—what d'ye mean, old pal?"

"Nay, ask Peregrine," answered his lordship, shaking his head. "Only very sure am I that love which is true and everlasting is infinitely unselfish."

And presently we took our leave, the Earl attending to see us into the phaeton and bid us adieu; and all the way back I must needs ponder his definition of love and wonder exactly what he had meant.

CHAPTER XXXV

OF A SHADOW IN THE SUN

And now ensued a halcyon season, dewy dawns wherein I bathed and sparred with Jessamy, long, sunny days full of labour and an ever-growing joy of Diana's radiant loveliness, nights of healthful, dreamless slumber beneath the stars.

Sometimes, when work was slack, I would walk far afield with Diana for my companion, or we would jog to market with the Tinker in the four-wheeled cart, hearkening to his shrewd animadversions upon men and life in general; and Diana's slim hand in mine.

Indeed this poor pen may never adequately set down all the happiness of these care-free, swift-passing days, and how may I hope to describe Diana's self or the joy of her companionship, a sweet intimacy that did but teach me to love her the more for her changing moods and swift intuitions, her quickness of perception, her deep wisdom, her warm impetuousness and the thousand contradictions that made her what she was.

So grew my love and with it a deep reverence for her innate and virginal purity. It touched me deeply to note with what painful care she set herself to correct the grammatical errors and roughness of her speech; often she would fall to a sighful despondency because of her ignorance and at such times it was, I think, that I loved her best, vowing I would not change her for any proud lady that was or ever had been; whereof ensued such conversations as the following:

DIANA. But when I am your wife we shall live in a fine house, I suppose.

MYSELF. Would this distress you?

DIANA. And meet grand folk, I suppose—earls and lords and—and that sort of thing?

MYSELF. It is likely.

DIANA. Shall we—must we have—servants?

MYSELF. To be sure.

DIANA (dismally). That's it! I shouldn't mind the earls s' much—it's the grand servants as would bother me. And then—O Peregrine—if ever I talked wrong or—acted wrong—not like a lady should—O Peregrine, would you be—ashamed o' me?

MYSELF. No, no—I swear it!

DIANA. I never wanted to be a lady—but I do now, Peregrine, for your sake.

MYSELF. You are good and brave and noble, Diana, and this is better than all the fine-ladyishness in the world.

DIANA (wistfully). Well, I wish I was a lady, all the same.

MYSELF. You will soon learn, you who are so quick and clever.

It was at this period that she began to purchase books and study them with passionate earnestness, more especially one, a thin, delicate volume that piqued my curiosity since, judging by her puckered brow and profound abstraction, this seemed to trouble and perplex her not a little.

"Peregrine," she enquired suddenly one morning, as I leaned, somewhat short of breath, upon the long shaft of the sledge-hammer, "Peregrine, what's a moo?"

"A moo?" I repeated, a little startled, "why, the sound a cow makes, I should think."

"No, it can't be that," said Diana, shaking her head and frowning at the open page of that same slim book I have mentioned, "it can't have anything to do with a cow, Peregrine, because that's what a grand lady does when she enters a ballroom; it says she moos slightly—"

"Lord, Ann!" exclaimed the Tinker. "What's she want to do that for? A moo's a beller, as Peregrine says, but who ever heard of a grand lady bellerin' in a ballroom or out—"

"I said moo!" retorted Diana. "And it's in this book."

"May I see?" I enquired. Obediently Diana rose and tendered me the volume, marking the paragraph with her finger, and at her command, I read aloud as follows.

"'UPON ENTERING A BALLROOM. The head should be carried stately, the bust well-poised, the arms disposed gracefully. The gait should be swimming, the head graciously aslant and the lips slightly *moue*.'"

"Well?" demanded Diana, glancing at Jeremy defiantly. "Now what's it mean, Peregrine?"

"'*Moue*?' I explained gravely, "is a French word signifying 'to pout' the lips."

"Which be a bit different to bellerin'!" chuckled the Tinker. Diana merely glanced at him, whereupon he began to hammer away lustily, in spite of which I fancied I heard him chuckle again. Turning to the title page of the little book I saw this:

ETIQUETTE FOR THE FAIR SEX
BEING HINTS ON FEMININE MANNERS & DEPORTMENT.
BY AN ACKNOWLEDGED SCION OF THE BON TON.

"It's a rather terrible book, I think," sighed Diana.

"Not a doubt of it," said I. "What do you think, Jerry?"

"Aye," he nodded, "I used to sell that book once, or one like it—"

"I mean," explained Diana, "it will be terribly hard to teach myself to do everything it says—"

"Indeed, I should think so," I nodded.

"You see," she mourned, "I—I didn't act a bit right when you—told me you—loved me—"

"Ah, but you did, Diana—"

"No, Peregrine, I was quite wrong and oh, most unladylike!"

"How so?"

"Well, I didn't tremble with maiden modesty or yield my hand coyly and by degrees, or droop my lashes, or falter with my breath—or—"

"Why in the world should you?"

"Because all ladies must do that—let me show you." So saying she took the book, turned over a leaf or so, and putting it into my hand, bade me read aloud, which I did, as follows:

"'UPON RECEIVING A PROPOSAL OF MARRIAGE. On this trying occasion, should the answer be in the affirmative, yield the hand coyly and by degrees to the passion of the happy suitor's lips; at the same time the lashes must droop, the whole form tremble with maiden modesty, the breath must falter and the bosom surge a little, though perceptibly—'"

My voice faltered and in spite of my efforts I burst out laughing, while Jeremy began to hammer again; whereupon Diana wrested the book from me and stood, flushed and angry, viewing me in lofty disdain.

"O Diana," I pleaded, "don't be offended, and don't—do not trouble your dear head over that foolish book—"

"Foolish!" she exclaimed indignantly. "Why, it's to teach ladies how to behave, and written by—"

"By a snuffy old rascal in some pothouse, like as not, Diana—" Here she turned and hasted away, but I sped after her and seeing the quiver of her lips and her dear eyes a-swim with tears, my own grew moist also.

"O Peregrine," sighed she, "I thought the book was foolish too—but for your sake—to be a lady—"

"O girl!" I cried, clasping her to me. "Dear goddess of the Silent Places, you are above all such silly pettinesses as this book; no woodland nymph or dryad could ever learn such paltry affectations and Diana herself would look a fool with a fan or a reticule. It is your own sweet, natural self I love, just as you are and for what you are."

"But you're a gentleman and I ought to be a lady."

"Be my own goddess Diana, and let me worship you as such."

"Why, then, let me go, Peregrine, for your goddess has the supper to prepare!" Reluctantly I obeyed her, and coming back, found the Tinker seated upon his anvil, lost in a profound meditation.

"What is it, Jerry?" I asked him, for he had sighed deeply.

"Ah, Peregrine," said he, without lifting his head, "oh, lad, lad—I've missed more than I thought—Love's a wonderful thing, far better and more beautiful than I ever dreamed it; pain and grief lose half their bitterness when Love looks at us from a woman's eyes and Death itself would come kinder—less dreadful, for the touch o' the loved hand, the sound o' the loved voice when the shadows gather. And—I might ha' had this blessing once—for the takin'—ah, Peregrine—if I'd only known, lad, if I'd only known!"

O joyous season of sweet simplicity, of homely kindliness and good-fellowship! Would to God this carpet beneath my feet might change to velvet moss and springy turf, these walls to the trees and whispering boskage I grew to love so well, this halting pen to the smooth shaft of sledge hammer or the well-worn crank of the Tinker's little forge, if I might but behold again she who trod those leafy ways with the stately, vigorous grace of Dian's very self, she who worked and wrought and sang beside me with love for me in her deep eyes and thrilling in the glory of her voice; she who sped light-footed to greet me in the dawn, who clung to kiss me "good night" amid the shadows. O season of joy so swiftly sped, to-day merging into yesterday (how should I guess you were so soon to end?), gone from me ere I had fully realised.

A hot, stilly afternoon full of the drowsy hum of insects and droning bees; birds chirped sleepily from motionless tree and thicket; even the brook seemed lulled to a slumberous hush.

Jessamy was away hard on the track of his Satanic antagonist, the Tinker had driven off to buy fresh provisions, and I sat watching Diana's dripping hands and shapely brown arms where she scrubbed, wrung out, and hung up to dry certain of our garments, for it was washing day.

"Dear," said I at last, "when shall we be married?"

"Lord, Peregrine, how sudden you are!" she answered, as if I had never broached the subject before.

"Shall it be next week?"

"No, indeed!"

"Well, then, the week after?"

"No, Peregrine, not—not until I am fit to be your wife—"

"That of course is now, Diana, this very moment!"

Here, having tossed back a loosened tress of glossy hair, she shook grave head at me.

"I must be sure I am—I must know myself a little—more fit—"

"A month, Diana!"

"Two, Peregrine!"

"We will get married in a month and camp hereabouts in these silent places all the summer. And when winter comes, I'll buy a little cottage somewhere, anywhere—wherever you choose—"

"Even then I—shouldn't be quite happy, Peregrine."

"Why not?"

"Well—because!"

"Because of what?"

"Just because!"

"Now you are provoking!"

"Am I, Peregrine?"

"And very stubborn."

"That's what old Azor used to say—"

"Why won't you marry me and be done with it?"

"Why should I? Aren't you happy as we are?"

"Of course, but to know you mine for always would be greater happiness."

"Oh, be content—a little longer. There's lots o' time—and I'm learning—I speak a—bit better, don't you think?"

"Is this your reason for delay, Diana?"

"Some of it. I want you to be—a little proud of me, if you can—if you ever grew ashamed of me—it would kill me, I think—"

"Sweet soul!" I cried, leaping to my feet to clasp her in eager arms.
"Why are you grown so humble?"

"It's love, I think, Peregrine—oh, mind the basin!" But I was not to be stayed and, sure enough, over went the great tin basin, scattering wet garments and soapy water broadcast.

"There!" sighed Diana tragically.

"What of it?" said I, and kissed her. "Why will you kiss me so seldom, Diana?"

"I ought to have done the washing in the brook like I always do."

"Don't you like me to kiss you, Diana?"

"Yes—and you've spilt all the water—"

"I'll bring you more. But why will you so seldom suffer me to—"

"Because—and take the large pail, Peregrine, and take it now—here's these four shirts ought to be hanging out to dry—so hurry, hurry! Get the water from the pool beyond the big tree, the stream runs clearer there!"

This pool was at some little distance, but away I went, happy in her service, swinging the heavy bucket and humming to myself, as carefree and light-hearted as any youth in Christendom, and presently reached the pool. I was stooping, in the act of filling the bucket, when I paused, arrested by a sudden, vague indefinable sound that puzzled me to account for and set me idly speculating whence it came and what it might be; so I filled the bucket and then, all in a moment, though why I cannot explain, puzzlement changed to swift and sudden dread and, dropping the bucket, I began to run, and with every stride my alarm grew, and to this was added horror and a great passion of rage. Panting, I reached the dingle at last to behold Diana struggling in the arms of a man, and he that same fine gentleman who had accosted her at "The Chequers." They were swaying together close-grappled, her knife-hand gripped in his sinewy fingers, his evil face smiling down into hers; and I burned with wilder fury to see her tumbled hair against his coat and her garment wrenched from throat and white shoulder.

Then as I sprang, with no eyes but for this man, a masterful hand gripped me, a commanding voice spoke in my ear.

"Back—stand back, boy!"

Turning to free myself, I beheld the Earl of Wyvelstoke, but now in his look and bearing was that which halted me in awed amaze.

"Devereux!" said he, not loudly but in voice so terrible that the man started and, loosing Diana, sprang back to glare at the speaker, heedless of Diana's blazing fury and threatening knife. "Stop, Diana!" commanded the Earl. "Come here and leave this unhanged ruffian to me—come, I say!" Humbly she obeyed, shrinking a little beneath his lordship's eyes, to creep into the clasp of my arm.

And so they faced each other, the stranger pale and coldly self-possessed, the Earl, his slender figure erect, one hand in the bosom of his shabby coat, his countenance placid, though frowning a little, but in his eyes a glare to daunt the boldest.

"Devereux!" he repeated in the same leisured, even tone. "Murderer—ravisher, I followed you, and by God you have betrayed yourself!"

"Ancient dotard!" smiled the other. "You babble like the poor, doddering imbecile you appear—my name is Haredale!"

"Liar!" said the Earl, softly. "I never forget faces, good or evil, hence I know you for the loathsome vermin, the obscene and unnameable thing you are!"

The stranger's pale face grew dreadfully suffused, his lips curled from gnashing teeth and, snatching up the heavy riding-whip that lay at his feet, he strode towards his lordship.

A deafening report—a gush of smoke, and the oncoming figure stumbled, checked uncertainly and stood swaying, right arm dangling helplessly, and I saw blood welling through the sleeve of his fine coat and dribbling from his finger ends; but he stood heedless of the wound, his burning gaze fixed upon the grim and silent figure before him. Once it seemed he strove to speak but no words came, and slowly he reached a fumbling hand to clasp uncertain fingers above the gushing wound.

Slipping from my hold, Diana took a step towards him, but his lordship's voice stopped her.

"Leave him, girl! Touch him not—do not sully your maidenhood with thing so vile. Let him crawl hence as best he may. Begone, beastly villain!" he commanded, with imperious gesture of the smoking pistol, "and be sufficiently thankful that my bullet sought your dastardly arm and not your pitiless black heart! Go, and instantly, lest I be tempted to change my mind and rid the world of thing so evil!"

Speechlessly the stranger turned, hand clasped above his hurt to stay the effusion of blood, and lurched and stumbled from our sight.

"Sir—O sir," I stammered, "who—what is that man?"

"A creature so unutterably evil, Peregrine, that only music could adequately describe him. He is one who should be dead years ago and consequently I am somewhat perturbed that I did not slay him outright instead of merely breaking his arm. It was a mistake, I fear, yes, a grave omission, yet there may offer another opportunity, who knows? Pray God his black shadow may never again darken your path, Peregrine, nor sully your sweet purity, my goddess of the woods. Forget him, my children. See, I have come to renew my youth with you, to talk and eat with you here amid God's good, green things, if I may.

"Yonder comes the excellent Atkinson with the tea equipage. Will you be my hostess, Diana?"

"Old pal—dear," she answered a little tremulously, "I'd just love to."

"Why, child," said the Earl, while I assisted the grave and decorous Atkinson to unpack the various dainties and comestibles, "why, child, how beautiful your hair is!" and lifting a silky tress in gentle, reverent fingers, our Ancient Person kissed it with stately gallantry.

CHAPTER XXXVI

TELLS HOW I MET ANTHONY AGAIN

"What with banns and certif'cates and this and that and t'other, they don't make it very easy for people to get married, do they, Peregrine?"

"No!" I answered.

We were jolting Tonbridge-wards in the Tinker's cart; the afternoon was very hot, and Diogenes, hearing the murmur of our voices, subsided to a leisured amble like the knowing, four-footed philosopher he was.

"Seven pounds seems a lot to pay for just one gown—even if it is to marry you in, doesn't it, Peregrine?"

"In three weeks!" I added.

"And four days!" she nodded.

"Twenty-five days—it's an age, Diana! Much may happen in such a time—"

"It will, Peregrine!"

"Pray what?"

"Lots of things, banns and certif-icates and—my new dress as will cost so much—"

"Seven pounds is ridiculously cheap, you dear child! And talking of banns, it may seem strange, Diana, that I have never troubled to enquire your surname, nor should I bother you now but that the parson must know—"

"Well, it's not so very strange that I've never bothered to tell you my name, Peregrine, because I don't know it. Old Azor often told me I had no name, but the Folk I lived with, theirs was Lovel—that'll do, won't it?"

"Of course! Goddesses don't need surnames."

"Will you still think me a goddess when we're married, Peregrine?"

"No, as something infinitely dearer and more precious."

"What?"

"My wife! It—it sounds strange on my lips, doesn't it?"

"I love the way you say it!" sighed Diana, and with such a look in her eyes that I clasped her to me and she, all unresisting, gave up her lips to mine. So, for a space, we forgot all but ourselves and I grew blind to all but her beauty, deaf to all but her voice.

"O Peregrine!" she sighed. "O Peregrine, I never thought love could be so—wonderful!"

"In three weeks you will be mine utterly, Diana—in three weeks!"

"I am now, Peregrine. I could never love—never, never marry any one but you. I never meant to marry because I never thought I could love any man—but now—O Peregrine!"

"Dear," said I, "if—if anything should happen to separate us, could you—would you always love me?"

"Always, Peregrine, always and for ever. Hark, there is some one coming."

Faint and far rose the sound of hoofs and, glancing up, I espied the distant forms of two equestrians and also observed that the perspicacious Diogenes, quick to heed and take advantage of our lapse, had halted to crop and nibble busily in the shade of a great tree that stretched one mighty branch protectingly above us.

"People are coming, Peregrine."

"I know, but they are still very far off; besides we are in the shade—kiss me again, Diana."

The advancing hoofs sounded nearer and presently, obedient to the rein, Diogenes ambled on again; and now I saw that the approaching riders were a lady and gentleman and mounted on spirited animals for, as they drew nearer, it seemed to me that the lady had much difficulty in managing her fiery steed.

Now between us and these riders was another tall tree that cast a jagged shadow athwart the white road, noting which, I kept my gaze on the lady's mount somewhat anxiously.

My apprehensions were suddenly realised for, reaching this patch of shadow, the lady's horse shied, swerved suddenly, and hurled his rider into the ditch.

Diana cracked the whip and Diogenes broke into a gallop, but long before we had come up with them, the gentleman was off his horse, had lifted the swooning woman in his arms, and was pouring out a breathless farrago of endearments and prayers with curses upon himself, his helplessness and the jibbing horse.

"Barbara, dear love—oh, damnation and the devil, what shall I do—Barbara, are you much hurt, dearest—the accursed brute—a thousand curses—look at me, beloved, speak—O God have mercy on her!"

Now glancing at the beautiful, pale face of this swooning girl, I started, and looking from her to the athletic form and handsome features of this distracted youth who clasped her, I caught my breath; and then Diana had leapt from the cart and, pushing aside this miserable, helping being, had busied herself to recover the unconscious girl in her own quick, capable fashion.

93

"A woman!" gasped the gentleman. "O God bless you—thank heaven! Say she isn't dead—you'll want water—not a drop for miles, dammit—brandy—not a spot—oh, curse and confound it—say she isn't dead!"

"She's not!" said Diana briefly.

"God bless you again! Tell me what to do?"

"Go away and leave her to me."

"But how can I leave her?"

"I must loose her stays—you'll find a brook t' other side the hedge—in your hat!"

Scarcely were the words uttered than the gentleman was over the hedge and as quickly back again, slopping water right and left from his modish, curly-brimmed hat in his frantic haste; this he set down at Diana's command and, turning away, began to stride up and down, muttering agitated anathemas upon himself and scowling ferociously at the two horses, which I had taken the opportunity to hitch to an adjacent gatepost.

At last in his restless tramping he seemed to become aware of me where I sat, for I had climbed back into the cart, and he now addressed me, though with his anxious gaze bent towards the unconscious form of his companion.

"Good God, man—this is pure damnation! If you can't do anything, since I can't do anything, can't you suggest something I can do?"

"Only that you strive for a little patience, sir."

At this he turned to stare at me, then his grey eyes widened suddenly, and he leapt at me with both hands outstretched.

"Vereker!" he cried. "Peregrine—Perry, by all that's wonderful."

"Anthony!" said I, as our hands gripped.

"Peregrine—O Perry, we—we were married—not an hour ago—Barbara and I—and now—"

"Look!" said I and nodded where Barbara sat, her pale check pillowed on Diana's bosom.

"Anthony!" she called softly. And then he was beside her on his knees, his head down-bent, her arm about his neck.

"Perry!" he called suddenly. "Come here, man, come here! Sure you haven't forgot the angel who stooped to a miserable dog, who trusted a desperate-seeming rogue and lifted him back to manhood and self-respect—you remember my Barbara? And you, dearest, recall my friend Peregrine—the gentle, immaculate youth who was willing to trust and bestow his friendship upon the same miserable dog and desperate rogue—aye, and fed him into the bargain—"

"How should I ever forget?" said Barbara. "Indeed, Mr. Vereker, we have talked of you often—though always as 'Peregrine'—"

"Mrs. Vere-Manville," I began.

"It was Barbara at the 'Jolly Waggoner'!" she reminded me, smiling and nestling closer into her husband's encircling arm.

"Barbara—Anthony," said I, "it is my happy privilege to introduce Diana—Miss Lovel—who is to honour me by becoming my wife shortly—"

Anthony bowed to Diana, laughed, and drew his wife a little closer all in the same moment, it seemed; then Barbara turned to look into the vivid, dark beauty of Diana's down-bent face where she knelt, and for a long moment eyes of blue stared up into eyes of grey, a long, questioning look.

"May I kiss you?" said Barbara at last.

Swiftly, almost eagerly, Diana leaned forward, then hesitated, drew away, and glanced swiftly upon each of us in turn with a troubled look.

"Lady," said she in her rich, soft voice, and speaking with careful deliberation, "Peregrine has not told you—all. Please look at me—my dress—"

"Very pretty, I think, and quaint—like a gipsy's—"

"I am a gipsy, lady—one Peregrine met by the roadside! 'T is best you should know this—first—before—before—"

The soft, sweet voice faltered and stopped and there fell a silence, a long, tense moment wherein I held my breath, I think, and was conscious of the heavy beating of my heart, but with every throb I loved and honoured Diana the more. Slowly and gently Barbara loosed her husband's clasping arm and rose to her knees.

"Now—I *must* kiss you, Diana!" she said.

"O lady!" sighed Diana.

"Barbara, my dear! Barbara ever and always!"

"Barbara!" murmured Diana. And then they were in each other's arms and Anthony was on his feet and tucking his arm in mine led me where the horses stood tethered, with such disconnected mutterings as:

"Come away, Perry—true blue, 'egad—leave 'em together—angels of heaven both—too good for me—or even you—not a doubt of it—"

"Agreed!" quoth I.

"Peregrine," said he, pausing suddenly to grasp me by the shoulders in his well-remembered way, "O Peregrine, she is the loveliest, sweetest, tenderest creature that ever made a man wish himself better—"

"Anthony," quoth I, "she is the bravest, noblest, purest maid that ever taught a man to be better!"

"She is, Peregrine!"

"They are, Anthony!"

"For one frightful moment I thought she—was killed, Perry!"

94

"But God is good and—Diana was there, Anthony."

"A wonderful creature, your Diana, Perry, as capable as she is handsome!"

"She is beyond all description, Anthony!"

"Yes, I can find no word for Barbara, damme!"

Now as he looked down on me, his handsome face radiant, his powerful form set off by the most elegant attire, I could not but contrast him with the forlorn, down-at-heels outcast he had been.

"It seems I have much to congratulate you upon," said I.

"God, yes, Peregrine! And I owe you a guinea—here it is! My curmudgeonly uncle (Heaven rest him!) had the kindness to choke himself to death in a fit of passion. And to-day, Perry, to-day—we gave 'the Gorgon' the slip (Barbara's aunt)—got married and are now on our way to outface her father—a regular Tartar by all accounts—and there's the situation in a word."

"You haven't lost much time, Anthony."

"Nor have you for that matter, Perry. And I've ten thousand things to tell you, and questions to ask you and—Ha, thank God, she's on her feet! Look at 'em—did ever mortal eyes behold two lovelier creatures?" And away he strode impetuous towards where they stood, the dark and the fair, with arms entwined, viewing each other's beauteousness glad-eyed.

"My brave girl! How are you now?"

"Better—oh, much better, dear Anthony, though I fear I cannot ride—"

"Not to be thought of, my sweet—Gad, no—not for a moment!"

"Diana has offered to drive me in the cart, Anthony."

"Excellent! We can hire a chaise at Hadlow!"

So very soon, behold us jolting along in the Tinker's cart very merrily, Anthony and I perched upon the tailboard, the two horses trotting behind a little disdainfully, as it seemed to me, judging by the flirting of their tails, head-shakings and repeated snorts.

"And what might you be doing now, Perry?" enquired my companion, swinging his long, booted legs and stealing a backward glance at his fair, young wife seated on the driving seat beside Diana. "Isn't she perfectly wonderful?" he murmured.

"She is!" I answered.

"Her hair," he sighed; "her hair, you'll notice, is—"

"The most glorious in all the world!" quoth I.

"Absolutely, Perry! Beyond all doubt—"

"Though it is not really black, Anthony—"

"Black!" he exclaimed, turning on me with a sort of leap.

"No, not black, Anthony, sometimes it seems full of small fires—"

Now at this he laughed and I laughed, all unheeded by the two upon the driving seat who talked softly and questioned each other with their lovely faces very close together, while Diogenes the knowing slowed to his meditative amble.

"You must forgive me, Perry, I—I've only been a Benedict since two o'clock. But tell me of yourself; what you are doing, how you live and where?"

"I am learning the art of working in iron, Anthony, and of making and mending kettles—"

"Gad—a tinker, Perry?"

"Yes. And I am living in a wood with one Jerry Jarvis, Jessamy Todd, and Diana—"

"The famous Jessamy?"

"Yes. He is instructing me in the noble art."

"Good heavens! And your—your people?"

"They perforce acquiesce."

"In—in everything, Perry—your marriage?"

"What else can they do?"

"And when you are married, how shall you live?"

"Travel the country tinkering with Jerry—or buy a cottage until I come into my property."

"And then, Perry?"

"I—don't know. You see, Anthony, if—if the people in our world should make any difficulty about the pure angel who will be my wife, well, I'll see the people of our world damned and go back to my cottage."

"No, you shall come to us, Perry, to Barbara and me, we shall always be proud and happy to welcome you both—in country or town and as for—your Diana, such beauty may surely go anywhere, and my Barbara is in love with her already, 'egad. Look at 'em, Perry, look at 'em! Did ever eyes behold two such gloriously handsome creatures?"

Thus we talked of things that had been and of things that were to be, making many plans for the future, a future which, by reason of youth and love, stretched before each one of us in radiant perspective. So we talked and laughed, finding joy in all things, more especially in each other and were all a little sorry, I think, when the ambling Diogenes brought us to Hadlow at last. And here, at the "Bear" we sat down to a merry meal that ended all too soon.

"Good-bye—oh, good-bye, dearest Diana!" sighed Barbara a little tearfully, as she leaned from the chaise for a last caress. "If I have learned to love you so quickly don't let it seem strange—it is just because you are Diana—and I have so few friends, and none like you. So be my friend, Diana, will you, dear—and when you are married bring your husband to see us in London—or wherever we happen to be, only—oh, be my friend, because—I love you."

"I will," said Diana, "your friend always, because—I love you too."

So the chaise rolled away. And presently Diana and I jogged camp-wards behind Diogenes, through an evening fragrant with new-mown hay; from tree and hedgerow birds were singing their vesper hymn and we drove awhile in wistful silence. But suddenly Diana turned and caught my hand so that I wondered at the eager clasp of these fingers and the tremulous yearning in her voice when she spoke.

"O Peregrine—oh, my dear—if only God would make me—like her—a lady—like Barbara. Do you think He would if—I pray—very hard?"

"Of course!" said I, kissing her hand. "Though, indeed—"

"Then I will, dear Peregrine—this very night—and every night."

CHAPTER XXXVII

A DISQUISITION ON TRUE LOVE

"Love," said his lordship, laying down his fishing rod, "love, from the philosophically materialistic standpoint, is an unease, a disquiet of the mind, fostered in the male by hallucination, and in the female by determined self-delusion."

"Sir," said I, "your meaning is somewhat involved, I would beg you to be a little more explicit."

"Then pray observe me, Peregrine! An ordinary young man falls in love with an ordinary young woman because, for some inexplicable reason, she appears to him a mystery, bewitchingly incomprehensible. Suffering under this strange hallucination, he wooes, whereupon our ordinary young woman, shutting her eyes to the ordinariness of our very ordinary young man, now deliberately deludes herself into the firm belief that he is the virile presentment of her own impossible, oft-dreamed ideal. So they are wed (to the infinite wonder of their relations) and hence the perpetuation of the species."

"My lord, you grow a little cynical, I think," said I, "surely Love has dowered these apparently so ordinary people with a vision to behold in each other virtues and beauties undreamed of by the world in general. Surely Love possesses the only seeing eye?"

"The Greeks thought differently, Peregrine, or wherefore their blindfolded Eros?"

"Sir, the mind of man has soared since those far times, I venture to think?"

"Perhaps!" said his lordship, shaking his head. "But love between man and woman is much the same, a power to ennoble or debase, angel of light or demon of hell, a thing befouled and shamed by brutish selfishness or glorified by sacrifice. Yes, love is to-day as it was when mighty Babylon worshipped Bel. Yesterday, to-day and for ever, love was, is, and will be the same—the call of nature coming to each of us through the senses to the soul for evil or for good."

"But, my lord," said I, stirred beyond myself, "ah, sir, be love what it may—no two ever loved as Diana and I, so truly, so deeply—"

"O my lovely, loving lover—O sublime egoist!" exclaimed my companion. "How many other lovers through the ages have thought and said and written the very same?

'Others may have loved mayhap,
But never, oh, never as thou and I.'

"This is the song of all the amorists of all the ages. Man has been saying this since ever he was man. Here is love's universal, deathless song, written or sung to-day and by lovers long, long forgotten,

'Whoever loved like thou and I,
No lovers ever loved as we!'"

"Nor did they, sir!" I maintained doggedly. "My love for Diana is a thing wholly apart, an inspiration to all things good and great."

"Then prove this, my egoist, prove it!"

"But sir—sir," I stammered, nonplussed by his words and the piercing look that accompanied them, "how—in what manner would you have me do this?"

"By forgetting yourself in your love for her! By foregoing awhile your present joys for her future good. Give her into my care for two years."

"My lord!" I exclaimed aghast. "I—indeed I do not understand."

"Peregrine, God has bestowed on her a mind capable of great things—a wonderful voice. Place her in my charge for two years—I am solitary and very rich—she shall see the world and its wonders; I will have her educated, bestow on her all the refinements that great wealth can command. Nature has given her a glorious voice, Art shall make her a great singer. Forego your present happiness for her future good and your gipsy maid shall become a great lady and a peerless woman. Do this, Peregrine, and here, truly, shall be love indeed."

Now at this I was silent a long while, staring down blindly at the hurrying waters of the brook; glancing up at last, I found him regarding me with his keen, bright eyes and was struck anew by the strength of his personality, his resolute face with its indomitable mouth and chin, his serene air of dignity and assured power.

"She would be safe with me, Peregrine," said he gently, "secure from every evil—and from every chance of molestation."

"I know that, sir."

"She would be cherished and loved as sacredly as—my own daughter—might have been."

"I am sure of it, sir—and yet—"

"Well, Peregrine?"

"Two years, sir," I faltered. "It—it is an age—"

"You are both children, Peregrine, but in two years, as I understand, you will be of age, a man, master of your fortune—and she a woman, clever, accomplished and perhaps famous."

"And may have forgotten me!"

"Do you think so, Peregrine?"

"No!" said I. "No!"

"Nor do I, boy. Such as she, being deep and reverent of soul, do not love lightly, and never forget. On the contrary, with her growing knowledge and experience, surely her love for you will grow also; it must do. If she loves you to-day, child of nature as she is, how much greater will be her capacity for love as an educated woman, knowing that it is to your unselfishness, first and foremost, that she owes so very much?"

After this was silence again wherein I watched my companion disjoint his fishing rod.

"Sir," said I at last, "yours is a very noble and generous offer—"

"Tush!" he exclaimed a little sharply. "I am a solitary old man who yearns for a daughter."

"Sir, in less than a fortnight is—the day—our wedding day—"

"Then," said his lordship, rising, "God's blessing on that day, Peregrine, and on each of you."

"You ask of me a very great thing, sir!" I groaned.

"Indeed, yes, Peregrine, so very great that only the greatest love could possibly grant it."

Long after the Earl had limped away, I sat crouched beside the stream, my head bowed between clasping hands, blind and deaf and unconscious of all else but the tempest that raged within me, a wild confusion of doubt and fearful speculation with a passionate rebellion against circumstance, and a growing despair. Gradually these chaotic thoughts took form, marshalling themselves against each other, so that it seemed as two voices argued bitterly within me, thus:

THE FIRST VOICE. To give up Diana for two long, weary years—

THE SECOND VOICE. But for Diana's sake!

THE FIRST VOICE. To forego the joys of Diana's companionship for two, empty, desolate years.

THE SECOND VOICE. But for Diana's own future good!

THE FIRST VOICE. Why should Love demand such thing of any lover?

THE SECOND VOICE. Because he boasted his love beyond all other. Was it but an idle boast?

THE FIRST VOICE. No lover would ever do such thing!

THE SECOND VOICE. Except he be indeed greatly true and most unselfish.

THE FIRST VOICE. Diana would never leave me.

THE SECOND VOICE. Never, even though it were the passion of her life! For truly a woman's love is ever more unselfish than a man's.

THE FIRST VOICE. She loves me too much to endure such parting.

THE SECOND VOICE. She loves you so much she would endure even this to become your comrade as well as wife, to fit herself that she may take her place beside you in your world, serene and assured, to become the woman you can revere for her intellect and refinement.

THE FIRST VOICE. All this I can teach her, all this she shall acquire after marriage.

THE SECOND VOICE. Never! She will devote herself to you rather than to herself.

THE FIRST VOICE. Howbeit, I love her well enough as she is—

THE SECOND VOICE. O selfish lover! And what of the future? You cannot live out your life in her world of the Silent Places, and in your world your gipsy maid will find small welcome or none.

THE FIRST VOICE. Then her world shall be mine also—

THE SECOND VOICE. O foolish lover! Think you she shall not grieve that by her love you should lose caste—

THE FIRST VOICE. She need never know—

THE SECOND VOICE. The eyes of a loving woman are marvellous quick to see.

THE FIRST VOICE. Then Love shall comfort her.

THE SECOND VOICE. Yet still must be her dark hours. Is two years so long a time?

THE FIRST VOICE. Too long! In two years she may find a thousand new interests to come between us. In two years she may meet with dashing gallants richer, higher placed, more versed in knowledge of women and far more intellectual than myself, who am but what I am. So, having won her to my love, what folly to let her go—to be wooed perchance by others.

THE SECOND VOICE. O most despicable lover! Will you be content to win a maid through and because of her ignorance of all other wooers better placed than your poor self?

THE FIRST VOICE. Yes.

THE SECOND VOICE. Then is yours a pitiful love, base and most unworthy.

THE FIRST VOICE. No matter—she shall not go!

THE SECOND VOICE. In such a love can be no true happiness.

THE FIRST VOICE. However, she shall not leave me!

THE SECOND VOICE. How if at some future day, her eyes be opened to see your love for the petty, selfish thing it is?

THE FIRST VOICE. She will be my wife!

THE SECOND VOICE. So God pity her.

THE FIRST VOICE. Come what will, she shall not leave me! I cannot, will not part with her!

"Why, Peregrine!" exclaimed a sweet voice. "My dear—my dear, what is it? Why do you sit here sighing with your dear head between your hands—this head that I love so! Peregrine dear, what is it?"

She was beside me on her knees, had drawn my face upon her bosom, and I thrilled to the soft caress of her mouth and the touch of her gentle fingers in my hair. "Why are you so troubled, my Peregrine?"

"O Diana! Beloved, I imagined a foolish thing—that being far from me you forgot our love—these dear Silent Places, and learned—to love—some one more worthy—more generous—altogether better than I. For Diana—I am—"

"My Peregrine!" she whispered passionately. "My brave lover that is so fine a gentleman he don't know anything of evil and has treated me always as if I was a proud lady—as if I was a very holy thing instead of only a gipsy girl to be kissed and—and—oh, you are so different—and so it is I love you—love you, worship you, and—all'us shall, my Peregrine, and long and yearn to be a lady for your sake and worthy of you—"

"O child," I whispered, "my Diana—hush! You don't know how vilely, basely selfish I am really—"

"Never—ah, never say so, Peregrine, it hurts me. There now, smile! I wouldn't ha' left you all the afternoon—not even wi' our pal—no, not even to try on my wedding gown if I'd thought you'd ha' grieved. Come, dear, Jessamy's back an' ready for you with the muffles—there, he be calling!"

So I arose, but stood a while to look into her eyes that met mine with such sweet frankness.

"And you still wish to learn all those graces and refinements that make what is called a lady, my Diana?"

"Yes," she answered, a little breathlessly. "Yes—oh, more than ever—more than anything else in life—except you—"

"Then—God helping, you shall!" said I, between shut teeth. And so we went on together.

"But, Peregrine," she questioned a little wistfully, "dear Peregrine, why is your face so stern and why must you sigh still?"

"Because to be unselfish is sometimes—an agony, Diana."

"Dear heart—what do you mean?"

"Only I know now that I do most truly love you."

CHAPTER XXXVIII

A CRUCIFIXION

"Where are you taking me, Peregrine?"

Birds were singing joyously, the brook chuckled and laughed merrily amid the shallows, the morning sun shone in glory, and all nature seemed to rejoice, as if care and sadness were things unknown.

"Where are we going, dear Peregrine?"

"To seek your heart's desire."

"That sounds very lovely!" said Diana, laughing gaily and giving my arm a little hug. "But everything seems so—wonderful lately!"

After this we walked in silence awhile, for when I would have told her whither we were going and why, I could not, try how I would.

"Barbara was telling me how she first met you and Anthony; she is very beautiful, don't ye think, Peregrine?"

"Very!"

"So beautiful that I wonder you didn't fall in love wi' her."

"I waited to fall in love with Diana, who is much more beautiful, I think—"

"Do you, Peregrine, do you think so—really?"

Here, of course, I stopped to kiss her.

"The wonder is," said she, "the great wonder is that she didn't fall in love wi' you, Peregrine."

"I'm very glad she didn't! Besides, there's Anthony, so strong and tall and handsome, so altogether different to myself and much more likely to capture a woman's fancy."

"Not all women, Peregrine."

Here she stopped to kiss me.

"Barbara is a much—gentler sort of fine lady than—your aunt, I think—"

"Aunt Julia can be gentle also—sometimes, dear—"

"When she gets her own way, Peregrine!"

"You will learn to love her very much some day, I hope, Diana."

"I hope so—but it'll take her a mighty long time learning to love me, I think," sighed Diana. "Lord, what furious fuss she'll make when she finds out we'm married. Not as I shall care—if you don't, dear. Why, Peregrine—yonder's Wyvelstoke Towers!"

"Yes," said I, "it is there we are going."

"But why—what for?"

"Dear, have patience—just a little longer," I pleaded.

At this she was silent, but her hand tightened on my arm, and I was aware of the sudden trouble in her eyes. So, having crossed the park, we came into the pleasaunce, a place of clipped yew hedges and trim walks. And here who should meet us but the sedate Atkinson, who, having saluted us gravely, led the way to a rustic arbour where sat his lordship engaged upon the perusal of a book. At sight of us, he rose to welcome us with his wistful, kindly smile.

"Ah, Peregrine," said he, viewing us with his keen gaze as we sat beside him, "I perceive you have not told her."

"Not a word, sir," said I, a little hoarsely.

"Old pal," she questioned, glancing from me to his lordship and back again, "what d'ye mean? Peregrine, what is it?"

"Diana," said I, finding my tongue very unready, "dear—what is your greatest wish—what is your most passionate desire?"

"You!" she answered in her sweet, direct fashion.

"And—what next?"

"To be a lady! Oh, you know that and you know why—to be done wi' this fear that sometimes I may shame you by my talk or by acting wrong; you know, don't you?"

"This is why I brought you here, Diana. My lord has offered to—have you taught all this and—much beside."

"Oh!" she sighed rapturously. "You mean to teach me to be a lady? Oh, dear, dear old pal—can you, will you?"

"Child, it would be my most joyful privilege."

"But, Diana," I continued haltingly, yet speaking as lightly as I could and keeping my gaze averted, "to learn so much you must—stay with his lordship—travel abroad—meet great people—be instructed by many skilled teachers and—there will be your music—singing—"

"Will they teach me everything a lady should learn, grammar an' deportment an' dancing—?"

"Everything, Diana."

"But, Peregrine, while I'm away learning all this, where will you be?"

"I shall remain—here!"

"Oh, well, that's done it! I shall stay with you, of course!"

"That would be impossible," said I, as lightly as I could, "quite impossible; such love as ours, that demands so much, would be a great hindrance to your progress, don't you see? All the time you were studying, I should hover around you most distractingly. No, we must part—for a little while—"

"For how long, Peregrine?"

"Only two years, dear!"

"So long—so very long! Two years! Ah, no, no, I couldn't bear it!"

"Two years will—soon pass!" said I, between clenched teeth. "And of course you will be—too busy to—miss me—very much—"

"Ah, how can you think so?"

"And you will be working for me as much as for your dear self, Diana, and—our love—our future happiness. So you will go, dear heart—?"

"For two years? No—it's too long—you might die—O Peregrine!"

"The contingency is remote—I—I mean—"

"But I can't leave you! I mustn't—I won't! I shall be your wife!"

"No, Diana, that—that must wait until you—come back."

"Wait?" she gasped. "Peregrine—O Peregrine—"

"I want you to be free, Diana—"

"Well, I won't be! I'm not free and never shall be because I belong to you and we belong to each other for ever and ever."

"Oh, my dear—my dear, God knows it!" cried I and clasped her to me in yearning arms. "But I want you to go into this new life quite free and unfettered, because it is a great and ever-growing wonder that you should love me who am neither very handsome nor strong nor brave—so I want you to meet men who are—fine gentlemen, and compare them with poor me. And O Diana, if you can return so much cleverer and wiser for all you have seen and learned and can still love me—why, then, Diana, oh, then—" my voice broke but in this moment her arms were about me and stooping her lovely head she mingled her tears with mine.

"Dear foolish boy," she murmured passionately, "how can you think there could ever be any other but just you. Ah, Perry dear, don't send me away; I should hate to be a lady now. Oh, be content with me as I am—don't send me away—"

"I must—for your sake," I groaned, "for your future, to help you to the better thing. Though God knows I love you well enough as you are, and want you, Diana, want you with every nerve and fibre of me, with every breath. Oh, sir, sir," I cried, "help me to be strong for—her sake!"

"You are, boy!" answered his lordship, and I saw he had crossed to the doorway and stood with his back to us. "Diana," he continued after a moment, "in this world of change, of doubt and uncertainty, one thing is very sure and beyond all cavil and dispute: Peregrine loves you far better than he loves himself, since he is strong enough to forego so much of present happiness for your future welfare. He honours me by placing you in my charge, I who love you as a daughter and will treat you as such. So, Diana, will you give yourself to my care awhile, will you become my companion and loved child?"

"Must I, Peregrine?" she sobbed. "Oh, must I?"

"Yes!" said I, looking at her through blinding tears. "Yes!"

Obediently she arose and, crossing to his lordship, placed her hand in his.

"I'll go wi' you, old pal," said she.

Now as our Ancient Person turned to smile at her, I saw his furrowed cheek was wet with tears also.

"Sir, when—when do you start?" I enquired.

"At once, Peregrine. We shall be in London to-night."

"Then this is—good-bye, sir?"

"Yes, my children!"

"My lord," said I, rising wearily, "I am leaving with you all I possess, my present joy, my—hope for the future, my loved Diana."

"God make me worthy of the charge, Peregrine."

All in a moment she was at my feet, upon her knees, her arms fast about me, her face hidden against me, her body shaken with convulsive sobs.

"O Perry, I can't—I can't do it—no, no—don't let me go—"

At this I knelt also and thus we faced each other on our knees, as when Love first had found us. And so I clasped and kissed and strove to comfort her, until the passion of her grief was abated. "Must I go, dear Peregrine—must I go?" she whispered, beneath my kisses.

"Yes, for the sake of the future—yours and mine. God keep you and—good-bye, my own Diana!"

Then I arose and left her there upon her knees, looking after me through fast-falling tears and her loved arms stretched out to me in piteous supplication.

"Peregrine," she pleaded, "oh, my Peregrine!"

But I turned away and rushed from the spot, never daring to look back; but ever as I went, that desolate cry rang and echoed in my ears.

CHAPTER XXXIX

HOW I CAME HOME AGAIN

"Two years! Emptiness! Loneliness! Two years!" It was in the hurry of my footsteps, birds sang it, leaves whispered it, my heart throbbed to it.

"Two years! Emptiness! Loneliness! Two years!" Sometimes tears blinded me, sometimes anger shook me, but always was the pain of loss, the yearning for that loved and vanished presence.—"Two years!"

More than once I turned to hasten back—to end this misery—back to my Diana, this maid who was more precious, more necessary to my life than I had ever dreamed. I should have but to lift my finger, nay ... one look and she would be in my arms ... so very easy, and therefore ... so utterly impossible.

Sometimes I hurried on at breathless speed, sometimes crept on slow, unwilling feet, sometimes stood motionless to stare blindly about me, raged at and torn by conflicting thoughts ... agonising ... irresolute.

How long I wandered thus I cannot say, but the sun was low when, amid the leafy whispering of familiar tree, I heard the cheery ring of the Tinker's anvil.

At sight of me he dropped his hammer and fell back a step.

"Why Peregrine," said he. "Why, Perry lad—don't look so! Is aught wrong?"

"Only my heart is breaking, I think!" said I, and casting myself down at the foot of a tree, I covered my face.

"God love me!" exclaimed the Tinker; and then he was kneeling beside me. "What is it, lad, what is it?"

"I've sent my Diana from me!"

"Sent her from ye, lad?"

"For two years, Jerry. Two weary years ... emptiness ... loneliness. I have placed her in the Earl of Wyvelstoke's charge ... they start for London at once ... leave England as soon as possible ... she is gone ... two years, Jerry ... two weary years ... desolation!"

"Peregrine," said he in hushed voice, "this was her great wish—to be a lady for your sake. She's told me so many's the time ... an' I caught her in tears over it once."

"I have sent her away, Jerry, for two years!"

"Peregrine," said he, "'t is a fine thing to be a gentleman, but 't is a grand thing to be a man big enough an' brave enough to do such act as this here. God bless ye, lad!"

"O Jerry—O Jerry, I love her so...! Yearn and hunger for her so much ... it is a pain!"

"Aye, but 't is such pain as makes the strong stronger! 'Tis such love as do be everlasting and reaches high as heaven—"

"Two years, Jerry! Two long, weary years to wait … to yearn … to live through without her … emptiness!"

"Ah, but you've done right, lad, you've done right. And then—what's two years? Lord, they'll soon go! And her love for you'll be a-growin' with every month—every day an' hour, lad, an' she'll come back t' ye at last, only more beautiful, more wonderful an' more loving than ever she was—"

"O Jerry," said I, grasping at him with sudden hands. "You don't think … death … you don't think she may die?"

"Die? What, Ann—s' strong an' full o' vig'rous life? Lord, not she, lad, not she—never think it!"

"Or … forget me, Jerry?"

"What—Ann? Lord love ye—no! She ain't one to forget or change—never was, an' I've knowed her since a little child. An' she's never loved afore—hated men! An' why? Because 't was always her beauty as they wanted—her body—an' never a thought of her mind, d'ye see! An' now—she's to travel to see the world, is she! An' with the Earl—an' him such a great gentleman! 'T is wonderful good fortun' for her, Peregrine, wonderful!"

"Yes, he is a very great gentleman and a truly noble man, Jerry."

"An' now, what o' yourself, lad?"

"I shall continue to live with you, Jerry; I shall go on smithing and tinkering—yes, harder than ever—"

"No!" said the Tinker, sitting back on his heels and shaking his head at me with the utmost vehemence. "Tinkering ain't for you, Peregrine, an' you can do better things than swingin' a sledge—ah, a sight better!"

"What do you suppose I can do?" sighed I miserably.

"Paint pictoors!"

"Impossible! I shall never be a real painter, Jerry."

"Well, then—write!"

"Impossible! I shall never be a poet, Jerry."

"Well, have you ever thought o' writin' a nov-el?"

"Never!"

"Well, what about it?"

"Impossible! Of what should I write?"

"Why, about HER—Anna, for sure, your Diana as would ha' made a better goddess than the real one, I reckon."

"Why, yes," said I, lifting my head, "I might do that, no matter how badly. To write of her would be better than to talk of her. To try to tell all her loveliness, her sweet, strong, virginal soul, her wisdom, her purity, her brave independence, to picture all this in words, no matter how inadequate, I shall see her with the eyes of Memory; she will be back with me in spirit…. A book! Jerry, O Jeremy, this is an excellent thought…. to see her again … to talk with her by means of pen and ink!"

In my eagerness I started up to my feet; then, the hot fit, passing, gave place to the cold, and Doubt leapt to seize me. "But I've never tried to write a book! Who am I to write a book?"

"Lord, don't be down-hearted afore you try, lad!" admonished the Tinker, for I had spoken this doubt aloud. "There's times in all writers' lives when they haven't writ a line, yet books are written all the same. Books ain't made, lad; they happen and they happen because a cove has an eye to see a little way beneath the surface o' things and an ear as can hear voices in the wind, an' a mind as discovers sum'mat in everything to wonder at. So he goes on lookin' an' listenin' an' wonderin' till one day out it has to come—an' there's your book. Now you're full up o' love, ain't you?"

"Yes, Jerry."

"Good! Well, write it down. There's nothing goes better in a nov-el than love, except blood—a splash or so here an' there, battle, murder an' sudden death—just a tang or so t' season it. I know, for I used t' sell nov-els once, ah, an' read 'em too! But love's the thing, lad! Everybody loves to read o' love—'specially old codgers, d'ye see—gouty old coves as curse their servants, swear at their families and, hid in corners, shed tears over the woes o' the hero an' heroine o' some nov-el an' stub their gouty toe a-kickin' of the villain. An' then there's the ladies—'specially the very young 'uns, God bless their bibs an' tuckers! Lord, how they sigh an' tremble an' toss their pretty curls an' weep an' languish. I heard o' one as always read wi' her smellin'-salts handy, but then, to be sure, she was a maiden lady of uncertain age as wished she wasn't an' was smitten wi' love for Tom Jones, besides, poor soul!"

"But my book—if I ever do write one, will not be read by any one."

"O? Mr. Perry—an' why not?"

"Being all about Diana, it will be too sacred for the perusal of all and sundry."

"There you're wrong, lad; no book can be too sacred for all folks to read, if it's writ honestly and sincerely. An' what a book you ought to write. First there's Anna an' yourself—folks would like to read about the two o' ye—you're such strange children. Then there's Jessamy—a wonderful character for any book. Next comes your uncles an' aunt—Lord, Peregrine, an' there's for ye—'specially your aunt! And last—" said he, a little wistfully, "if you want some one to fill in, kind of—to keep th' pot a-b'iling as it were, why—there's me. Not as your readers will be downright eager to read about a tinker—no, but you might work me in as a literary cove, d'ye see. How about it? What d'ye think, Perry lad?"

"Excellent well!" I exclaimed. "You inspire me with such strange confidence, Jerry, I almost feel I might manage a book—of sorts."

"Then go and try, lad."

"When—where—how?"

"This minute! At home! By hard work!"

"You mean leave—go back to Merivale—to-night?"

"Aye, I do. You can catch the mail at Tonbridge and you'll be home afore the moon's up."

"Do you know Merivale then, Jerry?"

"O' course. I'll harness Diogenes an' drive you in."

And so, within the hour, behold me upon the stage-coach that would carry me within a mile of home; behold Jerry standing below, gazing up at me with his wistful smile, a Jeremy whose form and features were blurred suddenly by hot tears as the whip cracked, hoofs stamped, and the London Mail lurched forward with a shrill and jubilant fanfare on the horn that drowned my cry of farewell, as Jeremy's blurred image waved blurred arm and, what with my tears and the dust, was blotted from me altogether.

With the small incidents of this short journey I will not worry the reader. Suffice it that the moon was high-risen when at last I reached Merivale. The lodge gates were shut for the night, and being in no mood to disturb any one, I clambered over the wall at an easily-accessible, well-remembered spot, and going by familiar paths, presently beheld the house, its many latticed casements winking ghostly to the moon, and a beam of soft light striking athwart the terrace from that chamber wherein my aunt Julia was wont to write her letters and transact all business of the estate. So thither came I to find the window wide open, for the night was hot, and to behold my aunt, as handsome and statuesque as ever, bent gracefully above her escritoire, pen in white fist, like an industrious goddess.

"Aunt Julia," said I, "pray don't be startled—I have come home—"

At this, though I had spoken softly, she dropped the pen, rose and, clasping hands to bosom, uttered a scream, though sweetly modulated and extremely ladylike. Then we were in each other's arms and she was weeping and laughing over me in a very ecstasy of welcome.

"Dear Peregrine—loved boy, at last! How brown you are! You're taller, bigger—handsomer, I vow—and you have come back to me. O Peregrine! You have come back to my loving care, dearest. Your wanderings are over?"

"Yes, dear aunt," I answered, stifling a sigh, "my wanderings are over."

"Oh, heaven bless you, dear boy! God be thanked—"

"And what of my good, generous uncles, dear Aunt?"

"I have banished the wretches—forbade them my presence—"

"Dear Aunt, pray why?"

"Because they are wretches."

"Then to-morrow we will write and bid them welcome."

"Never, Peregrine!"

"To-morrow, dear Aunt."

"Peregrine!" she exclaimed, starting and frowning a little, "I said, 'Never'!"

"And I said 'to-morrow', dear Aunt!"

"Boy!" she cried, lovely head proudly aloft.

"Aunt!" said I. "How very beautiful you are!" and drawing down that lovely head, I kissed her; at this, she flushed, and drew away, drooping her lashes like a girl.

"Why, Peregrine!" she murmured.

"They both love you so truly and faithfully, dear Aunt, and no wonder! And they are such—men! So to-morrow we will write to them?"

"Very well, dear Peregrine!" said my proud aunt, softly and not in the least proudly. "But you are hungry, thirsty—you must eat—"

"Thank you, no—only weary—"

So hand in hand she led me to my chamber.

"See, dear boy, I have kept everything as you left it; your bed is quite ready, the sheets aired, all waiting for you when you should choose to come."

She led me about the great chamber, showing me all things as they had been on the night of my departure, even to the pen where I had tossed it upon an unfinished manuscript. And no mention, never one word of Diana; for the which I loved her and was grateful.

"Dear Aunt," said I, and kissed her. "O dear Aunt Julia!"

But when at last she was gone and I alone in the soft luxury of this chamber, desolation filled me and I yearned bitterly for the discomforts of the little camp within the copse; the rustle of leaves, the soft, murmurous gurgle of the brook, the winking stars overhead; for Jeremy, and Jessamy Todd and my loved Diana. And coming to the open lattice, I leaned there to look upon the moon, this other Diana so placid and serene. And thinking that perhaps my Diana looked upon her even now, a Diana not at all placid and serene but with sweet, grey eyes a-brim with tears and heart full of yearning tenderness—even as mine, I fell upon my knees and stretching out my arms, whispered words of love with passionate prayers:

"O Diana, beloved … O God of Heaven—God of Mercy, bring her back to me at last with heart as sweet and pure—teach me to be worthy, fit me for such happiness…. O loved Diana of the Silent Places, my love goes with you always, and for ever, strong, sweet goddess of my life.

… Two years!"

102

TO THE READER

Here then, do I end this book, because this is the Book of Diana and she is gone out of my life.

So do I lay down my pen for a while, uneasily conscious of my narrative's many imperfections and greatly fearing that I have fallen very far short in my description of Diana.

But what work of man may hope to be utterly perfect? And who shall recapture the vanished glory of the dream?

Here, then, do I let fall the curtain; when it rises, the world and I shall be two years older, two years wiser, two years better, or the worse.

Book Two
SHADOW

CHAPTER I

THE INCIDENTS OF AN EARLY MORNING WALK

I remember waking to find myself very miserable in a ghastly dawn, where guttering candles flickered in their sockets, casting an unearthly light upon bottles, silverware, and more bottles that stood or lay amidst overturned and broken glasses; an unseemly jumble that littered a long table whose rumpled cloth was plentifully besplashed with spilled wine and flanked by empty chairs.

Into my drugged consciousness stole a sound that might have been wind in trees, or a mill race, or some industrious artisan busied with a saw, yet which I knew could be none of these, and my drowsy puzzlement grew. Therefore I roused myself with some vague notion of solving this mystery and turned to behold in this ghastly light a ghostly face; a handsome face, but very stern, square-chinned, black-browed, aquiline, scowling upon the dawn.

"Uncle Jervas!" said I, a little thickly. "You look like a ghost, sir!"

At this he started, but when he turned, his face was impassive as ever.

"Shall I wish you many happy returns of last night, Nephew?"

"God forbid, sir!" said I, bowing aching head upon my hands.

"It is perhaps a blessing to remember, Peregrine, that one comes of age but once in one's lifetime."

"It is, sir!" I groaned. "Pray what—what is that sound, sir—so monotonous and—damnable?"

"It is rather an aggregation of sounds, emanating in unison from your good friends the Marquis of Jerningham, Viscount Devenham and Mr. Vere-Manville—they sleep remarkably soundly!"

"And—the others, sir?"

"Departed in the small hours, with your uncle George—and four of 'em in tears!"

"It was a dreadful night, sir."

"It was a night of nights, Peregrine. I remember only one to equal it."

"And that, sir?"

"Your father's coming of age. But talking of ghosts, Perry, I almost fancied I saw one—no longer ago than last night—on my way here. But then I don't believe in ghosts—and this one was seated in a closed carriage and accompanied by a rather handsome young woman—and she was weeping, I fancy. Your head aches, Nephew?"

"Damnably, Uncle Jervas. I hate wine!"

"Yet one must drink occasionally, boy."

"You can, sir," I groaned, "last night you honoured every toast—yet here you sit—"

"Looking like a ghost, Nephew."

"And utterly unaffected, Uncle."

"On the contrary, inordinate drinking afflicts me horribly, Nephew, stimulates me to thought, harrows me with memory, resurrects things best forgotten! Ah, there's the sun at last. I'll leave you, Peregrine—I'll out to greet the day."

"I should like to walk with you if I may, sir."

"By all means, Nephew, 't will ease your head, perhaps."

And so, moving softly lest we disturb the three sonorous sleepers, a wholly unnecessary precaution, we took our hats and surtouts and stepped out into an empty street swept by a clean, soft wind that cooled my throbbing temples, and my sick heaviness was lifted somewhat in the sweet, pure breath of dawn.

"You have been about town for nearly a year, haven't you, Peregrine?"

"Yes, sir, long enough to teach me I love the country better than I thought."

"You are sufficiently dissipated, I trust?"

"I endeavour to be, sir. Her Grace of Camberhurst shakes her head over me, though I do my best—"

"Does it require so great an effort?"

"Somewhat, sir. You see, I find dissipation a particularly wearisome business."

"Wearisome, Nephew? You surprise me!"

"And depressingly dreary, Uncle."

"You astonish me!"

"Indeed, dissipation thoroughly distresses me."

"You amaze me! But you gamble, I presume?"

"When nothing better offers, sir."

"Well upon me everlasting soul—!"

"I hope I do not shock you, Uncle Jervas?"

"Worry would be the more apt word, perhaps; you worry me, Nephew. Such impeccable virtue naturally suggests an early death—a harp—a halo! And yet you appear to enjoy robust health. Pray to what do you attribute your so great immunity from those pleasant weaknesses that are so frequently a concomitant of strength and youthful vigour—those charming follies, bewitching foibles that a somewhat rigorous convention stigmatises as vices—abhorrent word!"

"You mean, sir, what excuse do I offer for not being politely vicious as seems so much the fashion?"

"I confess you puzzle me, boy, for you are anything but an angel in pantaloons. I have occasionally thought to remark in you a hint of unplumbed deeps—of passions as hot and fierce as—"

"Your own, Uncle Jervas?" At this he turned to glare at me rather haughtily, then his eyes softened, his lips twitched.

"So women do not appeal to you, Peregrine. Pray why?"

"Because woman appeals to me so much—one, sir!"

"Ah, your roving gipsy?"

"Precisely, sir."

"Where is she, at present?"

"I believe in Italy, sir."

"Hum! Your friend Vere-Manville ran across her in Rome, I believe. When did you hear from her last?"

"One year and ten months ago, sir."

"Painfully exact! And how many letters has she written you, may I ask?"

"One, sir."

"Hum! You know that the Earl of Wyvelstoke has made her his ward and heiress, Peregrine?"

"His lordship informed me of the fact, Uncle."

"He corresponds with you, then?"

"Every month without fail."

"Then of course you know he is returning to England shortly and holds a great reception at his place in town, a fortnight from to-day, I think?"

"Yes, sir."

"And in the space of two years you have received one letter from your beautiful gipsy?"

"Only one, sir! Though his lordship has kept me informed as to her welfare and progress."

"Such sublime patience argues either indifference or stupendous faith, boy!"

"Sir—sir," cried I, stirred at last. "Oh, sir, how may love be—how endure without faith?"

"Yours is a strange love, Peregrine, exceeding patient and long-suffering! You practically compelled her to—accept his lordship's offer, I believe?"

"Uncle—Uncle Jervas," I stammered, "how should you know this?"

"I have the honour to number the Earl of Wyvelstoke among my few friends, he writes to me also—occasionally. You are an immensely confiding lover, and your patience is almost—superhuman."

"However, my waiting is nearly over, I shall see her soon—soon!"

"In company with every buck, Corinthian and Macaroni in London, Peregrine."

"Still—I shall see her, sir!"

"If the reports of her singing, her wit and beauty are but half true, Peregrine, she will be the rage, the universal toast."

"Still—she will be—Diana, sir!"

"But two years, Nephew—wealth, rank, adulation—can these have wrought no change, think you?"

"Only for the better, sir!"

"Oh, the sublime assurance of Youth!" murmured my uncle. "Have you no doubt of yourself, now that you are no longer the—the—ah—'only Richmond in the field'?"

Here, though I strove to speak, I could not, but walked with head bowed, but very conscious of his keen scrutiny.

"You are so intense, Perry," he continued after a moment, "so very, damnably intense that I confess I grow a little fearful lest you be disappointed, and therefore take the liberty to annoy you with my dismal croakings, if I may—shall I proceed?"

"Pray do, sir!"

"Then, Peregrine, I would warn you that, considering her new attitude towards life, her very altered views upon the world in general, it is only to be expected your gipsy may find you very different from her first estimation of you—"

"Ah, there it is, sir—there it is!" I groaned. "The haunting fear that to-day—measured by the larger standard of her new experiences, she may find me fall very far short of what she imagines me—"

"And if this be so,—how then?"

"Do not ask me, sir,—don't!"

"The ordinary, impassioned youth, under such unpleasantly frequent circumstances, Peregrine, would seek oblivion in bottles or fly instantly to all manner of riot and dissipation and be cured sooner or later—but you? Knowing what I do of your devilishly intense nature, I must admit I am a little disquieted. You see, Peregrine, I have learned, though I grant you a little painfully, still I have learned at last to—ah—to care for you so much that your unhappiness would affect me—rather cursedly, boy—yes, rather cursedly."

"Uncle Jervas," said I, "indeed—indeed I am proud to have won your esteem; I shall endeavour to be worthy of it."

"Why then, Nephew," said he, slipping his arm into mine, "whatever damnable buffets Fate sees fit to deal you, whatever disappointments are in store, you will of course meet them with a serene fortitude—eh, boy?"

"You may trust me, sir. Not," I continued hastily "not that I anticipate any change of heart in Diana. Could you but have known her, sir—!"

"Pray tell me of her, Peregrine, if you will."

Our walk had brought us to Vauxhall, and skirting the gardens with their groves and walks, their fountains, temples and grottoes, we went on beside the river, I talking of Diana, my uncle listening, and both watching the sun rise over the great city, to gild vane and weathercock of countless spires and steeples and make a broad-bosomed glory of the noble river. Suddenly my uncle halted to point before him with tasselled cane where two rough-looking men, unconscious of our approach, were crouched among the sedge beside the water.

"Let us see what these fellows are doing!" said he. So we advanced until, being very near, we halted, for now indeed we saw only too well.

She lay where they had dragged her, just above the hungry tide, a slender, pitiful thing, young and beautiful, yet now dreadfully pale and still, shrouded in her long, wet tresses; a mute and beautiful thing, all heedless now of the rough hands that touched her, or the kindly sun's tender beam that showed the pitiful droop of pallid lips and motionless lashes, and the slender fingers of the small, right hand clenched in death. Even now, as I stood bareheaded, my breath in check, one of the fellows grasped this hand, wrenched open these delicate fingers with brutal strength, and finding within them only a wisp of crumpled paper, swore a hoarse oath of baffled cupidity that changed to a howl as my uncle's cane rapped him smartly across bull-neck.

"Detestable savage!" exclaimed my uncle, scowling down into the man's startled face. "Learn reverence for the dead! Now pass me that paper!"

The man snarled a threat, whereupon my uncle rapped him again.

"The paper—do you hear—animal?"

The man rubbed his neck, muttered an oath, and gave the wisp of paper to my uncle, who, without glancing at it, took off his hat and bowed his head.

"Poor soul!" he sighed gently, his impassive face transfigured by an extraordinary tenderness. "Poor frightened, weary soul—so young, so very young, and now fled—whither? Poor—poor child—Stop! Keep your beastly hands off her!" This to the bull-necked fellow, who flinched and drew away, snarling.

"Lumme, me lord!" whined the second man, a small, mean person. "What's ye game? She's ourn—we found 'er, Job an' me—seen 'er out in th' race, us did, floatin' s' pretty, an' folleyed 'er, us did, 'til she came ashore. She b'longs t' us, me lord, as Job'll swear—to diskiver a corp' means money, an' corpses, 'specially sich pretty 'uns, don't come often enough—"

"Pah!" cried my uncle. "There is a hurdle over yonder, fetch it—you!" The bull-necked fellow rose, but, instead of complying, turned short and sprang, an open knife in his hand; my uncle Jervas stepped lightly aside, his long arm shot out, and the bull-necked man went down heavily; he was in the act of rising when my uncle set his foot upon the man's knife-hand, placidly crushed and crushed it until he roared, until the gripping fingers relaxed their hold, whereupon my uncle kicked the knife into the river.

"And now—beast—fetch the hurdle yonder!" said he.

So the men brought the hurdle and my uncle, stripping off his fine surtout, made therewith a pillow for the beautiful, piteous head.

"And now, where shall we take her?" he demanded.

"There's an ale-'us down yonder, me lord, nice an' 'andy," answered the little man. "Us gen'ally takes 'em theer."

"Ah, do you mean you find many such?"

"A tidy few, me lord, but not s' many as us could wish, d'ye see—"

"Pah! Let us take her there. And be gentle with her."

"Gentle!" growled the bull-necked man. "'Er's dead, ain't 'er—gentle!"

So we moved off in mournful procession until we came to a small waterside tavern, whose inmates my uncle peremptorily awakened, and soon had forth a gruff, sleepy fellow to show the way and unlock a tumble-down outhouse, into which they bore their silent burden, followed by my uncle, bareheaded.

As for me, I walked to and fro in the sunshine, feeling myself cold and shivering. At last I heard the doors close and turning, beheld my uncle's tall, immaculate figure striding towards me.

"A sad sight, Perry, a dismal, woeful sight—and on such a glorious morning. Come, let us go." So saying, he put on his hat, sternly refusing the offer of my outer coat, and taking my arm, we began to retrace our steps. Suddenly he checked, and feeling in his pocket, brought forth that crumpled wisp of paper and, smoothing it out, glanced at it and I saw his eyes grow suddenly fierce.

"Haredale!" said he thoughtfully. "Haredale?" and passed the paper to me whereon I read these words, blotched with water, yet still legible:

You are unreasonable, but this is feminine.
You anger me, but this is natural.
You weary me—and this is fatal.
Adieu,
HAREDALE.

"Haredale!" said I.

"Haredale?" sighed my uncle. "The name is unfamiliar, I know none of the name in London. Do you, Peregrine?"

"No, sir!" I answered. "No—and yet—it seems as if—yes, I have heard it, Uncle, but not in London. I heard it mentioned two years ago—in a wood. It was spoken by a scoundrel who named himself Haredale though Lord Wyvelstoke addressed him as—Devereux!"

"Devereux!" said my uncle in so strange a tone that I lifted my gaze from the scrawled name and saw that he had removed his hat again and was staring at me with an expression as strange as his voice, his eyes fixed and intent as though they stared at things I could not see, brow wrinkled, nostrils expanded, chin more aggressive than usual. "Devereux! Nephew, you—are sure it was—Devereux?"

"Absolutely, sir."

"Hum!" said my uncle, putting on his hat. "I'll trouble you for that scrap of paper, Nephew. Thanks! Now let us go on. Your headache is better, I hope?"

"Much better, sir. But pray take my coat, you are shivering."

"Thank you, no—there is nothing like the early morning, it fills one with a zest of life, the *joie de vivre*—though I will admit I am seldom abroad at this hour."

Now despite his light tone, I noticed two things, his eyes were still fixed and intent and a thin trickle of moisture gleamed beneath his hat brim.

"Poor child!" sighed my uncle. "Let us hope her bruised spirit has found rest, a surcease from all troubles. Let us hope she has found the Infinite Happiness if there be such in the Great Beyond. Haredale—hum! Have you any recollection of this man, Perry; his looks, air, voice—could you describe him?"

"He was tall, sir, as yourself, or very nearly—looked younger than his years—a cold, imperturbable man, dark, but of pale complexion, with deep-set eyes that seemed to glow strangely. A man of iron will who fronted Lord Wyvelstoke unflinchingly even after his arm was shot and broken!" And here I described the incident as fully as possible.

"And what was the name Lord Wyvelstoke used?"

"Devereux, sir."

"Hum!" said my uncle. And thereafter we walked in silence through streets beginning to stir with the busy life of a new day.

Reaching my uncle's chambers in St. James's Street, he paused in the doorway to glance up and down the street with that same expression of fixed intensity, that faraway look of absorption.

"This," said he, speaking almost as with an effort, "this has been a—somewhat eventful walk of ours, Peregrine. I will not invite you to breakfast, remembering you have guests of your own. Au revoir."

"Uncle Jervas," said I, as we clasped hands, "this has indeed been an eventful walk, for to-day I have learned to know you better than I ever expected, or dared to hope—sir, are you ill?" I questioned anxiously, for despite that trickle of moisture at his temple, the hand I held felt deadly cold and nerveless. "Are you ill, sir?"

"Never better, Perry!" he laughed, clapping me lightly on the shoulder. "Get you to your guests. And by the by—talking of ghosts and grimly spectres—egad, Perry, I almost believe they do haunt this sorry world, sometimes!" So saying, he laughed, turned, and was gone, leaving me to stare after him in anxious wonderment.

CHAPTER II

INTRODUCING JASPER SHRIG, A BOW STREET RUNNER

"Ham, Peregrine?"

"Thank you, no, Anthony!" said I, shuddering slightly. "But where are the others? Asleep still?"

"Gone, Perry. At sight of this ham Jerny shied like a wild colt, Devenham moaned, and together they tottered forth into the bleak world. Did you say ham, Perry?"

"I—did—not!"

"Beef then—beef looks excellent! Beef?"

"Horrible!" I exclaimed, turning my back on the breakfast table. "Eat if you can, Tony, but talk you must and shall."

"Of last night, Peregrine?"

"Of Diana. I've scarcely had a word with you since your arrival."

"Which was last night."

"How is she, Anthony? Is she indeed handsomer—lovelier? Did she seem happy? Did she talk about—did she—happen to mention—"

"She did, Perry, talked of you frequently, very much so! Won't you try a cup of coffee and a crust—"

"Tell me how—where you first met her."

"It was at the ambassador's ball and mark you, Perry, there were some uncommonly fine women there, though none of 'em, no, damme, not one to compare with my Loveliness, of course—"

"You mean Barbara?"

"Of course. Well, my boy, we'd made our bow and here was Loveliness worrying in her pretty fashion because my cravat had shifted or some such, and here was I pulling at the thing and saying, 'Yes, dear,' and making it worse when, as the poet says, 'amid this glittering throng of lovely women and gallant men' my charmed eye alighted upon a haughty beauty, a ravishing creature condescending to be worshipped by a crowd of fawning slaves, civilian, soldier and sailor of all stations and ranks, from purple-faced admirals and general officers to pink, downy-whiskered subalterns. 'Egad, Loveliness,' says I, jerking at my cravat, 'what asinine fools brave men and gallant gentlemen can make of themselves for lovely woman—look yonder!' 'Where?' says she. 'There!' says I, 'the dark, dazzling beauty yonder!' So Loveliness looks, and at that very moment Beauty breaks from the abject circle of her fawning slaves and comes running. 'Diana!' cries Loveliness. 'Barbara!' cries Beauty, and they are in each other's arms—and there you are, Perry. Astonishing how they love each other. So when I left to attend this birthday of yours, Loveliness must stay with her Diana—I miss her most damnably!"

"Has she so many admirers?" I sighed.

"Hordes of 'em, Perry! Troops, squadrons, regiments, begad! So has my Loveliness, for that matter."

"And are you never jealous?"

"Devil a bit, dear fellow. Though," said he, slowly clenching his right hand into a powerful fist and scowling down at it, "given the occasion—I could be, Perry, y-e-s, madly, brutally—I could kill—do murder, I believe. Oh, pshaw! My Barbara is so sweet, so purely a thing of heaven that sometimes I—I hate myself for not having been better—more worthy. Women are so infinitely better than ourselves, or so infinitely—worse. And she sent you a letter—here it is!"

"A letter? Diana? Where?"

"A snack of ham or beef first, Perry, love letters don't go over-well on empty stomachs—" But here I caught the letter from him and sat with it in fingers that shook a little, staring at the superscription.

"Her writing has improved amazingly!" said I.

"Dear fellow," he answered, sharpening the carving knife quite unnecessarily, "go away and read it, seek some quiet spot and leave me to eat in peace."

"Thanks, Tony," said I gratefully, and hastened into the next room forthwith, there to read and re-read the superscription, to commit all those tender follies natural to lovers and finally to break the seal.

DEAR, DEAR MY PEREGRINE: Very soon we shall see each other, and this thought makes me tremble with alternate happiness and dread. Yes, dread, my Peregrine, because these years have changed me in many ways—oh, shall I please you as I am now? Will you love me as you did when I was only your humble Diana of the Silent Places? For Peregrine, you loved me then so very much, so truly and with such wonderful unselfishness that I am afraid you may not love the Diana of to-day quite so well as the Diana of two years ago. But dear Peregrine, know that my heart is quite—quite unchanged; you will always be the one man of all others, the Peregrine whose generous love lifted me high above my girlish dreams but never oh, never any higher than his own heart. So Peregrine, love me when I come back to you or these long two years will have been lived in vain and I shall run away back to the Silent Places and die an old maid. Perhaps I shall seem strange when we meet, but this will only be because I fear you a little and doubt a little how you may feel towards this new Diana—so love me, let me see it in your eyes, hear it in your voice. It is so much easier to write than to say, so I will write it again—Love me, Peregrine, love me because I am yours—now and always.

DIANA.

Having read this letter I laid it down and took from an inner pocket another letter, somewhat worn and frayed by over-much handling, which bore these words, smudged and blotted a little, though written with painful care.

DEAR PERRYGREEN: Your letter has made me cry dredfully. I cannot bear to think of you so lonly because I am lonly to. I cannot bear to think of you on your nees I would rather think of you as I saw you last so brave and determined. Pray for me as I pray for you only don't rite to me or I shall run back to you because I am not very brave and want you so. O dear Perrygreen always love

YOUR DIANA.

"You're looking confoundedly glum, Perry; I hope the *billet* is quite sufficiently *doux*?"

"Quite—indeed, quite!" said I, starting out of my reverie. "It is a letter such as only Diana could have written—"

"Then your woe undoubtedly proceeds from stomach; for the emptiness of same I prescribe ham, shall we say mingled—judiciously blended—with beef—"

"Abhorrent thought!" I exclaimed. At this moment, after a discreet knock on the door, my valet Clegg entered.

"Sir," said he in his soft and toneless voice, "the groom is below; shall you ride or drive this morning?"

"Neither!" I answered, whereupon Clegg bowed and withdrew.

"Excellent!" nodded Anthony. "Nothing like walking to make an empty stomach aware of its vacuity. By the way, queer article that Clegg fellow of yours—face like a mask! Where did you pick him up?"

"I don't remember. He had excellent references, I believe. Why do you ask?"

107

"Fancy I've seen him before. Come, let us adventure forth in search of your appetite."

To us in the hall came Clegg to bring our hats and canes.

"Were you ever in the service of a Captain Danby?" enquired Anthony, his keen gaze on Clegg's impassive face.

"Yes, sir, I was valet to Captain Marmaduke Danby—two years ago."

"I saw you with him once at a small inn called 'The Jolly Waggoner.'"

Clegg bowed deferentially, but when he looked up his pale eyes seemed to glow strangely and his pallid cheek was slightly flushed.

"Yes, sir, Captain Danby sent for me to attend him there—I found him in bed exceedingly—unwell. He was—suffering, sir. He suffered quite a—good deal of—pain, sir—of pain."

Saying which, Clegg bowed us out into the street with a deeper obeisance than usual.

"Strange!" said Anthony, taking my arm. "You have probably forgotten this Danby, the fellow I had the pleasure of thrashing, Perry?"

"I shall never forget how you stood on him and wiped your boots, Anthony."

"I did chastise him somewhat severely, I remember. But I learned something more of his villainy from Barbara, as we drove away, and I returned next day to give him another dose but found him in bed bandaged like a mummy and this Clegg fellow of yours beside him. I learned afterwards that he was friend to that same scoundrel Barbara's father was forcing the sweet soul to marry, damn him!"

"The world seems full of unhanged villains!" said I, through shut teeth.

"Oh, is it, begad?"

"It is!"

"You're devilish gloomy, Perry."

"I fear I am."

"All stomach, ye know, dear fellow. I've noticed this poor old world is generally blamed most damnably, purely because of the night of the morning after—more especially upon an empty—"

"Don't say it again, Anthony, for heaven's sake!"

"But you're curst gloomy and devilish doleful—"

"Anthony, dear man, while you were snoring blissfully this morning I watched a poor, beautiful young creature dragged out of the river."

"Dead, Perry?"

"Yes. She was probably drowning herself last night while we drank and rioted—poor despairing child!" and here I described the dreadful incident very fully. "You have never met or heard of any one named Haredale, have you, Anthony?" I ended.

"No," he answered, "no! Gad, Perry," he burst out with a vicious twirl of his cane, "there are times when killing is a laudable act!" After this we walked in silence for some time.

"Where are we going?" he questioned suddenly.

Hereupon I glanced up, for I had walked with my gaze bent earthward, and saw that we were close upon the river.

"Since we are here," I answered, "I will show you where it—she lies. It was yonder they found her, and over there, beyond those trees, is a wretched tavern—"

"And on the other side of the hedge, Perry, is a small, unpleasant person who peeps and peers and follows. Let us investigate!"

So saying, Anthony turned suddenly and confronted a small, mean-looking fellow who starting back out of reach, touched a shaggy eyebrow, cringed, and spoke:

"No offence, my lords an' gents—none in th' world, s' help me true!" Having said which, he clapped fingers to mouth and whistled very shrilly. "Not by no means nowise meanin' no offence, my lords," quoth he apologetically, "but dooty is dooty—an' 'ere 'e be!" Glancing whither he pointed, I saw a man approaching, a shortish, broad-shouldered, square-faced, leisurely person in a broad-brimmed, low-crowned hat and full-skirted frieze greatcoat; a man of slow gait and deliberate movement but with a quick and roving eye.

"Th' little 'un's th' gent, guv'nor—'e's th' cove! whispered the mean-looking fellow hoarsely, and now I recognised him as one of the two waterside characters I had met that morning with my uncle Jervas. The man in the frieze coat removed his hat, bobbed round head at Anthony, at me, and spoke, addressing himself to me:

"'T is in ewidence, sir, as you an' another gent 'appened to be a-passin' by when a lately de-funct o' the fe-male persuasion vas took out o' th' river at the hour o' four-two-two pre-cisely, this 'ere werry mornin'. Am I right?"

"That is so," I answered.

"'T is also in ewidence, sir, as you an' your friend 'appening to pass—by chance or de-sign, so werry remarkable early in the mornin', stopped to ob-serve same de-funct party o' the fe-male persuasion. Am I right again?"

"We did."

"'T is furthermore in ewidence, sir, that upon ob-serving corpse, you an' your friend seemed werry much took aback, not to say overcome. Am I—"

"They was, Jarsper, they was—oncommon!" quoth the smaller man hoarsely.

"'Enery, 'old your tongue! Now, sir, am I right or am I not?"

"We were both very naturally shocked," said I.

"Vich feelin's, sir, does you both credit—oceans. But 't is further in ewidence as your friend did commit a assault upon the body o' one Thomas Vokins by means of a cane an' there an' then took, removed, appre'ended or ab-stracted ewidence in the shape o' a piece o' paper as 'ad fell from right 'and o' said corpse. Am I right once more?"

"Not altogether!" said I. "The man wrenched open the dead girl's fingers so brutally that my—companion very properly rapped him with his cane and noticing the piece of paper, ordered the man to give it to him."

"Good—werry good! Now I puts it to you, sir—vere is that piece o' paper?"

"Probably in my companion's possession."

"Good again! An' vere might 'e be?"

"That I decline to tell you!"

"Vy then, sir, dooty bein' dooty, I'll take a valk."

"As you will!" said I. "Come, Anthony!" and turning, we began to retrace our steps. But we had gone but a little way when I faced suddenly about, for the man was plodding at our heels.

"Why the devil do you follow us?" I demanded, greatly exasperated.

"Becos' dooty is dooty, sir, an' dooty demands same," he answered imperturbably.

"Who are you, fellow?"

"Jarsper Shrig, Bow Street officer—werry much at your service, sir!"

"And what do you want of me?"

"A piece o' paper, sir, as ewidence to establish i-dentifi-cation of de-funct young party o' the fe-male persuasion in a case o' murder or feller-de-see—"

Here I turned and walked on again in no little perplexity.

"What am I to do, Anthony?" I muttered.

"Bring the fellow to your chambers, despatch a note to Sir Jervas and leave it to his decision."

So we walked on, perfectly ignoring this very pertinacious Bow Street officer; but I, for one, was not sorry when at last we reached the door of my chambers, and halting, turned to behold the Bow Street officer, who had stopped also and appeared to be lost in contemplation of the adjacent chimney pots. And as he stood thus, I was struck by his air of irreproachable respectability and pervading mildness; despite the formidable knotted stick beneath his arm, he seemed indeed to radiate benevolence from the soles of his stout boots to the crown of his respectable, broad-brimmed hat.

"A re-markable vide-avake young man, yours, sir," said he gently, still apparently lost in contemplation of the chimney pots, "a re-markable vatchful young man an' werry attentive!"

"What do you mean, officer?"

"I mean, sir, as he's opened your door afore you knocked."

Glancing at the door, I saw indeed, to my surprise, that it stood slightly ajar; hereupon I reached out to open it when it swung wide and my man Clegg stood before us.

"I saw you approaching, sir," he exclaimed, bowing us in.

Reaching my small library, the officer seated himself at my invitation and depositing hat and stick very precisely beneath his chair, sat looking more unctuously mild than ever, there was about him a vague suggestion of conventicles, and a holy Sabbatarian calm.

"You said your name was Shrig, I think?" said I.

"Jarsper Shrig, sir, at your sarvice."

"Then perhaps, while I write my letter, you will take a glass of wine, Mr. Shrig?"

"Sir," he answered, "not beating about no bushes, I vill—Mr. Werricker, sir."

"You know my name?" I exclaimed a little sharply.

"I dedooce same, sir, from them three letters on your secretary as is a-staring me straight in the face, Mr. Werricker."

"Pray, Anthony, oblige me by ringing the bell!" said I, taking up my pen.

Soft-treading, the discreet Clegg duly brought in decanter and glasses, and Mr. Shrig, watching him pour out the wine, drew from his capacious pocket a little book and opened it, much as though he would have read forth a text of Scripture, but all he said was:

"Thank 'ee, my man!" and then, as the door closed upon the discreetly silent Clegg, "Your 'ealth, gen'elmen!"

The letter to my uncle Jervas being written and despatched, I turned to find Mr. Shrig busied with his little book and a stumpy pencil, much as if he had been composing a sermon or address, while Anthony, lounging upon the settee, watched him with lazy interest.

"A on-commonly taking cove, sir, that young man o' yourn!" said Mr. Shrig, pocketing book and pencil.

"Not more so than other servants, I believe," I answered.

"And all valets," murmured Anthony, "all valets are predatory by nature, of course—"

"I mean as he's a likely cove. Now, talkin' o' corpses—" began Mr. Shrig.

"But we are not!" said I.

109

"Axing your parding, sir, but I am and, perfessionally speakin', never 'ave I seen a prettier corp', than this 'ere young fe-male in question—"

"And your experience in such is vast, I take it?" murmured Anthony.

"None waster, sir! Wast is the werry vord for it."

"Do you think this is a case of suicide or murder?" enquired Anthony.

"Can't say, sir. But somevun's allvays bein' murdered, murderin' or goin' for to murder somevun, somevere or t'other."

"Sounds cheery!" murmured Anthony. "Do you catch many murderers?"

"Pretty fair, sir, pretty fair. I got a special aptitood for it; I can smell murder in the werry air, feel it, taste it—"

"Must be devilish unpleasant!" said Anthony.

"'Tis a nat'ral gift wi' me, sir. Lord love ye, gen'lemen, I can p'int you out a murderer afore the fact's committed—I've got the names o' four on 'em—no, five—wrote down in my little reader, five werry promisin' coves as is doo for the deed at any moment; I'm a vaitin' for 'em to bring it off, sirs. Lord, I'm a vatchin' over 'em like a feyther an' mother rolled into vun, an' v'en they do commit the deed, I shall appre'end 'em red-'anded an' up they'll go."

"Your methods are highly original, Mr. Shrig," said I, "but do they always work correctly?"

"Ever an' always, sir—barrin' accidents. O' course, there's many a promisin' murderer died afore 'e could do the deed, death 'as no more respect for vould-be murderers than for their wictims. But whenever I sees a cove or covess with the true murderer's face, down goes that cove or covess' name in my little reader, an' I vatches an' vaits for 'em to bring it off, werry patient."

"Have you written down the name of Haredale in your little book?" I enquired.

"Haredale, Mr. Werricker, sir? V'y no, I ain't. V'y should I, sir? Vot ha' you to tell me about any party, name o' Haredale?"

"Only that you will find such a name on the piece of paper you are after."

Mr. Shrig's roving eye fixed me for a moment.

"Haredale?" he muttered, shaking his head, "Haredale?"

At this juncture, with a soft knock on the door, Clegg presented himself, bearing the following letter from my uncle.

MY DEAR PEREGRINE: I am grateful for your forethought, but you may suffer the man to visit me, for the law is the law—besides, the man Shrig is an old acquaintance. Moreover I have learned all I desired from the scrap of paper and it is therefore entirely at Mr. Shrig's service. Should you still be suffering from spleen, liver or the blue devils, go for a gallop on your "Wildfire."

With which salutary advice to yourself and good wishes to your friend
Mr. Vere-Manville,

I REST, YOUR AFFECTIONATE UNCLE, JERVAS.

"Mr. Shrig," said I, "you have my uncle's permission to wait upon him at once. Sir Jervas is acquainted with you, it seems?"

"Sir Jervas?" repeated Mr. Shrig, reaching down for hat and knobby stick. "Ackvainted? I should say so, sir! A reg'lar bang-up blood, a downright 'eavy toddler—oh, I know Sir Jervas, ackvainted is the werry i-denti-cal name for it! So, with your permission, sir, I'll be padding on my vay."

"You will find him at his chambers in—"

"St. James's Street, nigh opposite to Vite's, Mr. Werricker, sir. Ah many's the drop o' French brandy, glass o' port or sherry as I've drank to the 'ealth o' your uncle in them werry i-dentical chambers, sir. A gent wi' a werry elegant taste in crime is Sir Jervas. No, don't trouble to come down, sir, your young man shall let me out. A reg'lar treasure that 'ere young man o' yours, Mr. Werricker! Good morning, gen'elmen both, my best respex!"

So saying, Mr. Shrig bobbed his head to us in turn, beamed as it might have been in benediction, and took himself away.

CHAPTER III

CONCERNING A BLACK POSTCHAISE

"Begad, Perry, but that's a vicious brute of yours!" cried Anthony. This as Wildfire curvetted, snorting, sidled and performed an impassioned dance upon the footpath.

"Not exactly vicious, Tony," I demurred when I had quelled this exuberance, "merely animal spirits. Wildfire is a high-strung creature requiring constant thought and attention and is consequently interesting, besides which—"

Here a shriek and hoarse shouts as, by means of whip and curb and spur, I swung the animal in question from the dangerous proximity of a shop window and checked his impulse to walk on his hind legs.

"Scarcely a lady's pad, Peregrine!" grinned Anthony, as I came perilously near upsetting a coster's barrow, to its owner's vociferous indignation. "Egad, a four-footed devil warranted to banish every other worry but himself!"

"Precisely," said I, when my steed, moderating his ardour, permitted me coherent speech. "And this is the reason I ride him. No one mounted on Wildfire can think of anything but Wildfire and this is sometimes a blessing."

"How so, Perry?"

"Well, I am harassed of late by two obsessions—the memory of that poor—drowned child—I cannot forget her face!"

"But, deuce take it, man—this was days and days ago."

"And the other is, strangely enough—Diana. The thought that I shall meet her so soon—a nameless doubt—an indefinable dread—"

"Dread, Perry? Doubt? What the dooce d'ye mean?"

"That's the devil of it, Anthony—I—don't know. But I have a vague fear—a presentiment, if you like. I feel as if there was a dreadful something impending—a shadow—"

"Oh, pshaw, man! Shadow? Tush an' be damned to it! You're in a devilish low state—indubitably stomach—"

Here further converse was ended for the time being by Wildfire taking it into his head to snort and start, to prance and shiver at a large man in velveteens and a leather hat, whereupon Velveteens backed hastily and swore; Wildfire reared and plunged at him, whereupon Velveteens dodged into a doorway, cursing vehemently; people, at a safe distance, shouted; boys hooted; and then, having thus drawn attention to himself, Wildfire trotted daintily on again, leaving Velveteens spent and breathless with indignant cursings.

So with such minor unpleasantnesses as roaring oaths, curses and personal vilification, we won free of the denser traffic and had at last left the great city behind us and Wildfire's scornful hoofs were spurning the dust of Kent Street.

We rode by New Cross and Lewisham, through Lee Village with its two "Tiger" Inns and the stocks upon the green, through Eltham with the timeworn gables of its ancient palace rising on our right, dreaming of past glories.

"To-morrow night, Perry—to-morrow night we shall see 'em! My Loveliness! Egad, I'm only just beginning to realise how damnably I miss her! Wonderful institution, marriage. To-morrow, Perry! And the day after—home at Nettlestead Abbey—she and I. She loves the old place—and the roses will be in bloom—she adores roses. This is why I'm dragging you down to Nettlestead—must see everything shipshape—the old place ready—with its arms out to welcome her home, d'ye see—as it were."

"It is a glorious old place, Anthony."

"A curst dreary hole without her, Perry! Nothing like marriage, Perry! You'll give up your chambers when you're married, of course?"

"I suppose so, Tony—when I'm married."

"Aha!" he exclaimed, evidently struck by my gloomy tone. "Is it your damned shadow again—the blue devils? Oh, curse and confound 'em, I'll race you t' the next milestone for ten guineas. Come on! Yoicks, boy—hark forward! A touch o' the persuaders—and away!"

With a clatter of eager hoofs Anthony's raking sorrel sprang ahead; but away in pursuit leapt my beautiful roan, shapely head out-thrust, snorting, quivering, passionate for the fray.

Off and away, with the rhythmic swing and beat of swift-galloping hoofs below and the rush of wind above—a clean, sweet wind, full of health and sanity, to banish haunting dread and gloomy doubts of the future together with the devils that begot them, be they blue devils, black, or any other colour.

Faster and faster sped the road beneath me, hedges spun by, tree and gate flitted past as, untouched by whip or spur, Wildfire fell to his long, racing stride, an easy, stretching gallop. And ever he gained upon the sorrel, creeping up inch by inch, crupper and withers and nose; and thus we raced awhile, neck and neck. And now above quick-thudding hoofs and creaking leather I heard Anthony's voice urging his animal to fiercer effort, for slowly but surely, we were drawing away; slowly the sorrel's great crest and flaring nostrils fell to the rear, back and back, level with my gloved hands, my knee, my elbow, out of my view, and presently, glancing behind, I saw Anthony riding like a centaur—a wildly-galloping figure blurred in a storm of dust.

But on I rode, heedless of all but the exhilaration of rushing wind, of back-whirling hedgerows and trees, on and on until before us was a hill up which a chaise was crawling.

Now as I watched this vehicle carelessly enough, out from the window came a hatless head—an arm that waved imperiously, and the postboy, glancing back, began to flog his animals to swifter gait. But Wildfire, snorting scorn on all hills and this in particular, never so much as checked or faltered in his long stride and thus we approached the lumbering chaise rapidly.

We were close upon it when once again the head projected itself from the window, but now the face was turned towards me, and in these features I seemed to read a very lively apprehension, nay, as I drew nearer, I saw above the bushy, scowling brows the gleam of sweat; but on I came with loosened rein, heedless of the gentleman's threatening look and wondering at his very evident perturbation; and now I saw that he grasped something half-hidden in the fold of his coat that bulked remarkably like a pistol. But all at once, as he peered at me through the rolling smother of dust, his apprehensive expression vanished and, next moment, his head also, and as I drew level with the chaise, I saw him leaning back in one corner, the pistol upon his knees, and in the other corner the form of a woman wrapped in a pelisse and heavily veiled and who, judging by her posture, seemed asleep.

It was but a glimpse I caught of the interior and then I was by, had reached the summit of the hill and was galloping down the descent, but even so it seemed to me that the gentleman's face was vaguely familiar.

Mile upon mile I held on at this wild speed until Anthony and his sorrel had diminished to a faint, oncoming dust-cloud and Wildfire began to abate his ardour somewhat; as he breasted a long and steep ascent crowned by a hostelry, I, blinking at it through dust-whitened lashes, saw it bore a sign with the words: The Porto Bello Inn. Here I dismounted from my chastened steed, who, if a little blown, was no whit distressed, and forthwith led him to the stables myself, to see him rubbed down and cared for, the while a hissing ostler knocked, shook and brushed from my garments clouds of Kentish dust. In the midst of which performance up rode Anthony.

"Well—damme!" he exclaimed, as he swung to earth, "I said a milestone—"

"True, Anthony, but I felt inclined for a gallop—"

"I believe you!" he laughed. "And now I'm more than inclined for a pot, a tankard, a flagon, Perry—or say a dozen. Damme, I've been breathing nothing but circumambient Kent for the last half-hour—Ale, Perry, ale's the word! This way! And by that same token, here's your money. 'T is a glorious beast, your Wildfire, and curst well ridden, begad!"

"And I ride stones lighter than you do, Goliath!" said I, following him into the sanded parlour.

"I never drink a tankard of ale," gasped Anthony, setting down his vessel with a bang, "no, never, Perry, without remembering the first drink we had together—the ale you paid for! And the ham and eggs—oh, curse and confound it, I shall never taste anything so delicious again, of course. Everything is vastly changed since then, Peregrine—everything except yourself."

"I am two inches taller!" said I.

"Ah, to be sure! And, thanks to Jessamy Todd, a man of your hands. What's become of Jessamy these days—and your friend the Tinker?"

"I shame to say I don't know. I used to see them frequently up to a year ago, but since then, London and its follies have engulfed me."

"We'll devote ourselves to looking 'em up one o' these days!" said Anthony. "Meantime I'm devilish hungry and I always dine at 'The Bull' at Wrotham, so if you're quite ready, let's push on. By the way," he continued, as I followed him into the yard, "did you notice that chaise we passed just beyond Farningham—a black-bodied chaise, picked out in yellow, with red wheels?"

"I did, Anthony—why?"

"Fool of a fellow seemed infernally agitated, actually had a pistol ready for me, or so it seemed."

"I noticed his desperate attitude also,—and thought it very singular."

"Demmit, yes, and what's more singular, I recognised the fool fellow for the fellow I thrashed two years ago at the 'Jolly Waggoner'—Danby his name is."

"Ah, to be sure!" I exclaimed. "I knew his face was familiar. Did you see he had a lady with him?"

"No, what was she like?"

"I only caught the briefest glimpse—besides, she was heavily veiled and seemed to be asleep—"

"Asleep!" exclaimed Anthony fiercely. "Asleep! By God, Perry, I'm half-minded to wait until that damned chaise comes up and see for myself."

"I beg you will do no such thing!" said I, abhorring the idea of violence and possible bloodshed. "If you are hungry—so am I. Let us get on to Wrotham and dinner." So we mounted and in due time descended the steep hill into the pleasant village of Wrotham.

The "Bull" welcomed us, or more particularly Anthony, with cheeriness tempered with respect; such a bustling of ostlers, running to and fro of serving men; such a dimpling and curtseying of buxom, neat-capped maids; such beaming obeisances from mine host, all to welcome "Mr. Anthony": indeed such a reception as might have warmed the heart of any man save your embittered, cold-hearted cynic or one who rode with demons on his shoulders.

Though the fare was excellent my appetite was poor and I ate and drank but little, to Anthony's evident concern; and when at last we took the road again, I rode with a jibbering devil on either shoulder, filling me again with nameless fears and vague, unreasoning doubts of I knew not what. Above and around me seemed an ever-growing shadow, a foreboding expectancy of an oncoming evil I could neither define nor shake off, try how I would.

Anthony seemed to sense something of this and (like the good fellow he was) strove valiantly to banish my uncanny gloom, though my attention often wandered and I answered at random or not at all.

"Clothes go a damned long way with a woman, Perry!" he was saying. "I'm married and I know! That evening suit o' yours with the lavender-flowered waistcoat is bound to rivet her eye—nail her regard, d'ye see! Then there's your new riding suit, I mean the bottle-green frock with the gold-crested buttons. She must see you in that and there's few look better astride a horse than yourself—" here I became lost again in the vile gibbering of my demons until these words of Anthony's brought me back again:

"—dev'lish solitary place with an unsavoury reputation. The country folk say it's haunted."

"I beg your pardon, Tony, but what were you telling me?"

"My poor ass," said Anthony, edging nearer the better to peer into my face, "I have been endeavouring to give you a brief description of Raydon Manor—the house peeping amid the trees yonder."

We were climbing a hill and from this eminence could behold a fair sweep of landscape, a rolling, richly wooded countryside very pleasant to behold, and, following the direction pointed by Anthony's whip, I descried the gables of a great, grey house bowered in dense-growing trees that seemed to shut the building in on every side, the whole further enclosed by a lofty wall.

"Ah, a haunted house, Anthony," said I, glancing at the place with perfunctory interest.

"So the yokels say hereabouts, Perry, but if half what I hear is true, it is haunted by things far worse—more evil than ghosts."

"Meaning what?" I questioned.

"Well, it is owned by a person of the name of Trenchard who seems to be a rich mixture of gentlemanly ruffian, Turkish bashaw and the devil. Anyhow, the place has a demned unsavoury reputation and abuts on my land."

"Indeed!" said I, stifling a yawn. "And what manner of neighbour is he—to look at?"

"Don't know—never clapped eyes on the fellow—nobody ever sees him. Fellow rarely stirs abroad and when he does, always in closed carriage—muffled to the eyes—queer fish and demned unpleasant, by all accounts."

"Evidently!" said I, then uttered an exclamation as Wildfire tripped and off spun his near foreshoe.

"Curse and confound it!" exclaimed Anthony ruefully. "And no smith nearer than five miles!"

"That being so," quoth I, dismounting, "confound and curse it with all my heart."

"There's the 'Soaring Lark' not half a mile away—a small inn, kept by a friend of mine."

"And a ridiculous name for any inn!" said I.

"Wait till you see it, Perry."

So saying, Anthony turned aside down an unexpected and rutted by-lane, I leading my horse; and, rounding a sharp bend in this narrow track, we came upon a small inn. It stood well back amid the green and was further shaded by three great trees; and surely the prettiest, brightest, cosiest little inn that the eye of wearied traveller might behold. Its twinkling lattices open to the sunny air showed a vision of homely comfort within; its hospitable door gaped wide upon an inviting chamber floored with red tile, and before it stood a tall, youngish man in shirtsleeves with the brightest eyes, the cheeriest smile and the blackest whiskers I had ever seen.

"O Mary, lass!" he cried, "Mr. Anthony!" And then, as he hurried forward to take our horses: "Why, Lord, Mr. Anthony, sir, we du be tur'ble glad to see 'ee—eh, old lady?" This last to her who had hurried to his call—a youngish woman, as bright, as cosy, as cheery, but far prettier than the inn itself.

"Oh, but indeed we be j'yful to see 'ee, Mr. Anthony; us was talkin' o' you an' your bonny lady this very day. She do be well, sir, I 'ope, an' comin' home to the great house soon, Mr. Anthony?"

"Thank you, yes, Mary," answered Anthony, baring his head and giving her his hand, "we shall be coming home next week. And here, George and Mary, is my friend Mr. Vereker. His horse has cast a shoe, send it to Joe at Hadlow to be shod. Meanwhile we will drink a flagon of your October."

So while George led away my horse, his pretty wife brought us into the sanded parlour, where, having despatched a shock-headed boy with my horse, George presently joined us.

The ale duly drunk, Anthony proposed he should ride on to Nettlestead while Wildfire was being shod and return for me in an hour or so, to which I perforce agreeing, he rode away, leaving me to await him, nothing loath. For what with the spirit of Happiness that seemed to pervade this little inn of the "Soaring Lark" and the cheery good humour of its buxom host and hostess, my haunting demons fled awhile and in their place was restored peace. Sitting with George in this low-raftered kitchen while his pretty wife bustled comfortably to and fro, we talked and grew acquainted.

"By the way, George," said I, "Mr. Vere-Manville showed me a haunted house called, I think, Raydon Manor, do you know anything of it?"

Now at this innocent question, to my surprise George's good humour vanished, his comely features were suddenly overcast, and he exchanged meaning glances with his wife.

"Why, sir," he answered at last, speaking in a lowered voice as if fearful of being overheard, "there's some as do say 't is haunted sure-ly."

"How?" I demanded.

"Well—things 'as been seed, ah, an' heerd in that theer ghastly wood."

"What things?"

"Well—things as flits an' things as wails—ah, fit to break your 'eart an' chill a man's good flesh. Ghost-lights has been seed at dead o' night, an' folks has 'eer'd music at dead o' night an' screams o' devil-laughter, ah, an' screams as wasn't laughter. Old Gaffer Dick 'e du ha' seed things an' there's me, I've 'eer'd an' seed things—an' lots o' folk beside."

"What did you see, George?"

"I dunno rightly, sir, an' never shall this side o' glory, but 'twere a shape, a thing—I might call it a ghost an' I might call it a phanitum; hows'ever 't were a shape, sir, as I seed a-floatin' an' a-wailin'—Lord, I'll never forget 'ow it wailed!"

Here he mopped his brow at the mere recollection.

"But do you never see any one about by day?"

"Aye, sir, there be a great, sooty black man for one, a hugeous niggermoor with devil's eyes as roll an' teeth like a dog—there's 'im! An' there's three or four desp'rit-seemin' coves as looks like prize fighters—though they ain't often seed abroad an' then mostly drivin' be'ind fast 'orses, sir—coach, sir."

"And what of the owner of the place, Mr. Trenchard, I think his name is?"

"Very seldom stirs abroad, sir, an' then allus in a fast-travellin' closed carriage; though there's a-plenty o' company now an' then, 'ard-ridin' gentlemen—specially one as usually travels down from Lunnon in a chaise wi' red wheels—"

"What—a black-bodied chaise picked out in yellow?" I enquired sharply.

"Aye, sir, the same."

"And are there lady visitors as well as gentlemen?"

"Aye, there are so, sir—coveys of 'em, very fine feathers an' pretty as pictoors t' look at but—"

"Ah!" said I, as he paused, "that kind?"

"Aye, sir, if ye know what I mean."

"I do! Raydon Manor seems haunted in many ways."

"Aye, sir, an' this is very sure—if Innocence ever goes in, it never comes out!"

Thus we talked, George the landlord and I, while his pretty, buxom wife bustled quietly to and fro or vanished into the mysteries of her dairy, whence came the creak of churn, the chink of pot or pan and suchlike homely sounds where her two trim maids laughed and chattered over their labours.

It was a glorious afternoon and, at my suggestion, George brought me into a garden behind the inn where flowers rioted, filling the air with their mingled perfumes, and so to a well-stocked orchard beyond, whence came the warm odour of ripening fruit.

"You have a very beautiful home, George."

113

"An' all thanks to my little old woman, sir. I were a soldier once an' a tur'ble drinker, but Mary—Lord, sir, 'tis wonnerful how good a good woman can be an' how bad a bad 'un can be—though she's generally made bad, I've noticed! Damme, sir, axin' your parding but damme notwithstanding, there's some men as I'd like to 'ave wrigglin' on the end of a bagnet!" And he turned to scowl fiercely towards a stretch of dark woodland that gloomed beyond a rolling stretch of sunny meadow land.

"The sentiment is a little bloody, George," said I, glancing at this stretch of dark wood, "but under the circumstances, I think it does you credit. And now, seeing I have a full hour to wait for Mr. Vere-Manville, I will take a little stroll and waste no more of your time;" and smiling down his protestations to the contrary, I sauntered off through the golden afternoon.

To-morrow the term of my patient waiting was to be accomplished; Diana was coming back to me! At this thought there rushed over me such an eager, passionate joy that my breath caught and I paused to lean across a gate, endeavouring to picture her to myself as she now was, 'a changed Diana and yet the same', even as she had written. And as I stood thus, down to me through the sunny air came the song of a mounting lark who, as if knowing my thought, seemed striving to sing forth something of the ineffable happiness that thrilled me. The song ended, I went on again, walking slowly, my head bowed, lost in a happy dream. And presently I found myself walking amid trees, through an ever-deepening shadow, and, looking up, saw I had entered the pine wood. For a moment I hesitated, minded to turn back into the sunshine, then I went on, picking my way among these gloomy trees, the pine needles soft beneath my tread; thus, since there was no wind, I walked in silence broken only by the faint jingle of my spurs and the rustle of my advance, a silence that affected me with a vague unease. There seemed something stealthy in this uncanny stillness so that I grew stealthy also and set myself to keep my spurs from jingling, for unseen eyes seemed to be watching me. The deeper I penetrated this dismal wood, the darker it grew, and I advanced, cautious and silent, and with a vague sense of expectancy though of what I could not determine. With the glad sunshine my joyousness had vanished, in its stead came again doubt and foreboding with my devil that gibbered upon my heels; demons and evil things seemed all about me.

But suddenly I came out upon a narrow track or rather footpath and though the kindly sun contrived to send down a fugitive shaft ever and anon, yet my depression was in no wise abated and I began to hurry my steps, anxious to be out of these dismal shadows. All at once I halted, for before me was a lofty wall and I saw that the path led to a low-arched doorway or postern, a small door but of great apparent strength, that seemed to scowl upon me between its deep buttresses. And now as I gazed there grew within me an indefinable feeling, a growing certainty of something very threatening and sinister about this door, and turning, I hasted back along the path, turning neither to right nor left, hurrying as from something beyond expression evil. Nor did I stop or glance back until I was out in the pure sunshine and the cosy inn of the "Soaring Lark" seemed to smile at me beyond broad meadows, blinking its bright casements like so many bright eyes in cheery welcome. But even so I shivered, for the gloomy shadow of the wood seemed all about me still and therewith a growing depression that would not be banished but held me in thrall despite sunshine and cheery inn. What was it that I feared? I asked myself, and why— why—why?

I found Anthony awaiting me, but even his cheer presence failed to dispel my gloom. And so in a while, my horse being ready, we set out for London with hearty "God-speeds" from George and his wife Mary. But all the way back, my mind still laboured with these same perplexing questions:

What was it that I feared? And why—why—why?

And thereto I found no answer.

CHAPTER IV

OF A SCARABAEUS RING AND A GOSSAMER VEIL

"Ye're a little pale—yes, a trifle haggard, Perry, but there's nothing like a romantic pallor to attract the feminine regard and captivate the female heart, my boy—I'm married and I know! But your dress is a thought too sombre, I think, considering your youth, though I'll admit it suits you and there's a devilish tragic melancholy Danish-air about ye as should nail the female orb—"

"Don't be an ass, Anthony. How is my cravat?"

"Work of art, begad! How are my pantaloons, Perry? My tailor's made 'em too loose, the damned scoundrel. I'm wrinkled like a rhinoceros, by heaven! Keep your eye on 'em when I bend—"

"My dear Anthony," said I, "if they were any tighter you couldn't bend—"

"Well, my coat, Perry—how is it behind?"

"Admirable!"

"Feels like a sack, demmit! My Loveliness has the eye of a hawk, you'll understand—hasn't seen me for a whole month—nothing like first impressions, begad. Feels like an accursed sack, I tell you—"

"Gentlemen, the carriage awaits!" murmured Clegg from the doorway.

"What—already?" cried Anthony, clapping on his hat and reaching for his surtout.

"You forget we're Lord Wyvelstoke's privileged guests.—Come, Anthony!" and I led the way down to the carriage.

"Ain't you nervous, Perry?" enquired my friend, as we rolled smoothly away.

"No."

"Queer fish—I am!" said he, fidgeting with his cravat.

"You're deuced cool, devilish serene and enigmatical at times, like your uncle Jervas."

"You flatter me, Tony."

"Devil a bit—and this coat of mine feels like a—what the devil are we stopping for?"

We had reached the top of St. James's Street and glancing through the window, I saw our progress blocked momentarily by converging traffic; I was about to lean back in my seat again when my careless glance was arrested by an elegant closed chaise going in the opposite direction; the light was still good, and thus I saw this for a black-bodied chaise picked out in yellow with red wheels. The window was down and thence fluttered a lady's scarf or veil, a delicate gossamer thing spangled with gold stars; as I watched, from the dim interior of the chaise came a woman's white hand to gather up this glittering scarf, a shapely hand sparkling with gems, amongst which I saw one shaped like a scarabaeus; then the chaise rolled away and was gone.

"What the dooce are you staring at, Perry?"

"Nothing!" I answered, frowning. "Nothing!"

His lordship's house was ablaze with lights and, though we were so early, in the street immediately before it was a crowd that pushed and jostled as we mounted the carpeted steps and were ushered into the lofty hall. Here, the footmen having relieved us of our hats and coats, we found the sedate Atkinson as gravely imperturbable as I remembered him two years ago, who acknowledged my greeting with sedate smile and grave obeisance and brought us forthwith to a chamber where I found Lord Wyvelstoke in confabulation with my two uncles.

At our entrance they rose, and his lordship limped forward to welcome us; and looking upon his slender, elegant figure, beholding his impassive face with its air of serene and conscious power, I warmed to the kindness of his smile, even as I had done two years ago.

Our greetings over, his lordship slipped his arm in mine and led me apart.

"Well, Peregrine," said he, with his old, keen look, "I perceive your two years of self-sacrifice have not been in vain; you are grown in every sense. And to-night unselfishness shall have its full reward. To-night, Peregrine, I render back to you your Diana, but a Diana glorified—a woman, and one who has endeared herself to me by her great-hearted and noble qualities. In her is nothing paltry, education has not stunted or narrowed the soul of her. She has been faithful to her task for your sake and faithful to you for Love's sake. By your unselfishness she has indeed become all that we hoped—and more, one to be proud of. But I grow garrulous in her praise—go to her and see for yourself. She is awaiting you in her boudoir with Mrs. Vere-Manville."

So saying, his lordship rang and the silent Atkinson appeared, who led us up a wide stairway and so to a dainty chamber where, bowing, he left us.

A faint perfume was in the air, elusive but sweetly intimate. Upon an ottoman lay a fan and a pair of lace mittens.

"Begad," murmured Anthony, sniffing, "there's nothing like perfume to give a fellow palpitations, and palpitations always make my cravat too tight—devilish thing's choking me! A good woman, Perry, can be the most doocedly alluring, devilish engaging, utterly provoking creature in creation—far more so than—t' other sort. I'm married and I know!"

"Yes," said I, looking down at the discarded fan and deeply stirred by the elusive fragrance.

"Devil take this cravat!" exclaimed Anthony, wrestling with it before a mirror. "If they don't come soon, 't will be wreck, demmit! I wish to heaven they'd come."

"So do I, Anthony!"

"Finishing touches, I expect, Perry—they will do it! And mean to surprise us, of course." But as moment after moment elapsed, his impatience grew. "I wonder what's keeping 'em!" he exclaimed.

"I wonder!" said I.

At the end of ten minutes he was striding up and down the room in a very ferment.

"Damned strange!" he muttered. "Devilish incomprehensible! They must know we're here. Been waiting fifteen minutes now, begad! Getting beyond a joke—deuced exasperating, Perry, y' know. Dammit, man, why can't you say something, do something, instead of sitting there so devilish calm and serene, staring before you like an infernal sphinx?"

At the end of twenty minutes Anthony could wait no more and bidding me follow, jerked open the door and strode out. But I sat there staring before me at an empty fireplace and still all my thought was of the chaise with the red wheels.

But presently my gaze came by chance upon something that lay in a corner of the hearth, a piece of paper crumpled and rent as in passionate haste. For a while I viewed it idly, heedlessly, then all at once I saw a name, a scrawling signature plain to read; next moment the fragment of paper was in my grasp and I read this:

… confess to find you more bewitchingly beautiful than ever. And
therefore, having regard to what transpired between us in Italy, you
will come this evening without fail to
    Your ever adoring slave and master,
    HAREDALE.

How long I remained staring at this fragment of paper I do not know, but I started suddenly to see Atkinson bowing in the doorway and followed him from the room and downstairs and suddenly found myself in a polite tumult; silks rustled, feathers nodded, turbans bowed and jewels glittered.

But almost at once, amid all this throng, my eyes saw but one. Tall she was, with jewels that sparkled in her dark and lustrous hair; how she was gowned I cannot remember, but her white throat was unadorned save for a small gold chain whence hung a plain gold locket, at sight of which my heart seemed to swell within me.

Flushed and bright-eyed, she stood beside Lord Wyvelstoke to receive the many guests. And viewing her as I stood thus, myself unseen amid the crowd, beholding her serene and noble carriage, her vivid colouring, the classic mould of form and features, the grace and ease of her every movement, I saw she was indeed more beautiful than I dreamed and caught my breath in a very ecstasy. Here was Diana herself, yet a Diana glorified even as Lord Wyvelstoke had said, and with a thousand elusive graces beyond my poor description.

And now I was bowing before her, heard her tremulous murmur of "Peregrine!" and answered back as tremulously, "Diana!" and so, yielding place to others, I passed on, to bow and smile and chatter inanities with such of the guests as were of my acquaintance, but yearning for chance of speech with her alone.

Then, somehow, she was beside me, her hand upon my arm, and we were walking, though whither I cared not, my every sense thrilled by her gracious ease, her stately beauty and all the wonder of her.

I remember we sat and talked of the past two years, of much that she had seen and done; and she questioned me a little breathlessly and always of myself, and I, conscious of the many bewildering changes in her and of those deep, grey eyes looking at me beneath their level brows, or hidden by their down-sweeping black lashes, answered briefly or very much at random, so that she questioned me at last:

"Peregrine, are you listening?"

"Yes—no!" I answered. "How can I? You are so—wonderful!"

At this the rich colour deepened in her cheek and her eyes grew ineffably tender.

"And you," she murmured, "you are still my Peregrine of the Silent Places, the gentleman who stooped to teach me that love could be—a holy thing—"

From the distance stole the sound of music and suddenly, as if conjured up of these sweet strains, were eager gentlemen all about us, vying with each other for the honour of escorting her down to the ballroom.

"Miss Lovel," simpered a gallant young exquisite, his fashionably pallid features peeping out between the silkiest of glossy whiskers, "we are to be favahed, I think, to be charmed and delighted by your incomparable singing—aw, how do, Vereker! Miss Lovel, you behold me a humble ambassador, to beg, to entreat you to keep us waiting no longer—"

"The evening is young, my lord," she answered lightly, "though your impatience is flattering, I vow—"

"Impatience, Miss Lovel?" sighed a gorgeous being in scarlet and epaulettes. "Impatience—haw—is quite inadequate to express our—hum—I should say, my own sentiments; 'impatience' is a word too—ha—altogether too feeble! For my own part I should—haw—I should rather say we—"

"Passion, ma'm, passion!" exclaimed a square-faced gentleman in naval blue. "Speaking as a blunt sailor, passion's the word, Miss Lovel—passion. Passion's the only word, I think, gentlemen?"

"Indubitably!"

"Positively!"

"Per-fectly!"

Hereupon the Army retired a little discomfited but rallied sufficiently to suggest the word "languish."

"Behold us then, Miss Lovel, passioning—" said the Navy.

"And—haw—languishing, Miss Lovel—" sighed the Army.

"Behold us then unanimously beseeching you—aha, here comes Pevensey to add his supplication to ours."

The Duke shot his ruffle, fixed his eyeglass and bowed.

"Permit me, Miss Lovel, to add my petition! Vereker will spare you to us awhile, I am sure!" said he. "To behold a goddess is to be blessed; to hear her sing will be—"

"Joy!" suggested the Navy.

"Divine!" sighed the Army.

"Transcendent rapture!" quoth the Duke.

Diana laughed and rose, looking from one to other with that serene and level gaze I knew so well, and saluted them with a slow and graceful curtsey.

"Indeed you overwhelm me, sirs," said she, smiling. "Your impatience shall be satisfied, you shall passion and languish no longer!" And now as I bowed above her hand came her whisper, "I go to sing for you—to you, Peregrine!"

Then, giving her fan to Navy and her gloves to Army, she took the Duke's arm, and moved away.

And in a while, sitting in a corner of the great ballroom between my two uncles, I saw her stand before this august assemblage serene in her proud, young beauty; saw her calm gaze seek until it met mine and drew my breath a little quicker because of her very loveliness.

Then I felt the smart of sudden tears as from the orchestra whispered a loved and familiar melody that rose, little by little, into that wild and plaintive Zingari air she had sung so often in the Silent Places years ago.

And now from her white throat stole a murmur of sweet sound, swelling gradually to a full, round sweetness, rising to a passion of sorrow and heartbreak, and dying to a sigh, was gone.

For a long moment after the final liquid note had died away was utter stillness, an awed silence; then some one ventured to clap, others joined in, and upon this sound came shouts, cries, cheer on cheer—a frantic ovation.

"By Gad, Perry," exclaimed my uncle George, blinking moist lashes. "She—she can sing, ye know! What I mean is she can—sing, b'gad! What d' you say, Jervas?"

"That you are exactly right, George, she can sing!" answered my uncle Jervas softly. "She and her voice are one in beauty. And she signals you, Perry, I think!"

"Be off, Peregrine!" said my uncle George. "Be off, lucky dog—London will run mad—she'll be the reigning toast to-morrow."

The Army and the Navy yielded her to me with a somewhat bad grace, and her slim fingers on my arm guided me through the throng to a deep curtained window recess, and in this comparative seclusion she turned and faced me, and I saw that she was trembling a little.

"Peregrine," she murmured, wistful and eager, "am I changed very much—too much? I have worked—so hard and all—all for you—O Peregrine—dear—do I truly please you?"

"Please me!" I mumbled. "Oh, my Diana—!" Her lashes drooped and then, as she swayed to me, I clasped her in my arms and, tremulous, fragrant, vital with love and youth, she gave her lips to mine.

"Is it worth the years of waiting?" she whispered beneath my kisses.

"God knows it!" I answered and lifted her hand to my lips and then stood utterly still, cold with a sudden, horrible sickness—staring at this white hand, where, amid sparkling gems, I saw the dull oval of a scarabaeus ring.

"What is it, Peregrine?" she questioned, a little breathlessly. "This scarab? It is one my dear pal bought me in Egypt. Come away, dear, let us run from the crowd—let us steal away together, somewhere—anywhere—you and I." And speaking, she drew about her shoulders a scarf, a filmy thing of gossamer, spangled with gold stars. "Quick, Peregrine!" she breathed. "There is the duke—coming this way, quick—before he spies us!"

"Impossible!" I answered, wondering to hear myself speaking so lightly. "His Grace has seen us already—besides, your duty lies here to-night."

"Very well, dear Peregrine," she sighed, "but I had hoped you—you would have bade me forget duty—a little while."

So she turned away and indistinctly I heard the duke begging her to sing again; then I watched her go, smiling and bowing to her, but with a buzzing in my brain and all hell raging in my breast.

A black-bodied chaise—picked out in yellow—red wheels—Captain Danby!

For a long time I stood in the shadow of the window curtains staring out upon a moon hidden ever and anon in flying cloud-wrack; but at last I turned and wandered away with some vague idea of finding Anthony, and as I went, the lights and glitter, the sounds of voices and laughter grew ever more distasteful, and turning my back on it all, I found my way into a wide corridor. And here, in a shady alcove screened by curtains, I espied Anthony kissing his wife; her round, white arms were about his neck, crushing his cravat woefully, but seeing the rapture in their faces I stole away and left them.

Reaching the hall I bade a footman summon my carriage, but on second thoughts countermanded the order and, donning hat and cloak, set out to walk home to my chambers. A wind was abroad and I walked bareheaded to cool the fevered throbbing of my temples, but this wind found voices to mock me and at my heels ran demons, gibbering obscenities.

Reaching my door at last, I thundered on the knocker until it opened, and brushing past the pallid Clegg, bade him order my horse.

"Horse, sir?" he repeated, a note of interest in his usually toneless voice. "Do you propose to go riding, sir?"

"I do!"

"Yes, sir—which horse do you—?"

"Wildfire. Have him brought round at once!"

"Very good, sir!"

Not waiting for Clegg's assistance, I slipped off my evening garments and was pulling on my riding boots when I heard the tattoo of Wildfire's impatient hoofs upon the roadway.

"What time may I expect you back, sir?" enquired Clegg, as I jingled downstairs.

"I cannot say. I may be late or very early so—get to bed."

"If you are travelling far, sir, might I suggest that your pistols are ready in their holsters upstairs—"

"I shall not need them!" said I, and stepped out into the street where Wildfire danced and capered in the grasp of Tom, my groom.

"He do be werry fresh, sir," warned Tom.

"So much the better!" said I. "Hold him until I give the word."

So saying, I swung to saddle, settled feet in stirrups and gripped the reins short in gloved hand.

"An evil night, sir!" said Clegg. "And you won't take your pistols?"

"No! Let go, Tom!"

Back sprang the groom and, snorting joyfully, Wildfire sprang away.

CHAPTER V

STORM AND TEMPEST

A blusterous wind that fluttered the skirts of my long, caped coat, that filled the night with stir and tumult and flaws of sudden rain; a wind that whirled black masses of ragged cloud across a lowering heaven lit by a pallid moon that peeped stealthily and vanished, to peep again.

And glancing from desolate, wind-swept streets to flying cloud-wrack, I judged there was worse to come and knew a strange, unnatural joy therefore, as I bent my head to buffeting wind and reined the fiery animal I bestrode to less furious pace.

117

We crossed the river at London Bridge, a dark horror of moving waters swirling here and there in the ineffectual beam of lamp or lanthorn; on past gloomy streets and narrow courts where dim forms jostled, and ever and always the blusterous wind rioting 'twixt heaven and earth, booming in chimneys, moaning in dark corners, rattling windows, clapping-to crazy shutters and setting signboards a-swing on scolding hinges.

On and on through this ever-growing turbulence, while Wildfire tossed proud head, snorted defiance upon the elements, and bored eagerly upon the bit. But once the great city was behind us, I gave him his will and away we went headlong into the wind, the clatter of his galloping hoofs drowned in the universal uproar. But fast as he sped, the demon of doubt and suspicion and growing dread kept pace, and for once, riding Wildfire, I forgot Wildfire and all else save the hell within me.

A black-bodied chaise picked out in yellow!

And now came the rain to lash me and I bared my head the better to feel it. Before me in the swirling dark were twinkling lights lurching rapidly nearer, and down upon me loomed a stagecoach, a mountainous shape that flitted by me like a phantom. A phantom? The very night seemed peopled by phantoms; I sped past phantom wains and waggons, piled high with phantom loads, that moved with no sound of hoofs or wheels; spectral horsemen flitted by, soundless; in the shadow of hissing hedgerow and raving, wind-tossed trees crawled miserable, nebulous shapes, seen but to be lost again, swallowed in the howling murk.

Rushing wind and lashing rain; pale gleams of a fitful moon to show swaying trees that tossed wild arms to heaven, and a splashing quag below, mud and wind-swept pools, all lost again in the swirling dark. And buffeted thus, beaten by rain, smitten by unseen things, gasping in the wind's fierce gusts, my one thought was:

A black-bodied chaise with red wheels—Captain Danby!

How long I galloped at this wild and reckless pace I do not know, but little by little I became aware that the rain had ceased, the clouds were rent asunder and the moon looked down, pale and remote, upon a desolate countryside very ghostly and unreal and wholly unfamiliar. Before me was a winding road fringed with dripping, sombre trees and reining Wildfire to a standstill, I found that the wind had greatly abated its fury. But though the storm was over, the storm within me raged fierce as ever; therefore, heedless of where the morning found me, I spurred Wildfire forward and rode with slackened rein, leaving him to take me where he would.

A black-bodied chaise—What should bring Diana in company with such brutal satyr as Captain Danby?

Lost thus in agonising thought, I was riding with loosened rein and lax grip when Wildfire shied, swerved violently, throwing me from the saddle, and lying half-stunned, I heard him gallop away down the road.

For a while I lay there with no desire to move, but at last, summoning all my resolution, I scrambled weakly to my feet and endeavoured to follow, but after some while, wondered to see it so dark and found I was among trees that closed about me ever denser. Yet I struggled on, pushing my way haphazard through the undergrowth, being yet much shaken by my fall, until I came out into a narrow way lit by the moon; but scarcely was I here than I paused to lean against a tree, overcome by a sick faintness. And thus leaned I some while to recover my strength, and in my ears the dismal drip, drip of sodden trees and the mournful sighing of the wind in their branches, a sigh that rose every now and then to a low wailing, very dreadful to hear.

Now, all at once, I lifted my aching head, for, as my brain cleared, I knew that this wailing was not of the wind; thus I stood with breath in check waiting for it to come again. And suddenly I heard it, a low, murmurous cry, unutterably doleful.

"O God—O God—I want to be dead—I want to be dead!"

So I turned aside and, following the path, saw it ended at a frowning doorway set within a high and sinister wall; and recognising this door, this high wall and gloomy wood, I felt myself cold with that indefinable sense of impending evil which this desolate place had awoke in me before—

"O kind God—if I could only die!"

Going in among the trees I saw a shape of misery outstretched face-down upon the sodden earth, a shape that wrung pale hands and writhed in awful manner. Trembling, I sank on one knee beside her.

"Woman!" said I, laying hand lightly on her shoulder.

"Child!"

She raised a haggard face, its youthful beauty distorted by horror, its pallid cheeks stained with mire, and I blenched before the look in these wide eyes.

"Don't touch me!" she whispered hoarsely. "Don't look at me—I can't abide it—go away—let me die—"

"Child, where is your home?"

"None!" she whispered. "None! I durs'n't go back ... now. Oh, never no more ... they made me drunk ... when I woke ... ah, don't look at me ... I wish the sun 'ud go out for ever ... If I could only die!... I fought them as long as I could.... Oh, kill me, God.... I want to be dead ... but I want Tom first ... my Tom ... I want him to know 't weren't ... my fault. O Tom dear, Tom as I loved ... how can I tell 'ee. O God, I want to be dead!"

"Come, child," said I gently. "Come with me, you shall be safe, sheltered for to-night, and in the morning Tom shall be found for you—"

"Ah, no, no!" she panted, shrinking from my touch. "You're a man too—let me die!"

"Poor girl, poor child," said I, "there is an inn near by and a good woman to comfort you, come, you shall be safe, I swear, and find your Tom—"

Despite her feeble struggles, I got her afoot and half-led, half-carried her along that tortuous path and so at last out of that evil wood. Afar, across the meadows, I spied the chimneys of the "Soaring Lark" and, though dawn was not broken, to my joyful wonder saw its hospitable windows aglow and the beam of a moving light in the yard.

How we accomplished the distance I do not know, but we reached the inn at last and beheld a lanthorn borne by a stalwart form.

118

"Who's yon?" demanded a gruff voice.

"George," I panted, "if that's you—bear a hand with this poor girl—quick, she's swooning—"

"Why, Mr. Vereker!" exclaimed George's astonished voice, and next moment the fainting girl was caught up in powerful arms and borne into the inn kitchen, I staggering after.

"Mary—Moll—O Mary, old woman!"

A patter of quick feet upon the stair and George's Mary came running, seeming as bonny and buxom as ever, despite her scant *deshabille*, as she bent above the swooning girl.

"Poor maid—out i' the storm an' clemmed wi' cold an' 'unger, poor lass! Bring her upstairs—our warm bed, Jarge—an' then brandy, lad, an' the kettle on th' fire—up wi' you!"

Left alone, I filled the kettle from a bucket in a corner, and setting it upon the fire, drew up a chair and sat to dry my clothes and warm my shivering limbs, and presently, what with my weariness and the fire's comfort, began to nod. Opening unwilling eyes, I found George beside me, holding a steaming glass to my lips, and now felt myself deathly cold and shivering in every limb.

"Drink it, sir—hot rum an' a slice o' lemon—nought like it—drink it. Lord, Mr. Vereker, sir—'ere be a go sure-ly!" he exclaimed, smiling and nodding, as I sipped the fragrant beverage. "Awhile agone comes an 'orse into the yard, a-stampin' and a-neighin', so up I jumps and looks out o' winder. 'Lord, old woman,' I sez, 'yonder's Mr. Vereker's Wildfire,' I sez, 'I'd know 'im anywheers,' I sez; 'but what beats me,' I sez, 'there ain't Mr. Vereker.' So down I comes, rubs down the 'oss, takes the lanthorn an' is about to start lookin' for you when in you comes an' wi' you this poor lass—so wot I says now is, Lord, Mr. Vereker, sir, 'ere 's a go, sure-ly!"

"It is!" said I. "What of the girl, poor soul?"

"All right, Mr. Vereker, sir—she'm wi' my old woman, y' see, consequently she'll be right as ninepence in the morning, bless your 'eart, sir."

"I doubt it, George. You see, I found her—in the pine wood yonder, close beside that damnable gate in the wall."

"Did ye so, sir, did ye so?" said he in altered voice. Then, clenching his brawny fists, he raised frowning eyes to a bayonet above the mantel, a long, deadly-looking thing that glittered with constant cleaning. "Ah, by God!" he growled fiercely, "by God, Mr. Vereker, sir—there's them as I'd like t' have wrigglin' their beastly lives out on the end o' my old bagnet—"

"Hot water, Jarge!" commanded the buxom Mary from the stairs.

"Comin', old woman—comin'! Get a nap, Mr. Vereker, sir; your wet clo'es won't hurt 'ee now—I've slep' in wetter many a time in the Peninsula—nothin' like rum took 'ot an' plenty on 't sir. Comin,' old woman—comin'!" and whisking the heavy kettle from the fire, he nodded and hurried up the stair.

CHAPTER VI

I AM HAUNTED OF EVIL DREAMS

Either George was of different fibre to me, or the rum had been neither hot enough nor sufficiently strong, for on awaking I found myself full of pain, the least movement an agony, my head throbbing woefully and I burning with fever.

George looked at me and, shaking his head, hurried for his wife, who, having taken my pulse and felt my brow, clucked over me like a distressed and motherly hen and ordered me immediately to bed, whither, after some argument and faint reluctance on my part, I was promptly conducted by the indefatigable George, and where, having been duly physicked by his Mary, I sank to a restless slumber. And now ensued a dim period of troubled dreams and horrible nightmares.

I awoke to find my chamber full of the glow of evening; through the open lattice breathed an air sweet with a perfume of flowers; borne to my drowsy hearing stole a mingling of soothing, homely sounds, the snort of a horse from the stable, the clucking of hens, the faint rattle of a pail, to all of which peaceful sounds I hearkened in lazy content and with no desire to move. Vaguely, at the back of my mind, was a memory of some trouble now forgotten, nor did I seek to remember, content to stare out upon this summer evening; nor did I trouble to move even at the opening of the door and thus presently was aware of Anthony bending over me.

"Why, Perry, are you awake at last? How are you, old fellow?"

"Very well, Anthony," I answered, vaguely surprised to hear my voice so far off, as it were. "Very comfortable, Tony, only—a little weary—"

"And no wonder, Perry, here you've lain raving all last night and most of to-day."

"Raving, Tony?"

"Aye—all about some damned postchaise or other with red wheels."

"Postchaise?" said I, wondering. "Postchaise? How long have I lain here?"

"This will be the fourth day, Peregrine."

"Four days!" said I. "Impossible!"

"I rode down yesterday on the off-chance of finding you here—and here you were, begad, raging in fever and cursing and swearing very creditably, 'pon my soul! And all George could do to hold you down—"

"I'm better now, Anthony—get up to-morrow—"

"For which God be thanked!" said he fervently, and seating himself upon the bed, he grasped my hand. "Peregrine," said he solemnly, "you have honoured me with your friendship and as your friend I make bold to offer you a friend's advice,—in heaven's name, old fellow, be more discreet!"

"In what particular, Anthony?"

"There is but one, Perry—only one, dear fellow, and spelt with five letters—woman."

"You grow cryptic, Anthony."

"My dear Perry," said he, beginning to fidget with his stock, "my very dear fellow, as may be supposed, your extraordinary sudden and perfectly inexplicable flight from Wyvelstoke's reception and disappearance has caused no small consternation, and, to one person in particular, very much grief and anxiety. Under these distressing circumstances, I, as your friend, sought an answer to the riddle, the—the reason for your—very mysterious disappearance, and naturally arrive at the conclusion that it is a case of—er—*cherchez la femme*, Perry—"

"The devil you did!" exclaimed I.

"I haunted all the clubs, Perry, and with your uncles made discreet enquiry for you in every likely and unlikely quarter—yesterday, as a last possibility, I rode down here and learned from George how you came staggering in at dawn, plastered with mud, wet to the skin and accompanied by the lady who, I may inform you, had the good judgment to disappear as soon as possible—"

"The lady," said I, trembling and indignant, "was a poor distracted creature I found on my way—"

"Precisely, dear fellow! So here am I to lend you such assistance in the matter as a friend may. No reason to worry yourself, only in heaven's name be a little discreet, Perry—discretion's the word,"

"Discretion be damned!"

"Precisely, old fellow! And now only mention how I may assist you in this unfortunate situation?"

"By listening to me!"

"Ears wide open, Perry."

So I told him briefly of the storm, how, dazed and shaken after being thrown by Wildfire, I wandered into the wood and came upon the poor, distracted girl and brought her back with me to the "Soaring Lark." To all of which he listened, tap-tapping softly with his foot.

"Ha—outside that accursed house!" he exclaimed, when I had done. "The place should be burned down!" And then in a different tone, glancing at me somewhat askance, "But then, Perry—egad—don't ye see this does not explain your abrupt departure from the reception and flight from London—now does it?"

"Not in the least, Anthony. Nor can I offer any explanation."

Here Anthony pursed his lips to a soundless whistle and began his soft tap-tapping again.

"Diana was—deeply hurt," said he at last. "Every hour she is grieving for you—breaking her heart, Perry—as we sit here."

"For God's sake, Anthony," I cried passionately, "keep your feet still!"

"Eh? Oh, begad, forgive me, Perry! Consequently, she will be overjoyed to learn you are here safe. She will post down to you as fast as horses can bring her—"

"Need she know, Anthony?" At this he turned with a kind of leap and glanced at me with a startled expression.

"Lord, man—you are really ill!" he exclaimed.

"Ill or no, Anthony, if you are truly my friend and value my friendship, promise me—swear to me she shall not come near me!"

"Egad, Peregrine, you are damned ill!"

"Promise—promise! Swear me this, Anthony!" cried I, starting up in bed to grasp at him with eager hands. And then came Mary, running, to clasp me in eager arms and lay me back among the pillows.

"Mr. Anthony!" she cried. "Oh, Mr. Anthony, didn't I warn 'ee not to excite 'im then—oh, Mr. Anthony!"

Lying thus helpless, I felt myself shaken as by an ague fit, saw Anthony staring down at me fearful-eyed ere he crept from the room, felt an arm beneath my head, a cup at my lips and, drinking thirstily, lay awhile staring up at the ceiling, where red wheels seemed to spin through the mist of a gossamer veil spangled with gold stars.

It lay curling across my pillow close to my eyes, stirring gently as if endowed with life, a delicate, shimmering filament, never quite at rest, that glowed where the light caught it, and I watched it drowsily until, hearing a stealthy sound, I glanced up to behold my uncle George standing beside the bed.

"Why, Peregrine," said he softly, his handsome face unwontedly grave, "how are you, dear lad?"

"Thank you—I am greatly better and here is a hair on the pillow, Uncle George! This is neither your hair nor mine, and Mrs. Mary's is brown, as I remember. So whose hair is this, Uncle George?"

"Hair?" he repeated, fumbling with his whisker. "I don't see any hair, Perry."

"Here on my pillow, Uncle."

"Well, what of it, lad. Your Aunt Julia's, perhaps—"

"Hers is black. And this is—not black, you'll notice, sir, and—very long."

"Why, so 't is! But if it distresses you—there, away with it!"

"But whose is it?" I persisted.

"Lord, Perry, how should I know—why worry about such a trifle. Compose yourself, dear lad. I'll have 'em wake Julia, she was up with you all night—egad, she'll be overjoyed to see you so much better—"

"Pray no—don't disturb her. Have I been here long?"

"Nine days, Peregrine—touch and go—knocking at death's door, boy—and raving like any madman."

120

"What—what about, sir?" I questioned, beginning to tremble.

"A lot o' wild nonsense, Perry—"

"What, sir—what?" I demanded.

"There, there, lad—don't distress yourself. 'T was nothing to signify—mere sick fancies."

"Fancies concerning what, Uncle George?"

"Well, something about red wheels and a drowned woman in a wood, a wall, and a door, and suchlike idle stuff. Y' see, Perry, not content with getting yourself wet through, you must let that brute of a horse o' yours throw you on to your head; doctors say 't is a marvel you're alive, and begad, Perry lad, 'tis our firm belief, Jervas and mine, that you'd ha' died if it hadn't been for your wonderful aunt and Diana— watched over you like the angels they are—saved your life betwixt 'em—"

The room seemed to go suddenly black and from the awful darkness my uncle babbled cheerily, while I, smitten by a nauseous faintness, strove to speak yet could not.

"Uncle George," said I at last, "is—is she here—now?"

"Who, Diana? No, lad. But be patient, she's only out riding with Barbara—was with you here all day, she'll be back soon—be patient, she's never long away from you these days, b'gad—"

"No!" cried I, shuddering, "no! Don't let her come near me—don't let her touch me—send her away or I shall die!"

"Good God!" ejaculated my uncle George, glancing about helplessly.
"He's off again—this cursed fever—must call Julia."

"Don't!" said I, reaching out a feeble hand in supplication. "This is—not fever, sir. This is my conscious self imploring you to keep her away from me, or I shall truly die—or run mad—"

"O Peregrine—O Peregrine," he stammered, in choking voice, "this can't be you—to say such things—so cruel—this is your old delirium—you are raving again—you must be—"

"Before God, sir, speaking in all sanity, I beg and implore that you will—keep her from me."

"Oh, damnation—this is awful!" exclaimed my uncle, his handsome face looking strangely haggard. "Day and night in your delirium you have lain cursing Diana and with Diana's hand upon your brow and Diana's tears wetting your pillow—and now—O Peregrine, lad, tell me you don't mean it—that you are a little fevered, yes—yes, people at such times often turn against those they most love—will kill Diana else—"

"Or she me, sir—so keep her away—don't let her touch me—I'll not see her, I say—I'll not, by God—I'll not—"

"Hush—hush! Don't scream, lad, don't scream!"

He was on his knees, had clasped my trembling weakness in his great arms and was soothing me, and I weeping for my very impotence, when the door opened and Aunt Julia appeared.

"Dear Heaven!" she cried, bending above me. "What have you done,
George? What have you done to him?"

"O Aunt!" I cried. "Dear Aunt Julia, don't let her touch me again—don't let her come near me or I shall go mad—"

"No, no, my loved Perry, no one shall tend you but myself—there, dear boy, be comforted! O George, don't stand gaping—give me the draught yonder—quick!"

"Promise me, Aunt—swear she shall not approach me again!"

"I swear it, dear Peregrine. Come, drink—"

CHAPTER VII

CONCERNING THE SONG OF A BLACKBIRD AT EVENING

My uncle Jervas helped me carefully to the armchair by the open lattice and thereafter stood looking down at me with a certain bleak austerity of gaze.

"And you still refuse to hold any communication with her, Peregrine?"

"I do, sir."

"Or to afford her the least explanation, notwithstanding her devouring grief and distress?"

"Sir—I cannot," I answered, and shivered slightly.

"Do you feel the air too much, Peregrine?"

"Thank you, no, sir. But the topic naturally distresses me!"

"Strange," said my uncle Jervas musingly, "very strange that I should be pleading your gipsy's suit and find you so coldly, mercilessly determined to make that pleading vain! You are as stubborn as a Vereker and I think a trifle more merciless. Doubtless the reasons for your so sudden change are sufficient unto yourself, but to your friends they are profoundly incomprehensible, nor would I seek to probe the mystery; you are your own master and judge, and Diana is rich, has London at her feet, and may wed whomsoever she will, and small wonder! Indeed, with one exception, she is the most bewilderingly attractive and altogether beautiful woman I have ever had the happiness to know. So here's an end of the matter, once and for all. It is a painful topic, as you say; let us talk of other things—yourself, for instance. You will be up and about again soon, what do you propose to do with yourself, Peregrine? Now there is your friend Vere-Manville playing the devil about town—has not been entirely sober for a fortnight, I hear—I saw him myself, twice, very blatantly drunk—"

"Indeed, sir, uncle George mentioned something of this yesterday, though such conduct in Anthony is quite incomprehensible."

"Not content with this, the young fool is gambling desperately, haunts all the noted hells—I heard he dropped over a thousand recently in a few hours; his recklessness is becoming a byword."

"Good heavens, Uncle! Is he mad?"

"That you may ask him personally. I understand he intends honouring you with a visit this afternoon. He should be here shortly, unless he happens to be drunk. You are his friend, Peregrine; talk to him as such, endeavour to stem the tide of his folly, if only for his young wife's sake. Curb his madness if you can, it should be an occupation for your leisure not without interest."

Thus we conversed at large and upon many topics but spoke no further regarding her of whom we both were thinking; and thus, I believe, we were both of us a little relieved to hear a distant "view hallo."

"There rides your friend Vere-Manville, I think, Peregrine, and evidently a trifle hilarious!"

A trampling of hoofs in the paved yard below, and glancing from the window I espied Anthony sure enough, who, leaping from the saddle, reeled violently and clutched at the stalwart George to save himself.

"Aha!" he exclaimed, "seems something's matter wi' old mother earth, George—heaving damnably—up and down, George—unless it's my legs. Where's door, George? Aye, there 'tis. Seems dooced small—unless it's my eyes, George—ha ha!" So he blundered in and heavily up the stair, and after knocking thunderously, entered. At sight of my uncle Jervas, he halted, drew himself very erect and bowed profoundly and with a flourish, and when he spoke his speech was so thick that I dreaded lest he hiccough:

"Your servant, S' Jervas! Hope I see y' well, sir?"

My uncle's bow was extremely stately and distant.

"Peregrine," said he, "seeing you have—enlivening company, I will take occasion to go and meet your aunt Julia. Mr. Vere-Manville, I would venture to impress upon you that my nephew is still very much of an invalid." So saying, my uncle saluted us in turn with his grandest air and went out, closing the door behind him.

"Thinks I'm drunk, does he!" exclaimed Anthony, scowling after him. "Well, what the devil—so I am, damned d-drunk and so much the better—"

"So much the worse, Anthony!"

"Tush, you talk like a fool, Perry; better be drunk and forget than be sober and a s-suicide—felo—felo-de-se, buried at cross road—stake through your inside—devilish unpleasant business—"

"You talk like a madman, Anthony."

"And you like a f-fool, Perry! Here's you come back t' life like a fool, instead o' dying comfortably and respectably like—wise man. Here's you hoping and yearning to marry and that's the damndest folly of all. Much better be comfortably dead—"

"For shame, Anthony—for shame!" cried I angrily. "If you have so lost respect for yourself—at least think of and respect your wife—"

"Wife!" he exclaimed. "My wife!" and springing up out of the chair I saw him tower above me, clenched hands upflung, his comely features distorted and horribly suffused; then he lurched to the window and leaned, choking, from the lattice. Suddenly his bowed shoulders began to heave, and I heard him laugh in dreadful manner and when he turned his look was demoniac.

"Egad, but you will have your joke, eh, Perry, and devilish funny—aye, devilish! My wife, says you—ha! ha! says I. You're drunk, says you—I am, says I—so I can laugh, d'ye see—"

"Anthony!" I cried, rising from my chair. "O Anthony, here's more than drink—dear fellow, in God's name, what is it?" And I grasped at him with weak but insistent hands.

For a moment he made as if to throw me off, then his long arm was about me, his head bowed upon my shoulder, and when he spoke his voice had lost its wild, mad ring.

"D'ye think I like getting drunk, Perry? But there are worse things—madness and murder. A bullet would be quick, but I still have hope—sometimes—and death by drink is a slow business, so I've chosen death by drink—"

"Why, Tony? What is the trouble? Is it—Barbara—your Loveliness?"

"She has never been the same since she came back from abroad, Perry. Some secret trouble—all these weeks it has been getting worse—she has sometimes seemed afraid of me—of me, Perry! At last I taxed her with it—begged she'd confide in me. She told me there was nothing, laughed it off and I believed it, like a fool—but that night, Perry—that night, as she slept—and looking pure and holy as one of God's angels, she—cried on a name—a man's name. I woke her—questioned her, begged, implored, commanded—and still she laughed, but always with the fear in her eyes. And I know she lied! Then I took to watching her and she me—and so it went on until—there were times when I could have struck her—choked the truth out of her—O Perry! So I left her—went to London. Oh damnation, d'ye wonder I drink? Better drink myself to the devil than harm her—though drink will take a long time to kill me, I'm afraid—"

"Drink never shall, Tony! There, sit down, old fellow, calm yourself, for by heaven I think you are making much out of little—"

"Why did she lie to me?"

"Are you sure she did?"

"Certain!"

"What do you propose to do?"

"Go back to London."

"Then I will accompany you."

"Impossible; you're weak as a confounded rabbit!"

"I'm stronger than I look; I've walked regularly in the garden these last three days. However, if you go to London, I go too."

"Well, and if so—what could you do?"

"Remind you that a gentleman must endure unflinchingly and suffer with unshaken fortitude."

"Ha, would you preach at me?"

"Day and night, if necessary."

"Would you, begad!"

"I would! Indeed I would make myself a pestilential nuisance to help my friend."

"Friend!" he repeated. "Oh, curse and confound it, Perry, if I wasn't such a miserable, hopeless dog, I should be proud of such friendship—I am proud of it and always shall be—but here our companionship ends. There's but one course for me, and I intend to ride to the devil—alone!"

It was at this moment that the door opened and I rose to my feet, trembling, as Diana stepped into the room. She was clad for riding and her close-fitting habit served only to accentuate the voluptuous beauty of her form, yet her eyes seemed maidenly and untroubled, wide-opened and serenely steadfast as of old, and this of itself stirred within me a sullen resentment as she stood looking at me, a little pale, very wistful, yet radiant in her beauty; and when she spoke her voice was untroubled as her look.

"Mr. Vere-Manville, I beg you will leave us awhile!"

Even as she spoke, Anthony bowed, strode to the door and was gone before I could stay him.

"Peregrine?"

One word, softly uttered, yet in it a world of pleading—reproach and troubled wonderment, insomuch that, remembering that accursed black-bodied chaise, the ring and gossamer veil, my sullen resentment waxed to bitter anger, the whole thing seemed so utterly nauseous.

Evening was falling and from one of the trees in the orchard a blackbird was calling to his mate, soft and sweetly plaintive, and never, to the end of my days, may I hear such without recalling all the agony of this hour.

We stood very silent, looking upon each other, while the blackbird piped in the orchard below; and now I trembled no more, for my anger was passed and in its stead was a cold and purposeful determination.

"Are you better, Peregrine?" she questioned at last. "More yourself?"

"Thank you, yes."

When next she spoke her voice faltered a little, though her glance never wavered.

"Peregrine, why—why did you—drive me away? Why refuse to see me?"

"To avoid a painful scene."

"But what should cause a painful scene—between us, Peregrine? Oh, my dear, what is it—what has changed you? Is it your illness?"

"Let us suppose so."

"Have you no—no other explanation to offer me?" she questioned wistfully and stood waiting my answer, drawing her riding gauntlet a little nervously through her ungloved hand, on the slender finger of which I saw the scarabaeus ring. "Is there, O Peregrine, is there no other explanation?"

"None!" said I savagely, my eyes on that accursed ring. "None!"

"Peregrine—dear," she questioned humbly, "have you learned to—to love one more—more worthy than I in my absence?"

"God forbid!" I answered. "Love has become for me a thing abhorred and utterly detestable."

"Then God help me," said she in strange, passionless voice, "for without your love I shall be desolate!"

"But you are so beautiful—so very beautiful you will never lack for comfort, you could find scores of noble suitors to-morrow eager and willing. So why talk of desolation?"

Now at this she shrank a little, staring at me with a dawning horror in her eyes.

"Peregrine," she whispered, "O Peregrine, can this indeed be you? My loved Peregrine, my gentleman that was so chivalrous and gentle once, and now to hurt me so wilfully—so bitterly!"

"I am two years older, and—a little wiser, perhaps."

"Two years!" she repeated dully. "Two years I should never have left you—it was wrong! And yet—can two years work so great a change in any one? Ah, no, no—this cannot be you—so cold—so hard and cruel! Oh, if we might but have those two years back again when you were your own dear self and I your loving gipsy girl with no ambition but to be worthy of—just you! O Peregrine, is your love for me truly dead—so soon?"

As thus she spoke, all pleading, passionate entreaty, she came towards me with both arms outstretched, her eyes abrim with tears; but, frowning at her ungloved hand, I started back so hurriedly that she stopped and looked at me as if I had struck her; then she shrank away, her proud head drooped, her arms fell and she covered her face. "Then it is true!" she gasped, "all—dreadfully true." And upon the silence stole the sweetly plaintive notes of the blackbird calling, calling from the orchard below.

And as she stood thus, bowed and shaken with her grief, I kept my gaze ever upon that betraying scarabaeus ring. Suddenly she raised her head and I saw her tearless but very pale.

"Yes, you are changed," said she, in that strange, passionless tone, "quite changed; your eyes are cold, your face cruel and hard and yet—O dear God!" she cried, "O dear God, I cannot believe your love is truly dead—how can I? O dear, dear Peregrine, tell me you do love me still—if only just a little—oh, be merciful, dear—!"

And now indeed she was weeping but, blinded by her tears, choked by her sobs, she yet reached out her arms to me in mute appeal; and it seemed that somehow her tears were blinding me also, her passionate sobs shaking me, for I stood in a mist, groping for the support of my chair-back; indistinctly I heard a voice speak that I knew was mine.

"So you still wear the scarab ring—I've seen it before. But where is your veil with the gold stars? I did love you once—worshipped—reverenced your maidenly purity—your brave truthfulness but—that love is dead—crushed—crushed beneath red wheels, and I would to God I were dead with it. No—if you please, don't touch me—by your leave I will sit—and beg you to excuse me. I—would be alone."

"Ah, Peregrine—beloved, you are crying too!"

"Indeed yes. I grieve that I am not dead."

"But why—why would you be dead, my own?"

"Because—O Diana—I cannot help but—love you after all. And now, pray go—I beseech you, leave me ere the devil break loose and I speak the unforgivable thing ... Go, I entreat!"

With some such hysterical words as these and blinded by a gush of weak, unmanly tears, I sent her from me, unheeding alike her piteous entreaties and the clasp of her imploring hands. When she was gone I sank into my chair and suffered my tears to flow unchecked, while the blackbird voiced the agony of loss and disillusionment.

CHAPTER VIII

THE DEEPS OF HELL

Your Heroes of Romance from time immemorial have generally been large men, more or less handsome, superlatively strong, void of all fear, stalwart of body and steadfast of mind; moreover, being singled out by a hard fate to endure much and often, they suffer, unflinchingly and uncomplainingly, to extremity, like the heroes they are. To be sure, under great stress of mental or even bodily anguish, they are sometimes allowed to sigh, to tremble, or even emit an occasional groan, but tears, it seems, are a weakness forbidden them.

All of which foregoing is to lend additional point to the fact that in my last chapter I leave myself huddled miserably in my chair and dissolved in bitter tears; which of itself should sufficiently preclude the remotest possibility of my reader ever mistaking me for a hero, even if Nature had not done this already.

Behold me then, a high-strung, delicate, hysterical youth, weeping in an agony of shameful horror evoked of a perfervid imagination.

O Imagination! Whoso is possessed of thee is cursed or blessed by a fearful magic whereby the misty vision becomes real, unworthy suspicion changed to hateful certainty, the vague idea into a living horror to haunt us day and night until sweet Reason shrinks appalled; by imagination we may scale the heights of heaven or plumb the foulest deeps of hell.

So I, being not in the least like a Hero of Romance, wept miserably, staring through tears upon a countryside bathed in the glory of sunset; but to my jaundiced vision this radiance but made my circumambient shadow the blacker by contrast, a mephitic gloom wherein a chaise with red wheels bore Diana to her "slave and master"—a master whose power was such that he could force her, willing or unwilling, to obey his summons—his every behest ... horror on horror ... shame on shame, until my mind reeled sick with loathing.

And she who had driven with the profligate Danby to God alone knew what infamy—even she would return to act for me her part of sorrowing wonder—to weep and sigh. Oh, shameful hypocrisy! And with her would be my aunt and uncles to wonder also and shake grave heads over me, torturing me with their love while in my consciousness gnawed this undying horror that, like a demon raged within me, passioning for utterance, insomuch that day or night I had dreaded lest I babble the obscenities that haunted me. Better to die than speak! A bullet would be quick, as Anthony had said—and I had no fire arms! But I remembered that in the kitchen downstairs I had seen a pistol hung up in a dark corner and above the mantel hung George's bayonet, at whose keen point lay silence and oblivion; and this thought had in it a degree of comfort as I sat crouched in my chair, half-blinded by my unheroic tears.

The sun had set, the blackbird had ended his song, for evening was falling apace; against the glimmering dusk bats wheeled and hovered, and as the shadows deepened I watched the stars shine forth, while low down in the darkening sky was an effulgence that marked the rising moon.

Suddenly I arose, moved by a dominating purpose, kicked off my slippers, struggled into my boots and, taking surtout and hat, strode resolutely downstairs; by good hap there chanced to be nobody in the kitchen and, crossing to a certain corner, I took from the wall a small but serviceable-looking pistol, and having assured myself that it was primed and loaded, I slipped it into my pocket and stepped out into the fragrant dusk.

But as I crossed the yard, George suddenly emerged from the stables.

"Lord, Mr. Vereker, sir!" he exclaimed, touching an eyebrow.

"Any one about, George?"

"Nary a soul, sir—'cept me an' my little old woman. But 'bout a hour ago Mr. Anthony's lady rides up, all a-tremblin' an' pale—an' no wonder, poor soul, seein' Mr. Anthony galloped off lookin' like a devil an' a bottle o' my brandy in 'is pocket!"

"Had Mrs. Vere-Manville come to find him, George?"

"No, sir! He'd been gone a good 'arf-hour afore she came. 'O George,' says she, all a-gaspin' like, 'is Miss Lovel 'ere?' 'Upstairs along o' Mr. Vereker, ma'm,' I says. 'Oh, I must see her—I must see her!' cries she, a-shakin' wuss'n ever, so that I was afeard she'd fall off 'er 'oss an' 'im that gentle! 'Can I 'elp you ma'm?' says I. 'No!' says she, moanin' an' breathless-like. 'Oh, no, George—nobody can, O God, 'elp me, God 'elp me!' An' then, sir, down comes Miss Lovel an' runs to 'er. 'Why, Babs!' says she, anxious-like. 'Oh, what is it, dearest?' At this, Mr. Anthony's lady begins to sob—'eart-breakin', sir! 'O Di,' says she, all wildlike, 'O Di dear, 'e wants me! 'E says I must go—to-night—an' I'm afraid.' So Miss Lovel, she kisses 'er an' they whisper together. Then Miss Lovel calls for 'er 'oss, an' away they ride very close together, an' Miss L.'s arm about 'er. Lord, sir, who'd a thought it o' Mr. Anthony? So wild an' fierce-like 'e were—enough to fright any woman, 'specially such a beautiful, gentle creetur' as 'is wife! Drink 's a fearsome thing!"

"True, George. But Mr. Anthony would die rather than harm her, I am sure."

"Maybe, sir—but 'e looked 'orrible wild an' fierce when 'e rode off—an' drink du be a tur'ble thing."

"Now—touching a chaise, George—"

"Chaise, sir?"

"A black chaise picked out in yellow, with red wheels. You have seen such drive up to Raydon Manor, yonder, you told me once, I think?"

"I did, sir, an' I 'ave—frequent! It do have drove up theer this very evening. But Lord, Mr. Vereker, be you a thinkin' o' walkin' out—an' night comin' on?"

"I am, George."

"'T will be dark soon, sir. And you 'ardly yourself, yet!"

"No, George, there will be a moon."

"But, sir, wot am I to tell your lady aunt?"

"That I have taken a walk in quest of my health—and sanity, George."

"Be you a-goin' fur, sir?"

"No further than I need."

"Then I think I'll go along wi' you, sir."

"No, George, I may be back before the moon is up. At least—no, it will be high-risen when I return, most likely. Only pray assure my aunt that I am doing the very best for myself." So saying, I left the faithful George staring after me and shaking dubious head.

I walked at a leisurely pace, deliberating how best to contrive the desperate task I had set myself to accomplish, how best to bring it to a final and certain issue.

And presently up came the moon in glory and I stared up at her as one does who may behold her perhaps for the last time. Calm and serene she arose, and as I walked amid this tender light, I seemed to breathe in something of her passionless serenity and knew a strange exaltation of mind, placid and untroubled. Gone were my fever dreams, the foul horrors that had haunted me, and my obscene demons were vanished utterly away and with them, as it seemed, the inertia of my late sickness.

To die, and in so doing take evil with me, leaving the world so much the better? To die, and perhaps find for myself that oblivion, that untroubled rest that I so earnestly desired? Surely Death, after all, was the Great Good Thing? So I walked on at leisurely pace, serene, assured and utterly content.

Reaching the high road, I followed it until I espied a rutted byway bounded on the one hand by lofty trees and on the other by a high and sinister wall. At the same leisurely pace I strolled down this dark lane and thus arrived at a pair of tall and very massive iron gates.

Here I paused, and though the adjacent trees cast much shadow, presently discovered a bell handle to which I applied myself forthwith.

After some delay the door of the lodge opened and a figure appeared, though strangely vague and indistinct and then, peering at me through the bars of the gate, I saw a gigantic negro, his skin as black as his livery.

"Is your master in?" I demanded.

"Who yo' mean—mah master?" he replied in surly tone.

"I wish to see Mr. Haredale or Captain Danby."

"No sich names hyah!"

"Well then, I want Mr. Trenchard."

"Who's yo' se'f to see Mas'r Trenchard?"

"I am an—acquaintance of his."

"Well, ah don' know yo' face, so ah guess dey's bof' out fo' you an' so's yo'se'f—an' can stay out, fo' shure." Having said which, the negro laughed shrilly, and I saw the flash of his teeth ere he departed.

Balked thus but determined as ever, I turned away and began to follow the wall, looking for a place where I might climb it by means of some tree or rise in the ground. And with every step the sudden conviction I had formed that Trenchard was Haredale grew stronger; and Haredale, as I knew, was but another name for that evil rogue whose name had once been Devereux.

I went slowly, scanning every yard of the wall for a likely place, now in brilliant moonlight, now in shadow, while stronger and stronger waxed my determination that, supposing Trenchard were Devereux indeed, I would this night rid the world of him once and for all.

Presently, as I went, resolutely seeking a way to come at my desire, I found myself stumbling amid the dense gloom of tall trees; but I pushed on until before me, the moon being now high-risen, I saw the blackness cleft by a shaft of radiance and, coming nearer, stopped all at once to scowl at a small door in the wall that seemed to scowl back at me between deep buttresses.

Now suddenly, as I stood thus, I heard a sound of steps and voices on the other side of the wall, a key was thrust into the lock of this door, and instinctively I shrank back and back into the gloom of the trees; I heard the key turn, the drawing of heavy bolts, and then, as I crouched, hand upon the weapon in my pocket, the door opened.

And now at last I knew why this door had haunted my dreams, a thing of unutterable evil for, from beneath its frowning shadow, out into the moonlight, stepped Diana.

She was shrouded in a long, hooded cloak, but my sickened senses knew her even before she put back the hood to glance stealthily about her, like the shameful, guilty thing she was. Suddenly she shrank, cowering, as upon the air broke a strange, inarticulate cry that I knew for my own; an unseen hand plucked her back, the door closed, was locked and swiftly bolted, and I heard the sound of running feet.

And now, all too late, I sprang to smite this accursed door with maddened fists, to beat it with pistol butt and utter incoherent shouts and ravings. All at once my arm was in a powerful grip, the pistol twisted out of my hold and I glared up into the face of Anthony. His hat was gone, he swayed gently on his feet, and when he spoke his voice was hoarse and indistinct.

"What's t' do, old fellow—dev'lish din you're making—most infernal. Won't they open th' curst door t' ye then, Perry? Well—never mind—take a pull at this—nothing like brandy—"

From capacious pocket he drew forth a bottle and held it towards me, which I forthwith dashed against the wall.

"And now," said I, "give me the pistol!"

"What for?" he demanded, sobered a little.

"Because I purpose to shoot him."

"Who, Perry?"

"Trenchard or Haredale or Devereux or whatever he calls himself. Come, give me the pistol. To-night I make an end of him and his deviltries once and for all."

For a moment Anthony blinked at me in foolish amaze.

"Why, Perry—why, Perry!" he exclaimed. "B'gad, can this be you indeed?" And then, as if quite sobered by what he read in my face, he fell back a step, brushed hand across his eyes, peered at me again, and his slouching figure grew erect and purposeful.

"Give me that pistol!" I repeated.

"No, Peregrine!" said he, his voice sharp and incisive. "Killing is murder, and I am your friend. But if you wish to fight a fellow, or say twenty fellows, b'gad, I'm with you! The more the merrier—so speak the word!"

"Yes!" said I. "Yes, I'll fight, but kill him I will—it almost seems preordained that I should kill him from the beginning—"

"And whom did you say he was, Perry?"

"Trenchard he calls himself hereabouts—the damnable villain who lives here at Raydon Manor."

"A duel!" quoth Anthony, smiling grimly. "If you fight, Perry, I fight; b' God, I'll find somebody to accommodate me one way or another—a duel, oh, most excellent! Ha, dooce take me, but you're right, Perry, I never thought o' this. Oh, damme, the very thing—I'm with you heart and soul, dear fellow, so come on."

So saying, he ran at the wall and, leaping with long arms at full stretch, gripped the coping with iron fingers, drew himself up and reaching long arm down, had swung me up beside him, all in a moment.

"Ha, Perry!" he exclaimed, as we prepared to drop into the garden below, "I'm a curst, dull-witted ass—here have I been sedulously guzzling ale, rum, brandy and dooce knows how many kinds of wine, and what I really needed was blood, d'ye see? Blood, old fellow, no matter whose. And, begad, blood we'll have to-night, Perry, or know the reason why. Come on, old fellow, both together—now!"

Down he leapt and down I scrambled, and side by side we advanced towards the house that held for me all the nauseous evil and unspeakable shame of all the world.

CHAPTER IX

CONCERNING THE OPENING OF A DOOR

"Anthony, give me the pistol!"

"Damme, no—ha' patience! Meantime take this—more useful if it comes t' scrimmage!" And he twisted a stake from the flower bed we were trampling and thrust it into my hand. "Enemy's country, Perry,—qui vive! Hist! Attention and all the rest of it! Forward an' curse the consequences!"

So we stole forward like the madmen we were, but very silent and very determined.

The house stood upon a noble terrace, a large house of many gables and windows, most of these last being unlighted. Fortune seemed to favour us, for we met with none to oppose us, and mounting a broad flight of stone steps, reached the terrace unmolested. But as I stood glancing about for some door or likely window whereby we might force entrance, Anthony dragged me down suddenly into the shadow of the balustrade, as round a corner of the house two men appeared.

"Wot," growled one, pausing, the better to spit in passionate disgust, "put the 'orses to the phaeton, must I? And at this time o' night—an' all for a couple o' light country Molls as is afeard to foot it 'ome in the dark, curse 'em!"

"She ain't no country Moll, Ben, leastways not 'er as I see—a reg'lar 'igh-stepper—all the lady, Ben—such eyes, ecod—such a shape to 'er, Ben—"

"Well, dang 'er shape, I says! Why can't she go as she come?"

"Summat in the wood give 'er a turn, scared 'er like, an' back she run to the Guv'nor an' orders 'im to 'ave the phaeton round, which the Guv'nor does; an' there's 'im an' t' others a-toastin' of 'er this 'ere werry minute. Oh, she's a lady, Ben, an' mighty 'igh an' 'aughty, by 'er looks."

"'Aughty!" sneered Ben, spitting again. "Lady! We know th' kind o' ladies as comes a visitin' th' Guv'nor or the Captain 'ere a-nights—"

"Shut your trap, Ben, an' get to your 'osses, lady or no."

"Lady—ha, fine doin's—fine doin's! Shameless 'ussies—"

126

"Close up, Ben, close up—mum's the word hereabouts! The Guv'nor's got a quick eye for a fine young woman—ah, an' so's you an' me, for that matter! An' I tell ye, this 'un's a fine lady, even if a bit frolicsome. So git to your 'osses, Ben—an' sharp's the word."

The man Ben sniffed and, muttering evilly, slouched away, leaving his fellow to sigh gustily and stare up at the moon; a square-shouldered, bullet-headed man who, leering up at Diana's chaste loveliness, began to scrape and pick at his teeth with a thumb nail. And then Anthony sneezed violently. The man stood rigid, thumb at mouth, peering.

"'Oo's there?" he demanded gruffly, and began to advance, head bowed and arms squared in a posture of offence.

In one moment, as it seemed, Anthony was upon him; ensued a scrape of feet, a thudding of blows, a strangled cry, and they were down, rolling upon the gravel and with never a chance for me to get in a stroke with my unwieldy hedge stake. At last Anthony arose, panting a little and smiling grimly, looking from the man's inert form to his own bleeding knuckles.

"This," he whispered breathlessly, "this is doing me—power o' good! Toughish customer—forced to give him—tap with pistol butt. How about the fellow Ben?"

"No, no, Anthony! The door yonder—quick—this way!"

I remember a long, dim-lit passage, a narrow stair, and we found ourselves in a broad and spacious hall where shaded lamps burned and nude statues gleamed against rich hangings.

Borne to our ears came a jingle of glasses, the line of a song and boisterous laughter. A door opened suddenly and a man stepped into the hall, his bulky figure outlined against the lights of the room behind him, but he paused upon the threshold to glance back and flourish something triumphantly.

"Treasure trove!" he laughed. "The memento of a delightful hour!"

With the words upon his lips he turned, and I recognised Captain Danby. He was halfway across the hall when he espied us and stopped to glare in wide-eyed amazement; something fluttered to the floor and he began to retreat softly and slowly before us, but Anthony was pointing down at a small bundle of lace with hand that shook and wavered strangely.

"Look at it, Perry—look!" he muttered. "Look, man! Why—God's death, Perry—it's her lace scarf—belongs to my Loveliness, Perry—should know it anywhere—it's—hers, man—and here! Oh, damnation!"

In a flash he had picked it up and, roaring like a madman, hurled himself against the closing door. For moment was a desperate scuffling and frenzied straining and gasping, a creaking of stout panels, then the door swung violently open and we burst into the room.

A disordered supper table littered with bottles, three or four breathless gentlemen who panted and glared, and a curtained doorway in one corner; all this I was aware of, though my gaze never left the face of him who stood before this curtained door, a tall, slender man very elegantly calm and wholly unperturbed, except for the slight frown that puckered his thick brows,—a handsome face the paler by contrast with its dark and glossy hair.

For a tense moment there was silence but for Anthony's loud and irregular breathing; when at last he spoke his voice sounded wholly unfamiliar:

"Damned scoundrels—look at this! My wife's scarf—is she here? By God, if she is, I'll find her if I have to kill you one by one and wreck this hellish place—"

"Fellow's drunk!" suggested some one, whereupon Anthony cursed them one and all, and I heard the sharp click of the pistol as he cocked it, but I restrained him with a gesture:

"Mr. Trenchard," said I, "Mr. Haredale—Devereux or whatever name you happen to be using, I have forced myself upon you to-night to inform you that, knowing you at last for the foul and loathsome thing you are, I am very earnest that you should pollute the world no longer. Two years ago you struck me in the yard behind the Chequers Inn, at Tonbridge; I call upon you to account for that blow to-night—here and now!"

"Let any man stir and I shoot to kill!" said Anthony between shut teeth; his heavy tread shook the floor behind me, then he had swung me aside and fronted Devereux the pistol in his hand, face convulsed and murder glaring in his eyes.

"Trenchard," said he in strange, hissing whisper, "there is a curtained door behind you—whom are you hiding in there? Trenchard, I am yearning to kill you and kill you I will, so help me God, unless you draw that curtain and open that door—d'ye hear me?"

Trenchard's tall form seemed to stiffen, his mocking smile vanished, but his eyes never wavered.

Anthony levelled the pistol.

"Trenchard," said he softly, "I'll count three!"

Then Trenchard laughed lightly.

"Egad, sir," said he with a flourish, "drunk or no, you have a devilish persuading air about you. Behold then, and judge of my felicity!"

Thus speaking, he drew aside the curtain and reached white hand towards the door behind, but at this moment and before he could touch it, the door swung open and Diana stepped forth.

"Mr. Vere-Manville," said she, her soft voice calm and even, "pray give me my scarf, your wife made me a present of it days ago!" And she reached out her hand with the old, imperious gesture that I remembered so well. So Anthony gave her the handful of lace and turned his back upon us.

"O Perry!" he exclaimed with a groan, "O Perry, dear friend—what have
I done! God forgive me—"

"Heavens, Anthony!" quoth I. "Pray why distress yourself upon a matter so trivial—besides, I knew already. And now, Mr. Trenchard or Haredale or Devereux, if this lady will be so obliging as to retire, we can settle our small concern very comfortably here across the table."

"No, Peregrine!" said Diana in the same even tone.

127

"Mr. Trenchard—" I began.

"I say you shall not, Peregrine!" said she softly.

"Mr. Haredale—" quoth I.

"O Peregrine," she sighed, "suspicion has poisoned your mind against me or you would never stoop to doubt me—even here—"

"Mr. Devereux," said I, "will you pray have the courtesy to desire your charming friend to leave us awhile—"

"O Peregrine!" she gasped, and though I never so much as glanced in her direction, I knew she had shrunk farther from me. "Some day, oh, some day, Peregrine, you will regret this bitterly—bitterly—" Her voice broke, and in its place came Devereux's hateful tones:

"'My charming friend' is well aware that her society is my joy and delight, nor shall I cheat myself of one moment on your account, sir, whoever you chance to be."

"Why, then," said I, laying my card on the table, "the lady's presence need not deter us, I think. Let us be done with the affair at once."

"Absolutely and utterly impossible, sir!" he answered, taking up my card. "Since you desire me to kill you, I will do so with a perfect pleasure, but at my own time and place and—" Here he paused as he read my name, and stood a moment staring down at the pasteboard with that same faint pucker of the brow; then he laughed suddenly and tossed my card to Captain Danby. "Odd, Tom!" said he; then turning to me, "Mr. Vereker, I will meet you at the very earliest moment—shall we say five o'clock to-morrow morning? There is a small tavern called 'The Anchor' a few miles along the Maidstone road, a remote spot very suitable for a little shooting. And now, sir, pray begone. I am occupied, as you see—while my friends pour libations to Bacchus, I worship at the shrine of Venus."

Here, turning very ostentatiously, he bowed to Diana, viewing her with look so evil that I clenched my fists and made to spring at him, but Anthony's powerful hand arrested me:

"Come away, Perry," he whispered, "you can do no more to-night. Don't show 'em your pain—pride, man, pride! Come away, old fellow."

So I suffered him to lead me whither he would, following the impulse of his guiding arm like a blind man, for the shadow had closed in blacker than ever, to engulf me at last, and it seemed that my only escape from this horror was to grasp the kindly hand of Death.

Once clear of this accursed house I was seized of a great disgust, a nausea that was both mental and physical, and I groaned aloud in my extremity.

"O God, Anthony! Oh, my God!"

At this he clasped me in his arms and I stood awhile, shivering, my face hidden in his bosom.

"Dear fellow!" he muttered. "Women are the devil. I know—I'm married, d'ye see!"

Faint and far away a church clock struck the hour.

"What time was that?" I enquired.

"Eleven o'clock, Perry."

"Six weary hours to wait!" I groaned.

"B'gad, yes—only six hours!"

"Thank God!" quoth I fervently, and so we went on again, arm in arm.

"You mean to kill that damned fellow, Peregrine?"

"If they place us near enough."

"You are good for twelve paces, I suppose?"

"I don't know."

"But you—you shoot reasonably well, of course?"

"Very badly! This was why I was so anxious to do my shooting across a table—"

"But you—you—O Lord, Perry—you are familiar with the weapon—practised at the galleries occasionally?"

"I have shot once or twice at a target to please my uncle Jervas, but never succeeded in hitting it that I remember."

"Oh, damnation!"

"That is what my uncle Jervas said, I remember."

"But then—why how—oh, man!" stammered Anthony, viewing me in wide-eyed dismay, "how in the fiend's name d' you expect to hit your man?"

"I don't know, Anthony—except, as I say, across a table or a handkerchief. But what matter? After all, perhaps it is—yes—just as well—"

"Why, then 't will be rank murder! Ha, by heaven, Perry, you—you mean to let the fellow murder you—is this it?"

"I mean to shoot as straight as I can."

"It will be murder!" he cried wildly, and then tossing up his long arms in a helpless, distracted manner, he cried, "By God, Perry, you are as good as dead already!"

"Why, then," said I, grasping him by the arm, "listen to the voice of a dying man and one who has never accomplished anything as yet—indeed, I have been a failure all my life—"

"You, Perry? A failure—how, man, how?"

"Well, I yearned to be a poet—and failed. I tried to be a painter—and failed again. I endeavoured to become a man and have achieved nothing. I am a sentient futility! But to-night—ah, to-night kind fortune sent me—you. And you were drunk again!"

"I'm sober enough now, b'gad!"

"Drunkenness, Anthony, as you know, is the refuge for cowards and weaklings, and all unworthy such a man as Anthony Vere-Manville—"

"Egad, will you preach at me, Perry?"

"Call it so if you will, but to-night is something of an occasion and here is a setting excellently adapted to the sermon of a dying man."

And indeed it was a night to wonder at, very still and silent and filled with the splendour of a great moon whose peaceful radiance fell upon the sleeping countryside like a benediction.

"Look," said I, "look round you, Anthony, upon this wonder of earth and heaven! Does it not wake in you some consciousness of divinity, some assured hope that we in our nobler selves are one with the Infinite Good?"

"Why, to be sure, now you mention it," he answered easily, glancing from me to the radiant heaven and back again, "it is a very glorious night!"

"Yes!" said I. "'In such a night stood Dido with a willow in her hand upon the wide sea banks and wafted her love to come again to Carthage!'"

"Eh?" exclaimed Anthony, peering at me anxiously.

"'In such a night Medea gathered the enchanted herbs,'—and in such a night your friend, who may never see another—takes occasion to ask a promise of you."

"What is it, Perry?"

"That henceforth you will be drunk no more. Give me your word for this, Anthony, and come what will, I shall not have lived in vain."

"Why, Peregrine," he mumbled, "dear fellow—not quite yourself—very natural—quite understand—"

"On the contrary, I have never been so truly myself as now, Anthony. Grant me this and—if death find me to-morrow morning, I shall indeed have accomplished something worthy at last. So, Anthony—promise me!"

For a moment he stood very still, gazing up at the moon, then, all in a moment, had caught my hand to wring it hard; but the pain of his grip was a joy and the look on his face a comfort beyond words.

"I—I Swear it!" said he between quivering lips. "God's love, man, I'd promise you anything to-night! And now—laugh, man, laugh—oh, dammit!" Here he choked and was silent awhile.

"Where are you taking me, Anthony? I cannot return to the 'Soaring Lark.'"

"Of course not. You're coming with me to 'The Bear' at Hadlow. I have a room there. And you'll promise to be guided by me until this—this cursed affair is over—place yourself and the affair in my hands, Perry?"

"Most thankfully."

"Then I stipulate for supper and bed as soon as possible."

"Very well, Anthony—though I ought to draw up some sort of a will first, oughtn't I?"

"Yes, it is customary, dear fellow."

"There's my Wildfire, I'll leave him to you—if you'll have him."

"Of course—and thank you, Perry."

"You'll soon grow to love the rascal in spite of his mischievous tricks—"

"I hope to heaven I never have the chance—oh, curse and confound it—don't be so devilish calm and assured. You—you talk as if you were going out to your execution!"

"No, no, Anthony," I answered, slipping my hand within his arm, "let us rather say—to my triumph."

CHAPTER X

TELLS HOW A MYSTERY WAS RESOLVED

I opened my eyes on a bleak dawn full of a pallid, stealthy mist, to find myself cramped in my chair before the open lattice and with Anthony bending over me, his comely features haggard in the sickly light.

"Ha, you didn't go to bed then?"

"Evidently not!" I answered, shivering. "But I slept—"

"Well, I did—and never a wink, confound it! And here's you basking before an open window—and on such a perfectly damned morning—have you ill again!" and, shivering in his turn, he proceeded to close the lattice and light the candles.

"Pray what o'clock is it, Anthony?"

"A quarter to four. I have ordered a chaise to be ready in half an hour; seems this 'Anchor' Inn is some eight miles away—and better be a little early than late."

After a somewhat hasty toilet, during which Anthony contrived to cut himself, we descended to find a goodly breakfast and a cheerful fire; but scarcely were we at table than Anthony tugged at the bell rope.

"Good morrow to thee, Thomas!" quoth he to the portly and somnolent landlord who responded to the summons. "Chaise will be round soon, I hope?"

"Whenever ye do so wish, Mr. Anthony, sir."

"Excellent! Then pray, Tom, take hence this stuff!" And he pointed to a bottle at his elbow.

"Stuff, sir! Oh, Mr. Anthony—stuff?" exclaimed the landlord in sorrowful reproach, his somnolence forgotten in surprise. "It be brandy, sir—best French—your very own particular—"

"Aye, Tom, I know it is, and begad, I'm lusting for a mouthful—that's why I bid you take it away—drink coffee instead, confound it! So hence with it, Thomas—away!"

Very round of eye, the landlord took up the bottle and wandered off with it like one in a dream.

Anthony gulped his coffee, but, though the fare was excellent, ate little, fidgeted with his stock, shuffled in his chair, glanced frequently and stealthily at his watch and, in fine, discovered all those symptoms that indicated an extreme perturbation of mind.

"Devil take it, Perry—how you eat!" he exclaimed at last.

"The ham is delicious, Anthony—".

"Dooced stuff would choke me! Oh, by heaven, I'd give anything—everything, to take your place for the next hour!"

"But then, Anthony, it would probably be I who could not eat!"

"Tush, man, I'll hit you the ace of spades six times out of seven at twelve paces! Four o'clock, by heaven! I wonder if that confounded chaise will be ready yet!" And up he sprang and hasted away into the yard and almost immediately came hurrying back to tell me the vehicle was at the door.

Outside the mist seemed thick as ever, though the east was brightening to day; so I entered the chaise, followed by Anthony growling disgust, the door slammed, and through the open window came the round head of Tom the landlord to bob at us in turn.

"'T will grow finer mayhap by an' by, sirs," quoth he, "hows'ever, good luck an' good fortun' to ye, gentlemen—all right, Peter!" he called to the postillion. Whereupon a whip cracked, the chaise lurched forward and landlord and inn vanished in the swirling mist.

For a while we rode without talking, Anthony scowling out of his window, I staring out of mine at an eddying haze which, thinning out ever and anon, showed vague shapes that peeped forth only to be lost again, spectral trees, barns and ricks, looming unearthly in the half-light.

"Perry, you—you are confoundedly silent!"

"You are not particularly loquacious either," I retorted, slipping my hand within his arm.

"Why, no—no, b'gad—I'm not, Perry. But then, it's such a peculiarly damnable morning, d'ye see."

"Well, it will mayhap grow finer later on, remember."

"Hope to heaven it does!"

"It would make things—a little pleasanter, Anthony."

"Peregrine, if—should anything—anything—er—dooced happen to you, I'll—aye, by God, I'll fight the fellow myself."

"I beg you will do no such thing—I implore you Anthony."

"Oh? Damme and why not?"

"For the sake of Barbara—your Loveliness—your future happiness—"

"Tush, man!" he exclaimed bitterly. "That dream is over!"

"And I tell you Happiness is awaiting you—will come seeking you very soon, I feel sure."

"How should you know this?"

"You may have heard, Anthony, that people in such a position as mine—people who are facing the possibility of speedy dissolution, are sometimes gifted with a clearer vision—an intuition—call it what you will. However, I repeat my assurance that Happiness is awaiting you, coming to you with arms outstretched, if you will but have faith and patience—a happiness greater, fuller, richer than you have ever known."

At this, he turned to scowl out of the window again and I out of mine, and thus we came to an end of the rutted by-lanes we had been traversing and turned into the smoother going of the main road.

We had gone but a mile, as I judge, when, borne to our ears came the faint, rhythmic beat of fast-galloping hoofs growing momentarily louder.

"Someone in the devil's own hurry!" exclaimed Anthony, letting down his window. "No man would gallop his horse so without reason! Hark—hark, he must be riding like a madman—and in this fog! What the devil? Nobody to lay us by the heels—eh, Perry?"

"God forbid!" I exclaimed fervently, as Anthony leaned from the window.

"Nothing to see—mist too thick!" said he. "But road's dooced narrow hereabouts, yet hark—hark how the fellow rides!" And indeed it seemed to me that there was something terrible in the relentless beat of these wildly galloping hoofs that were coming up with us so rapidly. Anthony was peering from the window again; I heard him shout, felt the chaise swing jolting towards the hedge and the horseman was by—a blurred vision that flashed upon my sight and was gone.

"Missed by inches—dooced reckless, by Gad!" exclaimed Anthony, and I saw that his frown had vanished.

"What kind of a person was he?" I demanded.

"Muffled up to the ears, Perry, hat over his eyes—big horse—powerful beast. Going to clear up and be a fine day after all, I fancy."

"And it is nearly five o'clock!" said I, glancing at my watch.

"Hum!" sighed Anthony. "And here you sit as serenely untroubled, as placidly assured, as if you were the best shot in the world instead of the worst."

"Listen, Anthony!" I cried suddenly. "Do you hear anything—listen, man!" A faint throbbing upon the air, a pulsing beat growing louder and louder. "Do you hear it, Anthony, do you hear it?"

"No—yes—begad, Perry, it sounds like—"

"Another horse at full gallop, Anthony—and coming up behind us. Another horseman—from the same direction!"

"Dev'lish strange, Perry. How many more of 'em?"

"There will be no more!" I exclaimed bitterly, and then, the chaise beginning to slow up, I thrust my head from the window to demand why we were stopping.

"Turnpike, sir!" answered the postboy. And peering through the haze before us I saw the tollgate, sure enough, and I turned to stare back down the road towards the second hard-riding horseman, and presently beheld a vague blur that resolved itself into a rapidly oncoming shape that swept down upon us through the swirling mist; the flutter of a long cloak, a spurred boot, a shadowy form bowed low in the saddle—all this I saw in one brief moment; then rose a hoarse shout from the eddying mist ahead; the jingle of flung coins and, lifting his animal at the tollgate, the horseman cleared it at a bound and, plunging into the haze beyond, had vanished like a phantom.

And now I was seized with a passion of haste and began to shout fevered orders at our postboy.

"Hurry—hurry! A guinea—ten guineas for your best speed! Drive, man, drive like the devil. Whip—spur!"

I remember tossing money to a hoarse-voiced toll-keeper in a fur cap, and we were off in full career, the light chaise rocking and swaying. I remember Anthony's look of surprise and my answering his half-hearted questions at random or not at all, for now I rode, my head out-thrust from the window, hearkening for the sound of galloping hoofs ahead of us.

And so at last, after an eternity as it seemed, the chaise slowed again and came to an abrupt standstill before a dimly-seen building and, peering out, I made out the sign:

THE ANCHOR INN.

Next moment I had sprung out into the road and, not waiting for Anthony, hastened into the place, opened a door at random, and found myself in a small room where smoked a miserable fire over which lounged two languid gentlemen well coated and muffled against the chill of dawn.

"Sirs," said I, acknowledging their bows, "pray have you seen two horsemen pass lately?"

"Horsemen, sir?" repeated a dashing gentleman who seemed all whiskers, teeth and greatcoat. "'Pon my honour, no—stop a bit—yes, I did! They rode towards Maidstone, I fancy, sir."

"Did they stop to make any enquiries—either of them?"

"Stop, sir? No, sir—devil a bit!" answered the gentleman, flashing his teeth and shaking his whiskers to such a degree that I doubted him on the spot. At this moment Anthony appeared, whereupon ensued more polite bows and flourishes; and now the other gentleman addressed us, a plethoric, red-faced man in a furred, blue frock.

"Our friend Trenchard desired us to await you, gentlemen, to inform you that he has changed the ground. The—the—ah—affair will not take place behind the inn here as first intended, but in a place somewhat more secluded. If you will pray have the goodness to accompany us, we will—ah—show you the way."

So we set out accordingly, I, for one, little heeding or caring whither we went.

Now it chanced we came to a narrow way where but two might go abreast and I found myself walking beside the whiskered gentleman who prattled to me very pleasantly, I believe, though of what I cannot recall. After a while the path brought us to a rough track hard beside a little wood and here stood a roomy travelling-chaise and beside this the man Trenchard or Devereux, talking and laughing with Captain Danby and another.

I remember returning their salutes with a perfunctory bow, but recollect little else, for now that my time was so near, a numbness seemed to cloud my brain and I could think only that this little copse, full of the grey mist of dawn, was perhaps the last object my eyes should ever see.

"I told one of 'em," said Anthony in my ear, "fellow in blue frock yonder, that you were the dooce an' all with a hair trigger—almost as dead a shot as your uncle Jervas or Gronow of the Guards, and begad, it's set 'em all by the ears, Perry, especially that scoundrel Danby."

At this I laughed, I think, wondering the while if Anthony would ever know how much I loved and admired him.

I remember a stretch of green turf screened by trees; a solemn pacing to and fro by various grave-faced persons; a careful measuring of distances and selection of ground.

I remember some objection that Anthony made as to the light, whereupon the solemn measuring and pacing was gravely done all over again. I also recall that Anthony, while discussing or overseeing these grave proceedings, would often lift his head and glance hastily round about with a swift, keen-eyed expectancy.

I remember the sun peeping forth at last to make the world glorious and warm the chill in my bones.

And then Anthony came towards me, carrying a pistol, and I noticed that his hand shook as he offered it to me.

"God love you, Perry," he said, a little huskily. "You look as unconcerned, as cool as—as a confounded cucumber! And now, Perry, remember to aim low, all pistols are apt to throw high—so, for heaven's sake aim low, old fellow."

"Do I stand here, Anthony?"

"Yes—damned fellow insists on twelve paces!" said he, his voice sounding hoarser than ever, and I saw his glance wandering again, here and there, to and fro, in almost desperate fashion.

"Mr. Vere-Manville," called Devereux's second, "may I trouble you a moment, pray?"

Left alone, I stood watching the play of sunshine amid the leaves, when I was roused by a touch and found Captain Danby beside me.

"Your flint looks a trifle loose, sir," said he softly, "Suffer me!"

I relinquished the weapon with a murmur of thanks and stood again absorbed until I felt the pistol thrust into my grasp and heard a loud voice speaking.

"Pray attention, gentlemen! Take notice, the word will be 'one—two—'"

The loud voice faltered suddenly, was lost in the trampling of horse's hoofs and into the grassy level between Devereux and myself rode my uncle Jervas with my uncle George close behind.

My uncle Jervas reined in his horse and sat glancing serenely round about him, his lips curling in his bleak, sardonic smile, his prominent chin something more aggressive than usual.

"Ah, gentlemen," said he gently. "Your humble servant, I bid you good morning. Sir Geoffrey Devereux, we are very well met—at last. This is a pleasure I much desired when—we were younger, as you will doubtless remember, but I imagined, until very recently, that you were dead, sir, and damned, and necessarily out of my reach. You have hidden yourself surpassingly well, sir."

Very deliberately my uncle Jervas dismounted and proceeded to tether his horse to an adjacent tree, while Devereux watched him, head bowed and black brows puckered slightly above his smouldering eyes, his snowy cravat stained with a small mark of blood from an ugly scratch beneath his chin and which, despite his icy assurance seemed to worry him, for he dabbed at it now and then with his handkerchief. And now my uncle Jervas approached me, his hand outstretched imperiously, but when he spoke his voice was strangely gentle:

"Peregrine, dear boy, oblige me with that pistol."

"God bless you, Uncle Jervas!" said I fervently grasping that hand. "I thought I recognised you when your horse leapt that tollgate, but fate elected I should arrive here first, as I prayed."

"We were wilfully misdirected and went astray. And now, Peregrine, give me the pistol!"

"No, sir! Indeed you cannot, shall not take my place. This quarrel is wholly mine—a quarrel, sir, of two years' standing—"

"But mine, Peregrine, is of twenty-one years'."

"None the less, sir, you shall not shield me thus—none other shall take my place, I am here to meet that scoundrel yonder—"

"Ah, Peregrine," said my uncle, speaking very slowly and distinctly, "the scoundrel yonder, Sir Geoffrey Devereux, is the man who foully murdered your father and my brother! Give me the pistol, boy!"

As he spoke he grasped my wrist and had possessed himself of the weapon or ever I could prevent. Then he turned and faced Devereux, his eyes very keen and bright.

"George," said he in his quiet, authoritative voice, "pray give us the word."

My uncle George, still sitting his horse, lifted his right hand and I saw that he also held a pistol.

"Devereux," said he, his handsome face very fierce and grim, "if—this time—you fire before the word, even by one fraction of a second, I shoot you where you stand for the vile murderer you are—by God, I will! Now mark me! The word will be 'One—two—three—fire!' Is this understood?"

"Yes, George!" said my uncle; Devereux nodded.

"Ready!" said uncle George distinctly. "One—two—three—fire!"

A single sharp report and my uncle Jervas, lurching slightly, stared down at his weapon that had merely sparked and, letting it fall, staggered aside to a tree and leaned there.

In an instant uncle George was off his horse and together we ran to him.

"Aha, George—" he gasped in a horrible, wheezing voice, "it—it was unprimed—lend me—yours!"

"O God!" groaned my uncle George. "You're hit, Jervas—are you hurt?"

"A little, George—your pistol—quick!"

But even as he spoke and despite all his resolution and indomitable will, he seemed about to swoon; I saw his knees slowly bending under him, his stately head sank, and crying out in horror, I reached out to clasp him in my arms.

"No, no, Perry!" he gasped. "Don't touch me—yet—I have sufficient strength—dear boy." For a moment he closed his eyes and when next he spoke his voice was strangely loud and clear.

"Devereux, if ever you prayed—pray now!" Yet as he uttered these words, he sank to his knees and leaned feebly against the tree, his pallid face suddenly contorted by a dreadful spasm, so that I could scarcely bear to look. Then, sweating with the agonising effort, slowly—slowly—he raised his arm, dwelt a moment on his aim, and fired; the smoking weapon dropped from his lax fingers and, swaying sideways, he sank down, his face among the grass.

I remember my uncle George running to aid me lift this heavy head; and glancing from these dreadfully pallid features, the pitiful helplessness of this once strong form, I saw a group of pale-faced men who knelt and crouched above a twisted thing that had once answered to the name of Devereux.

"Dead, George?" questioned my uncle Jervas faintly.

"Dead, Jervas!"

"The right eye, George—I think?"

"Yes, Jervas. How is it with you, dear old fellow?"

"Very well—I'm going on—ahead of you, George. Don't—don't grieve, George—'t is none so terrible. And the great conundrum is answered, the mystery is solved, George—I mean—our Julia—she will—marry you, George, after all—I think she always loved you—

best. God bless you—both! And Peregrine—my dear lad—your gipsy—a strong—angel of God—Diana—" and with this word his noble spirit passed.

And thus even death was denied me and I, it seemed, was doomed to be no more than an idle spectator.

I remember helping to bear him back to the "Anchor" Inn—laying him reverently upon a settle. And then, because I could not bear to see him so pale and still and silent, I covered him with my cloak.

I remember the tears wet upon Anthony's haggard face and my uncle George crouched in a chair, clenched fists beneath square chin, staring wide-eyed on vacancy.

"Dead!" he exclaimed in an agonised half-whisper. "I mean to say he's dead, d'ye see. Jervas—dead—seems so impossible! If it could only have been me—it wouldn't ha' mattered so much, d'ye see. There never was any one like old Jervas. And now he's—dead, my God!" The agonised whispering ceased and silence fell that was almost as terrible. But suddenly upon this awful hush broke a sound of wheels—quick footsteps; then the door swung open and Diana stood upon the threshold.

"Peregrine!" she cried. "Oh, praise God you are alive—Peregrine—speak to me! Ah—dear God in heaven! What is it?" And hasting to me, she caught my hand, clasping it to her bosom. "Oh, what is it, Peregrine?" she whispered.

So I brought her to the settle, and reverently turning back my cloak, showed her what it had hidden.

"This!" said I. "Look upon your handiwork and go—wanton!"

Uttering a soft, inarticulate cry, she cowered away, shrank back and back across the room and out into the road beyond.

Then, treading as softly as I might, I crossed the room also and, closing the door very silently, locked and barred it securely.

CHAPTER XI

WHICH SHOWS THAT MY UNCLE JERVAS WAS RIGHT, AFTER ALL

A fortnight has elapsed and I sit here in my study at Merivale, idly adding these words to this book of mine which it seems is never destined to be finished. As my pen traces these words, I am conscious of the door opening softly, but, pretending absorption in my task, I never so much as lift my head but glance up surreptitiously to behold my aunt Julia, a little pale, her proud, full-lipped mouth not quite so firm as of old, but handsomer, lovelier than ever in her black gown, it seems to me.

"O Peregrine, do you really mean to go?"

"I do!"

"Ah, will you run away again, from us—from your duties—will you leave Diana to break her heart?"

"Can hearts break, dear Aunt?"

"Oh, poor Diana, poor child—after all she has done for you—"

"Indeed, Aunt, she has done a great deal for me, I admit—but—"

"You know how she came in the dead of night to warn your uncles of your peril—your mad folly? You know this?"

"Yes, yes, dear Aunt," said I, a little impatiently. "I know, too, how my noble uncles very nearly quarrelled as to which of them should risk his life for unworthy, miserable me—"

"It was George rode away first that dreadful morning," said my aunt, clasping her shapely hands, "and I shall never forget the look on the face of Jervas when he found that George had stolen away before him—poor, brave Jervas!"

"Yes, Aunt! If the place of meeting had not been altered—it would have been—uncle George, perhaps."

"Ah, yes!" sighed my aunt, shuddering and bowing pale face above her clasped hands. "But Diana—saved you, Peregrine."

"At least, Aunt, she caused a better man to die in my stead. As he is to-day, I would be—at rest!"

"Hush, oh, hush, Peregrine, you talk wildly! Indeed, sometimes I think you have never been quite the same since your illness, you are so much colder—less kind and gentle. And now you mean to go away again! What of the estate—your tenants?"

"Surely I cannot leave them in better, more capable hands than these, dear Aunt Julia!" and stooping, I kissed her slim, white fingers. "But go I must—I cannot bear a house; I want space—the open road, woods, the sweet, clean wind!"

"Where shall you go, Peregrine?"

"Anywhere—though first to London."

"And what of your book?"

"I shall never finish it, now!"

"And what of me? Will you leave me lonely? O Peregrine, can you leave me thus in my sorrow?"

"Hush, dear Aunt—listen!"

Through the open casement stole a soft, small sound—a jingle of spurs, the monotonous tramp of one who paced solitary upon the terrace below.

"Your uncle George!" she breathed, her hands clasped themselves anew and into her pale cheeks crept a tinge of warm colour. "I did not expect—your uncle George today!"

"He is lonely too, Aunt Julia. He does nothing but grieve! Indeed I think he is breaking his great generous heart for the brother he loved and honoured so devotedly."

"Poor—poor George!"

133

"Being a man of action, uncle George was never much of a talker, as you know—but he is more silent than ever these days. In London he would sit all day long in a dreadful apathy, and all night long I would hear him go tramping, tramping to and fro in his chamber—"

"O Perry dear—if he could only weep!"

"Aunt Julia, there is but one power on earth could bestow on him such blessed relief, and that is your love, the certain assurance that you do love him—the touch of your lips—"

"O Peregrine—oh, hush! Do you mean—" and my goddess-like aunt faltered and sat there, lovely eyes downcast, blushing like the merest girl.

"Yes, you beautiful Aunt," said I, "this is what I mean—this whose simple mention has turned you into a girl of sixteen, this wonderful truth that uncle Jervas had divined already." And I told her of his dying words: "'You will marry her after all, George—our Julia. I see now that she always loved you best!'"

"Oh, dear Jervas!" she murmured.

"He has left uncle George who loved him so greatly, very solitary—listen, dear Aunt!"

Up to us through the open lattice, borne upon the fragrant air, came that small, soft sound where my uncle George paced ceaselessly to and fro amid the gathering dusk.

"Poor George!" she whispered tenderly.

"He is so—utterly forlorn, Aunt."

"Dear George!"

"And so very much a man, Aunt!"

"And such a child!" she murmured. "So big and strong and such a helpless baby! Dear George!"

Here I turned to my writing again, heard the door close softly and, glancing up, found myself alone. Then, tossing down my pen, I arose and from a cupboard reached forth a hat and well-filled knapsack which last I proceeded to buckle to my shoulders; this done, I took a stout stick from a corner and stood ready for my wanderings. Thus equipped, I crossed to the window that I might see if the coast was clear, since I meant to steal away with no chance of tears or sorrowful farewells.

They were standing on the terrace in the gathering dusk; as I looked, Aunt Julia reached up and, taking his haggard face between her gentle hands, drew it down lower and lower; and when she spoke, no ear save his might catch her soft-breathed words.

And then his great arms were fast about her and there broke from him a sobbing cry of ecstasy.

"O Julia—at last. He was right then—our Jervas was right!"

And so my uncle George learned to weep at last and found within her loving arms the blessed relief of tears.

CHAPTER XII

HOW I WENT UPON AN EXPEDITION WITH MR. SHRIG

I had been ringing ineffectually at the bell of my chambers for perhaps five minutes and was about to visit the adjacent mews in quest of my groom, when a voice spoke my name, and turning about, I beheld Mr. Shrig, the Bow Street officer.

"Mr. Werricker, sir," said he, touching his low-crowned, wide-brimmed hat with a thick forefinger, "it ain't no manner o' use you a-ringin' o' that theer bell, because there ain't nobody to answer same, your young man Clegg 'aving took a little 'oliday, d'ye see, sir."

"A holiday, Mr. Shrig! Pray how do you know?"

"By observation, sir. I've a powerful gift that way, sir—from a infant."

"This is very extraordinary behaviour in Clegg!"

"But then, sir, your young man is a rayther extraordinary young man. 'Owsoever he's gone, sir, and I appre'end as he ain't a-comin' back—judgin' by vat 'e says in 'is letter."

"What letter?"

"The letter as 'e's left for you a-layin' on your desk this werry minute along o' my stick as I 'appened to forget—but you'll be vantin' to gain hadmittance, I expect, sir."

"I do."

"Vy then, 't is rayther fortunate as I did forget my stick or I shouldn't ha' come back for it in time to be o' service to you, Mr. Werricker. By your leave, sir." Saying which, Mr. Shrig took a small, neat implement from one of his many capacious pockets, inserted it into the keyhole, gave it a twist, and the door swung open.

"Ah—a skeleton key, Mr. Shrig?"

"That werry i-dentical, sir."

"Is this how you gained admittance to my chambers?"

"Ex-actly, sir."

"And, being there, read my private letters?"

"Only the vun, sir—dooty is dooty—only the vun. And I've a varrant o' search—"

Entering my small library, I espied Mr. Shrig's knobbed staff lying upon my desk and beside it a letter laid carefully apart from a pile of unopened missives.

"Is this the letter?"

"The werry same, sir."

"But if you have read it, how comes the seal unbroken?"

"By means of a warm knife-blade, sir."

Wondering, I opened the letter and read as follows:

SIR: I regret that I am forced by circumstances to quit your service at a moment's notice, but trust you will find all in order as regards tradesmen's accounts, your clothes, linen, napery, etc. The key of the silver you will find under the hearthrug.

Hoping you will find one as zealous as the unfortunate writer,

I remain, sir,

Yours respectfully,

THOMAS CLEGG.

"Very strange!" said I.

"Ah!" sighed Mr. Shrig. "But then life generally is, Mr. Werricker, sir, if you'll take the trouble to ob-serve; so strange that I ain't never surprised at nothing—nowhere and nohow, sir. For instance, if you a-peepin' from the garret winder o' the 'ouse opposite—yonder across the street—'ad 'appened to ob-serve a young fe-male on her knees—here beside your werry own desk and veepin' fit to break 'er 'eart, pore soul—you'd ha' been surprised, I think—but I wasn't, no, not nohow—"

"Do you mean you actually saw a woman here—here in my chambers?"

"Aye, I did, sir!"

"Who—who was she?"

"A wictim o' wiciousness, sir."

"What in the world do you mean? Who was she?"

"Well, d'ye 'appen to know a young woman name of Nancy Price, sir?"

"No!"

"And yet you've 'ad same in your arms, Mr. Werricker, sir."

"What the devil are you suggesting?" I demanded angrily.

"I suggest as you found same young woman in a vood at midnight and carried 'er to a inn called the 'Soaring Lark.'"

"Good heavens!" I exclaimed. "That unfortunate creature?"

"That werry same i-dentical, sir—a wictim o' wiciousness as your late lamented uncle, Sir Jervas, God bless 'im—amen!—saved from des'prit courses—"

"My uncle Jervas—" I exclaimed.

"Saved from des'prit courses!" repeated Mr. Shrig. "Himself, sir. Lord love him, 'e was always a-doin' of it; many a pore soul, male and female, 'e's saved from the river—ah, and worse as well, I know—ekally ready wi' fist or purse, ah, by Goles, an' vat vas better, with 'ope for the 'elpless an' 'elp for them as it seemed nothin' nor nobody could reach 'cept the law—a friend to them as thought they 'ad no friend but death. A fine gentleman, sir—yes, a tippy, a go, a bang-up blood, a reg'lar 'eavy-toddler, but most of all—a man! And I says again, God bless 'im an' 'is memory—amen!"

"Amen!" I repeated, while Mr. Shrig, tugging at something in the depths of a capacious side pocket, eventually drew thence a large, vivid-hued handkerchief and blew his nose resoundingly; which done, he blinked at me, surely the mildest-seeming man in all the world, despite the brass-mounted pistol which, disturbed in its lurking place by the sudden extrication of the handkerchief, peeped at me grimly from his pocket.

"Mr. Shrig, I should like to shake your hand," said I.

"'Eartily an' vith a vill, sir!" he answered.

"You see, I loved and honoured him also, Mr. Shrig."

"Verefore an' therefore, sir, I make bold to ask if you're partic'ler busy to-day?"

"I am here to meet a friend and then I am for the country."

"Tonbridge vay, sir?"

"Yes, why do you ask?"

"Because I've a call thereabouts myself to-day, an' if you vas minded to go along, I'd be honoured, sir, honoured."

"Thank you, Mr. Shrig, but—" I paused, for among the pile of unopened letters I espied one addressed in a familiar hand and, breaking the seal, read:

MY DEAR PERRY: Strong drink is raging, so am I, and London is the devil! Temptation dogs me, but a promise is a promise, so I have scuttled off ignominiously. You will find me at the Chequers Inn, Tonbridge, if I am not there to meet you, wait for me.

By the way, ale is exempt from your proscription, of course.

Yours to command now as ever,

ANTHONY VERE-MANVILLE.

"Mr. Shrig," said I, pocketing this letter, "when, pray, do you propose to start Tonbridge way?"

"This werry moment, sir."

"Why, then I shall be happy to accompany you."

135

"Are ye ready, sir?"

"Quite; let us go!"

So side by side we stepped out into the street; here Mr. Shrig, setting two fingers to his mouth, emitted a shrill whistle and round the corner came a tilbury behind a likely-looking horse driven by a red-faced man, who, at a sign from Mr. Shrig, descended from the lofty seat, into which we climbed forthwith.

"T'morrer mornin', Joel!" said Mr. Shrig, taking up the reins; and flicking the horse, away we went at a sharp trot.

"Do you propose to stay the night at Tonbridge, Mr. Shrig?"

"Vy—it's all accordin' to Number Vun, sir. Number Vun set out for Tonbridge but might be goin' further; v'ether 'e does or no, depends on Number Two."

"I fear I do not understand you, Mr. Shrig."

"Vich is 'ardly to be expected, sir. Y' see, perfeshionally speakin',
I'm arter two birds as I 'opes to ketch alive an' dead."

"But how can you catch anything alive and dead?"

"Veil, then, let's say vun alive an' t' other 'un dead."

"Ah—what kind of birds?"

"Downy vuns, sir—'specially Number Vun!" and here my companion smiled and nodded benignantly.

Mr. Shrig drove rapidly, threading his way through the traffic with the ease of an experienced Jehu, and soon in place of dingy roofs and chimneys my eyes were blessed with the green of trees shading the familiar road which led, as I knew, to those leafy solitudes where one "might walk with God." And now there rushed upon me a memory of Diana—Diana as she once had been—my Goddess of the Silent Places; and I yearned passionately for the irrevocable past and despaired in bitter hopelessness of the present and the long and lonely future.

From these gloomy thoughts I was aroused by the sound of my companion's voice:

"I am a-goin' on this here hexpe-dition, sir, with the expectation—I may say with the 'ope sir, of finding a body—"

"A body of what?" I enquired absently.

"Lord, Mr. Werricker, sir, vat should it be but a hum-ing body—a corpse, sir."

"Horrible!" I exclaimed. "Who is it? Where did he die?"

"Vell, sir," said Mr. Shrig, consulting a ponderous watch, "to the best o' my judgment 'e ain't dead yet, no, not yet, I fancy, but two hours—say three—should do 'is business neat an' comfortable; yes—in three hours 'e should be as nice a corpse as ever you might vish to see—if the con-clusions as I've drawed is correct. An' talkin' o' murder, sir—"

"Ah!" I exclaimed. Is it murder?"

"Sir," answered Mr. Shrig, "speakin' without prejudice, I answer you, it's a-goin' to be, or I'm a frog-eatin' Frenchman, vich God forbid, sir. An' speakin' o' murder, here's my attitood towards same—there's murder as is murder an' there's murder as is justifiable 'omicide. If you commits the fact for private wengeance, windictiveness or personal gain, then 't is murder damned an' vith a werry big he-M; but if so be you commits the fact to rid yourself or friends an' the world in general of evil, then I 'old 't is a murder justifiable. Consequently it will go to my 'eart to appre-'end this here murderer."

"Who is he?" I demanded.

"Ex-cuse me, sir—no! Seein' as 'ow this cove, though a murderer in intent, ain't a murderer in fact, yet—you must ex-cuse me if I with'old 'is name. And here's Eltham Village an' yonder's the 'Man o' Kent' a good 'ouse v'ere I'm known, so if you'll 'old the 'oss, sir, I'll get down and ax a question or so."

And I, sitting outside this sleepy hostelry in this quiet village street, thought no more of Mr. Shrig's gruesome errand, but rather of shady copse, of murmurous brooks and of one whose vivid presence had been an evergrowing joy and inspiration, waking me to nobler manhood, filling me with aspirations to heroic achievement; and to-day here sat I, lost in futile dreams—scorning myself for a miserable failure while the soul within me wept for that Diana of the vanished past—

"Right as ninepence, sir!" exclaimed Mr. Shrig, beaming cheerily as he clambered up beside me. "My birds 'as flew this vay, sure enough!"

Thus as we drove I sat alternately lost in these distressful imaginings or hearkening to my companion's animadversions upon rogues, criminals, and crime in general until, as the afternoon waned, we descended the steep hill into Wrotham village and pulled up at the "Bull" Inn, into whose hospitable portal Mr. Shrig vanished, to pursue those enquiries he had repeated at every posthouse along the road.

Presently as I sat, reins in hand, an ostler appeared who, grasping the horse's bridle and heeding me no whit, led us into the stable yard. And here I found Mr. Shrig leaning upon his knotted stick and lost in contemplation of a dusty chaise beneath which lay a perspiring and profane postboy busied with divers tools upon the front axle.

Now as I glanced at the vehicle, something about it struck me as familiar and then, despite the dust, I saw that it had red wheels and a black body picked out in yellow.

"Ah, Mr. Shrig," said I, "if this is the chaise you are so interested about, I think I can tell you who rode in it."

"And who would you name, sir?"

"Captain Danby," I answered.

"Aye, to be sure, sir. Then just step into the stable wi' me!"

Wondering, I obeyed and beheld a hissing ostler rubbing down a dusty horse.

"Why, this animal is mine!" I exclaimed. "This is Caesar, one of my saddle horses."

"Aye, to be sure, sir!" nodded Mr. Shrig. "Wiciousness has been a-ridin' in that theer chaise an' Windictiveness a-gallopin' arter on your 'oss. P'raps you can likewise tell me who't was as rode your 'oss?"

"No," I answered, "unless—good heaven, can it be Anthony—my friend
Mr. Vere-Manville?"

"Name sounds familiar!" said Mr. Shrig, rubbing his nose thoughtfully, while his keen gaze roved here and there.

"Where is Captain Danby—I want a word with him," said I, stepping hastily out of the stable.

"The Cap'n, sir," answered Mr. Shrig close to my elbow, "havin' partook of a glass o' brandy an' vater, has took a little valk a-top of it, an' the evenin' bein' so fine or as you might say balmy, I think we'll go a-valking too—"

Reaching the narrow street I espied the tall, lounging form of Captain Danby some considerable distance ahead and instinctively hastened my steps.

"Verefore the hurry, sir?" enquired Mr. Shrig, laying a finger on my arm.

"I must speak with yonder scoundrel."

"Scoundrel is the werry i-dentical vord, sir—but bide a bit—easy it is."

As he spoke, the Captain turned out of the street into a field path shaded by a tall hedge; in due time we also came to this path and saw a shady lane ran parallel with it, down which a man was walking. We had gone but a little way along this path when Mr. Shrig halted and seating himself upon the grassy bank, took off his hat and mopped his brow.

"A be-eautiful sunset, sir."

"Yes!" I answered, turning to view the glowing splendour.

"So werry red, Mr. Werricker, sir, like fire—like blood."

But I noticed that his keen glance was fixed upon the little wood that gloomed some distance before us, also that he held his head aslant as one who listens intently, and had taken out his ponderous watch.

"Why do you sit there, Mr. Shrig?" I enquired, a little impatiently.

"I'm a-vaitin', sir."

"What for, man?"

"Hush, sir, and you'll soon—"

The word was lost in a strange, sudden, double concussion of sound.

"At ex-actly twenty-two minutes to eight, sir!" said Mr. Shrig, and rising to his feet, set off briskly along the path. We had almost reached the wood I have mentioned when Mr. Shrig raised his knobbed stick to point at something that sprawled grotesquely across the path. The hat had fallen and rolled away and staring down into the horror of this face fouled with blood and blackened with powder, I recognised the features of Captain Danby.

"So here's the end o' Wiciousness," said Mr. Shrig and as he leaned upon his stick I saw his bright glance roving here and there; it flashed along the path before us; it swept the thicker parts of the hedge behind us; it questioned the deepening shadow of the copse. "Aye, here's an end to Number Vun, and if we look in the vood yonder, I fancy we shall see summat o' Number Two. This vay, sir—you can see the leaves is bloody hereabouts if you look—this vay!" Like one in an evil dream I followed him in among the trees and was aware that he had halted again.

"What now—what is it?" I questioned.

"Number Two, sir, and—look yonder, and—by Goles, 'e's dodged me likewise—burn my neck if 'e ain't!"

As he spoke, Mr. Shrig parted the kindly leaves and I beheld the form of my servant Clegg, as neat and precise in death as he had ever been in life.

"Poor lad!" said Mr. Shrig, baring his head. "Ye see, 'e 'appened to love Nancy Price, sir—the wictim o' Wiciousness yonder, an' 'ere's the result. Even walets has feelin's—this 'un werry much so!"

"Dead?" I mumbled, feeling myself suddenly faint. "Dead—both?"

"Aye, sir—both! Vich is comin' it a bit too low down on a man an' no error! To ha' lost both on 'em—crool 'ard I calls it!"

Sick with horror, I was stumbling away from this dreadful place when
Mr. Shrig's voice stayed me.

"'Old 'ard, sir—bide a bit! If the con-clusions as I've drawed is correct, here should be summat o' yourn."

Turning about, I espied him on his knees, examining the contents of the dead man's pockets with a methodical precision that revolted me.

"Of mine?" said I, shuddering.

"Your werry own, sir. 'T was one o' the reasons as I brought you along—I do 'ope Windictiveness here ain't destroyed it—ah, 'ere it is, Mr. Werricker, sir—though the seal's broke, you'll ob-serve."

Dazed and wondering, I took the letter he held out to me, but no sooner had I glanced at the superscription than I forgot all else for the moment.

"How—how should that man—come by this?" I stammered at last.

"Took or pur-loined it from the young 'ooman Nancy Price, sir, according to 'er own ewidence, as stated to me in my little office this mornin'—an' her a-veepin' all over my papers, pore lass! Aha!" exclaimed Mr. Shrig, still busied on his researches. "He's got summat in

137

this 'ere 'ind pocket as I can't come at—p'raps you'll obleege me by heavin' Windictiveness over a bit, sir? Why, never mind, sir—done it myself—"

"How—did the young woman come by this letter?"

"'T is in ewidence as years ago she was maid to a lady—now Mrs. Vere-Manville, it was give her by that same. What, are ye goin', sir? Werry good, this ain't exactly a cheery spot at present. Will you be so obleegin' as to send a cart an', say, a 'urdle for these ere birds o' mine?"

And so I left him, sitting between his "birds" whose flying days were done, busily making notes in his little book, very like some industrious clerk posting his ledger for the day.

Reaching the "Bull" Inn, I despatched cart and hurdle as desired and, ordering rooms for the night, shut myself therein to escape the general hubbub and horrified questioning my news had called forth. And here, remote from all and sundry, I unfolded the letter a dead man's hand had opened and read these words:

> Knowing you vile, I should have grieved for you, pitied you, but loved you still. Believing me vile, you are pitiless, cold, and with no mercy in you. Indeed and you would have shamed me! But true love, being of Heaven, knows no shame and can never die. Oh, you poor, blind Peregrine.

TO MY PATIENT AND KINDLY READER

Here do I make an end of this Second Book, wherein shall be found overmuch of blood, of gloom and shadow, of misunderstanding and heartbreak engendered of my own perfervid imagination; and glad am I and more than glad to have done with it.

And here, since the longest road must end, since after storm and tempest must come peace and heavenly calm, and because "though heaviness endure for a night yet joy cometh in the morning"—here do I begin this Third, last, and shortest Book which those enduring Readers who have borne with and followed me thus far may see is inscribed

DAWN

Book Three

DAWN

CHAPTER I

CONCERNING ONE TOM MARTIN, AN OSTLER

I sat upon a hay pile in that same shady corner of the yard behind the "Chequers" inn where once had stood a weather-beaten cart drawn by a four-footed philosopher called Diogenes.

But to-day this corner was empty save for myself, and the yard also except for two or three wains or country waggons and a man in a sleeved waistcoat who chewed upon a straw and stared at the inn, the waggons and myself with a faded, lack-lustre eye and sniffed; so frequently indeed, and so loudly that at last it obtruded itself upon my notice.

"You have a very bad cold!" said I.

"I ain't!" he retorted gloomily.

"Yet you sniff very loud."

"Con-sti-tootional!" quoth he. "My feyther done it afore me, an' 'is feyther afore 'im, 'an 'is feyther afore 'im an'—but wot of it, my chap? Can't a cove sniff if so minded?"

"Certainly!" I answered.

"I ain't said nothink to you about wallerin' in that theer 'ay—'ave
I? Very well! Why can't you let a man sniff in peace?"

"Very well," said I, "sniff!"

"I will!" said he and immediately did so, louder than ever.

"Astonishing!" said I.

"A cove can sniff without a cold if so be 't is 'is natur' so to do, can't 'e?"

"So I perceive."

"An' 't is a free country an' such so bein', a man's at liberty to sniff or no, an' no offence give or took, ain't 'e? Very well, then!"

"Very well indeed!" I nodded. "I have never heard a man sniff better or louder—"

"You leave my sniffin' alone an' I'll leave you alone—"

"I hope you will," said I.

"Well, I ain't so sure as I will; you wags your chin too much to please me—an' let me tell ye, bold an' p'inted, I don't like the cock o' your eye! So s'pose you stand on your pins—"

"Well," I answered, stretching myself more comfortably, "let us suppose so—what then?"

"Why, then, my covey, I'll knock ye off your pins again—prompt an' j'yful!"

"Under those circumstances I much prefer to remain as I am."

"Why, then you're a weevil—a worm, ah—an' what's more, a weevily worm at that, an' I spits on ye!"

Here, perceiving that he was about to put his heinous threat into execution, I arose.

138

"Enough!" quoth I, buttoning my coat. "Now let Olympus shake, the caverns of ocean roar, the round earth tremble! If you have fists, prepare to use them now—come on, pestiferous peasant, most contumacious clod, and 'damned be he that first cries Hold—enough'!"

"Well, drown'd me!" exclaimed the ostler, staring. "Drown'd me if I ever 'eard sich 'orrid talk in all my days, an' I've groomed for a earl—ah, an' a markis afore now!"

Having said which, he clenched his fists, squared his shoulders and launched himself at me like a charging bull. But profiting by Jessamy Todd's many lessons and painful instruction, I danced nimbly aside, tapped him with my left, spun round to meet his second rush, checked him with a flush hit, swung my right beneath his chin and next moment saw him sitting upon the cobblestones, legs wide-straddled, gaping about him with a vacant air.

"'Oly 'eavens!" he murmured, glancing from the cloudless sky to me and back again. "An' sich a whipper-snapper—'oly 'eavens!"

"A—weevily worm?" I enquired.

"Sir, I takes it back!" he answered, tenderly feeling his chin. "There ain't a weevil breathin', no, nor yet a worm as could ha' knocked me off my pins so neat an' true! I takes back weevil an' likewise worm, sir."

"Good!" said I, and tossed him a shilling.

"What's this 'ere for?" he enquired.

"The exercise you have afforded me; it has done me good, chased the dusty cobwebs from my brain, stimulated more healthy thought. Life perchance is not all dust and ashes nor the world a pit of noisome gloom; some day even I may learn perhaps to be—almost happy—"

"Lord, sir, you sound as if you'd been crossed an' double-crossed in love, you do—"

"Ah—what do you mean?"

"No offence, sir! But y' see, I were in love once—ah, an' with a sweet purty lass an' she wi' me, but afore I could marry 'er she bolted along of a circus cove in a scarlet, laced coat an' whip, d'ye see."

"Extremely feminine!" said I, nodding.

"May be, sir, but one day she come creepin' back to me, very 'eart-broke an' shameful, pore lass; seems the circus cove, growin' tired-like, 'ad took to usin' 'is whip on 'er—an' so she come a-creepin' back to me."

"And what then?"

"Why, then, o' course I married 'er."

"Married her! But after—the disgrace—"

"There weren't no disgrace; I married 'er! Y' see, I loved 'er purty looks an' gentle ways."

"And you—married her—notwithstanding! You forgave her!"

"Aye, I did—years an' years ago! Ah, an' a danged good little wife she's been too—ah, an' mother—none better."

"Have you many children?"

"Nine!"

"And you feed them all?"

"Every one—an' very frequent, bless their little 'earts."

"And clothe them?"

"As well as I can, sir, though their clo'es gets uncommon wore an' 'oley, 'igh an' low—specially low, sir!"

"You provide a roof to shelter them?"

"Aye—such as it is—needs re-thatchin' bad."

"And are you happy?"

"Aye, I am—though times is 'ard."

"And pray what is your name?"

"Martin, sir—Thomas Martin."

"Then, Thomas Martin, you are a man—and a better, a far better man than I, for—hear me confess, Tom Martin, I have never performed any one of these man's virtues. You have done nobly!" And I thrust five guineas into his work-hardened palm.

"Well drown'd me!" he gasped, very much as if he were undergoing that watery ordeal. "Egad, sir! Lord love your eyes an' limbs—"

"For the children and their mother," said I.

"God bless ye, sir!"

"Indeed I hope He may. Heaven knows I have been a sufficing failure hitherto, a sorrow to myself and my friends. But you, Tom Martin, have inspired me to attempt a notable good action—perhaps the noblest of my life. So good-bye, Tom; let me hasten to perform the best act I ever did!"

Hurrying into the inn I called for pens, ink and paper, and sitting down forthwith, wrote this:

MY DEAR ANTHONY:

The wind has whispered, a bird has sung to me, and an ostler, by name
Tom Martin (long may he flourish) has shown me a man's work.

For who am I, poor finite wretch, to judge my fellows and condemn such as work me evil (and, inadvertently, themselves also, since Evil is double-edged and cuts both ways?) Who am I to despise or dislove them for the pain they cause me to endure (and, inadvertently,

139

themselves also?) Should I not rather seek to forget past wrongs, to cherish and comfort such as despitefully use me? Is not this the secret of true and abiding happiness?

My two uncles (whom God eternally bless!) waked in me the desire to be a true man; and what is there more manly than to forget a wrong, to forgive past trespasses and cherish the hand that has hurt us?

So to-day, dear Anthony, instead of awaiting you here, I do a better thing; to-day at last, I go seeking my manhood in the achievement of a nobler act than I ever thought possible of my accomplishment; to-day I go to Diana.

Your devoted friend,

PEREGRINE VEREKER.

This letter despatched, I ordered a horse to be saddled; very soon, thanks to Tom Martin's zeal, the animal was at the door and, though the day was far advanced, I mounted forthwith and galloped away for Wyvelstoke Towers.

CHAPTER II

I GO TO FIND DIANA

Birds were calling their melodious complaint on the passing of another day and the shadows were lengthening when I came to a cross-roads where stood a timeworn finger-post beneath which sat a solitary figure in weather-beaten hat and coat, head bowed over the book opened upon his knees.

Now at sight of this lonely figure I reined in so suddenly that this solitary person glanced up and I saw the white hair, keen eyes and pale, aquiline features of the Earl of Wyvelstoke. At sight of me he closed the book and rose, and in stern features, in every line of his slender, shabby figure was a stately aloofness that chilled me.

"My lord?" said I interrogatively, and taking off my hat, I bowed.

"Ah, Mr. Vereker," he answered, with a slight inclination of his head. "So you come at last. A charming evening. I wish you as well of it as you deserve!" And turning his back, he began to limp away; but in a moment I was off my horse and, hastening after, ventured to touch his arm, then fell back in sheer amazement before the ferocious glare of his eyes; yet his voice was as politely modulated as usual when he spoke:

"Sir, were you any other than Peregrine Vereker—old as I am, I would call you out—and shoot you with peculiar satisfaction—"

"My lord—sir—?" I stammered.

"Sir," he continued, "you will doubtless have very many excellent excuses to offer for your perfectly inexcusable conduct—but doubtless you will at least have the good taste to keep them to yourself. Whatever your reasons, you have been the cause of much pain and very many bitter tears to—to one I hold inexpressibly dear."

"My lord, I—I have been ill—"

"And it is, I believe, mainly owing to her devotion that you still—gladden the world, sir."

"My lord, I am here to—to give Diana my hand in fulfilment of my promise."

"Are you indeed, Mr. Vereker—you surprise me!"

"To marry her whenever she will, sir."

"Permit me to remark that you are perhaps a little tardy."

"None the less I am here, sir!"

"Your condescension, Mr. Vereker, is somewhat overpowering, such magnanimity I find vastly touching. But Diana, I am assured, had no idea of permitting you thus to immolate yourself on the altar of duty."

"That, my lord, by your favour, I mean to learn from her own lips—at once."

"Impossible, sir!" he retorted, smiling bitterly. "Quite—quite impossible."

"Impossible, my lord—impossible? Pray what—sir, what do you mean?" I stammered.

"That if indeed you are minded—a little late in the day perhaps—but if—after very mature deliberation—you at last think fit to fulfil your pledge to Diana, it will of course be necessary that you first discover her present whereabouts."

"Is she not here at Wyvelstoke with you, my lord?"

"Emphatically not, sir!"

"Then she is with Mrs. Vere-Manville at Nettlestead or in London—at least I will go there—at once."

"Then you will waste your time, sir. Diana has disappeared."

"Disappeared? Ah, you mean she has gone—run away? Pray, my lord, pray when—when did she go?"

His lordship looked at me keenly a while and when he spoke his voice seemed less harsh:

"The news would seem to disturb you, sir?"

"Beyond words, sir. Henceforth I shall know little rest until I find her. Pray when did she leave you—and how?"

"She fled—yesterday morning—stole from Wyvelstoke before daybreak—she was seen by one of the keepers stealing away in the dawn. She fled away to—hide her grief—leaving behind all her jewels and—a very—solitary, very old—man. She was all I had—my comrade, my Penthesilea—my loved daughter—"

His lordship's voice broke upon the word, his usually upright figure seemed suddenly bowed and shrunken, he looked indeed a very grief-stricken, decrepit old man as he stood fumbling in the pockets of his shabby coat, whence he presently drew a letter that shook and rustled in his fingers as he unfolded it.

"She left this also, sir," he continued with an evident effort, "pray read it—you will find some mention of—breaking hearts the which should interest you a little—read it, sir!"

So I took the letter and saw it was this:

DEAREST PAL AND NOBLEST OF MEN: My poor heart is breaking, I think, and knowing how true I and deep is your love for me I would not have you see my pain. So I have run away from you awhile—fled away to the Silent Places like the poor, hurt creature I am. There I mean to hide until my wound is a little healed and then I shall come back to you, my dear, that I may surround you with my love and teach you how inexpressibly dear you are to Your would-be daughter and ever loving, grateful, DIANA.

"Has she money, sir?" I enquired, returning the letter.

"Very, very little, I fear."

"Then she cannot have gone very far."

"Ah, Peregrine—" the proud, old head drooped and the hand that crept upon my dusty coat sleeve was very thin and tremulous; "ah, Peregrine, if you love her, find her again—find her for Love's sake—and the sake of a desolate—heartsick—old man!"

"Sir," I answered, covering this twitching hand with my own, "I will—bring her back to you—if I have to travel the world over—I will find her if it takes me all my life and every penny I possess!"

Then, mounting my horse, I swung him round and galloped away without further word of farewell or so much as one backward glance.

CHAPTER III

TELLS HOW I FOUND DIANA AND SOONER THAN I DESERVED

It was growing dark when I reached a part of the road that I seemed to recognise; therefore I checked my steed to look about me.

Surely it was here or hereabouts that, upon a never-to-be-forgotten day, I had acted the craven and, fleeing in panic, yet (heaven be praised!) had rushed back to be beaten into unconsciousness by Diana's brutal assailant. Surely it was beneath yonder tree that I had waked to find my head pillowed in her lap, her cool hand upon my brow, her lovely face stooped above me full of tender solicitude.

Remembering which, I was seized of a sudden passionate longing for the touch of her hand, to behold again this face radiant with love.

'My poor heart is breaking I think—so I have fled away to hide—'

As I sat my horse, seeing in fancy the blotted lines of this, her letter, to my yearning was added the triumphant assurance that in spite of everything she loved me still; but this thought in turn was 'whelmed in despair because of the well-nigh hopelessness of my search.

And in this moment my wandering gaze lighted upon the shadowy outline of a gate that opened in the hedge upon my right hand, upon a rolling meadow with a gloom of shadowy trees beyond.

Next moment I was afoot, leading my horse, for surely this was that gate through which she had led me, swooning with my hurts, across this meadow, amid trees and underbrush, to that ruined and desolate barn which, she had once told me, had ever been her haven of refuge.

After some little delay, I contrived to open this gate and, leading my horse, began to cross the meadow, glancing this way and that, often pausing unsure, fearful that my memory was at fault. In this hesitant manner I proceeded until I was dimly aware that the ground sloped down before me into a place of shadows thick with dense-growing trees and bushes.

All at once I halted, a prey to many swift emotions, but chief of these joy and a thrilling, hopeful expectancy, for amid the deep gloom before me I espied a faint beam of light, and I was praying within myself as, my gaze upon this blessed light, I descended into the deeper shadows. Of necessity I went very slowly and cautiously until, the trees thinning out somewhat, enabled me to make out a black looming shape that gradually resolved itself into a barn; and it was from the small opening or window beneath the gable that the beam of light shone forth.

A solitary place and dismal, far removed from the world, a very sinister place, such indeed as might well be the haunt of grisly spectres; yet, with my gaze upturned to that beckoning light, I would not have changed it, just then, for the most gorgeous palace in all the world. Suddenly I halted again, my breath in check, to stare at this dreadful place with eyes of horror, as from its impenetrable gloom came sounds that brought out the sweat upon my temples and set my hand quivering upon the bridle,—a succession of hollow knocks and rappings whose dull reverberations seemed to fill the night.

For a long moment I stood thus, grasping my horse's bridle, shivering from head to foot, and staring at the black and ominous shape before me in wide-eyed terror; then I heard that which brought me to myself—nay, transformed me into a cool, dispassionate, relentless creature, reckless of all harms and dangers, intent only upon the one desperate purpose.

Leading my horse in among the trees, I tethered him securely and began to approach the barn very cautiously and with every nerve and sinew strung to instant action, my heavy riding-whip grasped in ready hand.

The knocking had ceased and, creeping nearer, I found the doors open and, from the pitchy gloom of the interior, heard a hoarse gasping that spoke of vicious effort.

"Be damned t' ye, Dick!" panted a hoarse voice. "'Eave, man—'eave—her's a-laying across the trap—push, damn ye—"

"Aye, Tom—but her's got a knife!" panted a second voice. "Don't 'e forget 'er's got a knife!"

"An' what—good'll her knife be—once we get—our 'ands on 'er—'eave, I tell ye—both together—now!"

"Bide a bit, Tom—let's 'ave a light—"

"Light be damned—'eave, man!"

Fumbling my way to the wall, I began to creep towards the creaking ladder where these panting, wrestling, evil things strove so desperately. Once or twice came a swift beam of light, vivid in the pervading blackness, as the trap door was forced up an inch or so; brief, sudden gleams, that showed me the forms of two men crouched upon the ladder, their shoulders bowed in passionate effort; and I waited until, loud-panting with their desperate exertions, they began to force up the trap again.

"Now, Dick—now!" gasped a voice; and then as they strove again, I leapt and smote with all my strength. A squeal of pain and terror, the sudden slam of the trap closing out all light, the impact of a heavy body upon the rotting hay that littered the floor, and a feeble, whining voice.

"Tom—O Tom—there's summat in 'ere wi' us—hurted bad I be—there's summat in 'ere as 'ave cut my 'ead open, Tom. O Tom, come down an' 'elp a pal—"

"What are ye yelpin' over now—and be cursed!" panted the man Tom from the ladder. "Th' gal's got money, I tell ye, an' 'er's a 'andsome tit into the bargain, so it's up wi' this 'ere trap—"

"O Tom, summat 'it me—come on down! There's summat or some one 'ere wi' us—come down an' see—"

"'Ow can us see wi'out a light?"

"Well, I got my tinder box."

I heard the man Tom stumble down the ladder, heard the sound of flint and steel, saw their two evil heads outlined against the glow of the tinder as they blew and, leaping upon them, I smote with my heavy riding-whip again and yet again.

And now in the black horror of this ruined barn was pandemonium, a wild uproar of shouts and cries, the sound of vicious blows, the shock of groaning bodies.

If they were two, they fought a mad creature who, careless of defence, unconscious of his own hurts, sought only to maim and rend; whether reeling in desperate grapple or rolling half-smothered beneath my assailants, I fought as a wild beast might, utterly regardless of myself, with fingers that wrenched and tore, fists that smote untiring, feet that kicked and trampled, head that drove and butted—I was indeed a living weapon, as senseless to pain and as merciless—intent only on destruction.

All suddenly was silence, a blessed quiet, save for the hoarse pant of my own breathing. Stumbling to the doorway, I leaned there, vaguely glad the horrid business was over, since I found myself faint and sick. Afar off I heard lugubrious voices that called one to another, a snapping of twigs growing ever fainter, and a rustle of leaves that marked their flight.

Down my cheeks and into my eyes a sticky moisture was trickling that I knew was blood, but the sweet night air revived me greatly so that, my strength returning, I presently—stumbled back into the blackness of the barn, found my way to the ladder and leaned there a while. And after some time, I lifted heavy head and spoke:

"Diana—are you there—my Diana?"

Silence, and a sudden, sickening dread, a growing fear, insomuch that I made shift to climb the ladder and, lifting heavy hand, rapped upon the trap door:

"Diana—O Diana—are you there?"

An inarticulate cry, and next moment the trap door was lifted, revealing a square of vivid light, and in this radiant glory—Diana's face.

"Diana," said I, wiping the blood from my eyes the better to behold her loveliness, "Diana—when will you—marry me?"

"O Peregrine—oh, my beloved!"

And down to me she reached her strong and gentle arms to draw me up from the darkness into the glory of her presence.

CHAPTER IV

I WAIT FOR A CONFESSION

"O Peregrine! My dear—how they have hurt you!"

She was ministering to my scratches and abrasions, and I, sitting on the old hay-pile, watched her, joying in the gentle touch of her white, dexterous hands, her sweet motherliness and all the warm, vital beauty of her.

"Child," said I, "don't tremble so—the beasts are gone!"

"Yes, I know—I heard everything, Peregrine. And you down there—all alone—to fight them in the dreadful dark! And I once dared to call you coward!"

"So I was, Diana. So I am. It was you gave me courage, then and now—you and—my love for you."

"Your love?" she whispered, and now the tremor was in her voice also.

"It was Love guided me here to-night, Diana—brought me back to you—for ever and always if—if you will have it so."

"O Peregrine," she sighed, leaning towards me, "my Peregrine, then your love for me is not dead as I feared?"

"Nor ever can be," I answered, very conscious of her nearness, "surely true love is immortal, Diana."

"You speak rather like a book, Peregrine."

"I quote from your own letter, Diana."

"And this—strange love of yours, Peregrine, that I feared dead, has come to life again because you know at last how cruelly you misjudged me—you are here because you have found out?"

"I have found out nothing."

"Then—oh—why, then, you still think evil of me?"

"I love you!" said I, leaning towards her, for she had drawn from me a little. "I love you—more than ever, I think, yes, indeed it must be so—because I am here to shield you with my care—to make you my wife."

"Wife?" she whispered, shrinking yet farther from me. "Your wife? You would marry me in my—vileness—doubting my honour?"

"Your honour shall be mine, henceforth."

Now at this she sat back to regard me beneath wrinkled brows; once her scarlet mouth quivered, though whether she would weep or no I knew not, but before the sweet directness of her eyes I felt strangely abashed and knew again that old consciousness of futility.

"O Peregrine," she sighed at last, "how very—foolishly blind you are, how hopelessly masculine, and how nobly generous—my proud gorgio gentleman!" And stooping, she caught my hand ere I knew and kissed it passionately.

"O Diana!" I exclaimed, very ill at ease. "Why do—so?"

"Because—oh, my dear—because you would stoop to lift your poor, stained Diana from the depths and cover her shame with your love! Because, thinking me vile, you would still honour me with your name. Oh, my Peregrine, you love me more—much more than I ever dared hope—better than even you know!" And rising, she gave herself to my eager arms.

"O Diana," I murmured, "how wonderful you are!"

"Last time we met you called me—wanton!" she whispered.

"I was mad!" cried I remorsefully. "And yet—"

"And yet—you meant it, dear Peregrine! And tonight I am here upon your heart—oh, wonderful—kiss your wanton again—"

"Ah—hush!" I pleaded. "Don't—don't say it."

"Ah, Peregrine, beloved—don't think it!"

"But Diana," I groaned, "oh, my Diana, I saw you with—"

"Hush!" she whispered suddenly. "There is somebody moving down below—listen!"

From the pitchy gloom beneath came a heavy tread and a deep, long-drawn sigh; but even so I knew a happiness beyond all expression to feel how she nestled closer into my embrace as if seeking protection there.

"Are you afraid, my Diana?"

"Nothing could ever frighten me—here!" she whispered. And then the place suddenly reechoed with a loud whinnying.

"My horse—I had forgotten him!" said I. And then, as she stirred sighfully, I stooped and kissed her, ere, loosing her, I rose. "I'll go and make him comfortable for the night."

"And I will make you a bed, Peregrine."

"It will be like old times," said I.

"Yes—though we didn't—kiss each other—then, Peregrine," said she, looking at me with a glory in her eyes. "Ah, no—not again—look at the candle, it will be out in a minute or two and I haven't another—so hurry, dear."

Forthwith I descended into the dimness below and finding the horse, loosed off saddle and bridle; this done, I closed the doors and was making them as secure as might be when I heard her calling:

"Be quick, Perry, the candle is going out!"

So I climbed up the ladder and, drawing it after me, closed the trap—and as I did so, the light flickered and vanished; but, guided by her voice, I stumbled through the dark and, finding the hay-pile, lay down. And then, all at once, I began to tremble, for there rushed upon me the conviction that, lying thus beside me so near I might have touched her, yet hidden thus in the kindly dark, she was nerving herself to the confession of that which must be pain to speak and agony to hear; thus, tense and expectant, I stared upon the gloom, waiting—waiting for her voice and resolved that I would be merciful in my judgment of her.

Thus moment after moment dragged by and I in a very fever of anticipation, waiting—listening—At last she stirred, but instead of the broken, pleading murmur I expected, I heard a long, blissful sigh, a rustle of the hay as she settled herself more cosily, and when she spoke her voice sounded actually slumberous:

"Are you comfortable, Peregrine?"

"Thank you—yes."

"Yet you—sound very restless. What is it, dear?"

"O Diana—have you—nothing to—to tell me?"

"You mean—to confess? No, dear."

"Nothing?" I groaned.

"Only to bid you not worry your dear, foolish head over trifles—"

"Trifles?" I gasped, sitting up in my amazement. "Trifles?"

"Silly trifles!" said she with a strange, little, tremulous laugh. "You came seeking me. You wish to make me your wife because your love is nobler, greater than you or I ever dreamed. And I am yours, and we are together at last and this—this is all that can possibly matter to us—Fourteen guineas, a florin, one groat and three pennies—was that so very much to pay for me? Do you regret your purchase?"

"No."

"Then—have faith in your love for me, Peregrine. Give me your hand in mine—this dear hand that fought for me and would lift poor me out of the shameful mire. And now, good night, beloved—now, shut your eyes! Are they closed?"

143

"Yes, Diana."

"Then go to sleep."

And with this cool, soft hand clasping mine, I sank at last into a blessed slumber.

CHAPTER V

IN WHICH WE MEET OLD FRIENDS

Morning with a glory of sun flooding in at the small aperture beneath the gable and through every crack and cranny of timeworn roof and walls; a glory to dazzle my sleepy eyes and fill me with ineffable gladness, despite my cuts and bruises.

For a moment I lay blinking drowsily and then started to my elbow, my every nerve a-thrill to the sound of a soft and regular breathing.

She lay within a yard of me, half-buried in the hay that clung about her shapeliness; and beholding her thus in the sweet abandonment of slumber, so altogether unconscious of my nearness, it was with a half-guilty feeling that I leaned nearer to drink in her loveliness.

Her hair was disordered, and here and there a stalk of hay had ensconced itself in these silky ripples, and no wonder, for observing a glossy curl above her ear I had an urgent desire to feel it twined about my finger, and shifted my gaze to her face, viewing in turn her cheek rosy with sleep, her dark, curling lashes, her vivid lips, the creamy whiteness of her throat.

But—even now, even as I mutely worshipped her thus, something in the voluptuous beauty of her troubled me. Memory waked, Imagination burst its shackles and began its fell work:

Other eyes than mine had seen her thus ... other hands ... other lips.... Before me flashed a vision of Devereux's evil features hatefully triumphant. And yet ... Great God, was this indeed the face of a wanton? Could such horror possibly be?

In imagination the dead lived again, the past returned, and through my closed lids I saw Devereux—her "slave and master" lean to gloat upon her defenceless beauty, bold-eyed and on his cruel lips the smile of a satyr.... And bowing my sweating temples between quivering fists, I ground my teeth in agony.

Now as I crouched thus, plagued by the obscene demons of my imagination, I was aroused by a distant sound and opening my eyes saw how the sun touched Diana's sleeping form like the blessing of God. And yet ... what of that night at Raydon Manor? She had volunteered me no word of explanation—not one—and why?

Up to me, borne on the sunny air, came the sound of a whistle that brought me to my feet eager for action, for conflict or death itself—anything rather than the harrowing torment of my thoughts. Very cautiously I crossed the uneven floor and lifting the trap as silently as possible, I set the ladder in place and descended. The whistling had stopped, but in its stead I caught a sound of stealthy movement outside the barn, and glancing about, I presently espied my whip where I had dropped it last night, and with this in my hand I gently unbarred the doors and opening them a little way, stepped out into the radiant morning. And then, tossing aside my whip, I ran forward, both hands extended in eager greeting.

"Why, Jerry!" I exclaimed. "O Jerry Jarvis, you come like an angel of heaven!"

"Lord!" exclaimed the Tinker, grasping my hands very hard. "Lord love you, Mr. Vereker—"

"Call me Perry as you used."

"Why, then—here's j'y, Perry—but as to angels, who ever see an angel in cord breeches—an' patched at that! But God bless us all—what should bring you hereabouts—"

"Love, Jerry—love—"

"You mean—Anna?"

"Yes, we are to be married as soon as possible."

"What, you an' Anna?"

"Who else, my Jeremy?"

"But she's a-breaking her 'eart over summat or other—"

"No, she's lying fast asleep in the loft yonder and looking as sweet—as good and pure as—as—"

"As she is, Peregrine!"

"Yes, Jerry. But what are you doing here, God bless you!"

"Didn't you know as she wrote me two days since—app'inting me to meet her here—and here I am, a bit early p'raps, but then I thought she was lonely—in trouble, d'ye see—in trouble. And then, Lord, if you only knew how hungry—aye, ravenous I am for sight of her arter all this time—"

"Why, then, you shall see her—at once."

"Nay, let her have her sleep out; let's you an' me get a fire going.
I've a frying pan in my cart over yonder—ham an' eggs, lad!"

"God bless you again, Jerry—breakfast! And here among the trees it will be like old times, though Jessamy ought to be with us, of course."

"Well he's over at my little camp not so far away. I'm pitched t' other side Amberley wood."

"How is he, Jerry?"

"Mighty well. He's rich again, y' see—aye, richer than ever an' pursooed by several widders in consequence. He's come into a mort o' money, has Jessamy. But you know all about it, o' course?"

"Not a word."

"Lord, an' 't was your uncle, Sir Jervas, as done it! Left Jess five—thousand—pound! Think o' that!"

Thus, talking like the old friends we were, we set about collecting sticks and soon had the fire burning merrily. All at once we stood silent and motionless, for Diana was singing.

It was an Italian love song full of sweet rippling notes and trills but, as she sang it, a very ecstasy of yearning tenderness that changed suddenly to joy and rapturous happiness, her glorious voice ringing out full-throated, rich and clear, inexpressibly sweet, swelling louder and louder until suddenly it was gone and we standing mute with awed delight.

"She's a-doin' her hair!" whispered Jerry. "She allus used to sing in the morning a-doin' her hair, I mind, but never—ah, never so—wonderfully!"

And then she began again, this time that Zingari air we both remembered so well. Singing thus, she stepped out into the sunlight but, seeing us, stopped in the middle of a note and ran forward (even as I had done) with both hands outstretched in greeting.

"Jerry!" she cried. "My dear, good Jerry!"

But the Tinker drew back, a little abashed by the wondrous change in her.

"Why, Ann—why, Anna!" he stammered. "Can this be you—so—so beautiful? Speaks different too!"

"O Jerry dear—won't you kiss me?"

"Glory be!" he exclaimed, taking her outstretched hands. "Though so very different 'tis the same sweet maid—'tis the very same Ann as learned to read an' write s' wonderful quick—Glory be!" And so they kissed each other.

Then walking between us, busy with question and answer, he brought us where stood his weather-beaten, four-wheeled chaise with Diogenes, that equine philosopher, cropping the grass as sedulously as though he had never left off and who, lifting shaggy head, snorted unimpassioned greeting and promptly began to nibble again.

Butter, a new loaf, ham and eggs and coffee! What hungry mortals could desire more? And now the Tinker and I, sitting side by side in the leafy shade, watched our Diana who, scornful of all assistance, prepared breakfast with her own quick, capable hands.

What words are there may adequately describe this meal? With what appetite we ate, all three; how we talked and laughed for small reason or no reason at all.

"Lord, Ann!" exclaimed the Tinker, glancing from the piece of ham on his knife point to Diana's stately beauty.

"'Tis wonderful what two years can do! You don't need any book of etiquette these days—you look so proud, so noble—aye, as any duchess in a nov-el or out! Lord love you, Ann, it don't seem right any more as you should be a-drinkin' coffee out of a tin mug along of a travellin' tinker in patched breeches, that it don't! I reckon you've seen a lot o' the grand world an' plenty o' fine folk, eh Ann?"

"Enough to know the simpler joys are always the best, dear Jerry, and to love the Silent Places more than ever. And as for you, Jerry, there never was such a tinker before—"

"And never will be again!" I added.

"And so we mean to stay with you awhile, don't we, Peregrine?"

"Excellent!" said I. "We will shift camp to the old place—"

"The little wood beside the stream beyond Wyvelstoke," said Diana softly, "that dear place where Love found us—in the dawn—and you clasped the little locket about my neck, Peregrine."

"Which you don't wear now, Diana!"

"Which you shall put back—one day—soon, Peregrine."

"Why did you take it off, Diana?"

"Because!" she answered.

"Because of—what?" I persisted.

"Just—because!" she answered in the old tantalising way. And so we sat a little while looking into each other's eyes.

"By Goles!" exclaimed the Tinker so suddenly that we both started, having clean forgotten him for a while. "'Tis good to be young, but 'tis better—aye, much better, to be in love, that it is! And—you may be mighty fine folk up to London, but you'll always be just children to me—my children o' the woods!"

"And so, Jerry, we'll stay with you until we are married if you'll have us?"

"Have you?" he repeated, a little huskily. "Have you? Why, Lord love ye—I feel that proud, an' s' happy as I don't know what—only—God bless ye both—Amen!" So saying, he arose rather abruptly and hastened off to harness Diogenes.

"Diana," said I, drawing her to me, "Diana, what do you mean by 'because'?" And standing submissive in the circle of my arms she answered:

"Because you love me so truly, Peregrine, doubt cannot make you love me less. But because of your doubt I have grieved, and because I grieved I ran away, and because I ran away you came to find me, and because of this I am happy. But because I am—a little proud also, I will not wear your love-token until you know how unjust are your doubts, and because I am a woman you shall not know this until I choose. But because I love you in spite of your doubts as you love me because you are so nobly generous, I am yours for ever and ever. So here's the answer—here's the meaning of 'because' and now—won't you kiss me, Peregrine?"

Thus stood we awhile amid the whispering leaves, and by the touch of her mouth doubt and heaviness were lifted from me. Then hand in hand she brought me where we might behold the barn, no longer a place of evil, gloomy and sinister, but transformed by the kindly sun into a place of beauty, dignified by age.

"Good-bye, old barn!" she whispered. "Look, Peregrine, it is so very, very old, and cannot last much longer—and I love it because it was there my man fought for me; it was there he showed me how truly generous, how wonderful is his love for me—O Peregrine, my gorgio gentleman, what a man you are! Good-bye, old barn!" she whispered. "Good-bye!"

And when I had led forth my post horse and tethered him behind the four-wheeled cart, we clambered in all three, Diana sitting close beside me so that the kindly wind ever and anon would blow a tress of her fragrant hair across my lips to be kissed.

And so the dead went back to his grave and my demons fled awhile.

"Perry," said the Tinker as, turning from the highway, Diogenes ambled down a narrow lane, "you've forgot to ask about this here watch o' mine."

"Well, how is it, Jerry?"

"Never was such a watch! Look at it! Reg'lar as the sun! Which riles Jessamy. Y' see, his ain't to be depended on nowadays, owing to a boot—"

"A boot, Jerry?" laughed Diana.

"At Maidstone Fair, Ann! Jessamy was preachin' Brotherly Love when a large cove in a white 'at up an' kicked him in the watch, which is apt to be a little unsettlin' to any timepiece. Anyhow, Jessamy's has never gone right since."

"His watch again!" cried I. "Last time the trouble was a brick, I remember."

"But Jerry, what happened to the 'cove' in the white hat?" enquired
Diana.

"Well, arter it was all over, Jessamy took him aside into a quiet corner an' they prayed together."

"Jessamy was always a forceful evangelist!" she laughed.

"And there he is."

"Where?" questioned Diana.

"Listen and you'll hear him, Ann!" Sure enough from the boskages adjacent came the ring and tap of a hammer to the accompaniment of a rich, sweet voice unpraised in song.

Hereupon, setting two slim, white fingers to her mouth, Diana whistled loud and shrilly, to the Tinker's no small delight. Ensued a prodigious rustling and snapping of twigs and into the lane sprang the slender, shapely figure of Jessamy himself, as bright of eye, as light and quick of foot as ever.

I will not dilate upon this second meeting, but it was good to feel the hearty grip of his fingers, to hear the glad welcome in his voice, to see how gallantly he stooped to kiss Diana's hand, and how his sun-tanned cheek flushed beneath the touch of her lips.

"Why, Anna!" he exclaimed. "Well, well—you ha' become so—so—you look so uncommon—what I mean is—"

"Beautiful!" said the Tinker. "Be-autiful's the word, Jess!"

"Aye, aye, shipmate, so it is, comrade!"

"And the next word is strike camp, Jessamy, up stick an' away, Jess—"

"We're going to the old place, Jessamy!" nodded Diana.

"Where you instructed me in the 'noble art,' Jessamy!" said I.

"So it's all together and with a will, Jess!" added the Tinker.

"Aye, aye—and heartily!" laughed Jessamy.

I will pass over the labour of the ensuing hours wherein we all wrought cheerfully; but evening found us camped within that oft-remembered wood beside the stream whose murmurous waters seemed to find a voice to welcome us.

CHAPTER VI

WHICH, AS THE PATIENT READER SEES, IS THE LAST

The Tinker stood resplendent in brass-buttoned coat of bottle green which, if a little threadbare at the seams, made up for this by the astonishing size and sheen of its buttons.

At this precise moment (I remember) he was engaged in brushing it vigorously, pausing between whiles to pick carefully at certain refractory blemishes, to give an extra polish to some particular button, or consult the never-failing watch, for to-day Diana and I were to be married.

"By Goles, Peregrine, it's past twelve o'clock already!" he ejaculated. "They ought to be here soon and—"

He checked suddenly and stood hushed and mute, for Jessamy had appeared,—a glorified Jessamy, resplendent from top to toe; his boots shone superbly, his coat sat on him with scarce a wrinkle, but his chief glory was his shirt, prodigiously beruffled at wrists and bosom.

The Tinker eyed these noble adornments in undisguised admiration.

"Lord, Jessamy!" he exclaimed. "Lord, Jess!"

At this, Jessamy's diffidence vanished and coming to the little mirror that hung against an adjacent tree, he scanned his reflection with an appreciative eye.

"Aye, aye, Jerry," quoth he, "when I wears a frilled shirt—which ain't often, as you know, Jeremy—I wears one with—frills!"

"Jerry, dear—O Jerry!" called Diana from the dingy tent.

"Yes, Anna!"

"I want you to come and hook up my dress!"

"Lord, Anna! To do what?"

"Hook up my dress for me."

"But—Ann—"

"I can't possibly do it myself, so come at once, there's a dear!"

"Won't Perry do, Ann?"

"Certainly not!"

"But I never hooked up a lady in my life, Ann!"

"Then you're going to hook up this lady now. So come at once and don't be silly!"

"Why, very well, Ann! But if I do it up all wrong an' sp'ile ye—don't blame me, that's all!" Saying which, he disappeared into the dingy tent, leaving me to survey myself in the small mirror and find fault with my every feature and so much as I could see of my attire, while Jessamy hovered near, eyeing me a little anxiously.

"You don't feel anywise groggy or—shaky o' your pins, do ye, Perry?" he enquired solicitously.

"Not yet, Jessamy."

"Why, very good, brother! But if so be you should feel it comin' on, jest tip me the office—I've a lemon in my pocket. There's some, being groggy, as nat'rally turns to a sup o' rum or brandy, but the best thing as I knows on to pull a man together is a squeeze o' lemon and—here comes the rest o' your backers—hark!"

The crack of a whip, a jingle of bits and curb-chains coming rapidly nearer, and then the air rang with a cheery "view hallo!"

A rustle of petticoats and Diana was beside me, a radiant vision in the gown she could not hook up for herself, and side by side, we went to meet our guests, and thus beheld a coach-and-four galloping along the lane, the sedate Atkinson seated in the rumble and upon the box the tall, athletic form of Anthony, flourishing his whip in joyous salutation, a cheery, glad-eyed Anthony; and beholding her who sat so close beside him, I understood this so great change in him. Reining up in masterly fashion, he sprang lightly to earth and taking his wife in powerful arms, lifted her down, pausing to kiss her in midair, and then she had run forward to clasp Diana in eager embrace.

"Begad, Perry, old fellow, all's well at last, eh?" exclaimed Anthony, grasping my hand. "What I mean to say is—will ye look at 'em, begad! Did mortal eyes ever see so much dooced loveliness and beauty begad? What I say is no—damme if they did! And here's his lordship to say as much."

"Ah, Peregrine," said the Earl, limping forward, "if this is a happy day for you, to me it is no less so. How say you, friend Jarvis—and you, Jessamy Todd?"

"Peregrine," said Barbara, as we came within sight of the dingy tent, "has she told you—has Diana told you how nobly she stood my friend and at what cruel cost—has she?"

"Not a word!" said I, beginning to tremble.

"Ah—that was so like you, Di—so very like you, my brave, dear girl."

"There was no need, Barbara. Peregrine's love is such that—though he doubted, being human—he loved me still!"

"Then I'll tell him—here and now! No, over yonder by the brook. And you, Tony—Anthony dear, you must come and help me."

"Yes, tell him, Barbara," quoth his lordship; "tell him, as you told me, that Peregrine may know how brave and generous is she who honours him to-day."

And so, with Barbara's hand on one arm and Anthony's on the other, I came to that leafy bower beside the stream where I had known Diana's first kiss.

"You will remember," began Barbara, seated between us, "you will remember, Peregrine, how, when first we met, I was with Captain Danby? I fled with him to escape a worse man, I mean Sir Geoffrey Devereux or Haredale, as his power somehow, for even while I was at school he gave me to understand it was his wish I should marry his friend Haredale. I was very young, my mother long dead, and flattered by the attentions of a man so much older than myself, I wrote him letters—silly, girlish letters very full of romantic nonsense—Anthony has seen them. But the oftener I met Sir Geoffrey, the less I liked him, until my feeling changed to dread. Captain Danby, seeing this, offered his help, and deceiving his friend would have deceived me also, as you will remember—"

"Damned scoundrel!" snorted Anthony.

"It was while in Italy with Diana—Anthony had just left me—that I met Sir Geoffrey again. He dared to make love to me and when I repulsed him, threatened to show my silly letters to Anthony. Then, thank God, we came home! But he followed and upon the night of the reception sent Captain Danby to me at Lord Wyvelstoke's house with a letter—"

"Ah—it was your letter?" I exclaimed.

"Yes, Peregrine—a dreadful letter, repeating his threat that unless I went to his chambers that very hour he would send Anthony the letters—and I knew—I knew that if my Anthony ever saw them, he would fight Sir Geoffrey and be killed—"

"Not alone though, Loveliness!" said Anthony, between shut teeth.

"In my dread I confided in Diana—"

"And she—went with you," said I hoarsely, "in—Danby's chaise!"

"Yes. When Sir Geoffrey saw Diana she seemed to fascinate him—he refused to give up my letters—said he could not part with them. In this way he tortured me for weeks until at last he wrote from Raydon Manor, saying I should have the letters if I would call for them in person, but it must be at ten o'clock at night—and Diana must go with me. So we went—there were other men there—they had been drinking. When we entered the room, Captain Danby locked the door—I nearly swooned with horror—"

"Ah, my God!" exclaimed Anthony.

"But then—O Peregrine—before any one could move or prevent—Diana sprang upon Sir Geoffrey—I saw the flash of steel, and he lay back helpless in his chair, staring up at her—not daring to move, her dagger pricking his throat—yes—I saw the blood! 'Sir Geoffrey,' said she in an awful, whispering voice, 'give up the letters and order them to open the door, or I will surely kill you'—and I saw him flinch as the dagger bit deeper. But he laughed and obeyed her, and so with the letters in my hand, Diana led me out of the room and none offered to hinder us. We had been admitted at the door that gave into the wood and we had just opened it when some one among the trees groaned, and afraid of being seen, we locked the door and ran back to the house and asked Sir Geoffrey for a carriage. And then—Captain Danby hurried into the room, saying you and Anthony were outside—in the hall. Then we fled into Sir Geoffrey's study and—I think that is all?"

"Yes!" said I dully. "That is all!"

"And enough for one lifetime!" added Anthony. "No more secrets, Loveliness!"

"Never any more, dear Anthony, though it was all for you that I suffered, and Diana—my dear, dear Diana—kept silence and allowed you to think—to—"

"God forgive me!" I groaned.

"I wasn't worth it, Babs!" exclaimed Anthony, kissing her; and then his hand was upon my shoulder.

"What now, old fellow?"

"O Anthony, was there ever such a blind fool? Was ever angel of God so cruelly misjudged? My noble Diana!" Hardly knowing what I did, I turned and began to stumble along beside the brook, conscious only of my most bitter remorse. And then a hand clasped mine, and turning to the touch of these warm, vital fingers, "Diana," said I, "O Diana—"

"You know—at last, Peregrine?"

"I know that I dared to think you unworthy—doubted your sweet purity—called you—wanton. And I—miserable fool—in my prideful folly dreamed that in marrying you—mine was the sacrifice! Oh, I am not fit to live—Diana—O Diana, can you forgive me?—All my life I have been a failure!"

"Dear love, hush—oh, hush!" she sighed in weeping voice. But in the extremity of my self-abasement, I knelt to kiss her hands, the hem of her dress, her slender, pretty feet. "Peregrine dear, your—your mistake was very natural; you saw me—at Raydon Manor—"

"I should have disbelieved my eyes!"

"And I could not explain for Anthony and Barbara's sakes. And when I could have explained I would not, because I wished you to—yes, dear—to suffer—just a little—and because I wished to see if you were brave enough to forgive your Diana—lift her from shame and dishonour to—to the secure haven of—your love. And you were brave enough and—now, oh, now I'm crying—and I hate to cry, Perry—but it's only because I do love you so much more than I can ever say—so don't—don't kneel to me, beloved—come to my heart!"

So she stooped and raised me to the comfort of her gentle arms, to the haven of her fragrant mouth.

And thus the dead was buried at last, mountains deep, and my hateful demons vanished utterly away for ever and for ever.

"You would always have been mine, Diana!"

"And so it is I love you, Peregrine! And so it is I am yearning to be your wife—and yet here we stay and our guests all gone—"

"Gone?" I exclaimed.

"I told them we would follow—in Jerry's cart. Shall you mind riding to your wedding in a tinker's cart, dear?"

"My wise Diana, I love its every spoke and timber for your sake, so could there never be any other chariot of any age, on four wheels or two, so proper to bear us to our happiness, my clever Gipsy-Lady. Come, dear, hurry—for I am longing, aching to hear you call me 'husband.'"

"And are my eyes—very red, Perry?"

"Yes—no—what matter? They are lovelier than ever they were—my jewels—let me kiss them!"

"And now—this, dear heart!" said she a little tremulously, and laid the gold locket in my hand: and kneeling beside this chuckling stream as we had done once before, I clasped it about her white throat and kissed her until she bade me (a little breathlessly) to remember our waiting guests.

And thus at last, sitting with Diana's hand in mine, behind Diogenes, that four-footed philosopher, we rattled, creaked, and jolted away to our new life and all that the future held for us.

CPSIA information can be obtained at www.ICGtesting.com
Printed in the USA
LVOW09s1029091016

508018LV00013B/297/P